On Wings of Death

For Jim and for Sylvia,
too late.

On Wings of Death

David Oldman

CLAYMORE PRESS

First published in Great Britain in 2013 by
CLAYMORE PRESS
An imprint of
Pen & Sword Books Ltd
47 Church Street
Barnsley
South Yorkshire
S70 2AS

9781781593011

A CIP catalogue record for this book is
available from the British Library

Printed and bound in England
By CPI Group (UK) Ltd, Croydon, CRO 4YY

Pen & Sword Books Ltd incorporates the Imprints of Claymore Press, Pen & Sword Aviation,
Pen & Sword Family History, Pen & Sword Maritime, Pen & Sword Military, Wharncliffe
Local History, Pen & Sword Select, Pen & Sword Military Classics, Leo Cooper, Remember
When, Seaforth Publishing and Frontline Publishing

For a complete list of Pen & Sword titles please contact
PEN & SWORD BOOKS LIMITED
47 Church Street, Barnsley, South Yorkshire, S70 2AS, England
E-mail: enquiries@pen-and-sword.co.uk
Website: www.pen-and-sword.co.uk

Prologue
Cumulonimbus
Storm imminent - rain and squally winds - machines grounded.

August 7th 1913

He had been late and by the time he reached Laffan's Plain Cody was already up. Even now a knot of people were on Cove Common standing, heads back, watching the machine as it banked over Ball Hill to come around for another circuit. Miller joined them, experiencing once more that feeling of incongruity, that sense of the *otherness* of that wire and fabric contraption above the trees scoring the sky with its tracery of wing and wheel and wire. The machine was low enough that he could quite clearly see Cody at the controls, wrapped in his heavy flying coat and masked by goggles, and that behind him he carried a passenger.

Miller, glancing at the man standing beside him, saw he was one of Cody's mechanics.

'Who's he taken up?' he asked.

'I don't know,' the man replied. 'A stranger. A man from Reading.'

Miller looked back up at Cody and the new floatplane and, as he did, saw the machine give a sudden lurch and begin to wobble. The passenger, reaching forward, had grabbed Cody's shoulders and it was clear even at that height that he was hampering Cody at the controls. Then the wing crumpled and an instant later the machine and the men were falling.

1
Nimbostratus

Persistent precipitation - sun hidden - ceiling zero.

From fifteen hundred feet the remains of the Cloth Hall jutted like the stump of a rotten tooth out of the rubble of Ypres. Taking a fix in the deepening gloom, Miller checked the reference on the map spread across his knees, knowing he had badly miscalculated the strength of the wind whilst pursuing the two-seater. He had been feeling morose and tried to take it out on a Rumpler, drifting further east than he had intended. He had lost too much altitude chasing the Hun and now, allowing for the freshening wind, he made an adjustment as he recrossed the lines over the salient.

To his right, he could see evening approaching from the east like a spreading stain – a darkening so aptly analogous to the present situation that a phrase occurred to him that slowly built into a line in his head. He repeated it to himself several times to fix it in his mind even while knowing that, on the ground, it would dissolve into nothingness like the wisps of cloud beyond his wingtips. He had become convinced that he did his best work up here, where height gave detachment and a god's-eye view, and he had often tried to write the lines down, carrying a notebook and pencil for the purpose alongside the map and torch and revolver and all the other paraphernalia that cluttered the cramped cockpit. But on the ground the words always sounded flat and banal as if, while created in the three dimensions of the air, once grounded in two dimensions they lost that lightness of being that had made them float.

Now he made no attempt to record the thought; the map was on his knees and, besides, at that moment he was more concerned with his lack of fuel. On the bright side, at least Archie had finally given up chasing him across the sky. He supposed, with the approach of evening, the anti-aircraft gunners had decided they had done enough for the day and had retired to their dugouts for supper. He looked down at the ruins of Ypres again, banking the One-and-a-half-Strutter to the west and slowly losing height, allowing the machine to slip sideways for a moment as if sliding across an icy pond. Then he straightened her and eased back slightly on the throttle, listening to the persistent cough of the Clerget engine as it changed note.

Trying to take his mind off the fuel, he remembered Ypres before the war when he had come to Europe looking for Cody. He recalled walking along the site of the old town ramparts and the broad streets and pretty gabled houses, and how he had sat in the sun outside the Café du Sultan in the *Grand Place* drinking Bavarian beer beneath the great façade of *Halles* — the Cloth Hall. With its three turreted Gothic storeys and niches on the topmost occupied by statues of the great men of Ypres, the huge belfry had risen two hundred feet above the square, dwarfing even the tower of the Cathedral of St Martin on the other side. It had validated in stone — Miller recalled thinking at the time — the power and permanence of the cloth trade. It had been half-hidden behind scaffolding then, undergoing a restoration. Now, beneath him, it lay in ruins and beyond repair, a few eddies of stone amid a sea of rubble; over six hundred years of dominance reduced to aggregate.

Ypres receded behind him and the folds and undulations of ground that a few minutes earlier had been softened by altitude now deepened into harsher focus. A seemingly aimless scribble of trench and track hatched over a country of crumbling farm buildings isolated between the periodic cluster of ruined villages.

The airfield lay at the junction of two roads, laid out in what had been the grounds of a château. He remembered visiting it, although that had been the previous year before the present squadron had taken possession. The old building had been in one of the areas of the front where they had managed to regain some territory lost in the first few weeks, before everyone had got dug in and the attrition had begun. The château had suffered, fire having taken some of the roof timbers and blackened the walls of the east wing in the wake of the German advance. It was a time he now remembered (if he thought of it at all) as a hazy collage of different airfields when each dawn meant another retreat as they pulled back from field to field until at last the French, with their backs to Paris, had made a stand on the Marne. After the ground was retaken, they had requisitioned the château, and had only just finished laying out the airfield when he had taken his Vickers FB5 down after it looked as if he wasn't going to make it home. Caught over the lines by a Fokker Eindecker — the first he had ever seen — he had taken a mauling when his gun jammed.

The experience, he now realised, had been worse in retrospect than during the fight — ignorance being bliss as far as the new Eindeckers were concerned — and, given the necessity of having to avoid the Hun guns, he had been allowed little opportunity at the time to ponder the metaphysics of the situation. Still, it had been bad enough to send him, once on the ground, striding into the wrecked château and straight down into the cellars. The wine was long gone of course. Whether the owner had had the foresight to retreat with his stock or whether the successive armies had accounted for the bottles wasn't clear – the shards of broken glass and rust red stains on the cellar floor might have been clues but just then he had been in no mood to investigate. Instead, the officer in charge of the detail entrusted with constructing the airfield had, compassionately, produced a bottle of cognac from his hut. Miller had returned the favour two days later, leaving two bottles with the captain when retrieving his repaired machine. In war, he found, it was the small kindnesses that counted.

Now, as he cut his engine and glided towards the same airfield, he wondered idly how many kindnesses there might be to number ahead of him. Fewer perhaps than he was leaving behind and there were precious few of those.

He had not asked for the assignment but then asking, he had noticed, was an impertinence that rarely generated rewards under the present conditions. Orders were what counted. However it was phrased — *detail, transfer, re-assignment* — at bottom they were all euphemisms that invariably meant a change for the worse. And things were already bad enough. The casual slaughter had become a habit - something to which they had, almost unnoticed, become accustomed; to some of the men he had met it had practically become a profession.

He stopped that train of thought there, suddenly aware of just how ludicrous the idea would have sounded had he spoken it aloud. *Of course* it had become a profession: killing was the army's business. He wondered just when he had begun to acquire such precious principles. Perhaps that was what the army did for you: engaged you in the basest of brutalities while gilding them in the most uplifting of causes. In the air, he had always assumed that it would be somehow different, that flight would add something, something indefinable... that unknown quantity of — what?

What *was* a known quantity, he had recently come to discover, was his past — a commodity that seemed continually to precede him. There was something decidedly off-kilter about that, as if his life was permanently running in reverse and, like a locomotive engine, he was doomed to find himself forever shunting his past in front of him down uninvited sidings. It had happened again that morning when he had walked into Wing and listened to Maxwell with that familiar sinking feeling in his stomach as the story unfolded — a feeling that might be akin, he suspected, to being swallowed in the mud of a shell-hole.

The colonel had spent several minutes talking all around the subject as if it were a problem he had much rather outflank if at all possible and it wasn't until he had finally finished that Miller asked:

'They've cut him down, I suppose?'

Maxwell's ruddy face had assumed that expression of badly suppressed impatience Miller had come to recognise was never far from the surface in the professional soldier when dealing with the amateur. It tended to manifest itself in a hardening of the gaze and in the compressed line of the lips — like Maxwell's at that moment, tight as a vice, as if they had gripped something they suddenly found unpleasant.

'Well of course they've cut him down!' he had exploded. 'They're hardly likely to leave him dangling in the middle of the room, are they? Good God! He shared the billet. What's the man supposed to do? Dodge around him until you arrive?'

'All I meant — '

'American aren't you?' he had interrupted, the privilege of rank, Miller assumed, superseding good manners.

'British, sir. I was brought up there.'

'You were, were you?' Maxwell said in a tone of vindication as if the American connection explained everything — a national penchant for lynching, perhaps, and for leaving them dangling where they hung.

'All I meant,' Miller tried again, 'was that sometimes the way it was done can give an indication — '

'Yes, yes,' Maxwell cut him off again, 'I know.' He rapped his knuckles on the desk a few times, staring into Miller's belted midriff. 'Had experience of this sort of thing before, I understand.'

'I assumed that's why I was here,' he said, belatedly adding as Maxwell looked sharply into his face, 'sir.'

Maxwell cared for the niceties of rank, Miller supposed. It was always the regulars that liked to keep things on a firm footing so everyone knew where they stood — literally, that usually was, and generally to rigid attention. God help the conscript, he thought.

'Well, Brigade's keen on it. They seem to know you.'

'I thought Brigade knew everything, sir.'

Maxwell's eyes narrowed.

'What I meant was, Brigade must have a reason. Otherwise why me? Surely it's a job for the provost.'

'No,' Maxwell said firmly. 'We can't have the provost crawling all over this. Bad for morale. Bad enough as it is.'

'But surely regulations – '

'I don't need you to remind me of regulations,' Maxwell cut in again. 'Brigade would prefer this to be handled by Wing.'

'Well,' Miller said, returning to his point, 'that's what I mean. They must have a reason.'

'A reason?'

Miller raised his eyebrows in an expression that might, under other circumstances, have been taken for familiarity.

'To put it brutally,' he said. 'he's just one more dead man. They must have had a reason.'

'Oh, yes, I see.' Maxwell relaxed slightly into his chair as if prefiguring a confidence. 'Family connections, apparently.'

'Of course, sir.'

Maxwell looked him in the eye again, searching perhaps for a trace of cynicism in Miller's reply, but the censure seemed little more than habit.

'And as I said,' he went on, 'it doesn't do much for morale. Neither would leaving him strung up like a Christmas goose.' He leaned forward again. 'Why this Heyward chap couldn't have simply flown into the ground, Lord only knows. Quicker and cleaner for everyone concerned.'

'That did occur to me,' Miller said. 'Perhaps he was thinking of the machine.'

'It strikes me that he couldn't have been thinking of anything much but himself. Certainly not his room-mate.'

'He found him?'

'Yes. And you'll be glad to know that though they cut him down someone thought to take a photograph first, so you might find that helpful.'

'Officer commanding organise that did he? Sir.'

'Strouden, Major Strouden. Decent chap, regular army of course.'

'Of course.'

'I want you to take a look at him.'

'Sir?'

'A man hangs himself there has to be a reason,' Maxwell said. 'Strouden insists he doesn't know. I wondered if perhaps he isn't asking too much of them.'

Miller knew that they were both aware that it was Brigade and Wing that did the asking, but as the question had been rhetorical he didn't see much point in offering a reply.

'Something of a martinet, is he?' he suggested instead.

'No,' Maxwell said. 'Not at all. Probably just needs a rest. Him and his adjutant. His name's Budge. Queer bird. Lost a hand and should have stayed home but he insisted he was fit to work. Should have had a staff job but couldn't swing it – no hand.'

'No sir, I suppose not,' Miller said, assuming that Staff wouldn't want to be looking at a reproach like a missing hand every day, reminding them of just how far from the front *they* were. Unsettling.

'But that's Budge, not Strouden,' Maxwell said.

'So the major organised the photograph,' Miller said, getting back to the point.

Maxwell sniffed disapprovingly. 'No, he was over the lines when they discovered the body.'

'Ah,' Miller said, filing away his first hard fact on Strouden: squadron leaders were supposedly non-operational.

'One of the men thought of it,' Maxwell continued, shifting uncomfortably in his chair.

'Quick thinking.'

'Not really.' He sighed. 'They've hung the picture up in the mess. Heyward wasn't very popular, it seems.'

The sun had dropped to the western horizon, smearing the base of a cloud bank blood red. Miller turned his engine on again and levelled out. The ground beneath him was indistinct in the dusk and it was a minute or two before he made out the outline of the château and, beyond it, the dark silhouettes of a Bessonneau hangar, huts, stacked oil drums and all the other paraphernalia that gathered itself like discarded baggage around an airfield. The strip itself, rapidly disappearing in the evening gloom, looked to have barely changed, still no more than a rutted field.

He had done a little night flying before, restricted mostly to taking off in the pre-dawn darkness where gaining height soon lifted you above the black coverlet, but there had been a couple of night bombing raids up along the coast and, in retrospect, he now recalled how much he had disliked it. Even with a moon he had found the experience to be like flying blind where imagination proved an ever-ready substitute for sight. And on those occasions there had always been the reassurance of knowing the field would be lit with flares on your return. Now, in the deepening gloom, it was a different matter and the unbidden question of what he was doing there persisted in returning.

He circled the field once, then reached down into the cockpit and felt for his flare gun.

The ostensible reason he was there, over the field at that time — and the one he couldn't deny — was that he had spent too much time and too much fuel chasing the two-seater. But that was not the real reason. *That* went deeper and was more difficult to explain. That had been an odd amalgam of ambition and duty and desire.

None of that, of course, had been in his head at the moment of enlistment.

'Your accent,' the recruitment officer had said, 'it isn't English.'

As usual Miller had replied, 'I was brought up in America,' having used the sentence so often that it was beginning to sound like an excuse.

He loaded a green flare into the gun — the usual signal for a machine turning back — and fired it above his head.

Back then, of course, when he had first applied to join the Royal Flying Corps even those sentiments, the life and death ones, had not been uppermost in his mind. The principal factor that had made him join was that he had wanted the opportunity to fly — an opportunity that is, beyond the occasional turn on a Bristol BoxKite to which he was limited while helping to construct the things for his employers. Also, he couldn't deny, in the back of his mind was the feeling that it might be fun.

How he had ever conceived the notion that it might be fun was now so far beyond his comprehension that he was completely incapable of imagining himself ever thinking that way. But he supposed at the time he had been totally incapable of conceiving what war would actually be like. Yet he was not alone in that. Who could have imagined that, after a month or two of movement (generally backwards), the war would settle into a unsatisfactory stalemate of trench attrition interspersed by bouts of homicide? No one had ever experienced that sort of warfare before.

Around him the evening suddenly exploded in a glaucous phosphorescence breaking his train of thought. Below, the looming shape of the huge Bessonneau hangar was thrown into hunkering relief against the field. He banked and circled again as the arcing flare fell and died leaving a blackness deeper than before. A minute later two oil drum flares sprang into life and beneath him light from the squadron tenders threw tunnels of illumination along the landing strip. He straightened the machine and eased forward, dipping the nose as the engine coughed its last drop of fuel and died. He turned it off as he went down.

2

The ground crew were already dousing the flares as Miller climbed out of the cockpit and jumped to the ground. A barrel-shaped warrant officer edged around the wing of the Sopwith and executed a salute with an oil-stained hand. A smudge of the same oil had smeared his right cheek, darkening an already weathered complexion.

'Tidy landing if you don't mind me saying so, sir. Being dark and all.'

'Thank you, sergeant,' Miller said peeling off his gloves. 'See to her, would you? I'm going to be with you for a while.'

'Let's hope so, sir.'

Miller peered at him. Then the last of the light from the oil drums died and the man's face was lost in shadow.

'You'll be Captain Miller, would you sir?'

'That's right.'

'Warrant Officer Mackinnon, sir. The major told us to expect you. When you hadn't arrived by dinnertime I thought it best to get some flares ready, just in case.'

'Thank you, Mackinnon. It's just as well you did. I had another engagement so I got in a little later than I had planned.'

'Dinner, sir?'

'Hun two-seater.'

'Anything in particular we need to take a look at?'

'No, I never got close enough for any polite exchanges.'

'Better luck next time, sir.'

'You might take a look at the piston rings for me, though. Three hours is normally as much as I've been getting out of them.'

'Right you are. Clerget, isn't it? They've always been a bit of a problem in that area. Reliable engine, otherwise.' Mackinnon stroked the fuselage fondly. 'She's one of the new Sopwiths, isn't she?'

'That's right. The One-and-a-half-Strutter.'

'We haven't seen many around here. I didn't think the Navy was going to let us get our hands on any of them.'

'Ways and means, sergeant. You say Major Strouden's waiting for me?'

'Officers' mess, sir. In the big house.'

'And he told you to expect me?'

'Wing warned us you were coming. Main entrance of the château, sir. Just follow the noise.'

Miller nodded and turned towards the big house two hundred yards away.

So Maxwell had warned them that he was coming. It made him wonder how much of his personal rolling stock he was pushing into this particular siding.

He heard the mess before he saw it. The main doors of the château opened on to a large hall littered with the impedimenta of an operational squadron. The corridor was lit by electric lights strung on wires along the cornice although the sound of the generator powering them was lost beneath a cacophony of voices and the discordant notes of an untuned piano. Two flying coats and some helmets hung from pegs by the door and a pair of gauntlets had been casually tossed onto a table; maps and notices were pinned to the walls over what was left of the stained and torn wallpaper. Over his head discoloured paint peeled from the cornice and ceiling like a bad case of sunburn. Apart from the lighting, the place looked much as he remembered it.

He paused by a larger map of the sector that hung nearest the doors, as if it were meant to be a last reminder to those leaving of where they were supposed to return. Beneath the map, an old armchair sat facing the double doors onto the field. The lumpy upholstery was torn in places and singed and holed by scores of cigarette burns. A sign above it read: *Budgie's Perch*. Miller slapped his gloves against his flying coat, as if he suspected he had gathered dust at altitude, then walked down the hall towards the noise.

The room was large; the state of the decor much the same as the hall — except that here some embellishments had been attempted. A twisted propeller hung like an overgrown ceiling fan from where the plaster had been knocked down from the joists, one blade truncated and splintered near the boss and the other with its laminated layers open, lending it a resemblance to the gaping mouth of a crocodile, its stretched tendons of glue and shards of timber passing for teeth. Charcoal drawings enlivened one wall above half-a-dozen scrawled signatures; the other walls held photographs of men, machines, and men and machines. In one corner, propped against the wall by one splinted leg and a length of timber, stood a grand piano, the keys of which were being mercilessly beaten by a large officer with short centre-parted blond hair and fat round fingers. Miller was oddly struck by the resemblance the man's fingers bore to those inescapable sausages that every mess hall unfailingly served up for breakfast, popularly known as 'barkers' being commonly held to be made of dog-meat. He decided he must be hungry.

The pianist glanced in his direction as he stepped into the room, hit several off-key notes with his barkers and proceeded to launch into a chorus of one of the current popular songs. Three other officers gathered around him at the piano, drinks in hand, took up the refrain, bawling it across the room towards several more sitting at tables. Behind them stood a short and crudely engineered bar consisting of a large baulk of timber supported by old bully-beef boxes, the centrepiece of which was a small portion of an aeroplane wing bearing the Maltese Cross of the German Flying Corps. Had Miller been forced to bet, his money would have been on an Eindekker, the Fokker monoplane.

By the bar, two men stood watching him and as Miller met their gaze one lifted his elbow off the baulk of timber and placed his glass of beer down carefully as if he didn't quite trust the stability of the construction. He wore the Royal Flying Corps rank of a major and, although below average height, he was stocky enough to make fitting himself into a cockpit more uncomfortable than

16

was usually the case. He had a broad face to match his build, ruddy and suggestively agricultural, although Miller was prepared to allow that a preconception might have crept into his assessment as Maxwell at Wing — being the kind of officer whose description of any man always required an appendage — had outlined Strouden's background and social standing as being from Devon, landed stock — *gentleman* farmers, that is. But if something of Strouden's yeoman background still showed through, more disconcerting to Miller's way of thinking was the fact that the major's head, squat and square like the rest of him, had been given a cropped haircut which, put on top of an alternative uniform, might easily have passed him off as a Prussian *Junker*.

Miller crossed the room towards him and, upholding the informalities of the mess, forwent a salute.

'Major Strouden?' He held out his hand. 'Miller. I'm told you've been expecting me.'

Strouden pursed his fleshy lips disapprovingly. 'You cut it fine, Miller. We expected you earlier. We're not equipped for night flying.'

Take a look at Strouden, Maxwell had told him. He looked now, trying to judge the squadron leader's age. Experience told him that it was never an easy characteristic to guess in men engaged in daily combat. Added to the usual strain of discomfort, irregular and often uneasy sleep — and a diet that generally included a high intake of alcohol — there was also the allowance to be made for the stress of watching those around them die, allied to the knowledge that arithmetic was ceaselessly gnawing at the odds of their own survival. It was a phenomenon that Miller had not only observed in others but one he recognised daily in his shaving mirror. Even if Strouden was no longer flying operationally, he must already have served his time as a pilot and had now, instead, shouldered the responsibility of the squadron, sending others to do what he was no longer allowed to do personally.

Regarding him, Miller decided he looked forty and was probably no older than twenty-seven.

'I try not to make a habit of it myself,' he said to Strouden by way of an apology. 'Thanks for the flares. You've a good man in Mackinnon.'

'He runs the squadron really,' the officer standing at Strouden's shoulder put in, 'but we keep that between ourselves.'

He wore a captain's insignia, looked older still than Strouden but naturally so. Lines had etched themselves deeply into his unnaturally long face, more prominently towards his eyes where the skin lacked the tell-tale paleness of protection that the frequent use of flying goggles offered against the sun and the wind. It highlighted instead the pattern of lines that radiated almost completely towards his right side where the skin had pulled tighter into the semblance of an embryonic smile, giving an odd sardonic cast to his face.

'Frank Budge, our Recording Officer,' Strouden said.

Budge turned a few degrees sideways as he stepped forward and extended his left arm, twisted outwards from the elbow so that his hand faced outward and could be grasped in a right-handed shake. His right arm remained immobile, the hand tucked out of sight in his tunic pocket.

Miller took Budge's left hand and gave it a tug.

'Archie,' Budge said, catching Miller looking at his right arm. 'Took it off at the elbow.'

'Bad luck,' Miller said, meaning it. Anti-aircraft fire always looked — and felt — worse than it actually was and to get an arm taken off by a piece of shrapnel really *was* bad luck.

'Oh, I don't know,' Budge replied cheerfully, his face achieving a measure of equilibrium as the left side of his mouth turned up in a rueful smile, 'another few inches and it would have disembowelled me.'

'I'm surprised you managed to get down,' Miller said.

'I was spotting, old man,' Budge explained. 'All I had to do was sit there and let the chauffeur do the driving.'

Strouden gave him a sideways glance. 'It was your ticket home if you'd had the sense to take it, Frank.'

Budge laughed a little self-consciously. 'And what would I do at home?'

'Still,' Miller said. 'How did you persuade them to let you back?'

Budge shrugged lopsidedly. 'Can't manage a machine, of course, but I can still spot if I have to and the paperwork's no problem. Always could write with my left hand. Sort of party trick, so as soon as they saw I could still sign a chit they told me to report for duty.' He grinned. 'Anyway, *san fairy ann*, as they say — it doesn't matter. How about a drink? What's your poison?'

'A glass of beer, I think,' Miller said, aware of Strouden's eyes on him as Budge turned to the steward behind the bar who had been hovering near them.

'Corporal Grimshaw here will arrange for your mess privileges tomorrow, won't you corporal?' Budge said.

'Sir.'

'You missed your dinner, I suppose?' Strouden said.

'I'm afraid so.'

'Too late for the mess hall.'

Budge said, 'I dare say we can come up with a sandwich, can't you, Grimshaw?'

'Bung and bully beef, sir?'

'That'll do fine, thank you,' Miller said. He looked past the steward whilst the beer was being poured and then casually around the room, nodding amiably at the faces that turned his way. His gaze slowly returned to the glass of beer. There was no photograph of Lieutenant Heyward hanging by the neck on the walls of this mess.

Grimshaw, neat in his steward's jacket with narrow eyes above a thin and slightly predatory nose, dripped the last of the foam from the bottle into a glass. He stood it on the bar in front of Miller.

Miller picked it up. 'Cheers,' he said, and then to Budge, 'Here's to luck.'

Both Strouden and Budge watched as Miller drank down his glass and waited while he wiped the foam off his top lip. Then, as if satisfied he was presentable enough for official business, Strouden nodded towards the door.

'My office is down the hall,' he said. 'Then we'll get you settled in. What do you say, Frank?'

'I thought we'd put him in Heyward's hut,' Budge said, 'as it's vacant.'

'Heyward? Right,' said Miller.

The hanged man's hut. He decided in retrospect that it was probably just as well that they had cut him down after all.

Miller sat through the formalities of joining the squadron, Strouden standing at his shoulder whilst Budge retrieved the necessary paperwork from his adjoining office then sat himself behind Strouden's desk to complete the forms. The recording officer balanced himself, Miller noted, with his right arm braced against the desktop — or rather, a short cylindrical piece of timber protruding from his tunic sleeve in place of his arm, with a two-pronged hook, curved and ending in what looked to be particularly sharp points, fixed where his hand would have been.

'Useful little gadget,' Budge commented without having raised his eyes to Miller, as if aware of where the other man's gaze would be. 'It does have a nasty habit of impaling things, though.' He looked up quickly at Miller. 'Particularly good for fruit.'

Strouden had begun pacing up and down the small office, sucking on a cigarette with quick draws that burned it through in a matter of minutes. A moment later he was crushing the stub out into a tin ashtray, the smoke wafting up from the dying cigarette into Miller's face.

'Sorry,' Strouden said and moved the ashtray as Budge's left hand scrawled quickly through the forms.

The office was at the back of the château with a window screened by a piece of torn curtain. A bare electric bulb hung from the centre of the ceiling and from where he sat Miller could hear the steady chugging of a generator somewhere outside. A litter of papers spilled out of wire baskets on the desk which was just a trestle table like the ones used in the mess halls; their seats were the standard issue folding canvas chairs.

When he had finished, Budge stood up and Strouden took the chair. He pulled the forms Budge had completed towards him, signed them quickly and slid them towards Budge who collected each in turn. Miller watched. He had been transferred more frequently — for one reason or another — than was generally the case with other men, he supposed, and had served in most areas of the front, from the coast down to the Swiss border, at one time or another.

The paperwork was not onerous. Once registered with the squadron the papers would pass from the recording officer to his clerks in order that his pay would arrive in the right place at the right date, his entitlement to rations would be recorded and he would receive the accoutrements of a pilot from the quartermaster as and when he needed them.

'We don't generally get replacements with your experience,' Strouden said as he picked up Miller's paybook from the desk.

Budge had copied out Miller's relevant details but Strouden took a separate note of Miller's next of kin and the details of his will. Every soldier's paybook held these particulars as having them conveniently recorded usefully oiled the machinery of bureaucracy. But if the day ever came when Strouden needed to write to Miller's sister, he would need a separate note of the details should Miller have gone down in flames taking his paybook with him.

'San Francisco?' Strouden noted as he wrote.

'My sister married an American,' Miller said, leaving it at that.

Strouden nudged Miller's paybook across the desk towards him.

'Most of the men they send us,' he said, 'are pushed on out here if they've managed to take off and land half-a-dozen times without killing themselves.'

'We keep being told,' Budge said, 'that they're introducing a new training regime. Properly qualified instructors, that sort of thing. Heard anything about it?'

Miller shook his head.

'We lose more men in training,' Strouden complained, 'than we do in service. Any fool can see that using the pilots we send home on leave to teach new recruits is a mistake. We send them home because their nerves are shattered. How does making them train raw volunteers help anyone?'

'It's a difficult choice, I suppose,' Miller said, 'between keeping experienced pilots at the front and needing them at home for training. No doubt rotating the men was the obvious choice.'

'Well it doesn't work,' Strouden said, 'not when the men they rotate are suffering from nervous exhaustion. They need proper rest, not a daily ration of having to go up with men who can't handle a horse and cart let alone a flying machine.'

'You're probably right,' Miller agreed.

'You're the sort of man we need training,' Strouden said unexpectedly. 'You've been in since the beginning. You must have flown just about everything we've had. You've done your bit. Why not use your expertise to instruct others instead of keeping you here until — ' he stopped abruptly and didn't finish.

Miller had already done his stint training at a Home Establishment squadron and given the choice he preferred France. He had found the experience as hard on the nerves as operational flying. He looked across the desk at the major and, to avoid him having to give voice to what was obviously on his mind as to the inevitable consequence of operational flying, Miller said:

'As it happens, I've already spent several months training this year.' Then he added, 'Anyway, there are the other considerations.'

'Other considerations?' Strouden asked, frowning.

'For my being here,' Miller said. 'Heyward? I thought Colonel Maxwell had warned you I was coming?'

Strouden glanced at Budge then back at Miller, his mouth slowly closing over the exclamation, 'Ah,' as realisation dawned. 'You've come from *Brigade*.'

'Well, by way of Colonel Maxwell at Wing,' Miller said, 'yes.'

'But *you're* not a staff officer.' It sounded almost like an accusation.

'Staff? Good Lord, no.'

'We seem to have got the wrong end of the stick,' Strouden said, looking at Budge momentarily again.

Miller glanced from one to the other. 'Which end would that be?'

'We've been expecting someone from Brigade concerning Heyward's suicide and also a man to take his place. You appear to be one and the same.'

Miller had always supposed he was. He gathered up his paybook and buttoned it into his tunic pocket.

'So if you're not on the staff,' Strouden said, 'what exactly is it about Heyward's death that concerns you? If there is to be some kind of investigation, I would have assumed that the provost's office would send someone in an official capacity.'

'Investigation?' Miller repeated. 'Not as far as I'm aware. Colonel Maxwell told me Brigade had asked him to make sure there were no loose ends left, that's all.'

'Loose ends?' Budge echoed. He straightened and leaned back against the wall, his arms folded, hook uppermost. 'What kind of loose ends?'

Miller waved a hand to indicate vague generalisations.

'Talk, that sort of thing.'

'There's been talk?' Strouden asked.

'The colonel prefers that there not be,' Miller said.

'I don't see why there should be.' He glanced at Budge once more. 'You're aware that I've already written to Heyward's family.'

'Colonel Maxwell told me you wrote them that he was killed in an accident.'

'I thought it best.' Strouden lit another cigarette. 'Heyward had one — an accident, I mean — a couple of weeks before he... before it happened. I saw no reason to distress the family any more than was necessary.'

'The colonel's sentiments exactly,' Miller agreed.

'If that's the case,' Strouden said, 'I still fail to see why you're here.'

Miller scratched absently at his head as if to concur.

'According to Colonel Maxwell the boy's mother is acquainted with the minister.'

'The minister?'

'Field Marshal Kitchener.'

Strouden exhaled cigarette smoke noisily.

'And has *he* been informed?'

'I believe not, sir. But if the lady decided to make enquiries it was thought best that we have all the facts at hand so not to have the field marshal put in a compromising position.'

'I can see that,' Strouden agreed.

'Should it be necessary to acquaint him with all the facts,' Miller repeated redundantly.

'The boy hanged himself,' Budge said bluntly. 'What else is there?'

'The matter of why, I would have thought,' Miller suggested, looking up at the recording officer.

'Lost his nerve, I suppose,' he said. 'What else?'

'Well,' Miller said, 'I don't want to prejudge the case, but it seems odd that if a man loses his nerve and is afraid of dying he finds the solution in killing himself.'

'We're not going to suggest that Heyward was a coward, I hope,' Budge said.

'The case?' Strouden asked. 'So it *is* an investigation.'

'Just a figure of speech,' Miller assured Strouden. 'Was he?'

'Was he what?'

'Was he a coward?'

Strouden looked at him grimly. 'Every man can suffer a case of nerves,' he said. 'The constant strain of flying patrols tells on some men more than on others, that's all. Perhaps it was the strain more than the fear of death itself.' He ground his cigarette out in the ashtray again, keeping it away from Miller. 'It might be that Heyward was more sensitive to it than most. What do you say, Frank?'

'Sensitive? Heyward?' Budge sounded surprised.

'I was considering restricting him to observing, as a matter of fact,' Strouden continued. 'Perhaps I should have acted sooner but the fact is we're always short of men and to ease up on one means putting the onus on others.' He pushed some papers around the desk to no apparent effect.

'I'm sure the colonel feels that what happened is no reflection on the way you run your squadron, major,' Miller said.

Strouden eyed him sharply.

'I meant suicide is not that uncommon,' Miller explained. 'In the trenches — '

'We're not in the trenches,' Strouden snapped.

'Different pressures, Tommy,' Budge offered helpfully.

'That's all very well.'

'Colonel Maxwell merely asked me to talk to a few of Heyward's fellow officers,' Miller said, 'so the field marshal — if it ever came to that,' he added quickly, ' — so that he was in the picture.'

'In the picture?'

'Had all the facts,' Miller amended, wondering if that was an American colloquialism. Despite the length of time he had been in Europe he was still learning just what had and what had not crossed the Atlantic.

'Wing,' he went on, 'well, Brigade to be precise,' he amended for the sake of accuracy, 'wants the field marshal to have all the facts at hand if the real story gets back to Heyward's mother. If she finds out that he committed suicide, she'll naturally want to know why.'

'I still don't understand,' Strouden said, 'why Maxwell sent you. You're not a provo, so what are you?'

Miller tried the vague hand wave again. 'The instruction came from Brigade, apparently. Someone there thinks I've had some sort of experience in this sort of thing.' He shook his head as if it were all a mystery to him as well. 'I'm just a pilot, really,' he added disingenuously.

Strouden grunted as if unconvinced, then said:

'We're very stretched. I keep putting in for new men but I can't get as many as I need. I'm told they're being diverted to the build-up on the Somme.'

'That's where I've come from,' Miller said. 'It looks as if there's going to be a big push.'

'Well, while you're here,' Strouden told him, 'I'll expect you to play a full part in squadron operations.'

'Naturally,' Miller said.

'We're not a large squadron. Three flights, reconnaissance and artillery spotting mostly. Photography, that sort of thing. FE2bs. No doubt Wing told you.'

'Actually, no. Two-seaters, then.'

'Yes. Have you flown Fees before?'

'Not a 2b.'

'What have you been flying?'

'I brought my Sopwith One-and-a-half-Strutter.'

'That's one of the new jobs, isn't it?' Strouden said, impressed. 'With the engine at the front? They're two-seaters, aren't they?'

'Fortunately, I've got one of the single-seater scouts.' He leaned forward as though confidentially. 'The two seaters have the fuel tank between the pilot and the observer. The word is they were designed by a German.'

Strouden laughed on cue although his mind seemed elsewhere.

Budge grinned at Miller. 'In the Fee,' he said, 'you'll be sitting on it.'

Strouden scratched at his chin thoughtfully.

'On patrols and operations I'll expect you to fly an FE,' he said. 'We don't get many 'shows' and when we do it's likely to be a Hun observation balloon or a bombing run.'

He looked Miller in the eye and inclined his head slightly as if ready to concede a point. 'If you're providing escort you can use your Strutter. You're no doubt used to it, so you'll probably be of more use in it than in a Fee.'

'Thank you, sir,' Miller said.

'It *will* give us a little more flexibility,' Budge put in.

'I'll have to put you in C Flight,' Strouden said, 'to take Heyward's place. As it happens, tomorrow we've got a visiting general who's been attached to Brigade and we've been asked to lay on a demonstration of artillery spotting. We've arranged a show with the gunners against a Hun emplacement at Gheluvelt.' He smiled wryly at Miller. 'I'm not about to have a general shot down while visiting *my* squadron so there will be no crossing the lines. It'll give you the chance to get a couple of hours in on a Fee and familiarise yourself with the country. Been around here before, have you?'

'Yes.'

'Good.' He paused for a moment, then said, 'Look, I know you've got more experience than most of my men but I can't give you a flight right off the bat, regardless of rank. Last man in, you see. It just wouldn't be fair.'

'I don't generally insist on the privileges of rank,' Miller said.

'No slight intended.'

'None taken.'

'Well...' He raised his thick eyebrows inviting any comment and when none came pushed himself away from the desk. 'You'll be wanting those sandwiches.' He looked expectantly at Budge. 'Frank, perhaps you'll show Mr Miller to his billet when he's eaten?'

'There *was* just one other thing,' Miller said. 'Colonel Maxwell told me someone had been thoughtful enough to take a photograph of Heyward before he was taken down. If I might see it? I was told it had been pinned up in the mess but I didn't see it there.'

Strouden looked pained. 'What do you need that for if you're just here to talk to the men?'

Miller shrugged, suggesting it was nothing more than one of his idiosyncrasies. 'It would help me to know just who I'm talking about, I suppose.'

Strouden kept his eyes on Miller for a moment longer than seemed necessary as if the answer had been less than satisfactory. He leaned over and began rummaging in a box beneath the desk. He took out a photograph and passed it to Miller.

'Who took it, by the way?'

'I don't know where you got the idea it was in the mess,' Strouden said. 'Humour can become a little black under these circumstances, I grant you, but Heyward was one of the men and regardless of how he died that's how we think of him.'

'I must have been misinformed,' Miller said.

He took the photograph. It was underexposed and showed Heyward suspended by what looked like a length of rope from a crossbeam of the hut. His arms lay limply at his sides and the excess end of the rope hung beside the body. The angle of the shot was wide enough to take in a bunk behind the dangling legs and some of the hut's interior as well. A chair, knocked onto its side lay beneath the feet. Heyward's head, pushed sideways by the tension of the rope, was turned slightly away from the camera so that his features were seen only in profile.

'I'll keep it if you have no objection,' Miller said, rising.

'No, go ahead,' Strouden said. 'The sooner this is cleared up to the colonel's satisfaction, the sooner we can get back to normal operations.'

Miller followed Budge out of the office and back down the hall. The noise from the mess had increased as they walked into the room.

'Some of the men are in town,' Budge said, 'so it's a little quiet tonight.'

Miller smiled and pushed the photograph of Heyward into his tunic. As he did so, his finger brushed against the pinhole that he had already noticed had been made in the top of the photographic paper.

24

3

The huts stood to the west of the château. Beyond them, ranged around the Bessonneau hangar where the aircraft received maintenance and were kept under cover in bad weather, other smaller hangars, workshops and sheds, had been erected.

'The huts are small but comfortable enough,' Budge explained as he walked alongside Miller, a hurricane lamp clutched in his one good hand.

'I'm sure it'll be an improvement on my last billet,' Miller said. 'All we had there were tents.'

'Tents are fine in summer,' Budge allowed, 'but you don't want to be caught under canvas in winter. Fortunately we inherited most of this stuff from the previous squadron, otherwise you do what you can.'

Miller agreed about tents. He sometimes thought even a trench dugout would be preferable. But then, he had never spent much time in a trench dugout.

'And the Other Ranks?' Miller asked.

'Here and there,' Budge said. 'Some have quartered off areas in the machine shops. Quite snug, really.' They walked on a few more paces, shadows lengthening and shortening with the swing of the hurricane lamp. 'Here,' he said. 'This was Heyward's hut.'

It was timber-clad with rough-cut boarding darkened by creosote and reminded Miller of the mining huts in the goldfields in which he had grown up as a child. Then again, having lived in most variations on the theme as their father had dragged him and his sister from one mining camp to the next, nearly every wooden hut he encountered did.

Budge unlatched the door, stepped inside and held up the hurricane lamp so that the yellow light spread out into the hut's interior, throwing shadows against the walls.

'Bit of a mess, I'm afraid,' he said, frowning as he swung the lamp around.

Miller followed him in. The room was recognisable from the photograph except that the reality was a picture of disorder. Bedding had been half-stripped from the bunks and trailed onto the timber floor. A chest stood with the drawers half open like panting tongues, the few clothes inside rumpled and pushed aside. A picture in a gilt frame and a tin mug on top of the table had been knocked over. Beside them an unlit hurricane lamp stood next to a pen and an inkstand.

'Has someone been looking for something?' Miller asked.

'Damn the man,' Budge said.

'Who?'

'Jones. Heyward's orderly.' He put the lamp on the table and lit the other one. 'The man wants to be a mechanic but can't tell a piston from a crankshaft. He'll be on latrine duty unless he can explain this.'

'I wouldn't bother him tonight,' Miller said casually. 'I'll talk to him in the morning if it's all the same to you.'

'Sheer dereliction,' Budge said. 'I *ought* to have him running pack drill.' Then he looked at Miller and shrugged. 'Still, whatever you say, old man. He's your servant now.'

Miller dropped his gloves on one of the two bunks. 'Are Heyward's belongings still here?'

'Personal belongings are in my office ready to be sent home.'

'I'll take a look before it all goes, if you don't mind.'

'Of course,' Budge said.

'Who am I rooming with?'

'You're on your own until Foden gets back.'

'Is that who Heyward shared with?'

'Arthur Foden,' Budge said. 'The Old Man gave him some leave. He was overdue... Then what with Heyward committing suicide...'

'Sent home to train the next batch?' Miller asked sardonically.

'Actually,' Budge said, 'just a few days in Paris. He's a good man and Tommy didn't want to lose him.' He looked down at the tin mug on the table and stood it upright. 'Tommy...' he began hesitantly, 'the CO...'

Miller waited.

Budge smiled tightly. 'You mustn't mind if he seems a bit — short, if you get my meaning.'

'Not at all.'

'What with the squadron's responsibilities and then this business with Heyward. The build-up down south... Wing are on our backs pretty heavily for details of the Hun troop movements.'

'They've been preparing for weeks,' Miller said. 'It can't be too long now.'

'You've come up from there, you say?'

'The St Quentin sector.'

'Is it going to be as big as they say?'

'Big, yes,' he replied. 'The Hun *were* putting everything in against Verdun but lately the movement's been back north. I was hoping I was going to find it a bit quieter here.'

'I wish I could tell you it was,' Budge said. 'It has quietened down a bit since we got on top of the Eindekkers but of course we're all waiting to see what the old Boches come up with next.' He looked around the hut again. 'Are you sure you don't want me to give Jones a roasting over this? The little squit is probably in his pit now and it would give me the greatest pleasure to pull him out to clean this mess up.'

'Don't worry,' Miller assured him. 'I'll have a quiet word in the morning and see what reaction I get.'

'It's up to you, old man,' Budge said, 'but it doesn't pay to let the men get away with too much. They'll only take advantage of your good nature.'

Miller nodded. 'He'll find I'm not that soft a touch.'

'Good for you. The trouble is some of the young lads they send us don't know how to handle men. Aren't with us long enough to learn, either. Still...' he tailed off as if not wanting to pursue that line of thought. 'The general isn't due until mid-morning so it'll give you time settle in. What about your gear?'

'I brought all I need with me,' Miller said. 'Strapped to the Strutter.'

'I'll get it sent over,' Budge said. He picked up Miller's gloves from the bunk and smiled his tight smile again. 'The other one was Heyward's,' he said.

'Right,' Miller said. 'Looks a bit short for me.'

'Like cockpits,' Budge agreed. 'They don't cater for men of our height.'

'What about Heyward?' Miller asked. 'Was he a tall man?'

'Oh, about average, perhaps a little taller. Five foot eight or nine.'

'At least he had warm feet, then,' Miller observed.

Budge picked up the hurricane lamp. 'If there's nothing else? I'll let you get settled in. I'll make sure Jones knows you've arrived so you can arrange things as you like them in the morning.'

Miller let Budge get to the door, then said, 'I was told Heyward wasn't very popular. Why would that have been?'

Budge pulled a judicious face.

'I wouldn't exactly say he was unpopular. You know what it's like. You get all sorts in a mess. What you might call reserved. Most of them are hardly more than schoolboys,' he added by way of mitigation.

'Not Heyward?'

'No, actually he was a little older than most of the others. At university when he volunteered, I think.' He frowned. 'Cambridge, was it?'

'A swot?'

'No,' Budge replied thoughtfully, 'not so one would notice.'

'What was he reading, just as a matter of interest? At Cambridge, I mean.'

Budge shook his head. 'Haven't a clue, old man.'

'He came from a good family, I'm told,' Miller persisted. 'The right connections.'

'Must have if his mother knows the field marshal. I wasn't aware. Perhaps that was the trouble.'

'In what way?'

'Oh, you know, airs and graces.'

'Was he arrogant, then?'

'I wouldn't say arrogant.'

'What would you say?'

'Reserved,' Budge repeated. 'He tended to keep himself apart. Read a lot.'

'Bookish,' Miller said. 'Not a mixer.'

'Exactly. Or arty,' he amended. 'Arty rather than bookish.'

'A painter, you mean?'

'No, I mean the arts. Theatre, literature, that sort of thing.'

'Effeminate?' Miller asked.

Budge reacted as if he'd been slapped in the face.

'Good God, no! No, not at all. What gave you that idea?'

'But the theatre...' Miller suggested.

'More literature, I think,' Budge said. 'I didn't mean to imply...'

Miller shrugged. 'As you said... You get all sorts in a mess.'

'But not that... no.'

'What was he?'

Budge looked at him suspiciously. 'How do you mean?'

'Was he a pilot or an observer?'

'Oh,' Budge said, 'I'm with you. Heyward came to us as a pilot. As Tommy said, he was thinking of restricting him to observing.'

'Of course,' Miller said. 'So he did.'

'The way things have been, though,' Budge went on, 'the Old Man has us all muck in as needed. Don't be surprised if you have to turn your hand to both. Is that going to be a problem?'

'Not at all,' Miller said. 'Can it be?'

'You know what some of the pilots can be like,' Budge told him. 'But then observers usually regard themselves as the senior man in the machine. Actually,' he said, 'Heyward was a better observer than he was a pilot. He hadn't got many hours in before they sent him over, you see.'

'Usual story,' Miller said.

'I'm afraid so,' Budge agreed. 'Well, if there's nothing else, I'll see you in the morning and we'll arrange your mess privileges.'

Miller kept his eyes on the closed door for a moment after Budge had left then he took the photograph Strouden had given him out of his tunic and laid it on the foot of Foden's bunk, glancing at it once or twice as he positioned himself where he thought the photographer had stood. He looked around the room. The bunks appeared to have been moved a foot or two and the chair that Heyward had presumably stood upon had been righted and placed by the table. The chest of drawers and the other chair — by the wall — seemed to have been moved.

He began walking slowly around the hut. It was unlikely that there was anything left to be found but he looked anyway. There was little in the drawers but he slid them out of the chest and emptied the few contents onto Foden's bunk. He turned each upside down to see if anything had been taped to the underside. Finding nothing, he looked over the chest itself then worked his way methodically over the room. He was on his knees peering beneath the bunks when there was a knock on the door. Calling for whoever it was to come in, he got to his feet, dusting off his trousers.

'Your kitbag, sir,' an aircraftsman said, holding Miller's bag in front of him while his eyes took in Miller, the chest drawers and contents on the bunk and the moved furniture. 'Anything you need, sir?' he asked.

'Just drop it on the bunk, thank you. Jones, is it?'

'Robinson, sir.'

'Did you know Mr Heyward, Robinson?'

'The officer that 'ung 'imself? No, sir. I only arrived a couple of days before it 'appened. Never 'ad the pleasure, sir.'

'That'll do then, Robinson, thank you.'

'Yes, sir. Warrant Officer Mackinnon says to say your One-and-an-arf-Strutter will be ready if you wants 'er in the morning.'

'Tell Sergeant Mackinnon that I'll be taking up an FE when the general arrives tomorrow. Mr Heyward's machine, I presume.'

'Sir.'

After the door closed on Robinson, Miller climbed on one of the chairs and checked the top side of the roof purlings. When that afforded nothing, he pushed aside the rough matting and moved methodically over the timbered floor looking for loose boards. It occurred to him that he wouldn't have bothered to search the hut had not someone done so already. After all, he had no reason to believe that Heyward had not hanged himself — that it was anything other than suicide — but someone had been looking for something and he found that curious. Maxwell had not intimated that there was anything suspicious about the death, merely that it was a potentially embarrassing inconvenience, but if he wanted all the loose ends tied up Miller knew he had better make sure that none were overlooked.

After fifteen minutes, having found nothing, he dropped on to what had been Heyward's bunk and began rummaging through his own kitbag. He pulled out a carpenter's wooden rule, a ball of string and his Vest Pocket Kodak camera. There was certainly not enough light from the hurricane lamp to take any shots so it would have to wait until the morning although he doubted he could do any better than had the man who had snapped Heyward. He checked there were enough exposures left on the 127 film, then left the camera on the small makeshift table between the two bunks and walked back to the door.

He took the chair from where it stood by the table and placed it under the crossbeam from which Heyward had hung. He tied the string to the beam and placed the rest of the ball on the seat of the chair. With the rule, he measured the distance from the seat to the beam, then mentally subtracted sixty-nine inches — an approximation of Heyward's height. He picked up the photograph and tried to get some sense of the proportions between the rope showing in the photograph and Heyward's body. Finally, he climbed on the chair and measured the distance from the top of his own head to the beam where the rope had been secured, adding four inches for the difference in height between himself and Heyward.

He dropped the rule onto Foden's bunk and followed it. It was all a bit hit and miss, he knew, but even allowing for an extra inch — if Heyward had been five-eight rather than nine — it still seemed to him to be too little to play with. It gave — after kicking away the chair — a drop of at least two, but certainly not more than four, inches. Not enough of a drop to break a neck, he would have thought, although he assumed the medical officer would be able to confirm that either way. But it meant that if his neck had not broken, Heyward would have died through asphyxiation. That would have been an unpleasant way to die and slow enough to give him time for second thoughts... probably panic. He might have tried pulling himself up by the rope or reaching for the crossbeam. Either way, this should have left evidence on his hands. He wondered then if the MO had conducted a post mortem. He should have, of course, but with thousands

29

dying daily in the trenches and the squadron losing men on a regular basis perhaps one more body had hardly mattered.

And that thought led inexorably to another: was that meant to be the point? After all, where better to hide a death than in the morgue in which they were all living?

4

The officer was looking at him oddly as if he were a specimen of recruit he had not come across before.

'American? Why the devil do you want to join the RFC?'

'I'm English,' Miller began to insist. 'English! My father took me to America!' Tears of frustration pricked at his eyes and he was a small child again, looking up at the recruitment officer. 'It wasn't my fault...'

The recruitment officer peered down at him. 'Why the devil come back?'

Miller started explaining once more, but the officer began to laugh and the night around started exploding in a green phosphorescence and the machine was going down –

He woke with a start.

He was lying on Heyward's bunk still fully clothed. The hurricane lamp was burning on the table where Budge had left it and his bag lay on Foden's bunk, half unpacked. Looking at his watch he saw that it had gone midnight. Somewhere outside the sound of raised voices and laughter drifted across the field... men back from town.

Miller climbed off the bunk and undressed, snuffed out the lamp and lay down again. He had been dreaming, his subconscious activated, he supposed, by what he had been thinking before the flare had lit. His mind had been mulling over the circumstances that had brought him there, and then, logically, back to the moment of his enlistment. He could still remember how strangely the recruitment officer had looked at him when he had explained how he had grown up in America.

'Then why the devil did you come back?' he had demanded.

'I was interested in flying machines,' Miller had explained, quite reasonably he thought.

The recruitment officer had looked nonplussed.

'But they invented the damn things in America, didn't they? The Wright brothers? Don't they have opportunities there for flying?'

'Yes, sir,' Miller had said patiently. 'But my father was a friend of Samuel Cody, you see, and I came over to see if I might join him.'

'Samuel Cody? What's Buffalo Bill got to do with it?'

'No sir, that's William Cody. *Samuel* Cody was the first man to achieve powered flight in Britain.'

'First man? Was he, be damned!'

'Yes, sir. Cove Common. That's Laffan's Plain near Aldershot. 16th October 1908.'

'I know where Laffan's Plain is, Miller,' the recruitment officer had said wearily. 'Aldershot is where the Air Battalion was based.'

'Cody also won the trials on Salisbury Plain to supply the army with flying machines in 1912, if you recall.'

'Oh yes,' the recruitment officer had replied. 'Cody, of course. What happened to the fellow?'

'Killed on Laffan's Plain, sir. A year ago. He was testing out his new machine.'

The man had looked up from Miller's papers briefly. 'That was bad luck. Still, nothing stopping you getting back to America and flying, is there?'

'No, sir. I suppose not. It's just that...'

'That what?'

'I'd like the opportunity to do my bit,' Miller had said. 'My duty.'

He thought at the time how odd it was that the phrase had come so readily to the tongue and his hesitation had not been because he had been unaware of his own impulse, it had had more to do with how that sentiment would sound coming from *his* mouth. He wondered if that sort of talk had originated with the upper classes. He supposed that was the thing about rubbing shoulders with the upper classes: their manner of speech and habits rubbed off. It was like being subjected to a contagion, only one you *wanted* to catch. You'd never come down with the full-blown disease, of course, not unless you came into a substantial amount of money, but there was nothing to stop you displaying the symptoms. He had rubbed shoulders with a great many of them over the previous couple of years: army officers of good families looking for adventure; civilians with the time and money to devote to new interests.

He had been fortunate to have possessed a mechanical aptitude and ability that had opened doors for him that a lack of money would otherwise have kept closed. Working with and for those who had an interest in flying had eventually got him off the ground and given him the opportunity to get his ticket. And his ticket was what he hoped was going to get him into the RFC.

He knew that most of the men who had already joined had been drafted from the regular army – when the old Army Balloon and Air Battalions had been reorganised and the Flying Corps squadrons formed, volunteers had been taken from the existing services. The only civilians to get in — without, that is, having to join the regular army first — were those men who could already fly.

'Want to get in before it's all over, I suppose,' the recruitment officer had said.

'Yes, sir,' Miller had replied.

Everyone said it was only going to last a matter of months, probably be finished by Christmas. So, if he wanted to see anything of it, he had to get in at the start. Otherwise all the vacancies would be filled and he wouldn't get a chance to do any flying at all. Rumour had it that the army would probably commandeer all the civilian heavier-than-air machines, too, so that any private flying would be knocked out of court as well.

'Well, you appear to have got your ticket from the Aero Club. Fit?'

'Top form, sir.'

'Shame about your being a foreigner.'

'No sir, I'm English.' He relaxed long enough from the rigid attention at which he had been standing to gesture at his birth certificate on the desk beside his application.

'Oh, just so... just so. Background? Work?'

And that was when he had made his mistake.

At that moment, standing in front of the recruitment officer and looking back over a career of wrong turns and missed opportunities, he had thought his familiarity with flying machines and his ticket might not be quite enough. On the spur of the moment he had plucked an occupation out of his past that might – he had irrationally hoped – give his working life some weight, a basis of solidity upon which a structure of trust and worthiness might be built.

So he had told the recruitment officer of the time he had spent as a Pinkerton Detective.

From the way the officer looked at him, Miller wasn't sure that he knew exactly what a *Pinkerton* detective was. And the stupid thing, of course, was that he needn't have bothered.

He could fly.

That was enough. That would have got him in even if he had told them he had spent the past decade living as a vagrant. Applicants, it transpired, were dropping out of the sky like pheasants at a shoot; half of them weren't even making it through the training. They were being put into machines with only the most rudimentary idea of how they worked, without any sort of knowledge of just what was needed to keep the things in the air. Without that working knowledge of what wire did what, or just how much strain an engine could withstand, or exactly which manoeuvre was possible and which was not, they were all going to come down to earth a lot quicker and with a lot more violence than they had gone up.

And that was just the training. God help them when they were posted to France.

But, of course, he had not known that at the time. So he had told them he had once been a Pinkerton Detective.

In the event it had barely raised an eyebrow and he might have imagined that a small fact like that would have got lost somewhere in the bureaucratic jungle that was the army at the outbreak of war. But it had gone down on his application, an indelible entry that someone, somewhere, must have seen and noted. God only knew why. But there it was, a note that had come back to haunt him.

In the dark, the airfield around him silent and sleep having deserted him, Miller could far more easily see Heyward dangling from the crossbeam and he began to wonder exactly when it had been that suicide crossed the line from being unheard of to being not all that uncommon. In the Other Ranks, of course, self-mutilation was a more frequent occurrence than suicide — or was that a class view that had rubbed off on him as well over the past two years? He might have supposed that some ingrained sense of honour stopped the officer classes from putting bullets in their collective feet to get them home, or rather, it was probably more a fear of the *dishonour* of being caught giving themselves a

'Blighty wound' that caused the muzzle of the revolver to be raised from the foot to the head. But, beyond all that, it was the mechanics of the thing that troubled him. In the trenches there was always the revolver or the rifle to hand, or even, he had heard, the unscheduled climb over the top so that another man's finger pulled the trigger as if by proxy. In a squadron there was still the revolver and, most obviously, the machine; a rope seemed to him somehow unnecessary. Still, whatever the method, the motivation suggested that things had come a long way from the excitement and enthusiasm of those early days...

He could remember only too well his own sense of excitement and that of those around him as they had assembled at Swingate Downs near Dover during the second week of August 1914. The flying strength of 2, 3, 4 and 5 Squadrons had numbered only a little more than sixty machines although the full strength of the Royal Flying Corps was reputed to be 189 aircraft. Most of these, it had transpired, were either broken or worn beyond repair – or being used to train new pilots at the Central Flying School. What was left was an assortment of Farmans and Blériots, BE2s and Avro 504s.

He had been allocated a BE2 to take across the Channel — the machine that the designers had trumpeted as the first inherently stable aircraft. They were right, he had discovered, provided you only wanted to fly in a straight line. The first time he had attempted to bank and turn, the machine had fought him every inch of the way, continually trying to right itself like one of those children's toys with a lead weight in its base that, however it was moved, would always stand upright.

He had never flown over water before — apart from rivers — and for some unaccountable reason it had been arranged that they were to go, not in pairs or groups, but singly. He had suspected at the time that the powers that be had decided that to be seen ditching in the water would be deemed bad for morale. They were, however, instructed to climb to a height of three thousand feet before venturing across the water since from that height, it had been calculated, should the engine fail the machine would have enough altitude to glide to France. As it happened, there was so much shipping crossing to France in support of the BEF — their own lorry-loads of stores and equipment, men and machine spares included — that it had occurred to him it might be more difficult to avoid landing on a ship while looking for a stretch of empty water than actually ditching.

Being in a squadron that included the reservists — those men who had joined the RFC directly as opposed to having already been in the army — he was one of the last to cross. They were to rendezvous at Amiens and were then to fly to Maubeuge which was to be the RFC's base, ten miles behind the line then held by the British Expeditionary Force. He had already decided — once he had safely navigated the Channel — to do what he could to get himself reassigned onto a Farman or a Blériot, something at least that could be manoeuvred and didn't appear to have a mind of its own.

As it was, the flight had proved uneventful. He fancied he might have taken a nap and still have trusted the BE2 to fly him straight on without mishap. Even the airfield at Amiens had been easy to find and, by the time he reached it, was so crowded with the machines of those who had preceded him and what seemed like hundreds of sightseers gathered to witness the spectacle, that it would have been difficult to miss. On landing, he reported in and found to his relief that he had done no more than ferry the BE2 across the Channel. They were to wait for the rest of the corps to rendezvous — the transport and men having embarked from a variety of ports to steam to Boulogne before making their way to Amiens — and then move as one body to Maubeuge. In the meantime, there was all the bureaucratic paperwork to contend with.

In retrospect it had all been something of a lark. The war was still some way off, out across the country, and somehow — if he were to be truthful — not quite real. Had he then possessed his facility for introspection (acquired later, he suspected, following a series of close shaves and a more than nodding acquaintance with death) he might have seen himself as someone who had always been subject to the whims of chance — like a leaf (it was quite clear to see now) who had gusted this way and that depending upon the prevailing wind at the time.

He had not been entirely truthful with the recruiting officer and coming back to England had been no more than a whim, a puff of chance, he had decided upon after his sister, Catherine, had married. Their father had died and he had knocked around for a while to no particular purpose before learning — out of the blue, for his informant had been unaware of the connection with his father — that Samuel Cody had taken a Wild West show to England. Cody had by then adopted the long hair and whiskers as well as the name — either (it depended upon one's point of view) in emulation of William F. Cody, or for the purpose of cashing in on an understandable confusion with Cody's fame as a frontiersman and the not inconsiderable success of *his* Wild West show. Of course, by the time Miller had raised the money and reached England — courtesy of that stint as a Pinkerton man — Cody (*his* Cody) had decamped, show and all, to continental Europe. He had followed — for the want of any better idea — and had found himself, instead of aimlessly knocking around the United States of America, aimlessly knocking around the disunited countries of Europe. And before he had managed to catch up with Cody, the restless showman had returned to England where, instead of a Wild West show in which Miller had thought he might find some sort of employment, he found Cody had flown (literally) off on another tangent and had developed an interest in powered kites and the new heavier-than-air flying machines. Miller had been considering returning to America until he had watched Cody go aloft in one of his machines.

That had changed everything; an argument hard to dispute, particularly later when at a height of ten thousand feet it gave him a view of the Western Front stretching from the Somme to the Channel. It was also hard to dispute that he had progressed from being blown by the metaphorical winds of chance towards a state of having to pay perpetual attention to the strength and drift of an all too real wind, one that often seemed only too ready to sweep him towards disaster. The one big difference now was that he had at his disposal an eighty horsepower rotary Clerget engine, a means other than an uncompassed mind to direct his progress. On the debit side, of course, was the fact that the winds of chance aided by the Clerget had put him squarely in the middle of a war, the whys and wherefores — never mind the rights and wrongs — of which he had little knowledge and, to be truthful, not much interest.

Later, for all the good that it did, he could goad himself to his heart's content that he had had every opportunity of avoiding it. He had been aware of the darkening clouds which for some time had been gathering — more apparent in Europe than they had been in England, admittedly. And while he could not have guessed just how quickly and completely England had become enmeshed (or he should say the British Empire, given the variety of backgrounds of those with whom he found himself serving) there *had* been that oppressive sense of an approaching storm in the air ever since the preceding spring. He could still have taken a ship from Liverpool and just about paid the fare, or perhaps have worked his passage had he had a mind to, had it not been for the fact that, a little more than six weeks after Cody's death, he had been at Brooklands to watch a demonstration by the Frenchman Adolphe Pégoud on his Blériot monoplane and had been astounded by what a machine could be made to do: vertical dives, a loop, tail slides... Although already mesmerised by flight, until that moment he had had no idea of the potential of aeroplanes. That had knocked any idea of ships out of his head and within a month he had scraped together the money and had taken his ticket at the Royal Aero Club.

He couldn't help wondering now where all that enthusiasm had gone; disappeared, he supposed, with an all but forgotten world. He had to admit that his brief flowering of idealism had disappeared with it, submerged under what had become the clinical business of killing. He could not remember that it had been anything other than a gradual process, (no Damascus road revelation for *him* while sheltering in a foxhole under bombardment). No, it was that slowly he had come to the view that he was not the same man who had volunteered in the summer of 1914. That man, it now appeared, had been nothing more than an outline sketch for a character; the intervening two years had fleshed him out. The problem now was that, whilst being coloured in so to speak, his background, – the world around him – had somehow lost definition. Or rather, it was *tangible* enough (he wasn't so stupid as to attempt to fool himself as to the reality of an artillery barrage) but it was the *meaning* that had begun to lack definition, a meaning, that is, that could transcend the war.

It wasn't that he had become squeamish; once in the air and faced with the enemy he was too much of a realist to believe it was anything other than kill or be killed. And whilst undertaking the other duties expected of him, like artillery ranging or bombing which he knew would result in the deaths of others whom he would never even see, he still suffered no qualms of conscience. The odd thing was that his conscience had taken an unexpected turn — like a sudden half-roll off an expected horizontal: instead of being troubled by what he *was* doing, his conscience began to prick over his not doing *enough*. No matter that the odds predicted, anyway, that it would all most likely end with his death, he could not evade the conviction that he was having an easy time of it. The conviction was that those poor benighted souls beneath him were the ones who were fighting the real war while he was doing no more than indulging himself in a selfish passion and this conviction dictated that, sooner or later, a bill for self indulgence always became due.

5
Altostratus
Dense opaque layers - intermittent precipitation - ceiling low to zero.

He awoke to the sound of engines.

Lying in Heyward's bunk, he listened to the familiar *whop whop* of a swung propeller as the pistons pushed through the valves waiting for the spark. Then it started to cough, like a smoker getting going in the morning *whop, cough, whop cough, cough* , and she caught and, a moment later, began to purr with the contentment of an oversize cat. Somewhere nearby another joined in, a duet, then another until a full abrasive orchestra was playing, the sound swelling, rising and falling as engines were run, listened to, tested and watched.

It was a sound that was in his head now, a sound that had greeted him almost every morning for the past eighteen months, ineradicable, a part of the linkages between his cells, like the oil that was now always under his fingernails and the smell of aeroplane fuel that was forever in his nostrils.

He rolled off the bunk and pulled on his clothes. He laced his boots and thumbed his braces over his shoulders, scratching at his scalp through his short, stubbled hair with stiff fingers. He pulled the hut door open and stepped into the pre-dawn darkness of a June morning.

The field was alive with movement. Shadows flitted in the half-darkness; the lights of lamps and torches winked and flickered. Men ran this way and that accompanied by shouts half-drowned under the roar of engines. He walked through the flattened grass around the huts past the Bessonneau hangar and onto the edge of the field. Men were scurrying around the planes, riggers and fitters, checking the tensions of the wire webs that held the frail-looking constructs together; listening to the purr of the engines for any tell-tale consumptive rattle that might betray the first onset of mechanical disease; checking pressures, armaments, loadings, giving a thumbs-up, a wave, a benediction...

Then the first machines made their lurching movements and the men around them scattered, running clear like small parasites fleeing larger, stirring animals. The aircraft moved off, slowly at first, bumping across the field, first one, then the next, bouncing over the uneven ground and, as they gradually gathered speed, straining forward tails rising, the wheels lifting, falling back to kiss the earth briefly, then off, incredibly, a foot, two, and up into the lightening sky like heavy birds suddenly lighter than air.

The dawn patrol was airborne.

'Captain Miller, sir?'

A small questioning man looked up at him from his elbow, intent narrow eyes above a pinched nose, neck muffled against the cool dawn. He offered up a mug, cupped in his two hands and steaming into the morning air.

'Tea, sir.'

There was a faint Welsh cadence to his voice, like a melody started with each sentence then abruptly abandoned.

Miller took the mug. 'Jones?'

'Yes sir, Jones, sir.' He reached into a pocket and took out a canister. 'Sugar, sir? Didn't know how you liked your tea.'

'Just as it is, Jones, thank you.'

He sipped, the tea still hot enough to burn.

'Just how I like it.'

'Yes sir,' Jones said. 'Hot water in your hut, sir. Breakfast in the mess hall when you're ready. Will there be anything else?'

Miller looked up into the paling sky. The machines had shrunk into little black toys as they climbed and circled, making their height. He glanced back down at Jones.

'Walk back with me if you've got a minute, will you?'

Jones followed as Miller turned and retraced his steps to the hut. The hurricane lamp had been lit and hung on a hook yellowly illuminating the interior. By the washstand his soap and shaving kit had been neatly arranged in front of the mirror, unpacked from the bag where he had left it the night before. A towel hung on a hook beside the stand. The drawers had been replaced in the chest, the furniture pushed back where it belonged. His camera, he noticed, had been placed on the small table between the bunks. There would be no point in using that now.

'I found the hut in a bit of a mess last night,' Miller said.

Jones stiffened. 'Mister Budge has already given me a bollockin' on that account, sir, if you'll pardon the expression. I told him I'd cleaned through after Mr Foden went on leave.'

Miller drank the tea, put down the mug and bent towards the mirror. That older face, a familiar man but somehow not quite *him* looked back. He cupped his hands into the water and ran it up over his face, feeling rather than seeing Jones standing stiffly a few paces behind him.

'You were Mr Heyward's orderly, weren't you, Jones?'

'And Mr Foden's sir, that's right.'

'Get on all right with him?' Miller stepped aside slightly so that he could see Jones's reflection in the mirror. The Welshman shifted his stance but his face betrayed no discomfort.

'Well, he was an officer, sir. Other Ranks don't "get on" with officers.'

'Quite right, Jones,' Miller said. 'Stupid question. Put it this way, how did Mr Heyward treat you?'

Jones's eyebrows went up and his mouth dropped open slightly, as if the question had surprised him.

'No complaints, sir. Long as I did my job he seemed happy enough.'

'Couldn't have been all that happy, could he?'

39

'No sir, I suppose not.'

Miller turned to face him. 'Under strain, was he?'

The private shifted again, this time the discomfort was plain.

'Not my place to judge the flying officers, is it sir?'

'No, but the men talk. They know who's getting jumpy and is likely to crack. I've even known one or two to run a book on it.'

'Run a book, sir?' he asked innocently. 'Whatever do you mean?'

'Bet.'

'I'm chapel, sir. We don't hold with gambling.'

'I'm sure you don't, Jones,' Miller said, hardly convinced, 'but you'd have known if the strain was getting to Mr Heyward, wouldn't you?'

'Well, if you're asking, sir, I'd have said Mr Foden was due for a rest more than Mr Heyward. That's why he's on leave, isn't it?'

'Quite. But you'd have said that Mr Heyward was coping?'

'Perhaps he just didn't show it,' Jones suggested. 'Major Strouden would be the one to ask, sir, if you want to know.'

'I was just curious. You know,' he said, 'sleeping in a dead man's hut.'

Jones shrugged philosophically. 'Seems to me, sir, that these days every hut's a dead man's hut.'

Miller stripped off his clothes again, sponged himself down, shaved and dressed once more. Skirting the activity around the field kitchen from where the aroma of fresh-baked bread and brewed coffee percolated into the early morning air, he was struck as ever by the amount of men and equipment that was required just to keep a couple of dozen men in the air.

He found the officers' mess hall in a barn across a cobbled courtyard behind the château. It had been scrubbed clean and filled with trestle tables and chairs. The tables were covered with laundered cloth and even a decent service had been found to set the tables. It was still early and only four officers sat along the length of one table and, hungry after only sandwiches the previous evening, Miller told one of the mess orderlies to bring him toast and a plate of eggs and bacon before joining them.

'Miller,' he said by way of introduction. 'I got in yesterday evening.'

A big and loose-limbed young man with a boyish clean-shaven and oddly circular face put down his knife and offered his hand. Miller took it, recognising the fat fleshy fingers of the piano-player from the night before.

'Chacksfield,' he chirped, a smile cracking his moon-face. He picked up his knife again, nodded to the man next to him and the one beyond and said, 'Breconridge and Denham.'

Miller asked the orderly for coffee and sat down.

'That's Gregory,' Chacksfield added, gesturing with the knife at a blond officer further down the table. 'Gregory's our DH2 pilot. Bit of a trophy, really. We don't take him out of the cabinet very often.'

Gregory smiled back good-naturedly. He had the delicate-boned look that reminded Miller of fine porcelain. His blond hair, centre-parted, was long and as fine as his features. He wore the rank of captain; the other three were all lieutenants.

Beside Chacksfield, Breconridge, perhaps slightly older and sporting a thin and well-tended moustache that Miller had noticed was beginning to oust in popularity the yard-broom Kitchener variety, gave him a cheery 'good morning' whereas Denham, sitting to his right, glanced first at Miller's rank before offering a curt, and somewhat supercilious, nod.

'First time out?' Breconridge asked.

'No, actually.' Miller said as his breakfast arrived.

'Thought not,' Breconridge said.

'The CO's put me in C Flight.' Miller said. 'Taking Heyward's place.' If he thought Heyward's name might have caused a reaction he was disappointed.

'Hard luck, Denham,' Chacksfield said, not looking as though he meant it.

'Denham here has been acting Flight Commander of C,' Breconridge explained.

'He's waiting to be gazetted captain,' Chacksfield added unhelpfully, making the point of looking around Breconridge at Denham. 'Won't make captain now, Denham, old man.'

'Chuck it, Chacksfield,' Breconridge said with a certain weariness as if he had heard it all before.

Chacksfield laughed through his eggs.

'I'm not taking the flight,' Miller assured Denham. 'The CO made it clear, last man in, that sort of thing. I'm just taking Heyward's place.'

This time Chacksfield said, 'Bit of a stink about that. The idiot hanged himself. Now Wing's sending someone over to find out why.'

Miller looked up from his plate. 'That would be me,' he said amiably. Then, while they were all still staring at him, he asked Chacksfield, 'Who was it that took the photograph?'

'Oh, the photograph,' Chacksfield said, eyes to heaven. 'That was that squit, Tozer. He thought it was a bit of a jape. He has no sense of decorum.'

'And you have, I suppose?' said Denham.

'Anyone see the *Gazette*?' Chacksfield called to no one in particular.

'And Tozer pinned it up in the mess?' Miller asked.

'The major took it down as soon as he saw it,' Breconridge assured him.

'No sense of decorum,' Chacksfield repeated.

'The fellow's dead,' Gregory put in from further down the table. 'I don't think we ought to be talking about him like this.'

'That's why Miller's here,' Chacksfield said, matter-of-factly.

'Even so.' Gregory pushed aside his plate, stood up and walked away.

'Back to your cabinet, Gregory,' Chacksfield called after him.

'Chuck it, Chacksfield,' Breconridge said.

Miller finished his breakfast then finding Budge in his office made arrangements for his mess privileges. That done, he drew what new maps of the sector he needed, studied them to familiarise himself with the area again, then checked through his equipment and wandered out towards the Bessonneau hangar where a DH2 was being wheeled out onto the field.

A single seat scout fighter, the DH2 was a pusher — its engine behind the pilot — but was more manoeuvrable than most. It had been developed to counter what had been labelled the 'Fokker Scourge', the dominance of the Fokker Eindecker — the Hun monoplanes that were the first production machines to boast a synchronised machine gun firing through the propeller. They had been causing havoc among the allied aircraft since the previous autumn, lowering morale to the point where the pilots and observers had started to refer to themselves as 'Fokker Fodder'. Miller had thought himself fortunate that, by the time he had returned from his stint of training, he had found that together with the FE2b and the Nieuport 11, the DH2 had finally begun to redress the balance. He had missed the worst of it and was not at all sorry for the fact.

The first DH2s had been dealt out singly among the existing squadrons to bolster their firepower, although new squadrons consisting only of DH2s had now crossed the Channel. Up to that point, single pilots like Gregory chosen from the squadrons for the DH2 had quickly come to be regarded as the elite — and the butt, it seemed, of Chacksfield's humour.

Miller walked alongside the machine as the riggers pushed her out. He had yet to get the opportunity to try one out and, although the DH2 reminded him of the old Vickers FB5 and did not look particularly prepossessing, its reputation made him hope he might soon get the chance.

'Is this Mr Gregory's machine?' he asked one of the riggers as they wheeled the machine past him.

'Yes, sir,' the man said. 'He wants to take her up this afternoon and give her a run through. She took a bit of a beating when he downed that Hun Fokker day before yesterday.'

'Downed one?' Miller said as he watched them out on to the field. 'Good show.'

Behind him the ground crew had begun pushing out the FE2bs ready for the general's visit. To anyone unlike Miller, who looked upon almost any aircraft with a regard close to love, the FE2b might have appeared more like a bathtub strung between wings with a metal frame for a tail than an aeroplane. Miller, though, had known what to expect. He had flown an earlier version of the FE and had been assured that the 2b was much improved. Like the DH2 it was a 'pusher' with the engine behind the pilot which, although sacrificing some speed and manoeuvrability and requiring a skeletal metal, rather than fabric-covered, fuselage due to the demand for airflow, allowed the nacelle in which the pilot and observer sat to extend forward from the wings and improve vision and field of fire. The nacelle itself looked more like a giant hip bath than anything else. Staggered, so the pilot sat higher than the observer for better visibility, the nacelle ended in a large bulkhead at the pilot's back directly behind which the engine was located.

The pilot had no gun — his job was to get the observer into a position to do whatever it was they were in the air for. The observer had the armament, one Lewis gun fixed on a horizontal bar at the front of the nacelle capable of being swung up and down as well as laterally, and a second Lewis behind him fixed on the top of a vertical bar so that it could be fired backwards over the top wing and the pilot's head. This necessitated the observer having to stand on his seat or even, if he were a particularly short man, on the combing of the nacelle itself — a somewhat precarious position if the pilot began throwing the machine around the sky. To some extent this gun covered the FE's blind spot — its rear — although Miller knew from experience that having something as large as an engine between his back and the enemy machine did afford the pilot some sense of security. All in all, the FE2bs were rated as all-round machines used for just about any task required of them and he was quite happy to fly one; the trick was trying not to think too much about the vulnerability of attack from the rear.

He was looking over one of the FEs when Warrant Officer Mackinnon ducked around the tail.

'Your Fee is out on the field all ready to go when you need her, captain. They're just starting them up for a last check through.'

'Thanks,' Miller said. He reached up and slapped the belly of the nacelle. 'I'm looking forward to giving one a spin.'

'I'm thinking you'll find them a little heavy after the Sopwith', Mackinnon said.

'I was flying Vickers FB5s before the Strutter,' he told Mackinnon. 'After them, I'm sure I'll get on with Fees just fine.'

Until he had got his hands on the Strutter he had been stuck for months on a Vickers, a machine he had never grown to care for. Like many of the engines up until then, the Gnôme-Monosoupape had no throttle and was flown flat out either on or off; adding to the awkwardness was the fact that it also required constant attention to the petrol/air mixture to keep it running smoothly, which wouldn't have been too much of a bother if the oxygen level didn't vary depending upon what height you were flying. As it was, the Vickers had a ceiling of only six thousand feet and in the gunbus, as it was disparagingly known, that had been high enough for him. Making adjustments were one thing when flying unopposed on a reconnaissance patrol or when artillery spotting, but quite another when attacked by a Hun fighter whose sole objective was to shoot you down. Miller had learned that there were only a certain number of things he was able to do at any given moment and flying an FB5 at the same time as defending himself was one too many. It was what had given rise to the feeling of being Fokker fodder. Some pilots loved the thing; he did not.

'I was told Mr Heyward had an accident before he died,' Miller said to Mackinnon.

'Accident? Oh, yes sir. But that must have been a couple of weeks before Mr Heyward died.'

'A fortnight? As long as that? Was it badly damaged?'

'Bad enough,' Mackinnon said.

'What happened?'

'Bad landing,' Mackinnon said. 'Came in too steep. Smashed the front up pretty badly but nothing we couldn't fix.'

'Was Heyward hurt?'

'Just bruised, that's all sir. Mr Dunne wasn't so lucky.'

'Dunne?'

'Mister Heyward's observer, sir. Broke his neck.'

Strouden had gathered all three flights in the mess hall. A Flight — back from patrol and already debriefed — was having breakfast with some of the other late risers and the CO was trying to make himself heard above the din. Miller poured himself another cup of coffee and watched with mild interest as Strouden stood at the end of a table, banging the flat of his hand on the top and raising his other hand as if trying physically to push the volume of noise down with his palm.

'Gentlemen,' he shouted. 'Gentlemen, if I may...?'

A Flight was attacking its breakfast with the sort of gusto that the general command would have liked employed in those sectors earmarked for the next big push. The man nearest Strouden was zooming his hands in the air above his plate of bacon and eggs demonstrating what looked like a roll out of the top of a loop.

'*Gentlemen!*'

Frank Budge, rising from his chair with a strained expression on his face, tried waving *his* arms then resorted to a whistle.

Strouden winced, his ear being closest to the shrill blast. The man next to him who had been demonstrating the manoeuvre froze momentarily, hand in the air with his poor pilot and observer presumably hanging on for dear life in the upturned nacelle. He glanced in astonishment at Budge then picked up his knife and fork and resumed strafing a fried egg.

'This morning, gentlemen,' Strouden half-shouted before turning down the volume, 'this morning, we are to receive a visit from General Bovington from Brigade.'

Someone booed the general in advance of his arrival and received a querulous glance from Strouden for his temerity.

'General Bovington,' Strouden continued, 'as you may know, is on the Corps General Staff and will be visiting us this morning to see a demonstration of the valuable work which this squadron does in this sector.'

A cheer ran up the table like an incoming tide.

'To that end a demonstration of artillery spotting has been laid on and the general has evinced a desire to go up in a machine...' more cheers, ' ...to watch. Accordingly C Flight...' audible groans, 'personnel will meet in ten minutes in the operations room for the briefing.'

A few shouts of 'Good show... good show' followed until Strouden raised his hand for silence again.

'General Bovington will, of course, be accompanied by members of his staff. These gentlemen will not, I assume, wish to emulate their commanding officer...' general pandemonium along the tables, '...but,' Strouden said, '*but* they will no doubt interest themselves in the day to day running of the squadron and therefore we will endeavour to demonstrate that we run an efficient and tidy — I repeat *tidy* — operation here.'

Shouts of 'shame... shame...'

'NCOs and Other Ranks,' Strouden went on, 'have been detailed accordingly and upon the conclusion of breakfast I am sure each officer here will want to retire to his billet and ensure that it is in such condition as to withstand the most rigorous of inspections. Captain Budge will be undertaking a random tour to satisfy himself to this effect.'

He looked up and down the table. 'Thank you, gentlemen,' he nodded curtly and left the room to resounding cheers.

Miller finished his coffee and found his way to the operations room. It had once been one of the château's receptions rooms, he supposed, high-ceilinged with the flaking remnants of gilded rococo decoration still visible on the walls. Maps of the sector now hung over cracked plaster on which a *trompe l'oeil* scene showed a garden through open doors. On the other walls aerial photographs of trench positions and Hun reserve and distribution camps had been pinned. A couple of dozen chairs of various kinds stood angled towards a table with an easel standing at one end. Strouden was balancing an enlarged map on the easel as Miller and the rest of C Flight filed in and sat down.

Satisfied his map was straight, Strouden cleared his throat.

'I've just been advised by Brigade that the general will be arriving at ten-thirty.' He looked at the men in front of him intently. 'Now we all know what generals are like in wanting to relive their glory days — ' he allowed himself a pause, ' — if they've had any. And that is by getting into the thick of the action. Our job, as undistinguished low-ranking officers, is to see that these cravings go unsatisfied. I'll not have this squadron go down in the history of the RFC as being the one that got a general staff officer killed on a routine visit. Understood?'

They laughed on cue and, when Strouden's intent stare did not waiver, muttered their assent.

'The general will be flying as observer with Mr Denham.'

Denham, in the front row and one of the men who had groaned in the mess hall, groaned again.

'Visibility is satisfactory for spotting at the moment but should it deteriorate to the point where you have to descend any lower than two thousand feet I have advised the gunners that we will scrub the demonstration. In this eventuality, Mr Denham, you will take our visitor to an altitude high enough to get him thoroughly chilled but not high enough to give him frostbite. The patrol will fly up and down our lines but will on no account cross them. With luck he should be able to get a good view of the enemy positions without any need for excursions into hostile territory.' He allowed that to sink in and to give them a chance to express a contrary view if they had one. No one had.

'Mr Denham,' he continued, 'is your Flight Commander and will be flying close enough to Mr Bartlett and Mr Hardy who will be doing the spotting so that the general can get a decent view of how it's done. Mr Moss and Mr Trueman will patrol at a respectful distance to the rear alongside Mr Parker and Mr Cliff.'

He looked up and caught Miller's eye.

'For those who haven't met him yet...' he gestured to where Miller was standing at the back of the room and paused while the men turned in their chairs and nodded in his direction, 'Captain Miller arrived yesterday evening and will be flying with Lieutenant Etherington, who also arrived yesterday and will be acting as observer. They will patrol a thousand feet above the rest of the flight and will keep a sharp lookout for enemy aircraft. I doubt that they will trouble you — they have shown a distinct lack of interest in crossing our lines of late — but we will not take any chances. At the first sign of the Hun, Captain Miller will alert his flight commander and the patrol will return to the airfield. Understood?'

'Sir,' they chorused.

'With luck, Strouden added, 'Archie will put on a little display for the general without getting a chance to do him any real damage.' He glanced around the room then added, 'Dismissed.'

A droop-eyed young man with large-lobed ears popped up in front of Miller.

'Captain Miller, sir?' he asked.

His features gave him the aspect of a rather disconsolate spaniel although somewhat spoiled, Miller thought, by a severe haircut.

'Etherington, sir. I'm with you.'

'Been out long?' Miller asked him.

'No, sir. Arrived yesterday.'

Chacksfield and Denham walked by and Chacksfield said:

'A bit thick giving my seat to the general. I would have thought, Miller, that he'd go with you, senior man and all that.'

'Denham's flight commander,' Miller said.

'*I* don't want to ferry the beastly general around,' Denham said.

'Just don't scare him, that's all,' Chacksfield advised. 'I don't want to find anything nasty on my seat when you get back.'

'Keen to get up, I suppose,' Miller said to Etherington.

'*Rather*, sir. First time over the lines.'

'We're not *going* over the lines,' Denham said. 'Didn't you hear the CO?'

'Been in an FE before?' Miller asked Etherington.

'No, sir.'

'Still,' Chacksfield brightened, 'give the old man a good spin and he might put in a word about your promotion, Denham.' Then he looked seriously at Etherington. 'I should watch that Fee of yours. Has a tendency to land on its nose.'

'All right, Chacksfield,' Miller said, deciding that perhaps it wasn't the best time to tell Etherington that it would also be his own first time up in an FE2b.

'Of course,' Chacksfield added to Denham, 'give the old man a rough time and he'll probably break you to fitter.'

Denham groaned again.

Miller returned to his hut. Jones, his orderly, had already been through, making the bed and tidying what few possessions Miller had brought with him. Miller idled away several minutes adjusting the spines of his books on the shelves and his toilet kit on the washstand by a quarter-inch here and a quarter-inch there, then looked around, satisfied by the general impression of neatness.

Passing by the hangars again, Miller exchanged a few words with the C Flight ground crew then checked on his Sopwith's piston rings. Finding everything in order, he asked directions to the medical officer's hut. He found a field ambulance parked outside and two legs protruding from beneath. He stepped over them as he passed and knocked on the door and opened it.

It was a large hut with two scrubbed pine tables, cots and a desk and was occupied at that moment solely by the medical officer who turned from inspecting a row of bottles and jars on a shelf and looked at Miller enquiringly.

'And what can I do for you, captain?' he asked without any apparent enthusiasm, dropping a clipboard onto the cot beside him and pocketing his pen. 'Cure for a hangover is it you're wanting, or have you sprained your ankle in a scrum in the mess?'

His name was Doyle, he was in his thirties and possessed of red hair above a freckled face that led, noticeably Miller thought, nose first with an air of enquiry and interference. His voice, by contrast, held an Irish lilt that had a kind of built-in mocking quality that Miller couldn't quite decide had been deliberately affected or was simply natural.

'Neither,' Miller said, introducing himself.

Doyle grunted. 'What are you, Miller?' he asked. 'A late starter or a more than usually proficient pilot?'

'I beg your pardon?'

'In my experience,' Doyle said, 'most pilots are dead by the time they reach your age. So you're either a good flyer, man, or a tardy recruit.'

Feeling a little affronted, Miller said, 'I've been in since the first week.'

Doyle raised an eyebrow as if feigning surprise.

'Then you'll be something of an awkward bastard, I'm thinking. If you haven't got yourself a cushy staff job by now and you're still having to go up in those cloth and wire contraptions they call aeroplanes, you must have something of the malcontent about you.'

Miller laughed. 'Is this an example of your bedside manner?' he asked.

'We don't run to those kind of niceties around here, Miller,' Doyle said. 'If it's care you're looking for I suggest you get yourself to a hospital.'

'I'll bear that in mind,' Miller said. 'As a matter of fact, I wanted to ask you a few questions about Lieutenant Heyward. How he died.'

'Poor Heyward, is it? And what's your interest in him?'

'Because I've been given his hut?' Miller tried optimistically.

'It's not because you were sent here to ask, then?'

'So you've heard?'

He waved Miller into the chair the other side of the desk and sat down himself. 'It's probably common knowledge all over the Hun lines by now. I'll lay money the only ones who don't know are the Intelligence Corps.'

'It'll save me having to make up some improbable story, I suppose.'

'Ah, why not? We're always short of light entertainment around here.'

'How did he die?'

'They found him hanging in his hut, man, how d'you think he died?'

'I mean, was his neck broken or was he asphyxiated?'

'Asphyxiated. The fall wasn't great enough to break his neck.'

'Were there any marks other than rope-burns on his neck?'

Doyle stared at him. 'If you're suggesting what I think you're suggesting,' he said, 'I saw nothing that was inconsistent with a man who'd hanged himself. Nobody asked me to look for ligature marks. Now what would it be that you're looking for?'

Miller raised his eyebrows. 'What makes you think I'm looking for something?'

'I'm a doctor,' Doyle said. 'Looking at you I'd diagnose a case of curiosity.'

'Did you perform an autopsy?'

'Look here, Miller, I'll bandage a wound if you've got one, give you a powder for a hangover and maybe splint a broken limb if I can remember how, but if it's autopsies you're after you'd be better off finding yourself a pathologist.'

'Did you at least notice any other marks on the body? His palms, for example.'

'No. Not other than the bruises I'd put some liniment on a few days before.'

'I'd heard he'd crashed,' Miller said.

'The way Heyward flew,' Doyle said, 'he was going to wind up dead sooner or later anyway. He was in and out of here like he was tied to a rubber band.'

'No other marks?'

'Like what?'

'Abrasions around his wrists?'

'As if he'd been tied?' Doyle asked. 'Now I think I would have noticed *that*.'

With time before the general's arrival Miller wandered across the field and walked in the sun for half an hour. Heavy cumulus was building in the west but there seemed to be no rain in it and he doubted it would interfere with the general's show. He sat on a gate and smoked, thinking of Heyward and how Doyle had said there had been no other marks on his body except for the rope burns around his neck. It was suicide. There was nothing to suggest otherwise. But then why did someone search the hut?

6

Miller walked towards the knot of men who had gathered on the edge of the field. He had been wrong about the cloud. It had thickened and was now blowing quickly on a stiff westerly breeze towards the lines. The ceiling was between two and three thousand feet and Strouden's mood had perked up. The worry lines that traversed his face in a complex system of tramways had somehow turned north, lightening his humour. Beside him, an even shorter and stouter man who had out-Kitchenered the Field Marshal in terms of luxuriant moustache growth while stopping short of any passable analogy to a walrus, was stamping up and down and liberally beating his thigh with his swagger stick.

'Nonsense,' he kept repeating, throwing his head back with every exclamation to look up at the sky. 'Nonsense.'

General Bovington gave his thigh momentary relief and placed his arms akimbo peering at the gathered pilots and observers. He jerked his chin at the staff officer heading his retinue, all red piping and braid in immaculate uniform and boots that would have been gleaming in the morning sun if there had still been any, and pointed the end of his swagger stick at the ground and then up to the base of the cloud as if to aid measurement.

'What would you say, Findlay? Eh?'

Major Findlay, aide to the general, pursed his lips judiciously (an expression that had the effect of bunching and pushing forward his own moustache — a quite splendid example of the breed taken in isolation but not in any way one that might be seen as rivalling the general's) and, after some meditative thought, told the general what he wanted to hear.

'Quite do-able, general. Yes, quite do-able.'

'There you are, Strouden,' Bovington said, turning on the major and being decent enough not to sound too triumphant. 'Findlay says do-able. He should know. He's been up.'

'But — ' Strouden began, only to be cut off by the general.

'What is it? Five? Seven thousand? What is it you chaps call it, ceiling?'

Strouden tried again. 'It really — '

'Oh, five,' Findlay said. 'Five at least.'

'You see? I've done my homework. Always come prepared. Like old Baden-Powell and his scouts, eh?'

'It really,' Strouden finally insisted, 'isn't much over two. The point is you won't *see* anything.'

'Nonsense,' Bovington said again. 'Nonsense.' He gave his leg a healthy thwack with his cane and took another look at the pilots. 'Which one's mine, then? Don't want a duffer, Strouden. I dare say there's some on the general staff that would like to see the back of me — old Bovington shot down in flames...' he stopped long enough to laugh at his own joke and was joined heartily by Findlay and the retinue.

Strouden's tramlines headed south.

Denham took a reluctant step towards the general.

'I believe I have the honour, sir,' he said, speaking slowly as if still hoping someone else might volunteer before he finished the sentence.

Strouden introduced Denham as the flight commander.

'Ripping,' Bovington said. 'Well, let's take a look at the machines.' He strode off towards the waiting line of FE2bs on the field, Findlay having to skip a step to remain in his wake and not be lost in the wash with the rest of the retinue and the flight. Budge led the way, pointing at Denham's machine with his good hand and explaining where the observer sat.

Strouden had caught Denham's arm and was holding him back. Denham winced under the pressure of his fingers.

'Get him above that cloud and make sure you stay our side of the lines, understand?'

'Perfectly, sir,' Denham said through clenched teeth.

Strouden looked up and saw Miller following a few feet behind.

'Miller, you patrol along the length of the line and keep the flight west of you. I don't like this wind.'

He ran his tongue backwards and forwards along his lower lip while he watched the general move among the machines, the retinue and the pilots and observers following behind like a pack of schoolboys chasing a soccer ball.

'If you get the chance of a hole,' he said to Denham after a moment's consideration, 'you can come down and give him a taste of Archie, just so he knows he's been up.' He gripped Denham's arm even tighter. 'But get back up in the cloud as soon as Archie's got your range. He never hits a damn thing but there's no point in tempting fate.'

'Absolutely,' Denham squealed, trying to free his arm.

There was a concerted movement towards the machines as Budge pushed the general's bulky frame into a flying coat, his hook — testament to Archie occasionally hitting *some* damn thing — catching awkwardly on the garment. Miller saw Etherington into the front nacelle and climbed into the cockpit behind him. Cliff, Parker's observer, began arcing his forward Lewis on its mount as if anticipating trouble, the attached leather pouch designed to catch the empty shell casings and stop them flying back into the propellor swinging like a chicken's wattle beneath it. Strouden was staring up at him with a black expression warping his face. The riggers gave a last check to wires and the aerilons and longerons, then the fitters shouted 'Contact' and spun the propellers. The engines coughed, spluttered, caught and roared and the aircraftsmen scattered like rabbits. Major Findlay stepped back alongside Strouden; he had been 'up' once before and hadn't seemed keen to repeat the experience. They watched as C Flight bounced out across the field and assumed their take-off positions.

At a wave from Denham to take the lead, Miller began to pick up speed, hoping he wasn't about to disgrace himself in a new machine in front of the whole squadron. The tail rose and, a moment later, he felt the machine break free of the shackling earth and lift its wheels into the air. He pulled back on the stick, glanced down at the grass of the field dropping away beneath him and felt a warm sense of relaxation spread through his body. He was up.

Making a wide arc around the field, he gave the thumbs-up to Etherington's turned face as he began to climb. The FE, he found, was not as manoeuvrable as the Strutter — he hadn't expected it to be — but it handled well enough although he had been forewarned that the machine dived like a brick. Still, it was responsive to the controls, had a decent turn of speed and a rate of climb that was reasonable. More to the point, if Etherington ever saw them coming, the FE had enough firepower to hold its own against anything the Hun had to offer.

Below, he saw Denham and the general were already up. Bartlett and Hardy were lifting off and, behind them, Cliff and Parker were accelerating across the field.

Miller found a gap in the cloud and, as Moss and Trueman cleared the trees at the edge of the field beneath him, the gap abruptly closed and he felt the sensation of having stepped suddenly into an impenetrable fog. Moisture filled his mouth and his goggles misted over. He wiped at them clumsily with his gloved fingers and pulled the nose of the FE up into a steeper angle, keeping up the engine's revolutions. Etherington turned to him, almost a ghostly figure in the swirling cloud, and Miller nodded encouragingly until they finally broke through the overcast.

Above the cloud, it resembled an ocean caught in one static moment of time. A brilliant sun threw shadows over frozen troughs. Wave tops wisped with fingers of foam that flew on an unfelt wind, caught as still as if in a photograph. To the east, the leading edge of the cloud bank had already crossed the lines although the rear of Hun territory still lay in clear sun. Behind their own lines some holes had appeared like wells plumbed in whipped meringue.

Miller climbed into the blue, the sky above free of every encumbrance except for the back of Etherington's head below him, turning this way and that, eagerly searching for Hun aircraft.

At six thousand feet he levelled out, taking a compass bearing north by northwest. The front was below and a little west of them and he flew on, picturing the towns beneath, grey under a leaden sky: St-Julien... Pilckem... Langemarck... North of where he estimated Bixschoote to be, he banked and turned southeast again, picking out the rest of the patrol as they breached the cloud and lined up with Denham and the general at the head of the formation. Flattened out from Miller's relative perspective, the diamond formed by the machines took on a rhomboidal shape against the clouds, Parker bringing up the rear.

Beneath and further east the target for the artillery spotting still lay visible and he watched as Hardy's machine pulled forward and saw Bartlett in the front nacelle signal that he was ready to wireless the guns. Miller banked again, dipping his wing and sliding east off his course, as if to outflank them and to mark the extent of the patrol. For a few minutes Denham seemed to hang motionless over the frozen peaks of the meringue while they waited for the agreed time of the shelling to start. Then the cloud, like a creeping barrage, spread over the target and Hardy, followed by Denham and the general, moved his FE closer to the lines beneath Miller. They flew up and down a little longer but the target had gone and finally Bartlett, drawing his thumb sharply back across his throat, called it off.

Hardy dropped their FE, sliding in a quarter-turn back west to where Moss was waiting, as Denham began to climb towards Miller, growing larger as he approached until Miller could see the almost waxwork figure of Bovington hunched over the Lewis gun in the front nacelle observer's seat. They flew on for several more minutes until Denham, still below, signalled that he was going to gain altitude. Miller, raising a hand in acknowledgement, had begun to climb when the waxwork figure turned in the nacelle to Denham, now hidden from Miller by the top wing, and suddenly dropped from view as the FE unexpectedly dived into the meringue beneath them. In another minute the rest of the patrol had been sucked out of sight after it.

'Bloody hell!' Miller cursed and put the FE's nose down, turning in the flattest of spirals into the overcast.

In front of him, Etherington twisted around, his face beneath the flying cap and goggles grinning inanely as wisps of cloud drifted through the struts and over the wings like fine muslin.

Miller glanced up but the cloud had shut out the dazzling morning and locked them into a fog as thick as soup.

For what seemed an eternity there was no sensation of movement, even the forward tilt of the machine was lost without any fixed point of reference. The vague chill of a westerly breeze he had felt upon his cheek above the cloud had been swallowed in the dank, oppressive cling of the moisture-heavy air. Breathing felt like sucking through a wet sponge. Etherington vanished as Miller's goggles misted over again and the cloud seemed to fill the cockpit as if intent upon smothering him. Rivulets of water streamed down his face over his coat and pooled in ponds in the folds around his legs.

Then, just as Miller had begun to suspect that the cloud cover had become a ground fog, the interminable grey blanket lightened and started to thin, finally parting as they broke through a haze of lengthening strands like pulled dough. The ground resolved from indistinguishable grey to a discrete mass of crater, wire, trench and earthwork, rushing to meet them like a suddenly overwhelming vision of Danté's Inferno.

The FE began to shake as if a terrier had closed its teeth around the tailplane, great grey globes of dirty smoke appearing out of nowhere as anti-aircraft shells exploded around them.

Miller cast around to get his bearings, the FE leaping and bucking like a rodeo horse. Below, at no more than five hundred feet, he saw a rubbled town with a blasted wood to the south and, to one end, what he guessed was the blackened peak of Hill 60. In front of him, beyond the head and back of Etherington, lay the Hun reserve trenches and behind them the roads and duckboard trails of the German rear, stretching out over a cratered mud moonscape. He looked around but couldn't see Denham or the other machines. Small, almost musical notes played in his ears ... *zing* ... *zing* ... and as he watched holes appeared out of nowhere in his lower left wing, the fabric puckering up like a dry wound and leaving the torn edges waving in the wind of his airspeed.

Zing... zing...

He was too low. Beneath them men were taking shots at the FE as if it was a fairground target. Etherington had opened up with the Lewis, but Miller couldn't see what he was shooting at. They crossed the old railway line that had run into Comines and Miller banked steeply to the left, pulling her round until the nose of the FE was pointing north. Archie from the emplacements in Sanctuary Wood had fogged the sky ahead of them with puffed balls of smoke coloured grey and black and dirty yellow. Shrapnel whined in his ears like irritated wasps and something tugged at Miller's sleeve like a pest trying to catch his attention. He snatched a look down and saw a tear in his flying coat and a smear of blood around it. He had been hit but felt nothing, just a sharp tug at his coat. He wondered suddenly if this was how it felt when, like Cody, the Man from Reading grabbed you by the shoulders and drove you into the ground.

In front of him Etherington had stopped firing the Lewis gun and just sat, hunched over it. Jammed gun, Miller thought. Then above Etherington's head, out of nowhere the lumbering outline of an FE jerked like a puppet on strings.

Miller kicked at the rudder bar and pulled back on the stick to climb above it, staring past Etherington at the machine. He thought it was Moss and Trueman. Hanging, he turned, almost in a tail slide, looking for Denham and the general as the FE fell back to the horizontal. Below them, south of Hill 60 and running parallel to the Hun trenches, he finally saw another FE, low — one hundred, perhaps only fifty feet above the ground — Bovington standing in the nacelle to get the maximum depression, swinging the Lewis's muzzle round from side to side, spitting fire and strafing the infantry in their muddy ditches.

Miller dived again and followed Denham's trajectory, cursing him for a fool. He reached forward to rap on Etherington's shoulder to start shooting, but Etherington seemed to have frozen. Hunched over the gun he didn't move, hoarding the stock to himself like a miser reluctant to spend shells.

Underneath him Moss's FE reared like a startled horse and Miller saw a glowing lump of shrapnel tear through the wing and climb in front of him. Denham, having reached the shattered rubble of St Eloi, was turning to run the length of the trench system again. As they closed on him Miller could clearly see Bovington changing the drum of the Lewis and flinging the spent one out of the nacelle as if, with luck, it might brain some unsuspecting Hun in his trench.

Miller zoomed with Moss on his tail. He climbed to the base of the cloud then shadowed Denham until, near Hill 60, the flight commander began to climb to their altitude, dodging Archie until he had reached the lower edges of the overcast. He slid up into it and vanished. Moss followed and, with a last glance down into the chaos below, Miller climbed to join them.

Over the field Miller watched Denham cut his engine and glide into a bumpy landing. He followed Moss down, wondering why he felt no pain in his injured arm. He kept flexing the fingers in his flying gloves trying to bring it on. There was no sign of Hardy and Bartlett or Parker and Cliff. Etherington still sat frozen over the Lewis. Miller decided the boy wasn't suited to the work. Apart from that initial burst, the observer hadn't fired the gun. It was all very well wanting to get up, but there was no point if the first bit of Archie scared you silly. Strouden would have to do something about him; a man who couldn't pull his weight was a liability. What would have happened if they had met a Hun formation? It was like flying a single-seater scout with no gun. There just wasn't room for passengers. You might as well be carrying the Man from Reading.

The ground crew came running up as he slowed the FE to a stop. Denham was out of his and on the ground, pacing backwards and forwards the length of the machine like a demented shop-walker. Strouden and Budge were running towards Bovington who was being helped out of the FE's nacelle by Sergeant Mackinnon. Beyond them Trueman was still scanning the sky.

'You've been hit, sir,' Miller's fitter, Tregoran said. He was a wiry Cornishman with a thin, wedge-shaped face who had told Miller that he used to maintain pump engines and had come out of a tin mine to volunteer. Miller had told him he should have stayed where he was.

'Get yourself to the MO, sir. I'll see to the machine.'

Miller stripped off his gauntlet and rolled up his sleeve, looking for the wound.

'It was a bloody mess up there,' he said to Tregoran.

'Let me, sir...' he helped Miller out of the coat but he wasn't bleeding.

Miller looked down at the bloody coat in amazement, then slowly felt the surprise drain out of him. He looked back up at the FE's nacelle. Etherington hadn't moved.

Tregoran climbed up and eased the observer back from the gun he was still clutching. The Cornishman looked down and shook his head.

'Gone, sir. I'm sorry.'

Miller clambered up beside him and helped pull Etherington out of the nacelle and lay him on the grass. His face was white and his skin already cold to the touch. His droopy spaniel eyes were wide open and empty. A neat hole — the size of a minié ball like the ones Miller used to collect as a boy — had been punched through his flying coat to the left side of his stomach. A bigger hole, below his shoulder-blade, showed where the shrapnel had exited. Miller climbed back into the cockpit and found the hole beneath the instrument panel where it had passed through to the pilot's seat and tugged at his sleeve, bringing some of Etherington's blood and guts with it.

Miller jumped down, swearing under his breath. Denham was still by his machine. Strouden, Budge, Major Findlay and the rest of the general's retinue had reached Bovington. Strouden was staring back towards Miller and Etherington's body on the ground.

Bovington was grinning hugely under his yard broom moustache.

'Good *show*,' he was crying. 'Good *show*! That gave the Hun something to think about, eh? First rate, Strouden, first rate!' He retrieved his swagger stick and cap from Findlay, put on the cap and tapped the peak with the stick. 'Half a mind to transfer myself to the Flying Corps. Eh?' He looked around for Denham, spotted him hanging back by the tail of his plane and roared, 'What d'you think, Denham? Would I do as an observer? Eh? Would I do?'

Denham had slumped to half his normal size, a picture of misery. Strouden was staring at him, his face a volcanic red, blood diffusing up through his cheeks to his nose. It had begun to glow like a beacon. Red didn't suit him. He was about to blow.

Budge threw him a look, took Bovington by the arm and began to waffle about lunch and a drink in the mess. He steered the general back towards the château, Findlay and the rest of the retinue in tow.

Miller reached Denham just as Strouden blew.

'Where are Hardy and Parker?' he shouted at Denham. 'What the *fucking* hell do you think you were doing? Miller! What the *fucking* hell did you think you were doing?'

'It was the g-general,' Denham stuttered, his composure in tatters. 'As s-soon as we got up above the c-c-cloud he insisted we d-drop down again and cross the lines.' He gaped at Strouden. 'B-Bartlett cut the spotting and the general ordered me down.'

'Why the hell,' Strouden shouted, 'didn't you pretend you couldn't hear what he was saying, man?'

'He kept p-passing me these notes,' Denham spluttered, spraying Strouden with a fine mist of saliva. 'He'd already written the beastly things out!'

Strouden beat himself on the leg with his cane. 'You should have dropped the damn things... anything...'

'He had reams of them,' Denham insisted. '*Lose height... Over the lines...* He had one for every occasion.' Denham whined on, 'Must have been up half the night writing the beastly things out.'

'No, that's what they have adjutants for,' Chacksfield suggested laconically as he joined the group.

'Where's Bartlett and Hardy?' Strouden demanded again. 'Parker and Cliff?'

They all looked over their shoulders as if the missing pilots and their observers might be standing behind them.

Moss and Trueman walked up.

'I didn't see them after they dropped through the cloud,' Miller said.

'They were supposed to stay on my tail,' Denham reminded Strouden hopefully.

'Bartlett?' Moss said, as if he had just picked up the thread of the conversation. 'He bought it over Sanctuary Wood. Archie took their tail off as soon as we came through the cloud. God knows where Parker is.'

Strouden groaned.

'Etherington is dead,' Miller added. 'He caught a piece of shrapnel.'

'Bastard,' Strouden said. 'Bastard!'

General Bovington was sitting at the lunch table as Miller and the others trooped into the mess behind Strouden. The room was full — Strouden having revoked all passes into the town for the duration of the general's visit.

'The squadron is a team,' he had insisted that morning. 'He'll see that we're all together and pulling our weight.'

They were all together now, Chacksfield had commented as they had filed through the door of the mess, only not quite as many as before.

They sorted themselves out and took their chairs and were no sooner seated than the general stood and raised his whisky and soda aperitif. They all stood again with a noisy scraping of chairs and raised their glasses.

'The King,' Bovington roared.

'The King,' they all muttered in reply. They knocked back their drinks and, following Bovington's example, sat down again.

Strouden remained on his feet.

'Lieutenants Bartlett and Hardy, Parker and Cliff and Etherington,' he said.

The squadron stood once more, raised mostly empty glasses and repeated the names with somewhat more enthusiasm than they had afforded the King.

Bovington looked questioningly at Strouden.

'The five men killed this morning on your patrol,' Strouden said.

The general raised a bushy eyebrow. 'Rotten luck,' he said.

'They wouldn't have been killed if Lieutenant Denham hadn't taken you below the cloud cover,' Strouden went on.

Budge tugged at Strouden's sleeve. 'Steady Tommy,' Miller heard him mutter.

Bovington's expression remained blank. He looked down the table to where Denham sat. 'That a fact, Denham? Would they?'

'Yes, sir,' Denham said. 'I mean, no sir.' He didn't look up, occupied as he was trying to stare a hole in his plate of roast pork.

Strouden took his seat. The bile of his anger, the lava of the explosion, subsiding. Now he was no more than white with contained fury.

'If you recall, general,' Strouden said to Bovington, 'I advised you before take-off that the cloud ceiling was around two thousand. I expressly ordered Lieutenant Denham not to fly beneath it.'

'Two thousand?' the general repeated, forking some pork through the hedge formed by his moustache.

'Captain Miller,' Strouden called down the table, not taking his eyes off the general, 'what is your estimation of the cloud ceiling this morning?'

'Fifteen hundred feet at most, major,' Miller called back equably. 'Down to no more than a thousand in places over the Hun lines, I'd say.'

The general grunted loudly and allowed his gaze to rest on Miller briefly. Then he turned to Major Findlay sitting beside him.

'Bit of a black mark, there, Findlay,' he said. 'Five and do-able was your opinion. I remember it distinctly.'

Findlay glanced at the general apprehensively. 'Came in thicker as soon as you were up,' he explained defensively, dabbing at his mouth with his napkin.

'There you are, Strouden,' Bovington said. 'No accounting for the weather.

We can't blame young Denham if conditions turn sour on us, can we?'

'I'm not blaming Denham,' Strouden replied tonelessly.

The general's eyes narrowed momentarily then he looked back down the table again.

'There you are, Denham,' he said. 'No blame attached to you at all.'

Denham muttered, 'Thank you, general.'

An awkward silence followed broken only by the clatter of cutlery until Budge cleared his throat and outlined a tour of the hangars that had been arranged for the general.

Bovington finished his lunch and sat back in his chair and squared his shoulders.

'Thank you, captain, but we won't have time for that. Pressing matters back at HQ, don't y'know. Pressures of command and all that.' He dropped his napkin and stood, the rest of the squadron following suit. 'If you give Findlay the names of the men killed this morning, Strouden, I'll see if I can't get something done for them.' He scratched pensively at his cheek. 'What can we do for them, Findlay?'

'DFC, general? Something like that?'

'I'm sure their families will appreciate that,' Strouden said icily.

Halfway down the table Bovington and the retinue stopped in front of Miller.

'You're Miller, the American chappie, aren't you?' he said. 'Heard about you up at Brigade.'

'English, sir,' Miller said.

Bovington frowned and turned to Findlay on his shoulder.

'You said he was American, Findlay.'

Findlay glared at Miller. 'His records say American.'

The general turned back to Miller. 'Well? What have you got to say for yourself, Miller?'

'Winchester, general.'

'School?'

'Born.'

Bovington grunted again. 'Black mark, Findlay,' he said as he walked out of the mess. 'Men who want to stay on my staff give me the right information.'

7

Miller stood a chair in the sun in front of Heyward's hut and sat down. The cloud cover that had ruined the patrol had disappeared down the same road as the general and his retinue, leaving behind the distinct impression that he carried it permanently over his head like some peripatetic gloom. Miller had watched the staff cars disappear towards an impromptu visit to the forward trenches, then had given his coat to Jones to clean but still found himself scraping listlessly at the front of his tunic as if trying to rid the last vestiges of Etherington from his clothes.

They had been halfway through the debriefing in the operations room when, in a minor resurrection, Parker and Cliff had turned up in a lorry belonging to a company of sappers. They had caught some shrapnel in the engine and had been forced down but had made it back over the lines. They had ended up nose down in a bomb crater. Shaken and bruised but otherwise unhurt, they had managed to cadge a ride back to the airfield.

'You'll probably get a DFC,' Chacksfield had observed sardonically, having gatecrashed the debriefing on the strength of being Denham's regular observer. 'The general thinks you're dead.'

Their reappearance, though, had done nothing to lighten Strouden's mood. He was still on edge, hearing little that was addressed to him and prone to staring into empty space; when he wasn't doing that, he glared menacingly at Denham and Miller in turn. Budge did his best to carry on as normal but even his usual equanimity had not been up to the task of finding much that was positive in Bovington's visit. Miller supposed that they might have disconcerted a few Huns when Bovington strafed their trenches, and the artillery had undoubtedly made a saving on shells when Bartlett had called off the spotting but, all in all, he couldn't see much else on the profit side of the ledger after the patrol.

'We were right in front of Hardy and Bartlett when they bought it,' Parker said laconically, suggesting there wasn't much point in elaborating. Slim and well proportioned, there was an effortless athletic grace about him that drew the eye whenever he moved. Staring vertically into a bomb crater from an upended FE didn't seem to have perturbed him unduly.

Cliff, somehow slow and gauche in comparison to his pilot, looked as if he thought duty demanded a little more detail and added, 'I'd lost sight of Denham, you see. I was looking back over my shoulder. Archie was as thick as... as...' he looked down at his hands as if the simile he was searching for might be found there, but settled for, 'Archie was pretty thick. Hardy must have flown right into a burst. Machine just fell apart. Rotten luck, I'd say. I think we must have caught a piece of something in our prop.'

'Stopped turning,' Parker added as if it was his last word on the matter.

Strouden stared at a spot of grease on the wall.

Budge said, 'Anything to add, Mr Denham?'

Denham had already delivered a second litany of excuses, trying to tread the fine line between absolving himself of blame and dumping it all on a senior officer. He began to explain about Bovington's notes once again, caught Strouden's stare falling back on him and dried up.

Miller outlined what had happened from his point of view, saying that he must have come down through some particularly thick cover having lost contact with the others.

'I was somewhere over Gheluvelt, east of the others,' he told them. 'Then I almost ran into Moss and saw Bovington — General Bovington,' he amended, 'loosing off at the trenches. Hardy must already have gone down and Parker have made for the lines. I think Etherington had already been hit. I thought it was shrapnel from the Archie but it might have been ground-fire. We were drawing a lot and we were diving. It wasn't easy to tell from the angle. I suppose the MO will know.'

Now, sitting in front of the hut, he felt the black despondency that he had experienced the previous evening descend upon him again. The day before he had tried to put it down to missing the Rumpler two-seater but he knew it wasn't that; he had already had it before he had even seen the Hun. Besides, the idea that he was out of sorts because he had failed to kill someone wasn't one designed to lighten his mood in any case. Etherington's pointless death hadn't helped. The boy had barely been out twenty-four hours and Miller couldn't help but remember with a sense of shame that he had been ranting at the dead man on the way back for not being up to the job.

Looking across the field at B Flight's FEs being pushed out and readied for the evening patrol, he tried to remember when that first early flush of enthusiasm had finally died. He wondered if things had turned sour when he had got back from his stint training at home (he called it *home* but he had to admit that there was little that seemed familiar, nothing he really cherished as a native land). But in truth, he hadn't found things that much different when he returned in the spring; if anything the situation had improved. Back in the previous autumn, even before he had left, the Eindeckers had almost cleared them out of the skies and they had had to start flying in formations to protect the reconnaissance and spotter aircraft. By the spring, with the introduction of the new machines, they had begun to redress the balance. No, it was the general *tenor* that had changed and he was aware that that had happened well before the previous autumn.

It was all so different from the way it had begun. It was almost callous to think it now, but back then it had been fun. Well, it wasn't fun anymore. For his part, despite beginning to feel some sort of guilty shame at the thought, looking back he remembered those first few weeks as being the best. Despite the lack of sleep and food, the exhaustion — not even being able to wash or get out of one's clothes — it could now almost be remembered fondly.

After rendezvousing at Amiens, they had moved as a body to Mauberge. It had been a war of movement then, and they were up constantly, looking for the

German advanced units and their artillery and often running across detachments of Hun cavalry doing the same on the ground. Then, after an hour or two of trying not to get lost, it was back to the field to deliver a report, generally to be told another reconnaissance was required somewhere else and to get straight back up. And at the end of the day it was not uncommon to find the field you had taken off from was now behind the advancing Hun army. There had been a brightly painted van, he remembered, with HP Sauce emblazoned on the side and if that wasn't on the field when you returned you flew on until you found it. Le Cateau... St Quentin... La Fère... They had retreated through them all in the first days, catching whatever they could to eat and sleeping wherever they could find to sleep – a barn, a hayrick, under a hedge on one occasion, he recalled. The weather had been perfect. Fine days with little wind and nothing more than a scattering of cloud drifting aimlessly like lost flocks of sheep. The country had been eerily deserted, empty fields and farmhouses, and one would hardly see a living soul until suddenly coming across a troop of Uhlans riding along some sunken road and a madness of rearing horses and wild rifle fire would break out as you passed over. Then, as often as not, you'd go back so you could take a pot-shot with a rifle or revolver or whatever you had thought to take up with you. But it was all harmless enough; no one had the skill then to hit anything from a moving aircraft.

Compiègne... Senlis... Juilly... Serris... Touquin... into September and it seemed as if they'd never stop. With the French and British in full retreat, flying over a column of men of any army would generally result in a blizzard of ground fire. The French, in particular, would shoot at anything. They had painted the union flag on the underside of the wings so that they could be identified but it made little difference. Later they painted on the roundels which proved easier to see.

It wasn't until they reached Melun, near the Seine south of Paris that they had finally stopped. The Germans unaccountably turned east to face the French, exposing their flank, and had found themselves trapped between two French armies on the Marne. Soon *they* were in retreat and the corps was back in Compiègne again, then Amiens. By mid-October they were in St Omer and that's where they were to stay.

After that, he remembered, things had settled down and at the time he had not been sorry. The flying had become almost routine. There were the reconnaissance sorties still and someone had come up with the idea of trying bombing to disrupt the Hun supplies. They'd developed a method of spotting for the artillery, wirelessing down to the gunners to range the target once they'd perfected it. They'd even amused themselves taking shots at the opposition machines with their rifles and revolvers, although generally to little effect. From his perspective now, it had all seemed like a game; a bit of a lark and not just for the younger men.

When had it all become so *earnest*? And even as he asked himself the question he felt that familiar pang of guilt run through him like the point of a bayonet. It had always been *earnest* for the poor bastards down on the ground. They'd had the rough side of it, the sharp end of the stick, right from the outset. He flushed at the thought of it. While he had been joyriding, quibbling over fancied moral objections to actually trying to kill someone, *they* had been up to their waists in mud and blood, shelled and gassed, cold and hungry and no doubt thinking longingly of a home to which *he* felt little but indifference. He couldn't help feeling that sometimes it was difficult to stomach his own self-absorption.

He got up, chucked the chair inside the hut, picked up his gloves and goggles and went to find Strouden. Perhaps a couple of hours up in the air would clear his mood. Then, he supposed, he'd better try to find out why Heyward had hanged himself. That's why he was there, after all.

Strouden was in his office, sitting in his chair staring grimly at a map on the opposite wall. Miller waited a moment in case he was interrupting some train of thought, then realised that Strouden wasn't actually looking at the map at all and that it just happened to be in his line of sight.

'I thought I'd take my Strutter up for a couple of hours if you've no objection,' he finally asked when Strouden showed no signs of stirring himself.

The CO tore his eyes off the map.

'Miller. Yes, yes go ahead.' He shifted in his chair and cleared his throat, pushed a piece of paper sideways across his desktop and looked at Miller again. 'I suppose,' he said abstractly, 'you've been allowed a fair bit of latitude in scout squadrons.'

'Latitude, sir?'

But Strouden didn't elaborate. He pulled out his watch instead. 'B Flight will be going up in an hour. They'll be taking some photographs along the Menin Road. Fly cover, will you? Gregory's DH2 still isn't quite right.'

'Will do,' Miller said.

'And you'd better let Mr Chatterton know you'll be up with them. I don't suppose they'll have seen a Strutter before and I wouldn't put it past them to try and put some holes in you before they notice the roundels.'

'Chatterton?'

'Flight commander.'

'Right sir.'

'And Miller?'

He stopped halfway to the door.

Strouden scratched at his forehead. 'You'll be up at dawn with C again. You'll need someone to replace... the chap this morning?'

'Etherington.'

'Etherington. Take up one of the other two that came in with him, will you?' He glanced down at the paper on the desk. 'Pollock. Neither of them has the faintest idea of what he's doing.'

'Right, sir.'

'I wouldn't mention Dunne or Etherington to him if I were you. Some chaps can be superstitious about that sort of thing.'

'The machine, you mean? I suppose they can.'

'No point in worrying the boy unnecessarily.'

'I suppose not.'

'How did you find it, anyway?'

'The FE?'

'Yes.'

Apart from its habit of killing observers?

'Fine.'

He told the C Flight sergeant — Greene, a taciturn stick of a man who looked as if he bathed each morning in oil — to get the One-and-a-half-Strutter fuelled and out onto the field, then he retrieved his flying coat from Jones. There was little trace of Etherington left on it, only a dark stain on the leather around the patched hole where Jones had sponged him off. He hoped that somewhere in the world the boy had left a more enduring mark.

He found Chatterton on the field next to his FE2b. At Miller's height, he had the good looks that other men had turned into stage careers. Budge made the introduction. Chatterton took his hand and outlined the patrol.

'I thought we'd cross the lines at Hooge at around eight thousand and follow the road through Gheluvelt to Menin,' he said. 'We'll just nip up and down the road a few times while Watson takes his snaps at around six-and-a-half. Two or three passes should do it. Glad to have you with us.'

He had a last word with his flight and pointed out Miller's One-and-a-half-Strutter to the men. Miller recognised one or two from the mess but on the field they all looked like variations on a theme under their helmets. He heard the name Tozer but wasn't able to single him out before they began to move off to their machines.

He climbed into the Strutter and went through the familiar take-off ritual, gunning his engine once it had started and listening for anything he might have to worry about later. He let the FEs rumble across the grass, then, as the first of the four machines lifted into the air, he waved away the man holding down the Sopwith's tail and moved off to follow.

He felt his mood lift with the Strutter's wheels and after a minute or two of circling and climbing he caught the rest of the flight and pulled above them. The One-and-a-half-Strutter was lighter than the FE2b with a better rate of climb and he was up at ten thousand feet and waiting while the others still wheeled below like clumsy birds on a slow thermal. He executed a few turns and rolls while he waited, checking how the machine handled. A new ground crew, he had sometimes found, would make adjustments to the way the machine had been set up by the previous crew. It was something he had grown particular about — having a machine do exactly what he expected it to do when he wanted to do it.

Far to the east the cloud bank that had departed with the general was now no more than a hazy band on the horizon. Around them in its place a confection of clouds was laid out like pastries, fluffy morsels likely to melt at the touch. To the north sunlight glinted on the Channel. Here and there he could see small formations of aircraft, bombers he thought, moving in the direction of Ostend, and, closer to their own position but still well to the rear of their own lines, a flock of Hun machines no doubt waiting for someone to stray towards them. That was one thing that had changed for the better, he reflected: they were no longer as keen to cross the lines if they thought they might meet some DH2s or FEs. He looked around but there were no other machines close enough for him to worry about except for a French Morane and a Neiuport moving towards him from the south and he deliberately spun the One-and-a-half-Strutter around in a half-roll to give them a good view of his roundels so there would be no mistakes. In the early days, rule of thumb insisted that every machine be treated as an enemy machine until one determined otherwise. It had taken some while to become used to the different machines, their shape in the air, and also to get used to the nasty habit of men on the ground — artillery as well as infantry — shooting at anything low enough to attract their attention.

Looking down over the side again he saw that one thousand feet below him Chatterton had gathered his flight and turned towards the lines. The sun had begun to dip, lengthening shadows on the ground. He picked up another formation away north near the coast, four perhaps five craft, moving east and below them the smudged explosions of anti-aircraft fire trying to gauge their height. Ahead, over the German lines, he could see no aerial activity and he glanced back over his shoulder, into the sun, wondering if the four Hun machines he had seen earlier had managed to get west of them and were now hidden there, within its glare.

Below, the FEs had moved into their layered formation at eight thousand feet, Chatterton's pennant streaming from a strut of the leading machine with Griffiths and Watson with the camera behind and the other two either side and slightly elevated. They had turned east crossing the lines over what was left of the battered town of Hooge, almost lying abreast of the opposing trenches, and were now following the old Menin road. Archie had opened up from his positions in Sanctuary and Polygon Woods as they ran the gauntlet between the two. The front line itself still ran through Sanctuary Wood on the southern boundary of the salient, the struggle having ebbed and flowed for two years through its shattered timber. What little of the wood that was left had been scorched black by artillery fire then bleached white in death, twisted this way and that like giant whale ribs exposed to the summer sun. Yet, even at his height Miller could see smears of fresh growth greening the carnage below; grass and weed, branch or twig straining into leaf in their agony with a tenacity that dripped its optimism into his pervading sense of hopelessness.

He pulled out his notebook and jotted the thought down, careful this time not to read or even over-think it into pretension or banality.

Polygon Wood, behind the German lines since the previous spring, had been flattened like its counterpart to deny cover for the guns. Archie, tucked away somewhere within its cratered and hummocked floor, began to find their range, bursting ahead of the FEs like dirty exploding balloons, spewing shrapnel in indiscriminate arcs. Knowing that it was only dangerous if you were close enough to get hit by a piece of the red-hot metal did little to calm the nerves and a heavy and co-ordinated fire would always be disconcerting enough to break up a formation. Miller, a thousand feet above and ignored, watched as Chatterton dipped and turned to throw off the range, leading the rest of the flight into a mechanical dance of 'follow the leader'.

Over the rubble of Gheluvelt, Chatterton took them down to allow Griffiths and Watson to find their optimum height for photographs. Archie, suddenly too high, sprayed the air indiscriminately for a minute of two then settled back into a tighter barrage. The formation broadened a little as they began to take the photographs and the machine on Chatterton's right wing — either Tozer or Royston, Miller thought — began to drift wide and he could see Chatterton moving south towards him like a sheepdog closing up the pack. The camera was strapped to the side of Watson's nacelle and, while Griffith had to ignore Archie and keep the machine steady, Watson took the photographs, allowing as he worked for their airspeed and drift as he timed the exposures. From above Miller could see Watson pulling one photographic plate out of the camera and inserting another as they flew along the Menin Road. Archie thinned as they left the woods behind, picking up desultory bursts from isolated pockets until the emplacements around Menin itself took up the barrage.

Chatterton took them the length of the road three times, Archie concentrating his fire on each turn with greater accuracy. One of the flanking machines was rocked by a burst and, as the smoke cleared, Miller could see the tattered fabric of its wing fluttering in the wind. Holding position above them, he scanned the sky, weaving east and west of the formation below as the sun sank slowly in the west. The four Hun machines he had seen were still missing and by now had had plenty of time to fly west above them, turn east again to keep the sun on their backs and the westerly wind in their tails. Caught fifteen miles behind the lines and facing a west wind to go home is how Miller would have wanted *them* if the rôles had been reversed.

On the third pass over Menin, Chatterton broke the pattern, took a bearing south and picked up the Lys where it flowed between Menin and Comines. The river, a blue and silver thread in the sinking sun, meandered through a moonscape, spilling here and there into craters that, by some strange alchemy, turned its waters a viscous green-brown that seemed to heave and shudder as if with its own independent life. Above it and slowly as if through water themselves, they followed the Lys over Comines picking up new bursts of hate from the anti-aircraft guns, all the FEs dodging now that Watson had taken his photographs.

Skirting north of Comines, Chatterton picked up the old railway line that had linked Ypres and Comines and turned to follow the tracks north. As he banked and turned a little ahead of the FEs below, Miller caught a movement in the sun and saw the four machines he had been waiting for. Closer now and using the glare of the sun, they were slightly below him and were diving on the formation. Two were Eindeckers and the other two Halberstadts. Dipping the Strutter's nose, he picked up speed and, with the Hun five hundred yards off, put her into a vertical dive, half-rolled and eased the stick back, coming out above the Hun machines. He squeezed the trigger of the Vickers as the top wing of a Halberstadt passed under his nose, then tried to keep her straight, raking down the length of the fuselage. He saw a little timber fly from the tail and the Halberstadt rolled out of the attack and dived, spinning as she went. Straightening out he came up behind the three remaining machines as they closed on Chatterton and the formation. Ahead he could see the observer in one of the flanking machines climbing up out of his nacelle, feet on the combing, as he reached up for the rear Lewis gun. Miller put a burst in behind one of the Eindeckers then had to pull up and zoom as he crossed over and above the formation. Turning in the climb and falling out in a roll he straightened again behind and below the turning Hun. With the FE observers covering their rear with their top wing Lewis guns, the Eindeckers and the remaining Halberstadt had dropped under the FEs to come up at them from their blind spot, below and beneath. Finding Miller to *their* rear, they thought again, put in a few hopeful bursts from too great a range and broke contact, putting their noses down and diving for home. The FE on the right flank seemed to feint to follow then thought better of it. Watching, Miller held his position behind them until they approached the Hun reserve trenches and Archie took up the refrain again, then climbed free of the smoke.

Crossing the lines to the east of St Eloi he replayed the fight in his head like a three-dimensional chess game, looking to see if a better advantage might have been gained. But they had moved well and he had been impressed by the way Chatterton had kept the formation together, the observers acting as rear gunners protecting each other with Miller covering the blind spot.

He suddenly thought of Cody and his death again; how fate had engineered the collapse of the machine and the grip of his passenger that had left him with no room to manoeuvre. It was as if the dead hand of the Man from Reading was always there, poised above his shoulder. In a dogfight he was sure he had sensed him at his back — although, of course, he was always too busy to turn and look the Man in the eye. But he *believed* he was there nevertheless, on his shoulder trying to interfere with those instant decisions, trying to cloud his judgement of tactics by making him turn the logical way when only the counter-intuitive manoeuvre would take him out of the enemy's sights.

But was it really only about positioning? He became dimly aware that there was something of importance there had he the wit but to grasp it, even while knowing that any insights he might have up here would inevitably dribble away as he dropped down. In the air, and particularly when flying over those peaks and valleys above cloud, it all seemed so clear, almost commonplace. It was clinging on to this understanding once he had his feet back on the ground that was so difficult and he cursed the vagueness, the fog, the *cloud* that seemed eternally to envelope him down there. It was as if the understanding drained out of him, pulled by gravity from his brain so that, by the time he knew what was happening, it was already too late.

No, there was only one certainty as far as Miller was concerned and that was that he was always up there. Watching in the cockpit behind him and waiting for that one slip, that one lapse in concentration that would give him the opportunity to put his hands on your shoulders and drive you down into the ground.

Watson's plates were taken off to be developed while Budge tried to impose some order on the debriefing during what sounded like a series of haphazard observations. Macmaster, Chatterton's observer, disagreed with Royston's observer, White — an NCO who had volunteered to observe when Strouden had needed a stopgap and had proved to have an aptitude for it — over the amount of Hun traffic moving south out of Menin. Tozer, a restless young man of only average height but whose athletic frame lent him the impression of size, maintained it was immaterial as the traffic leaving Menin was not the objective of the patrol. Chatterton told him curtly that *all* information was valuable. Griffiths and Watson who had taken the photographs sat through it all with an air of boredom having done what was asked of them, and Boyes, Tozer's observer, almost lost under the peak of his cap and within the folds of his flying coat, sat apart from his pilot as if he wished he was somewhere else. Once the arguments had been resolved, Royston claimed the Halberstadt on Miller's behalf.

'Saw him go down. Shot the tail off.'

'Damaged, but I don't think it was out of control,' Miller said.

'Playing dead?' Strouden asked, conspicuously happier now that he had got through the day without losing any more men.

'I think so.'

'You should have gone after it,' Tozer said. 'Sitting duck.'

'I'll log it as a 'driven down',' Budge said.

Miller said he was happy to take that and sat through the rest of the debriefing before waiting by the door for Tozer and catching the tail-end of a conversation he was having with Royston:

'...Boyes off to?' Royston was saying. 'He was out of here like a shot.'

'His nose is out of joint,' Tozer said. 'In a funk, if you ask me. Yesterday he actually had the cheek to go to the Old Man. He wanted — '

Miller put a hand on Tozer's arm as he passed.

'Sorry to interrupt...' he said.

Tozer glared at him.

Miller smiled indulgently. 'If you've got a minute, I'd like a word.'

'I wanted to get cleaned up,' Tozer said. 'Can't it wait? I'm going into town.'

'It'll just take a few minutes,' Miller assured him.

'What's it about?'

'Say the mess in half an hour?'

'Oh, all right,' Tozer said petulantly. 'If I must.'

Miller returned to Heyward's hut and stripped off his clothes. Jones had hot water waiting for him in the basin and Miller washed, trying to rid himself of the oil and fumes that always blew back from a tractor machine. It was one of the advantages that pushers had in that, back in England after a day's training, you weren't forever catching the puzzled expression above a wrinkled nose if you were lucky enough to find yourself in the company of a lady.

When he had scrubbed himself as clean as he was going to get, he walked back to the château and Budge's office. The head clerk, Donaldson sat at a desk just inside the door, tapping at the keys of a Remington typewriter and the recording officer was leaning over him going through the notes he had just made on the patrol. He looked up at Miller and smiled briefly.

'Hullo Miller, was there something else?'

'One thing. Would you have a list of the flying officers and the flights they're attached to? You know what it's like at a new squadron,' he added. 'I find it helps me remember names.'

Budge pursed his lips, tapped his hook on the desktop a few times then said, 'Should have, somewhere.' He sorted through some of the papers on his desk. 'I'm trying to get confirmation on that Halberstadt of yours but that far behind the lines... Royston was pretty sure.'

'He's keen.'

'You?'

'I'm pretty sure he would have made it down.'

The clerk cleared his throat. 'If you give me a minute, sir, I'll knock out a list for you.' He pulled the paper in his Remington out, rolled in a blank sheet and began typing.

'If you've got a minute?' Miller said to Budge.

'Right you are,' Budge said. 'While you're doing that, Donaldson, I think we'll have a drink in the mess. What do you say, Miller?'

Miller followed Budge out into the corridor.

'Heyward, I suppose?' Budge said. 'No point in having it all around the Other Ranks, is there?'

'When you put his things together for his family,' Miller said. 'I was wondering if there was a diary... or a journal?'

Budge gave it some thought. 'Well, you know keeping a diary is against regulations but there were a couple of exercise books. Poetry, I think.' He offered Miller a tight, self-deprecating smile. 'Not my cup of tea, to be honest. I did take a look — just in case there was something the censor might object to, you understand. Nothing I could make out, though.'

'You said he wasn't much of a mixer, did he have *any* friends?'

'Don't get me wrong. I didn't mean the fellow had been ostracised. It was just that he tended to keep himself aloof, that's all. He was a bit *literary*, if you get my meaning.' Budge emphasised the word as if it denoted a particular species with which he was sure Miller must be familiar. 'He'd have a drink with you in the mess, that sort of thing, but if you were looking for someone to go into town with for an evening you wouldn't pick Heyward as your first choice. Well, unless you were going to the theatre, perhaps.'

'But not the music hall?' Miller said.

Budge laughed. 'No.'

'What about his observer, Dunne?' Miller asked.

67

'Ah, poor Dunne,' Budge said a little wistfully. 'He wasn't exactly *Heyward's* observer. To be honest Heyward didn't get *up* that much. There was always one thing or another – engine failure or something not working as it should. And the Old Man sometimes likes to rotate the men where he can so Dunne didn't always fly with Heyward. To tell the truth, no one much liked going up with him. He didn't inspire one with confidence, if you know what I mean.'

'Was Dunne well-liked?'

Budge looked sideways at Miller as if the question surprised him. 'Bobby Dunne? Everyone liked him. First class chap. As for Heyward, I suppose Arthur Foden was closest to him. They'd been at school together, apparently.'

'Did you see the crash?'

'That killed Dunne? Oh yes, I generally watch the boys come home.' He smiled at Miller. 'I was on my perch.'

'What happened?'

'He cut his engine too soon on his approach and lost too much height. He could probably still have glided in on what he had but he didn't really have the confidence — I don't think he ever developed a real *feel* for a machine. Anyway, he opted for restarting his engine — to come around again I suppose — but he tried to climb before he had enough speed and stalled. He almost stopped in the air. His nose was up and with what little forward momentum he had it dropped, of course. He came down nose first and Dunne, being in the front of the nacelle, was thrown out. The MO said that hitting the nacelle probably dislocated his shoulder. It was the fall that broke his neck, though. If they'd come down any harder, the engine would have hit Heyward and killed him, too.'

They walked into the mess. It was empty except for a man leaning against the bar and looking disconsolately into his glass.

'Gracey!' Budge said. 'Have you met Miller? Gracey's the squadron's armaments officer,' Budge told Miller as they joined him. He was a thin, greying man whose slight stoop unaccountably brought a broken pencil to Miller's mind.

'You're the chap with the Strutter, aren't you Miller? Where the devil did you get that?'

'Off the RNAS, as a matter of fact,' Miller said.

'The Navy?' Gracey said in disbelief. 'They never give anything away. Especially their flying corps. Between them and the rest of the army I can't get my hands on anything worth having.'

'We were stationed near Calais,' Miller told him. 'The RNAS were issued with half-a-dozen Strutters and turned them down. They'd had some trouble with the original interrupter gear. Had a nasty habit of shooting off the propeller, apparently.'

'That's what I heard,' Gracey said.

'These had the new Ross interrupters so my CO snapped them up. Then we got transferred down to the Somme before the Navy realised their mistake.'

'And your CO let you keep one?'

'I'm only up here on loan,' Miller said.

'He's here about Heyward,' Budge explained.

'Heyward?' Gracey said, as if the name was familiar but he couldn't quite place it.

'Chap who hanged himself,' Budge added helpfully.

'Oh, right,' Gracey said. 'Didn't know the fella. What's he to do with you?'

'I've been asked to find out why he did it.'

Gracey look mystified. 'Does it matter?'

'Does to his family, I suppose,' Budge said.

'Oh yes, well I suppose it would, wouldn't it? Mother's probably all of a flutter to know why poor little Johnny did it.'

'Charlie,' Budge said. 'His name was Charlie.'

'Poor little Charlie,' Gracey amended.

'Well,' Miller said, 'actually she doesn't know.'

'What? No one told her?' Gracey said. 'That's a bit thick.'

A group of officers walked into the mess and Miller turned towards them. 'Not that he hanged himself,' he said.

'Looking for someone?' Budge asked.

'Oh, well,' Gracey mused. 'I can see it would be a bit heartless telling the poor woman something like that.'

'Tozer,' Miller said to Budge. 'I was supposed to meet him here.'

'Tozer? I saw him getting a lift into Pops about fifteen minutes ago.'

'How'd the Old Man explain it away, though?' Gracey wanted to know.

'Fifteen minutes?'

'Tommy told her he died in a flying accident,' Budge said.

Gracey harrumphed and waved his empty glass at Grimshaw behind the bar.

'With the number of "flying accidents" Tommy has to write home about these days,' he said, 'they'll begin to think we don't know what we're doing.'

8

The town was heaving. Like a rotting carcass left athwart the road, it pulsed with soldiers crawling like maggots feeding off whatever choice morsels it had left to offer. Disgorging themselves from the pupae of vehicles they swarmed along the streets heading for anywhere soft onto which they might attach their mouth parts.

Poperinghe sat on a railway junction and at the hub of five converging roads. Around it a constant stream of vehicles passed in a hooting cacophony through columns of marching men. Limbered guns and horses added to the anarchy as they moved along the main road. On the outskirts of the town vast canvas transit camps had been pitched to accommodate the new battalions arriving to replace those about to be pulled back from the front. Nearer the rail lines casualty clearing stations had been set up to ferry the wounded to hospitals or, for those fortunate enough to be going home, to Boulogne. German shelling had left craters like puncture wounds scabbed over by rubble along the streets; buildings either side seemed to totter towards the pits as if drawn magnetically into their depths. Men and vehicles skirting the craters spilled out across the road and around the barriers thrown up to deter those drivers inclined by sleepiness, or perhaps sheer boredom, to drive straight into them.

Miller threaded his way through knots of men walking, often arm in arm, in and out of the traffic toward the square at the centre of the town. Some were drunk, some were looking for drunkenness; they wove a meandering progress that only sheered off at sharp angles when confronted by approaching military policemen.

General officers, disdaining to travel by foot, rode in staff cars, sitting upright in attitudes stiff with authority; those of lower rank strolled, swagger stick at the ready to touch the cap in an acknowledgement of a passing fellow. Miller passed salutes thrown like confetti by eager young bridesmaids. Closer to the centre the tide of men on the pavement ebbed and flowed with its own rhythm. The cafés and bars, doors open, exhaled men onto the pavement with one breath and sucked in their replacements with the next. Sound swilled around him; engines, horns and shouts mixing in a contrapuntal dissonance that had, as a sort of base rhythm, an interminable drone of talk, indistinguishable as isolated words and atonal as a conglomerate whole. Miller grimaced at the almost physical pain of being in its midst. He pushed through as it flowed around him, attempting to swim to some isolated pool of calmness and silence that began to seem forever a stroke or two beyond his reach.

A hand grabbed his right arm and rushed him forward. Another took his left while he was trying to shake off the first.

'Miller, old chap,' a voice said in his ear.

He turned and looked into a pair of inquisitive eyes. Lieutenant Breconridge, the A Flight observer he had met at breakfast, parted his slightly, but apparently perpetually, amused lips and said, 'Out for fun?'

'As a matter of fact,' Miller said, startled, 'I was looking for Lieutenant Tozer.'

'We're looking for fun,' a voice on his other side said.

A grinning Chacksfield had him by the upper arm and was steering him across the road. Miller stumbled over a kerb and was pulled back sharply as a lorry lumbered past him. Then, before he could regain his balance he was propelled forward again, warping through the weft of the traffic to the other side.

He dug his heels in and pulled the others to a halt.

'Tozer,' he said again, straightening his tunic and suddenly seeing himself through another pair of eyes as one of those self-important officers he had instinctively disliked in his first months of service. Perhaps that's how they get you, he thought, by slowly absorbing you into the gut of their corps, dissolving you until you became part of their indistinguishable mass.

'Not a chance, old man,' Breconridge said. 'Not in this chaos. Better come along with us.'

'Where are you going?'

'Madame Poulon's,' Chacksfield announced.

'Where's that?' Miller asked.

Breconridge leaned towards Miller confidentially. 'If it was old Chacksfield here you were looking for I would have known where to look.' He winked ostentatiously. 'Old Chacksfield is always at Madame Poulon's.'

'I say!' Chacksfield protested.

'Who's Madame Poulon?' Miller asked.

'You make me sound like a sex fiend or something,' Chacksfield objected.

'He doesn't know Madame Poulon,' Breconridge said to Chacksfield, leaning across in front of Miller.

Chacksfield peered at Miller, shaking his head condescendingly. 'Just where have you *spent* the war?'

'Does Tozer go there?' Miller asked.

'Just about everyone goes to Madame Poulon's,' Chacksfield said.

'It's a brothel, I suppose.'

'Miller!' Breconridge said feigning surprise, stopping dead in the street and pulling Miller and Chacksfield to a halt.

Chacksfield muttered, 'Still, it's a bit thick making out I'm *always* there.'

'Do I detect a moral objection to a brothel?' Breconridge asked. 'I was given to understand that Americans spent half their lives in brothels.'

'I'm not American,' Miller said automatically. 'I was just brought up there, that's all.'

Blocking the path as they were, they were hit by a group of sappers stumbling along the street. The sappers staggered a few steps in retreat.

'I say!' Chacksfield exclaimed again. 'Watch where you're going man!'

The sappers mumbled an apology as they weaved past.

'I know *some* chaps have a moral objection,' Breconridge granted. 'Sons of parsons, mainly, brought up in a theological atmosphere, don't y'know.'

'Whorehouses,' Chacksfield decided. 'I think Americans prefer the term, whorehouses.'

'Chacksfield has an academic interest,' Breconridge confided. 'Your guv'nor wasn't a parson by any chance, was he Miller?'

'A schoolteacher, actually,' Miller said. 'And either term will do.'

'What?'

'Brothel or whorehouse,' Miller said.

'A gentleman,' Breconridge corrected, 'may visit a brothel. But I'm not sure a gentleman would enter a whorehouse.'

'If it's the same thing...' Chacksfield said.

'But that's just it, old man,' Breconridge went on. 'How *can* it be if a gentleman frequents one but not the other?'

'What do you say, Miller?' Chacksfield asked. 'From a disinterested viewpoint. That is, moral objections aside. You are disinterested, aren't you?'

'I say we should get off the street and discuss it over a drink,' he suggested, 'if only to avoid being knocked over.'

'Capital idea,' Breconridge said.

'We could have a drink at Madame Poulon's,' Chacksfield objected. 'All the girls will be taken if we don't get there soon.'

Miller said, 'I rather thought that was the point.'

'What point?'

'That the girls get taken.'

Chacksfield's face assumed a bewildered expression.

'I believe, old man,' Breconridge explained, leaning across Miller to address Chacksfield again, 'that the captain was making a joke. A play on the word "taken", don't y'know.'

'Was it funny?' Chacksfield asked.

'Moderately so,' Breconridge allowed. 'Moderately so.'

'Do Americans *have* a sense of humour?' Chacksfield enquired.

'Charlie Chaplin,' Breconridge said.

'But he's *English*.'

'But it's *Americans* who pay him to be funny,' Breconridge pointed out, 'so it follows that they must have a sense of humour, mustn't they?'

'Or a sense for business,' Miller suggested.

'Well,' Breconridge decided, 'since the suggestions are not mutually exclusive, I suggest we drink at Madame Poulon's, then. Unless,' he added to Miller, 'you *do* have some moral objections?'

'None,' Miller said, capitulating.

'But if gentlemen do not frequent whorehouses,' Chacksfield persisted, 'does it not follow that those who may not be gentlemen should not frequent brothels?'

'It's the academic in him,' Breconridge apologised. He grabbed Miller by the arm again and turned to his friend as he resumed his pace. 'Chuck it, Chacksfield.'

They stopped outside a house where groups of men had gathered, milling about on the pavement. They were, Miller could see, all officers and, as if to underline the observation, a sign hanging on the wall by the door proclaimed, *Officers Only*. Enlisted men, of course, would have had their own whorehouse and, if military protocol held, he supposed that NCOs had access to yet another establishment; a sort of middling place no doubt, where bluff no-nonsense competence held sway. It never ceased to astound him just how far military discipline and hierarchy reached. Then again, he could see that it wouldn't do for a private to see a general with his britches down around his ankles. That sort of sight wouldn't contribute anything to military discipline.

He looked at the building and saw it was a quite unremarkable French town house, square to the road behind the rusting stumps of what had been iron railings — the victim, as had been its neighbours, of the war's insatiable appetite for iron. It was protected now only by a small unkempt front garden. The front door was open and some dim light squeezed from the gaps in its shuttered windows — beacons, Miller thought, from a couple of thousand feet to enemy aircraft, although experience had shown that the safest place to be under a bomber was its target. A pair of officers had just issued from the door, smoking and talking together, and they shouldered their way past as Chacksfield and Breconridge, with Miller in tow, walked up the front path to the entrance.

From inside — from somewhere down the length of a gloomy hall — they could hear music and laughter and an occasional feminine squeal that might equally have been delight, surprise or alarm.

'It sounds devilishly busy already,' Chacksfield complained.

'How often do you come here?' Miller asked.

'Oh, not a lot,' Chacksfield said casually.

'Chacksfield has logged more hours in Madame Poulon's than he has in the air,' Breconridge remarked.

'That's a beastly lie,' Chacksfield said, leading them to a door at the end of the hall from behind which most of the noise was coming. He pushed it open.

Miller followed them and was hit instantly by a wave of cloying scent mingled with cigar smoke and stale alcohol. He began coughing as the fine mist of powder that hung in the air suddenly clogged in his throat.

The room was large, dimly lit by table and wall lamps and furnished with chairs and sofas deeply upholstered in plush reds and purples. Officers from a variety of units filled the room, standing or sitting, while girls, haphazardly-clad in diaphanous satins and silks, hung off them like pendant jewellery, heads thrown backwards with laughter to expose their white throats. As the three of them entered, some of the heads turned speculatively to inspect the newcomers.

An older woman, fully dressed yet still displaying a deep and impressive cleavage, detached herself from a group of officers and approached them. She was tall, elegant and not what Miller had expected. Older, he decided, than she probably looked, hollow cheeks under her prominent bones lent her face a natural expression of haughtiness. Her hair, short and neatly coiffured, was streaked by grey that can only have been by intention.

'Lieutenant,' she cooed in heavily accented English. She held out her arms, took Chacksfield's hands in hers and leaned toward him slightly to receive a kiss on either cheek. 'I am delighted to see you once again.'

'Do you see what I mean, Miller,' Breconridge said with an air of validation.

Madame Poulon turned to Miller and Breconridge. 'You 'ave brought your friends. 'ow nice.'

She took their hands in turn with a touch as light as the passing drift of a summer thistle.

'You will 'ave a drink, please.' She looked across at a group of girls and lifted her chin sharply. 'Françoise!'

A small girl joined them, hung momentarily on Miller's arm and looked up at him with a somewhat vacant expression. She was young and thin with a pale face that even her heavy rouge could not obscure. Through her negligée — muslin to the touch, not silk — Miller could see her small powdered and barely formed breasts.

'Cognac? Wine?' Madame Poulon asked. 'What will you 'ave?'

They agreed on cognac and Françoise padded on bare feet across the threadbare rug to a bar where a white-jacketed waiter poured their drinks.

Miller looked around at the other men in the room but could see no one else from the squadron.

'I don't see Tozer,' he said.

As he watched, a couple rose from one of the sofas and, the girl leading, walked though a door at one end of the bar. A moment later another officer emerged from the same door, crossed the room tugging rather self-consciously at his tunic and bowed curtly at Madame Poulon as he passed.

'Colonel,' she murmured. She turned back to them and, taking Breconridge by the arm, escorted them to a vacant sofa.

'Please,' she said. 'Sit down and relax. Per'aps you will see something else you might like?'

'Do many of the others come here,' Miller asked Breconridge.

'Some,' he said. 'Not the parsons' sons, naturally.'

'Heyward?'

'Who?'

'Lieutenant Heyward. The chap who hanged himself,' Miller said.

'Oh, him.' He leaned towards Chacksfield who was looking goggle-eyed at the girls and raised his voice above the general hubbub. 'Miller wants to know if Heyward ever came here, Chacksfield.'

'Heyward?' Chacksfield repeated. 'Oh *Heyward*. Yes, I remember Foden brought him here once. Why?'

'What about Dunne?'

'I say, are you always so full of questions, Miller?' Chacksfield said.

'Bobby came here with us once or twice,' Breconridge said. 'Thought it was awfully good fun. Parry, too, although between you and me I think he's a bit of a parson's son.'

Françoise returned with a tray and three glasses of cognac. She smiled at

Miller and her eyes widened expectantly. Miller reached for some money and put it on the tray.

'I don't think it's money she wants,' Chacksfield suggested laconically. 'At least not yet.'

Miller knocked back his cognac. 'What do you mean?'

'I think she'd like you to take her upstairs.'

'She looks like a child,' Miller said, 'She's too young to be working in a place like this.'

'Oh, you'd be surprised just how young some of them are,' Breconridge said.

Miller fidgeted on the sofa.

Breconridge leaned towards him and whispered, 'Your moral objections are showing, old man.'

'If you want to take Françoise upstairs,' Chacksfield said, pointing towards the door where the colonel had emerged, 'it's through there. The rates are very reasonable.'

Miller had decided he most certainly did *not* want to take the girl upstairs. 'Dunne,' he began again, 'I was told he was particularly popular.'

'What is it you're trying to get at?' Breconridge asked with a slight note of exasperation.

'It's about Heyward,' Miller said.

'My dear chap,' Chacksfield said with a heavy sigh, 'the fellow hanged himself. Can't we let that be an end of it?'

'You know Brigade has asked me to look into it,' Miller said.

'I can't see what difference it makes,' Chacksfield replied, making room for one of the girls to sit on his lap. 'He was such a rotten pilot that he was going to get himself killed sooner or later anyway.'

Françoise made to follow suit. Miller crossed his legs.

'*Monsieur,*' she complained.

'That's what Doyle said,' Miller told him.

'There you are, then.'

Françoise pushed herself onto Breconridge's lap and looked sullenly at Miller. Breconridge pecked her on the cheek and his fingers played with the ribbon that tied her gown together. Miller looked elsewhere.

The girl with Chacksfield stood up and pulled him after her. He allowed himself to be led to the door to the stairs.

'I'll see you fellows later,' he said with a sheepish grin.

'Don't forget we're due up at dawn,' Miller called after him, then shifted along the sofa to put some distance between himself and Françoise's legs. The girl slid into the vacant space with a giggle and linked arms with both Breconridge and Miller.

Breconridge said, 'I think she's got designs on both of us, old man.'

'For God's sake!' Miller said and stood up.

Françoise tugged at his sleeve, pouting.

'Sorry,' Miller said to her. 'Not tonight.'

Breconridge shook his head and said with a sigh, 'You'll probably find Tozer at a restaurant in the Priesterstraat. Just off the square. There's a waitress there he's taken a fancy to.'

'Priesterstraat,' Miller repeated.

'Give him my regards if you find him,' Breconridge said, the wry smile playing at his lips again.

Miller walked back along the street, breathing deeply. He supposed the way he had reacted would be all over the squadron by the morning. There was still dust in the air from the last shelling and even the tang of cordite but he found it preferable to the cloying scent and powder that Madame Poulon had to offer. He edged his way through the crowd on the pavement, noting the gold bands and braid of staff officers and wondering if this was as close to the front as any of them ever got.

Back on Ieperstraat, the flow of traffic had slowed. He walked towards the square and crossed the road, edging past the beginnings of a scuffle between a large corporal and two MPs that was only going to end in close arrest, court martial and a breaking to the ranks. It suddenly occurred to him that he had missed his dinner and that he was hungry. He walked through the square, found Priesterstraat and followed the street past a patisserie and a milliner's that looked as if it had gone out of business until he found the restaurant.

Inside was quiet after the street. Two NCOs were eating at a table, a large glass of beer in front of each of them, and at the bar stood a solitary drinker, a subaltern. He looked at Miller questioningly for a second as he walked in then averted his gaze when Miller frowned. At one of the rear tables a crowd of officers were drinking but Tozer wasn't among them so he took an empty table and watched the fat, aproned waiter plod across the floor towards him.

'*Je voudrais une omelette s'il vous plâit?*' Miller asked.

They were nominally just inside the Belgian border where the population had been Walloons whose language, he had discovered early in the war, was a curious version of medieval French and quite incomprehensible to him. Two years of war, however, had added an altogether odd mix to the pot and now most languages would get a response as would just about any currency.

The waiter looked at him and shrugged. '*Désolé monsieur, mais nous n'avons pas d'oeufs.*'

'*Qu'est-ce que vous avez?*'

'*Du pain, un peu du salade, peut-etre du fromage.*'

'*C'est bien,*' Miller said. '*Et du vin.*'

He sighed with a deep irrational dissatisfaction that had nothing to do with the lack of eggs and watched the waiter plod away. What was it about Madame Poulon's (he couldn't even bring himself to call it a brothel in the privacy of his own thoughts) that unsettled him so? Was he that much of a prude that the thought of such an establishment disturbed his sensibilities? He didn't think so. At least, he *hadn't* thought so. Good God! He'd seen far worse places than that on the southside of Chicago and around the docks on the East River in New York. In fact, there wasn't anything particularly offensive about the place at all. What was it then?

The waiter returned with a carafe of wine and a glass. Miller poured a little and sipped at it, his face souring at the taste. He wondered what they had started adulterating it with now. He drank a little more and thought again of Madame Poulon's. He didn't really have to ask the question: he knew what it was that he had found offensive. It had been the fact in general that the girls were selling themselves and in particular that Françoise had been so young. *Why* it mattered, he couldn't say. Boys of her age — younger probably — were getting themselves blown to pieces daily at the Front, so what did the exchange of a little sex in return for a few francs matter? It was probably keeping the girl alive. He was being irrational.

But he hadn't convinced himself. It wasn't the girl being there *per se*; it was Chacksfield and Breconridge and that colonel and *himself* being there that was the problem. If it wasn't for them and everything else they had brought with them, she wouldn't have had to be there at all. And what then? She'd probably have starved to death or have been overrun by the Hun. And serving in one of *their* brothels.

It was the war! It was the damnable war. That was the excuse that was generally trotted out.

But he knew he couldn't really hide behind that. His objections to places like Madame Poulon's began while he was growing up in the succession of mining camps that his father had dragged him through. Any camp of any size would have attracted those who supplied the services of bars, eateries and flop-houses, and almost certainly whorehouses — of some description — almost as if it were a kind of evolutionary requirement of camps dictated by a natural survival stratagem. He had always been aware of them, had grown used to their presence, although what he had never grown used to was the fact that they were accepted as places that offered merchandise in the same way that the dry-goods store did or a bar or a cheap hotel did. And yet, in another way, it *wasn't* the same. Men would use them without ever acknowledging the fact outside of the precise milieu in which the establishment existed. It was never talked about in polite society — not that the society of mining camps ever became *that* polite. What really disturbed him was that he had discovered that his own father had visited them.

The waiter returned with half a stick of bread that might have been fresh that morning, a small plate of limp salad and a piece of cheese that showed signs of having had a mouldy rind recently amputated. He glanced up at the waiter who was wearing a what-do-you-expect face.

'*Merci,*' he said with as much dignity as he could muster. He supposed the man deserved that; no doubt he got very little pleasure out of serving up such poor fare. It's the war, he told himself again. It's the war.

He broke a piece of the bread and dabbed it in what oil he could find in the salad and put it in his mouth. Perhaps it was as well that these poor bastards couldn't see how well they ate in the mess. Somehow the commissariat found good fresh food and plenty of it — barkers and bully beef aside. It couldn't all be shipped in from England. Anyway, by all accounts things were beginning to get pretty tight at home. He had heard that the German U-boats were hitting the shipping hard. Then where did it come from? Better not ask, he decided. One thing was certain, the poor beggars up at the front weren't eating as well. There weren't too many opportunities for cooking and serving decent hot meals in the forward trenches. Cold bully beef, bung and hard biscuits while dodging shells, all washed down with a mug of muddy tea were probably the best *they* could expect. He was far better off where he was.

Then, having manoeuvred himself into familiar territory — and as the game he played with himself demanded — he began to enumerate the dangers he faced that *they* did not. He folded some salad with his fingers and ate it while he numbered them.

First, there was always the danger of engine failure (you always had to begin with the difficulties of getting into the air in the first place). Cutting out on take-off with neither enough height nor speed to control your own landing always headed his list. What did that equate to? Coming up into the line and getting a shell on your head right off the bat? Perhaps. After all, the airfields took the occasional pasting from enemy bombers as well, so he thought it was a fair exchange.

Next there were the dangers from anti-aircraft fire and — when you were low enough — of ground fire. He would generally liken this to sniper fire. The snipers were always picking men off in the trenches, far more he supposed than there were machines brought down by Archie because it was just sheer bad luck to get hit by shells lobbed up on the off chance. But then, the blasted men could keep their heads down, couldn't they? Keep your head down below the parapet and the bloody snipers couldn't see you!

Going over the top in a push was much the same as going out on a show, in his opinion (not, he always had to concede, that he had ever gone over the top). You were up there for the Hun to shoot down and if you weren't damn careful you'd have one sticking to your tail like a leech on your backside trying to fill you with hot lead. And, of course, he didn't have to hit you personally. All he had to do was find a vulnerable spot in the machine. He thought that was pretty even as chances went.

But then there were the imponderables. Those awful craters filled with that greeny-brown liquid that couldn't really be described as water. That viscous ooze that waited like the saliva of some monstrous animal's mouth ready to suck you down if you put a foot wrong. That, in particular, he never cared to think too much about.

And the general conditions in the trenches – mud everywhere and no water to wash in. Rats and lice... Miller shivered, emptied his glass and refilled it again. There was all that. There was no way you could compare the living conditions. He could come back to a (usually) comfortable billet, clean clothes and hot food. No, there was no comparison there. On the other hand, after a couple of weeks in the line, the men were generally pulled back to the rear for a rest; in a squadron it might be months before you had the opportunity to stand down and then they generally wanted you to risk your neck trying to teach some imbecile how to fly back at a home establishment training base. No, the day to day conditions were just not comparable. There was nothing he could do about that. As to the relative dangers, that would require some statistical analysis of casualty figures compared to manning levels, the kind of thing that staff wouldn't let you near as it was probably a soft job that had been reserved for some draft-dodging civilian.

He drank a little more wine, regretting in some part of his brain his earlier harsh judgement of its quality. Then he played — holding back for a moment for effect's sake — his trump card. This was the ace he always kept up the sleeve until the end of the game. This always took the last trick.

The machine on fire.

Up there at several thousand feet, the cockpit burning around you... your clothes catching fire... the fuel tank at your feet... your skin starting to burn...

Miller dropped the imaginary card onto the table and sat back. What did they have to compare to that?

He wiped the last of the bread around the plate and finished the wine. It *should* win him the game but it never did. Afterwards there was still — always — this empty feeling of guilt. A feeling that, somehow, he was shirking. That somehow he had found an easy way of 'doing his bit'. He had even once, shortly after receiving his commission and in a fit of remorseful lunacy, put in for a transfer to a line regiment; until his CO had talked him out of it, that is, persuading him that his skills were needed and that the dangers of flying were increasing — and promptly going up himself and getting shot down as if he had needed to illustrate his argument. And it was true, over the last twelve months contact with Hun aircraft and their bloody 'Fokker Scourge' had become far more lethal. But that never really salved his conscience, his conviction that those lost souls living in the filth of their holes in the ground were waging the real war and that he was doing no more than playing at it, a damned shirker who sooner or later was going to get found out.

'Vous avez terminé?'

Miller started. A girl was standing over him looking at his plate. She was dark with curling hair and a face that looked no happier than the waiter's.

Since the plate, the carafe and the glass were all empty it had seemed a particularly redundant question.

'Oui,' he said. She was quite pretty in a sullen sort of way and he wondered if she was the girl Tozer had taken a liking to. He pulled some coins from his pocket. 'Qu'est-ce que je vous dois?'

The girl cleared the table. 'Sou quatre-vingts?' she said with a shrug. Almost a question.

He put four francs on the table. The habit of some of the French to continue talking in *sous* still confused him.

'Vous étiez dans un rêve. A quoi pensiez vous?'

'What?' he said.

'I say you were dreaming.' She fluttered a hand into the air. 'You were away?'

'Oh, I was just thinking. Je pensais.'

'Vous pensez chez vous?'

He looked up at her, into her questioning eyes. How could he tell her that he was thinking that instead of flying he should be in the mud of the trenches with the rest of the lunatics.

'Home?' he said instead. 'Yes, thinking of home.'

Her mouth turned down as she picked up the money. She pushed her chin towards the window and the street beyond.

'C'est chez moi,' she said. 'This is *my* country.'

9
Stratus

Fog likely - occasional precipitation - ceiling undefined - visibility poor.

Miller climbed in a long slow spiral in the wake of C Flight. At eight thousand feet a few puffs of hanging cumulus lay scattered like discarded cushions. Below, the shadowed patches cast on the churned earth seemed oddly unrelated to the cloud. Beyond the wire of no man's land, the Hun front line, reserve lines and communication trenches running between looked like marks scratched in dirty sand by a stick in an idle hand. The odd movement of vehicles could be seen further to the rear and, now and again, a puff of dull smoke rose where a gun emplacement was loosing off a few hopeful shells towards the British lines.

In the front of the FE's nacelle below him the rear of Pollock's head moved left then right then left again with a metronomic regularity that had started to annoy Miller. Pollock, along with Garfield were new second lieutenants who had arrived with the dead Etherington the same day as Miller. Like Etherington, it was Pollock's first time up over the lines as an observer and, judging by the boy's face as he had climbed up into the nacelle, he had spent a sleepless night thinking about Etherington and having second thoughts about the whole business. Miller had tried to be reassuring. He told the gangling schoolboy just to keep his eyes open and try to familiarise himself with the country. What he looked as if he was doing now was peering vertically down at the roiled wasteland beneath them, ground that was almost identical to the rest of the front from the Channel to the Swiss border.

Miller leaned forward and tapped him on the shoulder with his gloved hand. Pollock started, almost as if he had forgotten that there was a pilot sitting behind him, turned in the wicker tub that served as a seat and looked with wide eyes behind his goggles back over his shoulder at Miller. Miller arced his arm out over the country beyond the Hun lines, forked two gloved fingers out from in front of his eyes as a sign to look and made a general relaxing motion with his hand, palm-down, thinking he probably looked more like a tame Indian in one of Cody's wild west shows than a competent RFC officer. Pollock stared back at him with mystification, then went back to his metronomic see-sawing. Miller scanned the sky with the slow rotation of his head that had become second nature and hoped that Strouden was having better luck with Second Lieutenant Garfield. He had not flown an FE before — had only had a few hours in the air in any machine — and Strouden had been unwilling to send him over the lines first time out. Since Miller was there to make up the numbers, Strouden had elected to be taken up himself by Garfield for a trial flight, one well back to the rear of their lines.

'Just until you're familiar with the machine,' Strouden had explained before

81

the patrol. Garfield had been a mixture of eagerness and nervousness and looked as if he had not known whether to take Strouden's precaution as an opportunity or as an insult. Pollock had just looked scared stiff.

Ahead of them Denham had banked and was swinging to the north over the salient to cross the Hun line above Hooge. Archie opened up from their emplacements in Sanctuary Wood but the gunners were well short of their height as yet and, as soon as the explosive yellowing gouts of smoke began to get near enough to buffet the machines, Denham took them down a thousand feet to throw them off their range. Behind Denham and Chacksfield at the head of the diamond formation Moss and Trueman lay forward and to Miller's left.

To his right, Cliff and Parker were using a replacement machine that Sergeant Greene had had the C Flight ground crew up working on for half the night. Parker's FE was still nose-down in a crater just behind the lines east of Ypres, a new target for Hun mortars. Miller and Pollock brought up the rear where Hardy and Bartlett always flew until General Bovington had got them killed.

Denham, Miller was aware, still regarded him with distrust. Whether it was something to do with Heyward, Miller's rank, or some sort of class prejudice, he did not know. To discomfort Denham further, Miller had started to watch him — nothing particularly overt, just allowing Denham to find Miller's eyes on him when he looked up, in a game that he thought might prick anything on Denham's conscience that shouldn't be there. He was good-looking in a self-regarding sort of way and sported one of the thinner, well-tended moustaches that the younger men now favoured over the heavier Kitchener type which, by a year into the war had pretty well universally crossed the classes and was now almost *de-rigeur* for the older man. Miller had placed Denham somewhere in the upper-middle of the class system — public school, certainly, but untouched by any hint of aristocracy. He had developed an eye for these things and found he was seldom wrong. On the other hand, Denham's observer, the piano player Chacksfield, although from the same class as the flight commander was not noticeably put out by Miller's rank or social standing and, since the previous evening in Madame Poulon's had treated Miller with an undiscriminating familiarity. Before they had taken off, he had grinned at Miller out of his moon face and asked if he had found Tozer.

'Breconridge told me about a restaurant and a waitress he was keen on but he wasn't there.'

Chacksfield had winked lewdly.

'Oh, he's not getting anywhere with her. As a matter of fact, old man, I saw him upstairs at you-know-where. He was taking out his frustration on some poor little redhead. You should have stayed around.'

'I'll find him later,' Miller had said.

Chacksfield had then looked at Pollock and had repeated his joke about the tendency of Heyward's FE to land nose-down. Pollock had whitened at the news, adding another layer of concern to an outlook already thickly laminated with apprehension. Miller, himself, had merely smiled and assured Chacksfield that he would keep his eye on it.

Moss and his observer, Trueman, had looked on with schoolboy enjoyment at another's discomfort. Moss was a small pest of a youth given, like an agitated dragonfly, to making unexpected jerky movements and, to Miller's irritation, forever asking questions or making comments. Trueman, on the other hand, was an unruffled pipe-smoker who appeared as happy to observe as much on the ground as he did in the air.

'Come on, togs on, old man,' Moss had said to Pollock as they pulled on their flight boots and coats. 'If we don't hurry the Hun'll be back in their mess at breakfast.'

Pollock had given him a sickly grin then, goggled and gloved, alongside the rest of the flight he had trudged out to the waiting machines swathed like a deep-sea diver ready for the plunge.

Whilst making their height, Miller had given himself over to thinking about Budge's list. Donaldson, the clerk, had included Strouden and Budge as flying officers along with Gregory, the DH2 pilot; beneath their names he had listed the others under one of the headings, A, B or C, denoting the flight to which they were attached. He had by now met most of the men; only four or five names from A Flight were unfamiliar: Foden who was due back that day; Wynstanley, Bryce and Parsons; Parry — a friend of Dunne's who had accompanied him to Madame Poulon's (a parson's son, as Breconridge had described him) and Parry's pilot, a pilot-sergeant named Reynolds. Miller had held the rank of pilot-sergeant himself before being commissioned and knew what an awkward position it was; you flew and fought alongside the officers but still had to mess with the sergeants, caught in a sort of no man's land as far as the Other Ranks went.

He wondered if Heyward was the sort of man who was likely not to let Reynolds forget that he was still a sergeant even if he did fly with the officers, and it would be interesting to find out if, during one of Strouden's rotations, Heyward and Reynolds had ever flown together.

Although he still found it difficult to believe Heyward's death had been anything other than suicide — the medical evidence, such as it was, did not suggest otherwise — the fact that the hut was searched and the method Heyward had chosen still bothered him. From his own point of view he rather thought that either using his service revolver or deliberately crashing his machine would have offered a preferable death — although it had to be admitted that opportunities for Heyward to fly a two-seater alone would have been limited. This assumed, of course, that the man was not so self-absorbed as to be unconcerned about taking another man down with him. Even so, there was something about hanging that was off-key. Despite the lack of evidence, he still had not completely ruled out some sort of conspiracy among the other flying officers — some sort of quasi-judicial execution, perhaps, for causing Dunne's death — but he knew that that was grabbing at straws; there was no atmosphere of conspiracy at the squadron. No one seemed to be reluctant to talk about Heyward — with the possible exception of Tozer. It was more a case of their being bored by the subject, an attitude of 'the man is dead, so what?' and, given their particular circumstances, he could find nothing suspicious in that.

There was always the possibility of a conspiracy among the Other Ranks, of course, but that seemed to him even less likely. Beyond the chance of a sort of misplaced but 'fitting' revenge for his negligent — or rather, it seemed, his incompetent — contribution to the death of the popular Dunne, they had nothing in the way of a possible motive. And why would the Other Ranks take an exceptional exception to the death of yet another flying officer? It may have been that Heyward had upset someone by his manner, of course; 'gentlemen' could be jealous, he knew, of their perceived social standing and any slight Heyward may have felt could have made him vindictive towards the men. But it had been Miller's experience that a couple of weeks in an active RFC squadron soon knocked that sort nonsense out of one's head. Besides, if one of the NCOs or Other Ranks had had a grudge against Heyward a smart smack over the back of the head with a wrench would have been a more proletarian way to go.

What he really needed to do was to talk to Foden, the man who seemed to know Heyward better than most. Also to Reynolds. An NCO might well have a view of a man that differed to that taken by men of his own class. Perspective was what mattered, he had often found when trying to fathom the depths of the apparently unfathomable. It was like flying — the perspective of height often revealed features in a landscape that too close a familiarity generally obscured.

There was, he couldn't help reflecting as he became aware of Pollock's swinging head again, nothing unfamiliar about the landscape they were over at that moment. In some way it was like a giant midden reserved solely for the detritus of war — barbed wire, discarded battlefield accoutrements, tatters of uniform caught on the wire and flapping in the breeze, the odd baulks of timber and duckboard, and bodies, of course, in various stages of decomposition: those who at first could not be brought back with safety and then, later, were not worth the effort of shovelling up. Height, he was always pleased to find, soon rendered these accumulations of rubbish invisible as they dissolved into their background. The autumn rains, when they came, would soon make the remains indistinguishable from the mud they had died in. Everyone could then forget that they were ever there at all. He supposed collective amnesia was the best that they could ask for.

Pollock was pointing to something away to the south, so distant that it was surprising he had seen it at all. It was so far that it was unrecognisable and to Miller's mind presently so distant as to be of no consequence. He shook his head as the observer turned to him half in expectancy and half in agitation and Miller dismissed his concerns with a flick of his glove. It was to be no more than a routine patrol he had said to Pollock as they had set out. Denham was to cross the lines north of Sanctuary Wood, run up to St Julien then take a heading northwest over Pilckem towards Bixschoote. To the east of them, up to Bixschoote, was a bite that the Germans had taken out of the salient with the help of their introduction of gas in their push the spring of the previous year. In the intervening months they had repaired the smashed allied trench systems, dug their own new ones and extended their communication and reserve lines. The changes — together with the new artillery emplacements — had all been mapped once they had started to get the better of the Fokker Eindeckers, although there were always new developments to be noted.

To the north he saw that a speck Pollock had *not* seen had now resolved itself into several black smudges high over the horizon. He tapped the observer on the shoulder and pointed. Pollock frustratingly stared for a long while and, even when he finally began nodding his head, Miller was not sure that Pollock had seen the aircraft. A moment later, though, he leaned forward and grabbed the Lewis gun in preparation. Miller tapped his shoulder once more and shook his head.

'Miles away,' he shouted into the wind. 'Far too far.'

Pollock nodded vigorously again and Miller saw the man's shoulders relax. They were biplanes, Halberstadts or Rumplers and probably somewhere near their ceiling. Denham, he was sure, had already seen them and, although there were six machines as best as he could make out, they would probably think twice about tackling FEs, particularly as by the time they reached them Denham would have re-crossed the lines and the Hun of late had been windy about a fight anywhere but over his own territory.

The Archie around Bixschoote had got their range again and the sky started to thicken with smoke. Even as he watched a piece of shrapnel tore a hole in his port wing. Pollock had stopped swinging his head from side to side and was holding onto the rim of the nacelle with both hands.

Denham climbed again, then he banked and straightened, taking them around back over Langemarck. There was nothing left of the towns and villages below except the occasional scree of rubble amid the hills and craters created by the almost apocalyptic rain of high explosive. The mud had dried, crusting the surface and even greening the soil in places, although Miller could never accept the growth as a mark of health or regeneration, more of a gangrenous stain that had cursed a diseased body. Sometimes, on hot days, he could swear he could smell it.

Denham had straightened and was climbing again in a powered ascent with Moss on his tail, the wings of his FE tipping one way then the other in a rhythmic movement as if Moss were rocking in his seat to the beat of a ragtime piano roll. Ahead and above them he saw a lone two-seater, a Halberstadt, idling in the sky.

Miller alerted Pollock then swung further east to intercept the Hun's retreat. Denham and Moss parted as they neared the Halberstadt, Denham still climbing and coming up beneath it, while Moss with Parker now on his tail swung around, still climbing, to attack from the rear.

Seeing Moss and Parker's machines, the Hun rolled into a spin to lose height before the FEs could get on his tail, but he hadn't spotted Denham and spun into his path. The tracers from Chacksfield's Lewis arced around the spinning plane and Miller could see the observer swinging the gun to its lowest elevation as the Halberstadt dropped beneath them. The Hun pulled out of his spin at five thousand feet with his nose pointed east as Miller put the FE into a steep dive. At six hundred yards above the Halberstadt Pollock sat hunched over the Lewis, the

Hun running in the sights below them.

'Wait for two-fifty!' Miller shouted into the screaming slipstream.

Five hundred, four hundred... the staccato cough of the Lewis rattled over the noise of the engine.

'Not yet!'

Pollock's finger seemed to have ossified around the trigger. At three hundred yards from the Halberstadt the Lewis stopped. Pollock banged it with the flat of his hand, pulling on the trigger until it dawned on him that the drum was empty. He began fumbling at the gun, bullets whining past the nacelle as they came within the Halberstadt's range. Miller pulled the FE out of the dive and zoomed, climbed then rolled westward where Denham, Parker and Moss sat patiently watching. Beneath him the Halberstadt idled on at four thousand feet, the pilot glancing up at Miller in an invitation to follow. Pollock, having finally fixed a new drum on the Lewis, turned and pointed at the Hun. Miller smiled and shook his head, raising a hand at the Halberstadt and declining the invitation.

A slight westerly sprang up as the guns hidden in the remains of Polygon Wood threw a few hopeful shells their way. To the north Miller saw that the Hun formation he had seen earlier had closed the distance between them but seemed to show no real enthusiasm for the job. He fell in behind Parker and Moss as the flight commander raised an arm and signalled their return. With a larger target, Archie's comrades in Sanctuary Wood took up the refrain as they skirted its northern fringe and they recrossed the lines, buffeted by their explosive shells. Ahead an artillery barrage had opened up on Ypres again in the hope, Miller supposed, of levelling anything that might still be standing more than ten feet high. To the southwest, over St Eloi, an old Vickers FB5 stood up artillery spotting for some British guns, watched over by a couple of circling FE2bs. Miller stretched his back in the cramped cockpit and began thinking about Heyward once again.

'Why didn't we go back after him?' Pollock asked as Miller climbed out of the cockpit.

The riggers and fitters came running across the field to push the machines back towards the hangars. Miller jumped to the ground and began stamping his feet to get some feeling back into them. He stripped off his goggles and helmet, looking at Pollock.

'We were already too far over the lines to chase him,' he told him. 'He would have pulled us lower and the other formation we saw would have cut our retreat. If we'd had more height I might have chanced it.' He gave Pollock a tight smile. *And if you had been a better shot*, he might have added.

The observer slapped his gloves against his flying coat in disappointment, seemingly all eagerness now he was back on the ground.

'We needed to be closer,' Miller added as they turned to where Denham and Chacksfield were standing. 'Anything over two hundred and fifty yards is generally out of range unless you're lucky. Best wait for under two hundred.'

'I thought he *was* about two-fifty,' Pollock said.

'Better than twice that, I'm afraid.' Pollock scowled and Miller went on, 'Distance is deceptive up there. There's no perspective in the air. You'll get the hang of it. Just keep your eyes open and watch the others.'

'You had more chance of hitting the Adlon at that range,' Chacksfield said helpfully to Pollock as they joined him and Denham.

'The Adlon?' Pollock asked.

'It's a hotel in Berlin,' Miller told him.

Pollock's face reddened.

'I didn't see you put any holes in him,' Moss said darting up beside Chacksfield, slapping the bigger man with his gloves.

'Gun jammed,' Chacksfield said.

'You're the unluckiest man I know for jamming guns,' Trueman remarked. 'I don't know why Denham flies with you.'

Moss giggled.

'Let's report,' Denham said. 'I want my breakfast.'

They trailed across the field after Denham to where Budge was waiting at the château.

'How are you finding the Fee?' Trueman asked Miller, falling in beside him.

'Better than I expected,' Miller admitted. 'They can certainly dive.'

Trueman laughed. 'It's a bit unnerving at first but you get used to it. I just wish there was more to hold on to.' He turned good-naturedly to Pollock bringing up the rear. 'The worst thing I find is firing backwards with the top Lewis. Standing up like that I always feel as if I'm going to fall out, especially the way Moss throws the beastly thing about.'

Miller glanced back at Pollock.

The observer looked at him, a sickly grin wreathing his pale face. 'Why can't they fit belts?'

'There must be some reason,' Miller said. 'Perhaps they'd get in the way. They must have thought about it.' Although, upon reflection, he wasn't sure he felt much conviction that anyone actually had.

In the operations room he sat through the debriefing as Budge took notes. Chacksfield, Cliff and Trueman rattled through what they had seen on the ground — smoke from some dug-in artillery, a line of troops moving towards the front, the dust of vehicles well to the rear — and, when Budge looked expectantly at Miller's observer, Pollock began to flush.

'I told Mr Pollock just to familiarise himself with the area as it was his first time over the lines,' Miller said.

'I saw the troops on the road,' Pollock said hesitantly.

'Which road?' Budge asked. 'Travelling in which direction?'

'They'll be the ones moving towards Poelcappelle,' Trueman put in. 'Moving up the line.'

'Good,' Budge said. 'Mr Denham?'

Denham told him about the formation they had seen to the north and then about the lone Halberstadt.

'We all had a go at him but no luck.'

Pollock shifted uneasily in his chair.

Denham added, 'It looked to me as if he was spotting for the guns Trueman saw. They opened up on Ypres again as we crossed the lines.'

Budge looked up from his notes to see if there was anything else.

'Right, gentlemen,' he said. 'You'd better get some breakfast before they run out of barkers.'

They scraped back their chairs and chuckled and, stripping off the last of their gear, trooped to the mess hall. Budge hadn't been serious, Miller thought; they were never going to run out of barkers.

Falling in beside Pollock, Miller said, 'Done much shooting? Partridge, pheasant, that sort of thing?'

Pollock looked warily at him, suspecting, Miller supposed, another ribbing.

'A little. Why?'

'You know how you have to lead the birds by a few feet, so they're flying into the shot? It's the same with a Hun machine. Only the Hun's going a lot faster than a pheasant.'

'Of course,' Pollock said, as if it were obvious.

'But you're going equally as fast,' Miller said. 'And the Hun isn't always at right-angles to you as a bird might be.'

'They're usually coming over one's head,' Pollock said, 'in front of the beaters.'

'Yes,' Miller agreed, not having done a lot of pheasant shooting. 'My point is, that the angles — and the speeds — are always changing. That's why we have a tracer loaded every few shells. It gives you an idea of where your fire is going.'

'Mine seemed to be going everywhere,' Pollock confessed.

'They've estimated,' Miller said, 'that at around two hundred and fifty yards range the spread of shot will be in a thirty-foot diameter. That is a radius of fifteen feet around the pilot you're aiming at.'

'I was never too good at maths, sir.'

'What I'm trying to say is, that with a radius like that two-fifty is really the maximum distance you can afford to be if you want to hit the man. Closer is better. In fact, the tracers don't really become effective as a guide until you're at about a hundred yards.'

'The thing is,' Pollock said, 'I thought we *were* close.'

'Practice,' Miller said. 'It's the only way to get your eye in.'

They hadn't run out of barkers, of course, and Miller sat down with two of them, alongside his eggs and bacon. Moss kept up a continual chatter, fidgeting in his chair in much the same manner as he flew his machine, like a man with a nervous disorder. He pestered Chacksfield mainly but intermittently addressed all of them with some schoolboy inanity or other. Only Pollock didn't speak, still smarting, Miller supposed, from his action against the Halberstadt. Denham said little. The flight commander persisted on sliding away from Miller's eye contact and he rarely spoke, the little conversation he did allow himself being directed at Chacksfield. On a separate table, Miller saw Garfield and Strouden eating in silence. The CO's face looked as ominous as a lowering thundercloud and Garfield's expression of hurt indignation suggested that their flight together had not gone smoothly.

Strouden looked up and caught Miller watching him. He jerked his head curtly in the direction of his office.

Miller's heart sank. He excused himself and was waiting outside the office when Strouden arrived, squinting through the smoke of a cigarette clamped between his lips. He began without any preamble.

'Pollock,' he said. 'Any good?'

'A little nervous, first time over the line,' Miller admitted. 'Fired off a drum at a Halberstadt at five hundred yards but we all did that to start with. He'll learn.'

'If he lives,' the Strouden said.

'You took the other one up?'

He went into the office and sat behind his desk.

'Garfield,' he said, stubbing out the remains of his cigarette and immediately lighting another. 'Sit down, Miller.' He pushed the box across the desk, leaning forward slightly. 'Do you know how many hours he's got?'

Miller took a cigarette. 'I don't know what the requirement is now.'

'Eighteen hours,' Strouden announced as if he were counting down to the apocalypse. 'And most of them on an antiquated Maurice Farman, for God's sake!'

Miller worked at his cigarette until there was enough ash to flick. It didn't seem that long to him since Farmans were state of the art aircraft. Now they barely made the grade as training machines.

'Yet they're expected to come out here,' Strouden went on, 'get into a machine they've never flown before and go straight into combat.'

'They always seem keen enough to do it,' Miller observed.

'Of course they're keen!' Strouden exploded. His colour was rising again and for the first time Miller noticed a look in Strouden's eyes that resembled desperation. 'Their heads have been filled with how glorious and heroic it all is. Have you read the newspapers recently?'

Miller admitted that he hadn't.

'Well, it seems they've decided that we're chivalrous knights of the air, so you'd best get used to the fact before you go back on your next leave. The papers are full of how we shoot down the enemy in mid-air duels.'

'I know they made a bit of a fuss over Warneford last summer when he got the VC for downing that Zeppelin,' Miller said.

'That was the RNAS,' Strouden said dismissively. 'It has always been the policy of the powers that be in the RFC not to publicise individuals. That was my understanding.'

No, not unless it was *their* names in the stories, Miller thought.

'I don't know where they get their information,' Strouden said. 'Fabricate stories from what's in the *London Gazette*, I shouldn't wonder.'

'They always need heroes,' Miller said. 'If only as a counterweight to the casualties.'

'Like Etherington?'

Miller flinched.

'That was bad luck, sir.'

'Heyward, then,' Strouden said. 'An incompetent who fortunately killed himself before he killed anyone else.'

Except for Dunne. Still, he supposed that as a last resort he could always put *that* in his report to Maxwell.

'Good God!' Strouden continued, running on as if under some clockwork mechanism all his own. 'What would *you* rather do, waft around in the air having jousting matches with enemy machines, or get into the mud of a frontline trench and wait to go over the top into the teeth of a machine gun?'

Miller thought that that was hardly a fair question. Decidedly below the belt, in fact.

'Well, that's the result we're getting,' Strouden said, as if the argument were self-evident. 'Every Tom, Dick and Harry is volunteering to stick their head in our sausage machine and if they don't kill themselves in the first couple of weeks of training they ship them over here so we can do the job for them.'

'Garfield wasn't too good, then?' Miller surmised.

'He hasn't got the slightest feel for the machine at all. Not a Fee, anyway. I was lucky to get down alive.' He sniffed. 'Maybe he was better on Farmans,' he said, adding facetiously, 'Perhaps we can get one shipped out especially for him.'

'Perhaps when he's been up — '

'So an Eindecker can show him a trick or two? It'll be murder.'

Miller could think of nothing to add to that.

'And what is worse, I'm expected to send another man up with him.' He flopped back in his chair. 'I've got him on the gunnery range this afternoon to see if we can at least teach him to shoot straight. Then I'll restrict him to an observer rôle until he's got a few more hours in on a Fee this side of the line.'

'If you want me to go up and lead him through some manoeuvres...' Miller offered. He supposed that that was why Strouden had called him into his office, unless it was just to give him someone to rant at.

'You've been up a good deal already since you arrived,' Strouden said, although he didn't make it sound as if it was an impediment to going up again and taking Garfield with him. Then he added off-handedly, his mood suddenly swinging, 'This afternoon will do. Best give the boy a couple of hours off. I was rather hard on him this morning.'

Miller shrugged. 'I was only going to take the Strutter up anyway. One or two things I wanted to try out.' He was going to leave it at that, then became aware that Strouden was waiting for some kind of elucidation. 'Manoeuvres, that sort of thing,' he added.

'Manoeuvres?'

'Tactics.'

'Like Immelmann?'

Not really.

'I suppose so,' Miller said.

And it struck him as odd how they knew the name of a German flyer. He didn't suppose for one minute that the Hun knew any of them. They publicised *their* heroes, of course. No death in anonymity for them. So why *not* write stories about the British flyers? And if they gave some space to the number killed in training *that* might make the difference. They knew about Immelmann, of course, since he had given his name to a manoeuvre, even if other pilots had probably employed it before without possessing the arrogance of wanting to give it an eponymous appendage. But the really odd thing was that news seemed to cross the lines without any difficulty at all. They'd been butting their bloodied heads together across the front line for the better part of two years with nothing but a few muddy yards to show for it, yet news, rumour and speculation flew across the lines with the rapidity of high explosive. There was something exasperating about that. It was almost as if Hermes, the bloody winged messenger himself, was carrying it backwards and forwards unseen.

Well, Miller thought, if *he* ever came across him he'd give him a taste of the Strutter's Vickers gun as soon as look at him. See how the feathery bastard liked that!

10

The pilot-sergeant's nails, Miller couldn't help noticing, were edged in black with oil and grease. Despite becoming a pilot, it suggested that Reynolds had not given up tinkering with his engines. Miller sympathised with the compulsion; only a pilot who had worked on them could truly comprehend the capacity for failure that an aeroplane engine possessed; only a mechanic could do anything about it. Once you had become the former, you could never quite abandon being the latter. He himself had finally only desisted from getting his hands onto the cylinders and rocker-arms when he came to trust those who were there to do it for him. In his opinion, pilots who knew nothing about engines were doomed to a short career. That was something else any new boy like Garfield would do well to learn — a lesson Reynolds obviously knew well although, apart from his nails, he appeared to scrub up pretty well.

After his interview with Strouden Miller had gone to the Bessonneau hangar looking for Reynolds and had found Sergeant Greene overseeing the filtering of petrol through chamois leathers to sieve out the impurities. It was one more consideration for the ground crew: if the engine of a motor car ran rough or stalled through some impurity finding its way into the carburettor it was no more than a nuisance; at a few thousand feet it could well be lethal. Miller asked Greene to ready his and Garfield's machines for a flight after lunch and told him to have the observer's forward Lewis gun fixed in front of the cockpit.

'We'll need to adjust the trim if you're taking her up alone,' Greene had said. 'To take account of the loss of the observer's weight at the front.'

'You needn't be too precise, sergeant. I'm only going to lead Mr Garfield through a few manoeuvres.'

It was another possible reason to take into account, though, as to why Heyward had not chosen to commit suicide in a machine: he'd apparently had enough trouble getting a properly balanced machine into the air, let alone one out of trim.

'Right you are, sir,' Greene had said. 'How are you finding she handles?'

Miller said he'd like another inch or two of leg room. 'I'm a bit cramped on the rudder bar. If you can find any, it'd help.'

'You'll be a few inches taller than Mr Heyward. We can find a little bit extra somewhere, I'm sure.'

'And could you ask pilot-sergeant Reynolds if he'd come and see me? I'll be in Mr Heyward's old hut, if he knows which one that is.'

That done, Miller had gone to look for Garfield and Pollock to give them the good news about the afternoon flight.

Now Reynolds was in front of him — once you looked past the havoc that operational flying played with the face of anyone who had enough sense to be scared — Miller guessed he was in his twenties, about Gregory's age, although from the other end of the social spectrum. He had the build of a miner, short and wiry and somehow appearing muscular without the benefit of muscles. His face had a raw-boned look, as if the skin had been pulled too tight, making it redden in the areas where the skull threatened to push through. He was standing stiffly in the middle of the hut, on-guard and having adopted that self-effacing manner that only NCOs and Other Ranks adopt in the presence of an officer, as if they believed that was how officers wished to see them.

'What was it you wanted to see me about, sir?' Reynolds had finally asked when Miller didn't speak. His voice carried the interrogative intonations of the northeast of England.

Miller had been sitting on the chair by the table when Reynolds knocked on the door.

'Never mind rank, let's assume we're in the mess, shall we?'

'Which mess would that be, sir?'

'Why don't we make it the sergeants' mess,' Miller suggested. 'I came through it myself.'

Some of the stiffness ebbed from Reynolds's shoulders.

'What were you, sir, enlisted man?'

Miller said, 'I had my ticket from the Aero Club so I was taken on as a pilot-sergeant once I got my certificate. I was one of those who never got his seventy-five quid back.'

In the early days, the RFC had obliged prospective officers to pay for their own ticket from the Aero Club, reimbursing the £75 once they had been accepted into the service. The war seemed to have changed that — at least in Miller's case it had.

Reynolds smiled. 'Bad luck,' he said.

'Came through the army, did you?' Miller asked.

Reynolds rubbed a hand across his bony chin. 'Royal Engineers,' he said. 'I come from Durham. Started down the mines when I was a lad o'fourteen. I was good with machines, though, the pumps and all, so as soon as I had the chance I got out of the mines and took a job working on motor cars. Then the garage I worked for went out of business and I didn't want to go back down the mines so just as soon as I was eighteen I joined up.'

Miller offered Reynolds a cigarette.

'Thanks,' Reynolds said, lighting one and exhaling the smoke into the air towards the cross beam where Heyward had hung. 'I couldn't stand the mines,' he admitted. 'Cooped up down there, the thought of all that earth on top of you, like. First leave I got I went back home and saw someone who'd come up to Durham with a machine, an Avro biplane it was. They was giving a demonstration and I took one look at it and thought, that's what I want to do. The army had just formed the Air Battalion so as soon as I could I volunteered.'

'Did you work with Cody?' Miller asked.

'The colonel? Aye. At Farnborough at the balloon factory. He was working on kites. I worked on the *Nulli Secundis* and the *Beta* till they switched out of balloons onto aeroplanes.'

'You were in at the start, then?'

'I came over with the first squadrons.'

'Me too,' Miller said. 'Sit down.'

'I thought I recognised you,' Reynolds said, grinning. He drew up the other chair and sat down. 'There weren't many pilot-sergeants then and I knew if I was ever going to fly that's what I'd have to be.'

'I was with Cody when he was trying to get the army contract,' Miller told him. 'His Cathedrals were far too unwieldy but you couldn't tell Cody. When they didn't give him the contract I got work where I could around Brooklands. I knew all the theory so I took a course of lessons with Sopwith's school and put in for my ticket.'

'I couldna afford that,' Reynolds said.

'Nor could I, really,' Miller admitted, 'but at my age it was the only way I was going to get into the air.'

'I got onto the second course at the Royal Flying School at Upavon,' Reynolds said. 'That was three years ago, now. Most of us there were Royal Engineers except for the Navy men.'

'I've met some of them,' Miller said.

'When I saw you was a captain,' Reynolds said, 'I thought I must have been mistaken.'

'That's the war,' Miller said.

'You'll be getting your own squadron soon, I suppose?'

'I don't know about that. How long have you been sergeant?'

'Three months,' Reynolds said. 'I was put up for it a year ago but things take so long. It's only been since the Hun got the Eindecker...'

He didn't finish and Miller knew why. There was always the feeling of stepping into dead men's shoes when a promotion came to plug a gap.

'I was back home for six months training, then once I qualified they put me on teaching recruits, like. I could tell them how to strip an engine down but I could see no sense in getting me to teach them to fly when I hadn't got the experience myself yet.'

'How do you find it?' Miller asked. 'Being a pilot-sergeant, I mean? It's an awkward position.'

'It's not so bad,' Reynolds said with a shrug. 'When you're up there you've got a job to do and when you're down here you're expected to know your place. That's easy if you started out as an enlisted man. I mess with the sergeants and I'm used to that. Some of the men are a bit chary 'cause I fly with the officers but you always get some of that. It's the gentleman rankers that get the worst of it. They're stuck in the middle, if you see what I mean.'

Gentleman Rankers. It was a term Miller never heard anymore. Perhaps the sheer number volunteering for the war had diluted the expression. 'Are there any here?' he asked.

'One or two maybe. Proper gentlemen, like.' Reynolds leaned forward in the chair towards the ashtray and stubbed out his cigarette.

That was an aspect Miller had not considered. He still could not see what bearing any of it might have had on Heyward's suicide, but that is what it was like when you didn't have any answers. It was akin to flying through cloud: until you could see clearly in all directions you were never totally sure which way was up.

'Was it something in particular you wanted to see me about?' Reynolds asked. 'A Flight's up this evening. It looks like rain, but I want to check over the machine just in case.'

'I only wanted to ask you about Heyward,' Miller said. 'If you had had occasion to fly with him.'

'I wondered if that was it. Some of the men said you were here about Mr Heyward.'

'Colonel Maxwell at Wing asked me to tidy up a few loose ends for Heyward's family. He'd rather they didn't know that he killed himself.'

'That's understandable,' Reynolds said. 'No reason why they should carry the disgrace.'

'Disgrace?' Miller asked. 'Is that what you think it is?'

Reynolds shrugged. 'Not me personally, but that's how they'd see it, isn't it? Their kind.'

'Did you?'

'Sorry, sir?' Reynolds said, slipping unconsciously back into rank.

'Fly with Heyward? The major sent him up as an observer a few times, I believe.'

'Oh. Yes, once. He came up with me when we was short a few weeks back. At any rate, that's what Major Strouden told him.'

'How did he take that?'

'Well, to be honest, he wasn't too happy about it. Joined as a pilot, he said.' He shrugged again. 'No skin off my nose, though. Observer's senior man in the machine on a recce, so he told me what to do anyway. I mean, where to go and what he wanted to see. I did as he told me, then we came down.'

'Did he talk to you at all?'

'What about?'

'Anything. The recce – anything.'

'I don't think Mr Heyward ever said a word to me he didn't have to, when we was up, I mean. And he wouldn't talk to the likes of me on the ground, would he?'

'What about Mr Parry? He's your regular observer, isn't he? Wasn't he a friend of Mr Dunne's?'

'I wouldn't know about that,' Reynolds said.

'How did he take Dunne's death?'

'We all liked Mr Dunne.' He stood up. 'If that's all, sir, I'd like to check over my Fee.'

'Of course,' Miller said. Reynolds moved towards the door and Miller asked, 'What will you do if they offer you a commission?'

Reynolds turned.

'I don't know,' he admitted. 'I have thought about it, can't pretend I haven't. I suppose I'll have to decide when it happens — if I live long enough, that is.'

'Don't turn it down because you think you'll get stuck in the middle like the gentleman rankers,' Miller advised him. 'If they offer you a commission, it'll be because you deserve it. The war won't last forever and if you stay in, the RFC will need people like you. It won't always be full of public schoolboys. The ones that live will go back to their real lives.'

The windsock on the field had filled and was pointing towards the Hun lines like a fat admonishing finger rebuking them for dereliction of duty. Miller sat in the FE cockpit waiting for the fitter behind him to swing the propeller. Reynolds had been right about the possibility of rain and he had cut lunch short and chivvied Garfield and Pollock onto the field. He could feel the wind rising through the wings and lifting the machine as he waited, as if it was impatient to get into the air and hurl itself against the lines.

'Contact.'

'Contact!'

He felt the satisfying resistance as the propeller turned and gave that throaty roar, a hawking expectoration that was an inverse indication of health. He glanced again over his left shoulder to where Pollock sat in the front of the nacelle of the other FE. Behind him, Garfield was looking over his shoulder to see the fitter at his propeller. Provided they got up and down without mishap a bit of turbulent weather wouldn't do them any harm. As a pair, they were going to face worse than that.

'Just follow me,' Miller had told Garfield as they walked out towards the machines. 'Try to duplicate my manoeuvres but most of all try to relax and enjoy it. It's the quickest way to get the feel of a new machine.'

'It's a bit windy, isn't it?' Pollock had said, leaving Miller undecided whether he was describing the weather or his own state of mind.

'It'll be good experience in judging your drift. It's all too easy when you're concentrating on other things to find the wind's taken you too far over the lines. And the stronger the westerly, the longer it will take you to get back.'

Garfield had looked at him with a sort of grim determination. 'What sort of thing are you going to do?'

'Oh, nothing too difficult. Turns and banks, rolling out of a climb, that sort of thing.'

'I'll try to follow.'

'If it goes well,' Miller had suggested, 'I'll get on your tail and you try to shake me off. Have you been in a spin yet?'

'No.'

Miller had pulled on his gloves. It had only been earlier that year that someone had perfected a method of pulling a machine out of a spin; until then, unless the pilot had hit upon it by chance, the machine would dive into the ground.

'Do you know the drill?'

Garfield had stopped, as if he had needed to transfer that little mental attention needed in the act of walking into remembering the procedure.

'Straighten everything,' he recited, 'and centre the stick and rudder. When the machine has straightened into a nose-dive, pull back on the stick gradually until she levels out.'

'Good,' Miller told him. 'Above all, try not to panic. The modern machines can handle a spin without any trouble.' He had smiled with what he hoped had been encouragement. 'In a few days you'll be throwing your Fee into one deliberately to avoid the Huns.' He looked at Pollock. 'All *you* have to do is remember to hold onto something.'

Now, bumping across the field with the air under the wings, Miller remembered his first spin. It had been in a Vickers FB5 and it had scared the hell out of him. A Hun Aviatic had latched on to his tail while they were artillery spotting over Vimy Ridge. He had been concentrating on keeping the machine level through heavy Archie while his observer was signalling back the fact that their guns needed another thirty yards. Then the Archie had suddenly stopped and in that fleeting moment between its cessation and Miller asking himself, 'why?' the Aviatic had ripped several rounds into his tailplane. Fortunately for Miller, the Hun had come at him at an angle and had opened his burst too far to the rear of the FB5 and in the few seconds he had needed to straighten up, Miller had jerked the stick forward and kicked at the rudder thinking it had been shot off. The FB5 had put its nose down and started to spin and for days afterwards he could see the horror in his observer's eyes behind the goggles as the man had turned in his seat and shouted something that Miller had been unable to hear.

He had jiggled ineffectually at the stick as they lost height and it was purely by chance — when his hand had actually frozen over the controls — that it had been positioned perfectly centrally. The rudder, despite the damage, had responded and at about eight hundred feet the machine had straightened out. Miller had eased back on the stick and before he had the chance to breathe again he had had to start dodging ground-fire from the Hun lines. His observer had the presence of mind to start strafing the trenches with the Lewis to force their heads down and they hedge-hopped all the way back to the airfield. They had laughed about it afterwards over several drinks in the mess before both he and his observer had vomited their lunch into the latrines.

Now they reached five thousand feet in a series of long looping ellipses, Miller pushing the machine west with every turn into the wind to counteract the drift. Beyond St Omer he could see Boulogne and the Channel and the dark shadow of ships against the choppy sea. Long towers of cloud had drifted past on the wind and he could see more building to the southwest beyond Boulogne, a heavy bank of dark grey nimbus that promised a wet night.

Letting Garfield draw alongside, Miller waved, inviting him to follow then put the nose of the FE down into a shallow dive before executing a series of tight turns.

He didn't know what was needed to get an RFC ticket now but in his day the Royal Aero Club had required a series of figure eight turns and a landing on a mark. He assumed Garfield was competent enough for that. After executing the third eight, he put the FE into a thirty degree climb and rolled out to the right until the wings stood almost in the vertical, let her drift then steadied her back into the horizontal. When he saw Garfield capable of that, he turned the roll to the left keeping the machine in a tight spiral. Garfield followed, centripetal force and Pollock's own muscles keeping him in the nacelle. But then Garfield dropped the nose too much and he had to make a correction, slipping into an untidy dive. Miller performed the same manoeuvre to the right again, this time diving out at full speed, pulled the stick back into his stomach and, at the top, when the machine might naturally loop, dropped out, cutting the engine as the FE slid down into a glide.

He watched Garfield botch the first attempt, pulling up with insufficient speed so that the machine almost stalled on its tail. He held her, though, and dived again, holding the stick forward long enough to build his speed. As he came out at the top into the glide, Miller fell onto his tail and, with sufficient clearance to ensure he missed, gave him a short burst with the Lewis to concentrate his attention.

Garfield's machine shuddered as he jerked the controls and Miller closed in to 100 feet. He hung there as the new boy tried turning, rolling and climbing, coming up after each manoeuvre with Garfield's back within the gun's sights. He held him there for a few minutes until he judged Garfield desperate enough to attempt a spin, then, looking over the side at the green French country below, broke away and signalled their return. On his own he might have considered trying a loop. He had done them often enough in his Strutter, but he wasn't entirely confident that the heavier, slower FE would be quite up to it. And he certainly didn't think that Garfield was, not yet, anyway.

In the mess he stood the pair a drink. Pollock's face was a disturbing shade of green but Garfield was smiling. He had been a lot better than Miller had expected, guessing that having his commanding officer in the front nacelle that morning had scared what flying skill he had out of him.

'I couldn't shake you off,' he said as Miller raised his glass to them.

'You will,' Miller said, wondering if he would. 'If you can, try and think what the Hun would be thinking. Then do something he won't expect, even if you think it seems crazy. It always takes a second or two to react and, at speed, that can be enough to get you out of trouble.'

'I was going to try a spin,' Garfield said.

'I know. But we'd dropped to around three-and-a-half thousand and with the wind I thought we'd save that for another day. By the way,' he said to Pollock. 'How many ships could you see lying off Boulogne?'

Pollock looked blank.

'Never forget,' Miller said, beginning to tire of his own pontificating, 'that you're an observer. Even if you're joyriding, keep your eyes open and your brain working. Most of it is just habit. Get into the habit and it will soon become second nature.'

He finished his beer and left them in the mess before he ran the risk of acquiring a reputation as the squadron bore.

He was roused from a doze a couple of hours later, lying on his bunk with the book he had been reading — H.G. Wells's *Tono-Bungay* — having slipped from his hands, leaving a dribble of saliva wetting the corner of his mouth and his head full of odd images of aeronautical sheds and society ladies of doubtful virtue.

'Sorry,' a young man said. He was standing by the open door carrying a box. 'Didn't mean to wake you. I didn't know they'd put someone else in here.'

Miller swung his legs off the bunk and wiped the side of his mouth.

'You must be Foden,' he said.

He looked a thin and — as he stepped inside the hut and awkwardly dropped the box onto his old bunk — a somehow disjointed man, with bad skin and wavy brown hair that had been centre-parted but over which a few unruly strands appeared to be in dispute as to which direction they should run.

He had glanced, Miller noticed, somewhat involuntarily at the cross-beam where Heyward had hung and then stood in the middle of the hut, his mouth slightly open, looking around him.

'I've just got in on the tender from Boulogne,' he explained. 'I had some leave in Paris.'

Miller introduced himself and offered his hand.

'I just reported back and Budgie — Captain Budge — said he was moving me in with Springfield. I assumed... well,' he finished and began picking up things with clumsy, unpredictable movements, peering at them as if to establish ownership and dropping them in the box he had put on the bunk.

'He probably thought you'd appreciate the move,' Miller said, sitting upright on his own bunk and watching as Foden collected his belongings. 'Under the circumstances.'

'They told you? About what happened?'

'You knew Heyward quite well, didn't you?'

'Charlie and I were at school together.'

'Rugby, wasn't it?'

'Yes.' He peered at Miller for a second. 'How did you know that?'

'Wing asked me to talk to his friends,' Miller explained, lifting his shoulders slightly in a gesture that indicated that it was nothing. 'For the family,' he added.

'Oh,' Foden said, surprised. He stood still for a moment, apparently unsure of the identity of the person in the photograph he had just picked up. Then, satisfied he recognised them, he dropped it into the box and ran a hand through his hair to no discernible effect.

'You found him, didn't you?'

'I just walked in,' Foden said, bemused. 'He was...'

'The door to the hut wasn't bolted?'

'No. I just walked in.'

'The other thing I was wondering,' Miller said, 'Did Heyward keep a diary, do you know?'

'Charlie?' He stood still once more, presumably to give the question some thought. 'I don't think so. You know, regulations... Well, put it this way, I never saw him with a *diary* but he was always scribbling away at something or other. Bit of a literary chap, Charlie. Why do you ask?'

'I thought that if he had, it might give some sort of indication of what he was thinking. You know, of why he did it.'

'Major Strouden told me he was reporting Charlie's death as an accident. He particularly asked me not to say anything to the family. For his mother's sake,' adding, as if by way of explanation, 'Her father was Lord Breesdale.'

'You've met them?'

'I spent the summer holidays with him once at his family's place in Yorkshire.' He smiled a little wistfully. 'We fished mostly and walked the moors. Did a bit of shooting but mostly we fished.'

'Did anyone else in the squadron know him before he came here?'

'At school, you mean?'

'Or training,' Miller said.

'No, I don't think so. He never said. Why?'

'He didn't seem depressed to you?'

'Lord, no,' Foden said. 'He had too many plans for what he was going to do in the future to worry about the present. Do you understand what I mean? I think he thought the war was a bit of an inconvenience. He knew he had to do his bit, of course, if only for form's sake, but it was a bit of a nuisance.'

'What sort of plans?'

'As I said, he was something of a literary chap. Had the idea he was going to be a novelist or a poet.'

'Budge said he'd found some poetry among his things.'

'There you are then.'

Budge had sent Heyward's personal belongings over for Miller to look at before returning them to the family. They were under the bunk at that moment.

'He wrote his poetry in exercise books, it seems,' Miller said, 'but you never saw a journal or anything like that?'

'I'm afraid not,' Foden replied. 'He'd stop scribbling as soon as I turned up. Probably put him off with my incessant chatter.'

'What about Dunne's death? Did that affect him?'

Foden frowned, thinking. 'Difficult to say with Charlie,' he admitted. 'He made out it was a mechanical failure and not his fault. Hard lines on Dunne, anyway.'

'Did they get on?'

'Yes,' Foden said, 'as a matter of fact, they did. I often found them here chatting together. I think Dunne was a bit literary, too, but not the way Charlie was.'

'How do you mean?'

'Well,' he said, suddenly looking a little sheepish, 'to be honest I was never sure it wasn't a bit of a pose.'

'Charlie or Dunne?'

'Charlie.'

'Did you join the RFC together?' Miller asked.

'Oh no. My father has an engineering company in Derby,' he explained, taking some socks and underclothes from a drawer. 'Some sort of mechanical aptitude seems to run in the family. I've always been keen on aeroplanes. So, after the show started I applied for training as a pilot. I'd been up a few times — you know, as a passenger — and couldn't wait to fly a machine myself.' He stopped stuffing clothes into the box and looked across at Miller. 'Normally I would have had to come through the ranks but father's got a bit of pull and managed to wangle me a commission. Being at Rugby helped, of course.' He shrugged. 'Well, one had to get into the fight and I rather thought I could kill two birds with one stone, if you know what I mean.'

Miller nodded, knowing exactly what Foden meant.

'Not Charlie, though.'

Foden laughed. 'A man with less mechanical aptitude I've yet to see.' He patted his tunic pockets then looked questioningly at Miller. 'I say, you wouldn't have a cigarette, would you? I seem to have left mine in my new billet.'

Miller offered him the packet and took one himself. He struck a match and watched as Foden cocked his head to take the light, a hank of his hair falling over one eye and close to the match. Foden inhaled and blew the smoke out through his beak-like nose.

'As a matter of fact,' he said, 'that's reminded me. Mechanical aptitude, I mean. When you asked if he knew anyone else in the squadron... There's a chap here whose brother was a friend of Charlie's.'

'Oh?'

'Name of Woodward. He's a fitter. A Flight, I think.'

'A fitter?'

'Oh, I know. This chap's from a good family but he enlisted in the ranks for some reason. They were from up Yorkshire way. Charlie knew his younger brother.' Foden gave a shrug. 'Being Charlie, of course, he wouldn't have mixed with a fitter.'

'But he knew this Woodward was here?'

'Oh yes. He told me the chap owed it to his class to go for a commission. Couldn't understand choosing to be an enlisted man.'

'Not the sort of thing he would have done, then?'

'Good lord, no. Charlie joined the Yorkshire Hussars Yeomanry like his father. Decent chap, his father. He was never one to be down on you if your family wasn't quite... well, you know. Charlie's mother was not quite as egalitarian, if you know what I mean. I suppose it was her father being a lord and everything.'

'Condescending?' Miller suggested.

'Lord, yes,' Foden said. 'Oh, she was decent enough, civil, I mean. But one never felt as though one was really welcome. Bit sticky sometimes.'

'And Heyward?'

'Well, yes, in a way. Like his mother, grandfather being a lord, and all. Not that he was any trouble once you knew him. Being at Rugby I passed muster, I suppose, despite my background but he could come over as a bit cold — the grand manner, if you know what I mean. Distant, you might say.' He started to laugh again.

'What is it?' Miller asked.

'Oh, just something someone said at school once. About Charlie. Well, his family, really.'

'What was it?'

'Just that the Yorkshire land-owning gentry's noses had been out of joint for the past seventy-five years. Since the Brontë sisters had given the reading public an erroneous notion of society on the Yorkshire moors.'

He laughed again and Miller smiled.

'Pretty witty, I thought,' Foden said. 'Charlie wasn't impressed, of course. Not too keen on lady novelists, probably.'

'They gave him a tough time at Rugby, I suppose,' Miller said. Foden looked at him in surprise.

'No. Why do you say that? School was full of boys like Charlie. I caught it more than he did — my family being in business and all. *Trade*, they'd say, though where most of them thought their people's money came from I've no idea.' He pulled on the cigarette and leaned towards Miller confidentially as if he knew he'd understand. 'Still, not quite top drawer.'

Miller understood.

'I only mentioned it,' Miller said, 'as from what you said, I assumed Heyward was something of an aesthete.'

'Good Lord!' Foden exclaimed as if he hadn't expected to hear a word like 'aesthete' come out of Miller's mouth. 'I wasn't suggesting there was anything... anything effeminate about Charlie. Good Lord! No, not at all. He wasn't like *that*. What I meant was, to me it seemed that being the literary chap was more of an affectation. Perhaps I'm wrong. He wasn't like that at Rugby, anyway. Perhaps he was different at Cambridge — he got involved with the college magazine and theatre or something.' He looked intently at Miller. 'That sort of thing's all a pose isn't it? Just for effect, I mean?'

'You're probably right,' Miller said.

'I never ran with an arty set,' Foden explained, as if not wanting to leave any possible impression that he might have.

'Why did he transfer out of the Yorkshire Yeomanry?'

'His mother arranged it. She's got some pull, too, apparently.' He grinned. 'More than my guv'nor, I dare say.' The grin suddenly died. 'Charlie's father bought it last year.' He cocked his head in the general direction of the front. 'Not too far from here, as a matter of fact. Hill 60. They never even found his body, so Charlie told me.'

Miller remembered. The casualties around Hill 60 in the German offensive the previous spring had been appalling. The Hun had gained ground in Sanctuary Wood but Hill 60 had stayed firm.

'Charlie told me his mother thought she was going to lose him, too, so apparently she had a word in the right ear and the next thing he knew Charlie's name had gone forward for flight training. He was only too happy to be out of the trenches, of course, but I think it embarrassed him that his mother had arranged it. He probably would have refused — Charlie had quite a well-developed sense of honour, if you understand me — but after his father... well, he wouldn't have wanted to cause his mother any more pain.'

'But why the RFC, for God's sake?' Miller asked. 'Didn't she know the kind of casualties we'd been taking?'

He had been thinking she might have wangled him a soft job back at a training establishment until he remembered it was Kitchener's ear she was supposed to have; *he* wasn't the kind of man to afford *anyone* a soft option. He had probably thought a desire to join the RFC was a sign of keenness.

'I don't suppose she ever heard how many men we lose. They don't advertise it, do they? Anyway, I doubt it would have occurred to her at all if Charlie hadn't written that I had joined. She must have thought it was a safe billet.' His eyes moved heavenward. 'You know, up there, swanning around out of the mud and the trenches and the shelling. How he got through the training without breaking his neck I'll never know.'

'What makes you say that?'

'He was a rotten pilot,' Foden said. 'As I said, no mechanical aptitude at all. They really should have flunked him.'

But they wouldn't have, Miller thought. At the start of the war the really hopeless cases had been weeded out soon enough — at least, before they killed themselves or someone else. As the war had progressed, though, and the shortage of pilots had become critical anyone who managed to get up and down without breaking too many bones was given his ticket. Particularly if his family had 'pull'. It was driving the squadron commanders to despair. Once posted, half of the hopeless ones were dead within a fortnight, most of the rest within the month. If they managed to survive that long then they stood a good chance of saving their skins until the unexpected came along, although he didn't suppose anyone had expected what had come along for Heyward.

'I suppose Mrs Heyward fixed it for him to be posted here,' Foden went on. 'She wrote me, more or less asking me to look out for him but not in so many words, of course.' He gave Miller a crooked smile. 'She wouldn't have condescended to that.'

'How long had he been here?'

'Just over a month,' Foden said. 'About six weeks, that's all.'

'He must have been doing something right to have lasted that long,' Miller said.

'Well, to tell the truth he never seemed to be in the air that much,' Foden said. 'Always something up with his engine, according to Charlie. Turned back an awful lot. He'd got a bit of a reputation for it.'

'That couldn't have gone down too well with the other officers.'

'No,' Foden said. 'The major spotted he was a duffer in the flying stakes right off, of course. Shifted him to observing. Actually, Charlie had a good eye for that.' He laughed. 'All that shootin' and fishin' as a boy, I suppose. He thought he was being done down, though, I think. Probably thought being a passenger wasn't quite up to snuff.'

'Did he complain to the CO?'

Foden shrugged. 'Can't say. I know I tried to make out that being a pilot in a two-seater squadron was only being a glorified chauffeur. But Charlie...' he shrugged. 'Next thing I know is that I walk in here and there he is.' He raised his eyes to the cross-beam. 'Poor old Charlie.'

11

The mess hall was half-empty at dinner and Miller found himself sitting next to Doyle, the MO. The cloud bank he had seen to the west that afternoon had built into a weather front. Rain had washed out the late afternoon patrol and threatened to wash out the dawn flight as well. Many of the men, counting on a lie-in in the morning, had driven into town. Those left were scattered in loose knots around the tables, orderlies weaving between them with their dinner.

After talking to Foden, Miller realised he had had to reassess his picture of Heyward. He had initially formed the impression that the man had been something of a misfit, the kind that naturally became the butt of other men's jokes and was generally made to feel an outsider. It seemed though, to the contrary, that if Heyward had not made too many friends it had been more his own choice. In fact, he probably wouldn't have stood out from the crowd had he not hanged himself. Heyward's main fault — his deficiencies as a pilot aside — appears to have been an over-developed sense of his own social status and Heyward would not have been the first of that breed that Miller had met. Looking around the mess hall, he might have identified one or two at that moment.

Beside him, Doyle tipped a liberal amount of red wine into his glass, drank some and then scrutinised the label.

'What do you think?' the officer across the table from them asked.

He had a florid face with a heavy moustache and was forty years old at least. His belted and buckled body appeared contained within his tunic only with difficulty and some luck. Miller couldn't see how he could have squeezed himself into the cockpit of any machine he had ever seen. One of Cody's Cathedrals, perhaps...

'Now, that's what I call claret,' Doyle said. 'And where was it, if you don't mind my asking, that you found this little beauty?'

The florid face beamed with pleasure. 'A little fellow in the Rue Villiot,' he said through a mouthful of beef, 'near the Gare de Lyon. A chap in the Guards I know put me onto him. The fellow lost several of his best customers when the Hun looked as if they'd take Paris. Just up and cleared off. Left him over-stocked. Took two-dozen cases off his hands at a very reasonable price.'

'Did you now?' Doyle said appreciatively. He threw a glance up and down the table. 'A pity to cast it in front of some of these swine.'

The officer waved an admonishing fork at Doyle. 'Now, now,' he chortled. 'You can't expect to hog it all to yourself.'

'Very good, Fitz, very good.' He took another swig of the claret. 'I'll just have to learn to drink faster.'

The mess orderly poured some of the wine into Miller's glass and he sipped at it.

'Well, Miller?' Doyle asked.

'It's good,' Miller said.

'It's an educated palate you have, is it?'

'I wouldn't go that far,' Miller replied, 'but after two years in the country wine is one of the things you come to appreciate.'

'So, the longer you survive, the more you appreciate the grape,' Doyle said. 'By that reasoning, man, by the end of the war the general staff will be the only connoisseurs left. Them and Fitz, here.' He poked a fork across the table.

'We haven't met,' Miller said, addressing the officer.

'FitzHarris,' Doyle put in. 'He's a damned beneficiary of the Ascendancy, but the best mess officer you'll find in France. He'll tell you that himself. Isn't that so, Fitz?'

FitzHarris began to chortle again, his whole chest heaving up and down as if he were trotting a horse.

'He's nominally the transport officer around here so he never has to be using his legs,' Doyle went on. 'And he's the only man in the squadron who's got fatter since he was posted to France. When he goes home in civvies, they take him for an armaments manufacturer.'

FitzHarris roared, either enjoying or inured to the insults.

'The Ascendancy?' Miller queried. 'What's that?'

'Now I was told they had schools in America,' Doyle said pointedly. 'There's going to be a lot of disappointed Irishmen when they find out it's a land of damned ignoramuses.'

'He is referring to the Protestant Ascendancy,' FitzHarris said. 'The settlement of Ireland by the English and Scots. Maintains my family threw his off their farm a couple of hundred years ago, but that's bog-trotters for you.'

'Now I never said it was *your* family, Fitz,' Doyle argued. 'You're just a symptom of the whole malaise. Besides, if you'd just learn to talk properly and eschew this "bog-trotter" nonsense, you could almost pass as an Irishman.'

'*Eschew!*' FitzHarris appealed. 'Will you listen to that, Miller? Being pleasant to the rogue and buying him the odd drink only makes him worse.'

'And speakin' of drink,' Doyle said, 'I've got to pick up some supplies in town if you fellows fancy a little entertainment?'

'Not me,' FitzHarris said. 'Too much paperwork.'

'Paperwork!' Doyle said. 'I've spent the afternoon on latrine inspection and believe me, after an hour of that, a man needs to come up for air. How about you, Miller?'

'Yes, I'll come,' said Miller, 'and you can tell me all about the Ascendancy.'

'Don't say you haven't been warned,' FitzHarris said.

Miller brushed his teeth and combed his hair in his billet then walked over to the medical hut. Outside a large black soft-topped limousine was parked on which Doyle leaned as he went over a list with his orderly.

Miller walked around the not inconsiderable length of the car making appreciative noises, then unhooked the bonnet and looked over the engine.

'This is a Hansa-Lloyd Doppelphaeton,' he said to Doyle.

'So I'm told,' Doyle said matter-of-factly. 'Fitz said the Hun abandoned it when they got pushed back. Ran out of petrol or had a flat tyre or the like. It was liberated for the use of the squadron.' He looked up from his list with an interrogative glance. 'Now I wouldn't have said the Hun were a profligate race, would you? Seems oddly out of character to leave a machine as grand as this lyin' around.'

He tossed the clipboard into the front of the car. 'Still, when I can manage to pry it out of Fitz's grasp it gives me inordinate pleasure to ride around in a motor car that no doubt ferried the German High Command on inspections of their front-line cannon fodder.' He opened a rear door. 'Now come out from under that bonnet, will you Miller? Tell me, what is it about Americans that they've always got to be tinkerin' with engines?'

Miller climbed into the back as Doyle's orderly got behind the wheel. The rain had stopped temporarily but they kept the top up as they drove to town. They talked about the quality of the mess and the mental stability of the pilots and the filthy conditions of the roads but, Miller noted, they didn't talk about The Protestant Ascendancy.

At the medical supply depot Doyle oversaw the filling of his list and the loading and securing of the supplies in the front of the Doppelphaeton. Then they drove into the town proper and Doyle and Miller had a drink at a bar while Doyle had a glass of beer sent out to his driver who was sitting with the supplies. Then Doyle banged his empty glass on the bar top and announced that he had an appointment with a lady.

'You're welcome to join me,' Doyle said with a wink that intimated he'd used the term 'lady' as merely one of anatomical classification.

Miller declined and told Doyle that he'd meet him in the square in a couple of hours.

Doyle shrugged. 'All work and no play,' he said, 'makes Jack a dull, but possibly healthier boy.'

'You're the MO,' Miller said. 'I assume you know what you're doing.'

Doyle lifted a finger to the peak of his cap as he climbed into the back seat of the Doppelphaeton. 'If I do, Miller, I'm one of the few in France that does.'

Miller watched the driver slip the nose of the monstrous car into the stream of traffic then turned towards the square.

He still couldn't make up his mind whether or not he had visited the town before the war when he had come looking for Cody. The square, with its five roads converging around a central hub, had looked familiar, but he had been in Poperinghe when serving in this sector before and had visited so many other towns in the last two years and had found the war had seemingly stamped them with an odd universality so that they had merged, in the memory, into one another. He stopped for a cup of coffee in a small estaminet and watched the activity on the street, then looked over the wares on the roadside stalls. Mostly they offered cheap souvenirs for soldiers who still harboured the expectation of getting home, or household goods no longer new that had the air of having been looted from bomb-damaged houses.

After half-an-hour he found himself at the end of Priesterstraat where the restaurant in which he had had the limp salad the night before was situated. It had started to rain again and he walked down the street to the restaurant and opened the door. He was immediately hit by a barrage of noise, most of it emanating from a table near the bar where several flying officers from Miller's squadron were sitting. They were singing the song that had given anti-aircraft fire its nickname, over-familiar now after a year or more of repetition and growing as wearisome as the gunfire it had named:

A lady named Miss Hewitt got on friendly terms with me.
She fell in love with me at once and then fell in the sea.

Miller waved down two subalterns of the Ox and Bucks who rose from their chairs to salute as he passed their table. They were eating and pointedly trying to ignore the airmen at the other table. The voices were singing in ragged formation and somewhere, while importing the song from across the Channel, they had managed to ditch the melody:

My wife came on the scene as I threw coat and vest aside,
As other garments I slipped off to save the girl, she cried:
Archibald, certainly not!

There were five of them, too caught up in their own entertainment to notice Miller until he had reached the bar.

'Miller,' Chacksfield called as the others reached the chorus and their voices a crescendo:

Desist at once disrobing on the spot!
You may show your pluck to save Miss Hewitt,
But if you've got to strip to do it,
 Archibald, certainly not!

Beside him, with a glass held high and his chair tipping, Moss went over backwards with a cracking of timber and shattering of glass. A cheer went up and Moss jerked upright, giggling as he disentangled himself from the wreckage. With the same small darting movements Miller had noticed he somehow managed to extend to his flying, he turned the chair upright and sat down again, lurching slightly to the right where one of the stays had broken.

Chacksfield waved Miller over.

Miller said, 'Cognac,' to the portly waiter behind the bar then stepped to the table.

The other officers – Denham, wearing his habitual supercilious expression, Tozer and Foden's new roommate, the A Flight commander, Springfield – suddenly lost their party spirit. Miller pulled a chair from one of the vacant tables and edged it between Springfield and Moss who was canted over towards the wall. Bottles, empty plates and an overflowing ashtray cluttered the table.

Tozer was drunk. His unbuttoned tunic showed his shirt tight over a broad chest. His face was puffy with alcohol.

'I came in with the MO,' Miller volunteered. 'I wondered if I'd find you here.'
'Have you been looking for us?' Denham asked.
Miller said to Tozer: 'We were supposed to have a drink in the mess

yesterday, remember?'

'No,' Tozer said thickly, 'I don't.'

'Have one with us now,' Chacksfield said. He grabbed a relatively clean glass and dashed red wine into it.

'Thank you,' Miller said. 'What shall we drink to?'

'Victory?' Springfield suggested cynically.

Miller said, 'What about absent friends?'

'Tozer only drinks to Arlette,' Moss said.

'Who's Arlette?' Miller asked. 'The girl that works here?'

'A waitress,' Denham said with contempt.

Tozer glared across the table at him.

'A very pretty waitress,' Chacksfield allowed.

'Absent friends,' Miller insisted and drank. The others mumbled after him and drank some wine.

'Tozer's in love with Arlette,' Moss persisted.

'Is Arlette your girl?' Miller asked Tozer.

'Arlette's anyone's girl,' Denham said.

'Take that back!' Tozer shouted. He lurched at Denham, falling across the table and knocking the bottles over. One shattered on the floor. Wine spilled over Miller's tunic.

'Denham didn't mean anything,' Miller said to Tozer, looking pointedly at Denham and taking the opportunity to rattle him. 'Mr Denham is an officer. He wears the King's uniform. You wouldn't treat a lady with anything other than the respect she deserves, would you Denham?'

Denham stared back at Miller as if he was considering arguing the point, then deliberately turned away as Springfield pulled Tozer back into his chair.

'I didn't mean anything, Tozer,' Denham said, sounding bored.

By the next table Miller saw the dark-haired girl with black eyes who, the previous evening, had asked him what he was dreaming about. He wondered if this was Arlette and if she had understood the exchange. She was looking at him but there was nothing in her face to suggest she knew they had been talking about her. She turned back towards the bar. *This* was her country, she had said to Miller.

'So,' he said to Tozer again, 'is Arlette your girl?'

'She's not interested in a squit like Tozer,' Chacksfield said, righting the bottles.

'Shush,' Moss warned theatrically, leaning against the wall.

The girl came over to the table carrying a tray. '*Votre cognac, Capitaine?*' she asked Miller. She took the glass off her tray and placed it on the table in front of him. She began clearing the plates and bottles. He had not noticed the other evening but now he saw that she was hardly any older than the boys around the table.

Miller glanced at Tozer. He was staring at her with an open mouth.

'*Vous êtes Arlette?*' Miller asked her.

'*Oui, je suis Arlette.*'

'*Nous avons bousillé tout,*' he told her, apologising for the mess. Arlette's eyes ran around the eager faces staring back at her and she sighed volubly. '*Oui, monsieur.*'

Tozer almost fell off his chair turning to follow her passage back to the bar. Denham sat aloof, looking superior.

'Wonderful,' Chacksfield murmured.

Miller was aware that between waitresses and Madame Poulon's girls there weren't too many opportunities for officers to meet young women. In the two years he had been in France he certainly had not met many. There were always nurses and VADs, but they were generally chaperoned when not working and if you encountered one in a hospital you were hardly in any condition to take advantage of the fact.

He sipped his cognac and looked at Denham. His features gave the impression that they had been moulded with particular care, fine yet not delicate. Despite the evidence of the empty bottles on the table, his eyes were clear and comprehending, set above a discerning nose whose occasional twitch and flare suggested it did not always approve of everything it found placed beneath it. The general effect of his appearance, though, was in Miller's opinion spoilt by an almost permanently supercilious turn of the mouth.

Denham caught Miller looking at him and the nose flared again.

'You don't speak bad French for an American,' he remarked.

'Thank you,' Miller said. Aware that Denham was needling him he forewent his usual explanation concerning his nationality. 'How was Heyward's French? Does anyone recall?'

'Impeccable, as it happens,' Denham said.

'Was a rotten pilot,' Tozer slurred.

'Is that what you had against him?' Miller asked him.

'Who said I had 'nything against him?'

'That photograph? Why did you take it and then pin it up in the mess?'

'It was only a lark,' Springfield insisted.

'In rather bad taste, wasn't it?'

'I don't think anyone's ever tried to suggest that Tozer possesses taste,' Denham commented.

'Keep your beastly mouth shut, Denham,' Tozer warned, achieving some coherence with his vehemence.

'Just a lark?' Miller repeated. 'But you didn't like him much, did you Tozer?'

'Too damn superior,' Tozer said. 'Lording over 'veryone. Rotten pilot.'

'You never flew with him, I suppose?'

Tozer's slack features managed to pull themselves into an expression of incredulity.

'What about Dunne? Did you like him?'

Tozer squinted at him. 'Dunne's 'llright.'

'Everyone liked Dunne,' Moss interjected helpfully.

'So I'm always being told,' Miller said. 'What was it about him everyone liked?'

They all looked blank until Chacksfield suddenly announced, 'Enthusiasm. His enthusiasm.'

'For what? Flying?'

'For everything,' Chacksfield said, nonplussed. 'He was enthusiastic about everything.'

'I'm told he got on well with Heyward.'

'Until Heyward killed him,' Springfield said.

Arlette returned with her tray to clear the rest of the table. She leaned over Miller and he smelt a faint trace of eau de cologne from her body.

'*Merci, mademoiselle,*' he said.

'*Madame,*' she corrected.

'*Pardon, Madame.*'

'I'm afraid the lady is married, Tozer,' he said after she had left.

'Tozer doesn't care,' Moss declared. 'Do you Tozer?'

Tozer's eyes had taken on a glassy aspect. His lips had parted and his tongue was protruding slightly from between them as if he was beginning to lose control of his muscles.

'He's in B Flight, isn't he?' Miller said, nodding towards him. 'Is Chatterton in town?'

'He said he had letters to write,' Chacksfield said.

'Then perhaps you'd better get Tozer back to the squadron,' Miller said to Denham. 'The rain should clear by lunch and B Flight's got the midday patrol.'

'Is that an order, captain?' Denham asked.

'Just a suggestion, lieutenant.'

Moss began to giggle.

'Come on, old chap,' Springfield said.

Tozer grunted as Springfield hauled him to his feet. 'Time to go home or you won't be fit to fly.'

Chacksfield stood up and took Tozer's other side.

'Tozer's not fit to fly sober,' Moss said.

'I'm 'sgood as any you,' Tozer said, shrugging off Springfield and Chacksfield.

'Of course you are, old man,' Springfield assured him. 'You're as good as any of us.'

'I wanna say goodnight t'Arlette.'

'Arlette's gone to bed,' Chacksfield said.

'Then I'm goin' t'bed too,' Tozer said, breaking free of them.

'Get him back,' Miller said.

Denham hung back as the others steered Tozer out of the door, his face seeming to betray a struggle between a desire to maintain aloof from his drunken companions and an idea of duty to them owed by his rank of flight commander.

Miller waited. The singing began again as the door closed behind them. Duty appeared to win.

'There was nothing between Heyward and Tozer, you know.' Denham said eventually. 'Heyward was a bit disparaging about athletic prowess, that's all.

111

Thought it all a bit plebeian.'

'And Tozer's an athlete?'

'Cricket, rugger, rowing – all the usual things. But he's not too bright. Heyward had a way of making him feel inferior.'

Much like Denham's own, Miller thought.

'And the photograph?'

'Foden made a fuss when he found Heyward,' Denham said, 'and Tozer happened to have his camera with him. He'd been snapping the machines or something.'

'So he thought it would be a lark to take one of Heyward hanging from the roof.'

Denham looked at Miller frankly. 'I told you — not too bright.'

Denham followed the others and Miller picked up his cognac and moved to another table, brushing ineffectually at the wine stain on his uniform.

'*Capitaine,*' Arlette said, standing over him and holding out a cloth.

Miller took the cloth and dabbed at the stain to no effect. He gave it back to her with a shrug. '*Je suis désolé pour le degats,*' he said again. '*Je regrette la chaise est cassé.*'

She placed her tray on his table and pouted at him in a sullen fashion as if to convey that it was no more than she would have expected, then began to wipe down the other table. Miller took a five-franc coin from his pocket and placed it on her tray.

'*Pour la chaise,*' he explained again, pointing at the splintered stay on Moss's chair.

'*Oui, monsieur,*' Arlette said without enthusiasm.

Miller finished his cognac and smoked a cigarette, idly watching Arlette as she cleaned the tables, killing time until he was to meet Doyle in the square. The two subalterns got up to leave and he had just stubbed out the cigarette when he heard the whine of an approaching shell. The scream cut abruptly as if grabbed by the throat and a second later the street outside erupted. He grabbed the girl and pulled her to the ground as the floor shook and the window shattered, glass flying across the restaurant.

He dragged her towards the bar and squatted down behind it, arms spread over the girl's head, squashing in beside the waiter. A second shell exploded, toppling bottles from the shelf above them. One hit him on the head and he cursed. He could hear Arlette muttering under her breath as she trembled in his arms. He wondered if she was praying or cursing, but there was too much noise and his French was not good enough for him to make out the words. He could feel her shaking, but it might have been the earth.

Then, as abruptly as it had begun, the shelling stopped and a blanket of silence fell over the street. They remained crouching under the bar for a minute longer, the sound of their breath coming in short gasps that made a kind of syncopated rhythm. Then the silence outside erupted into a melée of shouts and roaring engines. Somewhere a horse was screaming. Miller stood up, pulling Arlette after him. His arms were still holding her and she was looking, from only inches away, into his face.

'Sorry,' he said automatically, taking a step back.

He picked a piece of broken glass out of her hair and some off his uniform. He became aware of a warm trickle of liquid running down his face. He wiped it away, expecting blood, but it had reached the corner of his mouth and he tasted cognac.

The waiter stood up beside them and filled three glasses on the bar. He passed one to Arlette and another to Miller. The girl drank, her pale face even whiter now.

'Are you all right?' he asked in English.

She nodded and smiled at him nervously. He moved back onto the floor of the restaurant. The door had been shattered and glass from the windows lay strewn across the room. He righted some upturned tables and chairs and wondered what had happened to the two subalterns. They must have been just outside when the shell hit. He picked his way onto the street but the only thing lying in the road was the horse. It lay on its side, still in the shafts of a splintered cart. One of its legs had been blown off and its blood was pumping onto the cobbles as it struggled to rise. As he watched, a major of artillery stepped out of a doorway, took out his revolver and put two bullets into the animal's rearing head. Traffic began moving again and men emerged from wherever they had sheltered. He looked back into the restaurant. The girl and the waiter had already started sweeping up.

Walking towards the square, he looked at the new damage that had been added to the old, the sign of a ceaseless persecution. He supposed the transit depots on the outskirts of town were the target; at any given time heaped dumps of supplies and armaments and thousands of camped men might be there — new detachments on their way up to the line and the exhausted ragged remnants of other battalions pulled down. Now, with the build-up to the south on the Somme, the frenetic activity around the camps resembled, from the air, an anthill kicked over by a malignant boot.

The camps were the favoured targets for German artillery and they lobbed shells over with a monotonous regularity. But, as the artillery spotters from the Hun balloons and aircraft had gradually been forced down by the increasingly offensive allied patrols, the shelling had taken on a spasmodic unpredictability, made somehow more lethal by its lack of discrimination, falling not only on the camps but also on the town, targets decided — it seemed — by nothing more than a cast of the dice of fate.

Passing a row of freshly ruined buildings, a low sloping hill of brick and rubble on the losing end of one of fate's throws, he wondered (it was a thought that had often occurred to him while spotting for artillery himself) what caused the differences in where the shells fell within a selected area? One supposed, once the desired range had been achieved, that shells from any particular gun would all fall in the same place — the gun barrels, after all, did not change. One had to account for the recoil, of course, but the guns were generally dug in so that, after the recoil, they would slip back into the same position they had occupied before firing. Was it, then, some small difference in the casting of the shell? If they were cast from a number of moulds they might, possibly, incorporate some seemingly insignificant variation that imparted a difference in spin or trajectory. Or perhaps it was a matter of atmospherics? A gust of wind, a slight variation in pressure. It was something that often occupied the mind when under shelling: a man crouches under whatever cover he can find and listens to the shells screaming overhead, shuddering in a kind of involuntary sympathy with the earth while that intolerable pressure on the ears builds until it feels as if it's going to crush the skull — and all the time praying that the next one lands somewhere else... on *someone* else.

And why shouldn't it? If the first shell fired from each gun missed, then didn't logic dictate that all should miss? Or perhaps it *was* that slight settling in the position of the artillery piece after the recoil? Was that it? A tenth of an inch here, a sixteenth there. And what dictated that, Miller wanted to know?

Why was the whole damnable show so incalculable?

12

It felt as if he hadn't slept. Yet he knew he must have because Jones was in the hut with a mug of tea and hot water for the washbasin. He watched him for a moment through half-closed eyes and then opened his mouth to speak and mumbled something unintelligible.

'Five hundred foot ceiling, sir,' Jones chirped, laying out Miller's uniform on the empty bunk. 'No wind but still raining.'

'Must be washed out,' Miller finally managed, pushing himself up on one elbow. 'I'm not due to go up, anyway. A's up.' The evening patrol had been washed out and Reynolds and A Flight had been bumped on to take the dawn flight.

'No sir,' Jones replied cheerfully, plainly pleased to be able to contradict him. 'Brigade's been on the blower.'

'What time is it?'

'Time you was up and dressed, sir,' Jones said. 'The major's waiting in the ops room.'

Miller fell back onto his pillow. It had been the middle of the night before he had got back to the airfield. The shelling in town hadn't lasted long but the result of the few that had fallen in the centre had been chaos. At one point he had found himself directing traffic so that the injured could be taken to one of the casualty clearing stations. When he had at last arrived at where he had arranged to meet Doyle, there was no sign of him. He had waited but, for all he knew, Doyle might have come and gone or been dead.

After an hour or so he began looking for alternative transport and finally found an obliging captain of the Scots Guards with an interest in aeronautics who went out of his way to drop Miller at the field. In return, all he wanted was the opportunity to sit in the cockpit of Miller's One-and-a-half-Strutter for a few minutes while Miller showed him the controls. It had been two o'clock in the morning by the time Miller finally waved him off and then, after he had dropped into his bunk and closed his eyes, he kept replaying the scene of the injured horse in the street. Over and over he saw the poor brute struggling to get to its feet despite its lost leg, the terror in its eyes and the screaming whinny of its distress playing soundlessly in his ears.

He crawled out of the bunk and as quickly as he could washed off the night's sweat before dressing. The rain was nothing more than a persistent drizzle but dawn had made no headway through the overcast and, as he made his way to the château, he kept catching vague movements out of the corner of his eyes like teasing phantoms flitting in and out of the darkness. An engine over by the sheds suddenly coughed into life, spluttered and died. Muted voices filtered through the lighted doorway of the château. He followed and filed into the operations room, nodding numbly at the sleep-puffed faces that turned to him.

'They've given us a sticky one this morning, gentlemen,' Strouden announced gloomily.

The CO looked to Miller as he always looked, as if he didn't undress or sleep but at the end of every day had been parked in a cupboard somewhere until next needed, brushed off and taken out again, spic, span and cleanly shaved. The only signs of passing time was a slight increase of the sagging jowl, a deeper hollowing of the eyes. He was standing by the easel, another map of the lines posted on it. Next to the easel, beside Gregory, the DH2 pilot, Budge leaned against the wall with his arms crossed and his hook resting in the crook of his left arm. He was looking down at it, frowning slightly, as if he had just noticed the modification to his hand for the first time.

'It's the Hun airfield at Rumbeke,' Strouden continued. 'For those who don't know, Poperinghe was shelled again last night and Brigade want to knock out the artillery they're using. To do this we need to spot it.'

'With respect, sir,' Watson said, 'you're not going to see anything in this murk.' The observer was sitting next to Chatterton, Wynstanley and Bryce. Springfield, the A Flight commander, and Denham and Chacksfield were there, looking no worse for their night out. Breconridge stood slightly apart on the other side of the room with Flight Sergeant Reynolds while Parry, Reynolds's observer, stood between him and the other officers. As he looked, Miller became aware of Foden stepping beside him.

'Flap?' he asked under his breath.

'That's the point,' Strouden said to Watson. 'They can't spot till the weather clears and once it clears the Hun will be up disrupting the spotting. The guns they're after are well behind their lines and it'll be the devil of a job letting our artillery know how they're doing with a squadron of Hun machines buzzing around. But we're not concerned with the spotting.' He smacked the map with his stick. 'We've been asked to bomb this airfield. The object of the exercise is to do as much damage as we can to their field and machines and generally disrupt their ops so that the boys doing the spotting will have an easier time of it.'

'Who's to lead, sir?' Chatterton asked. 'It's not going to be easy to find with a ceiling this low.'

It was a pertinent question. Along with A Flight and one or two other individuals, the commanders of the other two flights were also present.

'I thought I might,' Strouden said.

'Tally ho, sir,' Chacksfield cried.

Budge shook his head.

'I'm asking you, gentlemen, because you are the most experienced officers in the squadron and it seemed to me that together we have the best chance of getting the result we're after.' He ran the tip of his stick in a small circle on the map. 'Rumbeke Castle,' he said. 'It should be a good landmark if Fritz hasn't knocked it down. Last reports were it was still standing.' He turned back to them. 'Mr Foden?'

'Sir?'

'I'd like you to fly with Captain Miller. You've had experience with the bomb racks. Budgie, here, volunteered but he's as likely as not to get his hook caught in a bomb fin and keep hold of the damn thing.'

Budge looked suitably apologetic and the others laughed.

'Happy to oblige, sir,' Foden said.

'I'll be using Mr Griffith's Fee and Mr Watson has agreed to sit in as my observer.'

'Rather you than me,' Miller told Foden. 'I've never trusted those damn racks.'

They moved closer to study the map then gathered around a table where some old, indistinct photographs of the airfield had been laid out. Strouden pointed out the hangars they were to target as well as any machines they saw in the open. He indicated the line of approach he planned to take, offering the best targets, and gave them the formation order.

'And while you're dropping your eggs,' he finished, 'Mr Gregory will do what damage he can with hand grenades.' He waited a moment, then added, 'We're reliably informed that the weather is expected to improve so the idea is to get in and hit them hard while they're least expecting anything to be up. Any questions?'

Miller pulled on his clothes and tucked his scarf into his coat. Outside the sky had begun to offer the suggestion of lightening, but that only seemed to accentuate the thickness of the overcast and he found it difficult to judge the ceiling. He walked to his FE giving it an eyesight check then stopped by the bomb rack, an aluminium arrangement that had been fixed to the side of the nacelle. They used ordinary artillery shells that had been adapted with a fin and a detonator in the nose that went off on contact. The shells were held vertically in the rack by a pin through the fin and to release them the observer simply leaned over the side and withdrew the pin. It was an arrangement Miller had never liked. Particular care had to be taken when placing the bombs in the rack as the detonator wouldn't take any pressure at all. He had been on a field once when there had been an accident loading a bombing rack onto the side of a BE2. The man's name had been Borthwick, Miller remembered, an aircraftsman second-class who had only been out a week. He had either fumbled one of the bombs or the pin had failed. The shell had fallen through the rack. Borthwick tried to catch it but had knocked the detonator on the nose. The explosion had killed him outright. A man nearby had lost the lower part of his right leg and the BE2 had been destroyed.

Miller looked at the rack from every angle, finding it hard to resist the impulse to touch the bombs to ensure that they were not snagged. Foden stood beside him waiting to climb aboard. Across the field, Strouden squeezing himself into the cockpit of Griffith's FE, was almost lost in the murk.

'Let's hope it lifts a little before we get there,' he said to Foden as he climbed into the machine, 'otherwise when we come down we'll find ourselves flying through their hangars instead of over them.'

Waiting in line on the field watching Strouden in the FE bounce across the grass and lift off, Miller couldn't help thinking that not long before they wouldn't have entertained flying in these conditions. Getting up was not going to be a problem — after all, once you were off the ground you just pointed the nose up and kept going until eventually you broke through the cloud. Up there though, there was nothing except a white shifting ocean of cloud beneath the machine. There were no landmarks and no distinguishing features, none that lasted more than a few minutes, anyway. It was more like a gas caught in the bottom of a laboratory flask, a shifting, swirling fog, and, when the time came to descend through it, all one could do was pray that there still *was* a ceiling of some sorts, some gap between ground and cloud that would give you long enough to get the machine down.

Provided you were in the right place, of course. That was another problem altogether.

In front of him, Springfield and his observer, Breconridge, had begun to climb towards the cloud cover. Almost unconsciously Miller started counting under his breath as he opened up the FE's engine and began gaining speed across the field. Ahead, he saw Springfield's machine slice into the murk and disappear. He made a mental calculation based on the FE's rate of climb, then checked the figure against the altitude showing on the aneroid barometer as he hit the ceiling. He made it five hundred feet; the aneroid made it seven hundred. That was the trouble: the air pressure that operated the aneroid was a variable thing. But then, as often as not when distracted, so was mental arithmetic.

Pushing up, the Beardmore engine flat out, Miller began to experience that sensation of losing all sense of dimension. Beyond Foden in the nose and the tips of the wings on either side of him, nothing showed except a vaguely moving fog. Without the slight pressure of his body on the back of his seat and holding in his head the concept of 'up', he might easily have persuaded himself that they were diving, or even upside down. Sight, smell and touch were lost to him, leaving his one active sense, the perception of sound, swamped by the roar of the Beardmore behind him.

Water vapour had begun to soak into his clothes. He could feel drops running down the back of his neck under his scarf. It had begun to fog the glass of his instruments. Foden turned around, rivulets of water running over his face from the smooth skullcap of his helmet, and Miller could sense rather than see the wrinkles creasing his forehead under cap and goggles.

'We'll be through it soon,' he called to Foden.

Nimbostratus, he thought pointlessly. Knowing the classification for the type of cloud they were travelling through was not a great help. Except to know that the top might be as high as ten thousand feet. He smeared a gloved thumb across the glass of the aneroid barometer. They were at two-and-a-half thousand if the instrument could be believed. It was as thick as when they had first entered. Another machine might be twenty feet from his wingtip and he wouldn't have seen it. The noise of his own engine drowned out any sound of the others.

It was a matter of nerve, he told himself. Holding it until they broke through. That is why Strouden had chosen them. Any of the others might have panicked, thrown the stick forward and tried to find the ground again. And if they had, and found their way back to the airfield, would they have remembered that they still carried the bombs? Landing with them would be suicidal; one way or another, the eggs would have to be dropped and over their own lines unless they fancied a low-level sortie against the Hun trenches. No, turning back was not an option.

In front of him Foden began waving a hand and pointing upwards and Miller sensed the cloud had begun to thin. Beyond the wingtip he imagined he could see a few more yards. Cloud wisped ahead and, for a second, he glimpsed a splash of colour. Then, at four thousand, they were through, like a flying fish cresting the surface and soaring. Ahead he saw the tail and wings of Springfield's machine and, beyond him, those of Reynolds and Chatterton. Climbing to five thousand feet, he levelled out and caught sight of Strouden's machine a hundred feet above them. He looked back over his shoulder as the nose of Denham's FE crested the cloud and climbed to join him. Behind him, Wynstanley broke through.

A deep indigo-blue flooded the sky, cut here and there by faint stars. The sun, still lost below the cloud horizon ahead, had yet to rise above the mantle to dislodge the night. To Miller's right Denham made the 'all's well' sign and they flew on while Strouden above circled once to check his bearing then dropped the FE in front of Chatterton and MacMaster, his observer, and led them on a heading east-nor-east.

They had been in the air twenty minutes and by Miller's reckoning would be somewhere over Ypres. In a few more minutes they would be crossing the lines. Strouden was leading them by dead reckoning — air speed plotted on a compass bearing — and would have to allow for wind and drift as he found it. At around maximum speed at five thousand feet Strouden had calculated it would take them twenty minutes to approach the vicinity of Rumbeke where he would take them back down through the cloud. A ten-minute descent gave a journey time of fifty minutes. Roughly doubling that to allow for the return journey left a little over an hour for them to locate the Hun airfield, drop their bombs and turn for home.

'Ample,' Strouden had said as he had wound up the briefing. More than ample, Miller had thought, and twenty miles was no great distance to be over the lines. But, given the falling ceiling, Strouden had elected to run for home beneath the cloud cover. Twenty miles at five hundred feet over enemy lines was something else again.

He had never got used to cloudland. Perhaps it was the rarity of being above such dense cover. Flying through accumulations of cumulus one got used to the islands without ever seeing them; it was always the sea of sky between that captured the attention. Total cover never looked the same. Each visit revealed subtle changes to the topography, rills and ridges that shifted and twisted, towers of wisping vapour that defied gravity and logic. Now, as the sun crested the eastern edge of the milky horizon, indigo turned through crimson around him, tingeing the peaks and throwing shadow into the troughs that made canyons out of depressions. Ahead, where vision smoothed the surface of the cloudscape, plains stretched reassuringly with a siren invitation to land, to come and roll the machine onto the downy feather-lightness of its solidity and to step out and wander through the soft folds and undulations.

As if giving in to the hypnotic welcome, he saw Strouden tip his FE's nose down and slide into the ghostly white landscape. Then he was gone, swallowed, and as if in a trance the FEs behind were following, one after the other, pulled in on an impulse toward some collective destruction.

Miller eased the stick forward and the wraiths' fingers reached up and sucked him down, the deceitful fabrication of solidity dissolving into a smothering fog of vaporous water.

Blind again, the fog cleared from his brain as it thickened before his eyes. He wiped at the aneroid as it marked off their plummeting descent. The other machines had disappeared. His wingtips became indistinct, lost in vapour. There was nothing to do but concentrate on the fist that held the stick, make it become the centre of his world, resolute, unyielding, unaffected by the insinuating thought of the ground rushing up with increasing velocity to meet them.

Foden in front of him was still, as if a wax model had been placed in the nacelle as a counterweight. The cloud thinned and his grip on the stick began to loosen. Then it closed in again and he had to will his fingers to tighten. The aneroid showed they had broken beneath the thousand feet mark and still the fog swirled thickly around him. He concentrated on Strouden as if it was he who had his hand on all their sticks, controlling the formation as one and, as the image took hold and he accepted that other guidance, the vapours began to part. Through thick grey to greying-white, loose, free-floating tendrils formed over the wings and patches of darker colour appeared and swelled and suddenly the ground firmed in vision and came careering towards them.

Foden stiffened in front of him and a snatched glance at the aneroid showed under four hundred feet. He eased the stick back and levelled off beneath the ceiling, water streaming off the wings and the sides of the nacelle.

Through the rain he could just make out the FEs ahead. He looked behind and saw nothing. Below the country looked grey and empty. Roads lined with poplar and elm trees bordered fields that suggested an air of desolation. This ground had not been disputed. The Germans had come through against little opposition leaving only some small artillery damage to buildings here and there. The rest was the marauding consequence of an army on the move.

He looked behind again and saw Denham dropping from the cloud. His wings wobbled a little as if he were trying to regain his balance then he steadied. Behind him Gregory's DH2 appeared and as they closed up on the rest of the formation, Archie, as if disgruntled by being pulled unexpectedly from sleep, began throwing up a few desultory puffs of dislike. Miller peered over the side but there was little to see. His map, spread across his thighs was wet and he could make out nothing through his misted goggles. He pushed them up away from his eyes and wiped a glove over the map. The scrawl of line and contour meant nothing. He looked out again. It bore no relation to what he saw. He scanned around, looking for the castle at Rumbeke but it might have been anywhere. There was no sun and the compass bearing still showed a heading of east-nor-east. The country lay flat and still in the rain.

Strouden turned north and began quartering the ground in one methodical sweep after another that cost them thirty minutes of fuel until they found a road. Swooping down he followed its length to a group of grey buildings that rose out of the mist and resolved themselves into the scattered beginnings of a village. The anti-aircraft fire thickened and Strouden took them up again scraping the cloud ceiling, then banked and turned southeast. They crossed another road and a minute or two later, a cliff of dark crumbling walls loomed up above an outcrop of rock.

Heavy Archie buffeted them as they swung around the castle and Strouden, like a hound following a scent, took a new heading. A few minutes later Miller saw a collection of hangars and sheds ahead and, as they approached, the sky became peppered with exploding shells.

Under them, men came running out of the sheds and huts. Hangar doors were pushed back and, as he passed over, Miller saw the nose of a DFW emerge, men around it like bees around their queen. Strouden zoomed, banked and came around on the course he had shown them on the photograph. Archie followed, filling the air with the miraculously muted *puff puff* of detonating explosive. Following him, Chatterton and then Reynolds swooped in a dive over the hangars. Watson in Strouden's FE dropped two bombs onto the emerging DFW and Chatterton, behind, swung wide as MacMaster, in the front of the nacelle, released his bombs. Miller saw the hangar roof crumple under the blast and a gout of flame burst upwards. Smoke billowed after it, Reynolds and Parry lifted by the uprush of air. Then they were past and dropping their bombs on the sheds beyond. In front of Miller, Springfield was diving on a second hangar. From slightly above and behind, Miller could see Breconridge lean out of the nacelle and pull the pins on his bombs. Miller watched them drop as he approached the hangar, wobbling slightly as the fins bit the air, then he lost them as Foden in front of him cut them from view and released two of theirs.

The blast lifted them up, pushing the FE's tail in the air and running the whole machine forward as if they were riding an invisible wave. Miller kicked the rudder and slid off the turn to avoid Springfield's tail then straightened the stick again, coming around beneath and behind Springfield's machine. He looked over his shoulder and saw the two big hangars were both ablaze, billows of black smoke furling and unfurling into the sky. Across the field he could see a Halberstadt taxiing and above, at a bare fifty feet, Gregory's DH2 hovering like a predatory bird. He must have dropped a grenade for the ground in front of the Hun machine exploded in a shower of dirt and smoke. The Halberstadt swerved to the right, wing scraping the grass, then ran into a second grenade, rearing over the blast like a toy before collapsing into a crumpling of wings.

Beyond the field a collection of sheds burst apart, and he saw running men throw themselves to the ground as first Strouden and then Chatterton roared past strafing them from above. Ahead, Springfield veered off to the left and, below in the lee of a shed, Miller saw two parked Fokker Eindeckers. He turned and climbed to come in on an opposing axis to Springfield, straightening the FE as Springfield came over the Hun machines. He saw Breconridge leaning out of the nacelle again to pull the pins. A moment later the FE exploded in a sheet of flame.

The nacelle burst apart flinging shrapnel through the air. The wings spun away, fabric ablaze, in a mass of guttering fire. The blast met Miller's FE and lifted it over the sheds below, tears in his wings appearing from nowhere as the glowing shrapnel showered around them. He saw Foden twist violently, slump sideways then struggle upright again as Miller fought to keep the FE level, aware of the *zinging* sound of ground-fire as bullets sped past his ears. He slipped the FE sideways, seeing the wreckage of Springfield and Breconridge's machine falling out of the sky towards the Eindeckers. Smoke drifted up in the drizzle and dissipated across the open country. Clear of the burning sheds, Miller pulled back on the stick and climbed, turning and circling around the field again. He looked at Foden, sitting hunched in the front nacelle. He wasn't moving and Miller reached over and tapped him on the shoulder. Foden straightened and slowly turned. His ashen face had twisted into a grimace. There was a smear of blood on his chin.

'The eggs!' Miller shouted, waving his hand towards the bomb rack. 'Can you drop the eggs?'

Foden nodded slowly and reached his right arm out of the nacelle. Miller saw then that the leather below the shoulder of Foden's flying coat was ripped and that blood was running down his arm, mixing and thinning in the rain. Foden leaned over but his arm dangled uselessly out of the nacelle.

Miller wiped the back of a glove across his eyes and reached up for his goggles, feeling over the back of his helmet to the collar of his coat but they were gone.

'The eggs!' he tried again. There were still bombs left and he did not want to have to attempt a landing with them in the rack.

Foden had struggled around in the nacelle until he was facing Miller. His injured arm was hanging by his side and, from the front, Miller could see a pulpy mass of leather coat, skin and blood around the armpit. Foden's face was fixed in a rictus, his teeth bared at Miller like a snarling dog's. Kneeling on his seat, Foden reached over the side with his left arm, jerked at the pins above the rack then hung his head over to look. As Miller waited, he lifted his head slowly and with great effort nodded once. Then he fell backward and slumped into the well of the nacelle.

Above him a green flare lit the overcast morning and Miller aimed the nose of the FE towards the leading machine as Strouden signalled the return. Looking down over the airfield he saw burning sheds and shattered aircraft and running men. Scanning the sky he decided that no Hun machines had managed to get up until he saw a lone Rumpler with Gregory on its tail. He watched as it twisted and turned, unable to get away until, diving out of a turn, it crossed in front of Reynolds. Parry on the front Lewis gun raked the Rumpler from nose to tail and, as he watched, Miller saw it spin into the ground.

They ran for home skimming the countryside, following the road that ran towards Passchendaele and had once gone on to Ypres. Archie tried to follow them but they were too low and too fast. At Passchendaele the road terminated in churned earth and a pile of rubble. Beyond, there was little except a moonscape of craters etched over by trenches. It was land they had held until the spring of the previous year when the Germans had hit them with gas. Since then, the shelling had been ceaseless, pinning them in their holes and pounding the earth until the day came when they might reclaim the wasteland.

They spread out in a loose V formation, Strouden at the point. Flying over the rear lines, the ground-fire came up to meet them in a heavy inverse deluge of hot lead. Miller saw a strut shatter and the wing shudder. In front of him, Foden lay still in the nacelle. From somewhere an anti-aircraft battery must have got their altitude because suddenly they were flying into a low wall of Archie that peppered their machines with a molten rain. Watson with Strouden at the point was strafing indiscriminately around him. Behind him, Chacksfield, in the front of Denham's machine had lowered the snout of his forward Lewis as far as he could as they flew the length of a communications trench. To his left he saw Bryce trying to clear a jam on his gun. He pulled sharply at the drum and, even as Miller watched, he saw it slip from his gloved fingers and fly on the slipstream past Wynstanley's head into the propeller. The FE dipped alarmingly. She canted around at an angle and dived low over the mud. Miller followed with his eyes, turning to watch as he flew past, and saw the FE hit the ground. Then he was beyond it and approaching the Hun front lines.

Fire rose to greet them, as thick as starlings rising from the roost, and Miller gritted his teeth and flew through it, too thick to avoid. He felt a fumbling, like fingers, at his coat and almost simultaneously a sharp smack on the back of his head. For one heart-stopping moment he thought it was a warning from the Man from Reading, like the rebuke of a heavy-handed schoolmaster: *sit up straight... face forward... concentrate.*

He looked down but a fog had got between his eyes and what he was trying to look at. He shook his head but that set a lead weight careering through his skull. Then a raucous clanging behind his head focused his attention and the Beardmore engine changed note, hawking like a smoker in the morning, missing on a cylinder. He played the Beardmore, got a response as she picked up and pulled back on the stick, looking for height before the engine coughed up her valves for good. At three hundred feet he hit the cloud and skimmed the underside. He noticed that Foden had shifted position, was cramped deeper in the nacelle, but that might have been when he jerked at the controls as the engine was hit.

Crossing no man's land, Archie and ground-fire died behind him. Below heads appeared out of dugouts and arms waved as he passed over. He saw the stump of the Cloth Hall sticking proud of shattered Ypres and adjusted his course for the airfield. Below he saw the FEs of Strouden and Chatterton.

He pulled off a glove with his teeth and wiped the rain from his face, realising for the first time how dry his mouth was. He raised his face to the rain and licked at his lips. Somewhere in the cockpit was his water bottle but he suddenly felt too tired to search for it. The FE chugged discordantly and he momentarily wondered, if he had been rapped on the head by 'him', just where on a 'pusher' would the Man from Reading sit? Not on his shoulder, he thought, because the prop was there. Then perhaps the Man from Reading never flew pushers... but that couldn't be right for how else could you explain what had happened to Springfield and Breconridge?

Hadn't Miller watched as he grabbed their shoulders in that bright instant when they became an incendiary ball?

13
Stratocumulus
Rolling formations - possible precipitation - sun often hidden - visibility variable.

He could hear the commotion around him but he wasn't going to watch. He really didn't want to open his eyes. There was something so comfortable about just sitting there. That constant noise at his back had finally stopped; the rush of air and rain into his face had ceased; the intensity of concentration — something he was never actually aware of at the time — had ebbed away and somehow had only become real in its absence.

But now, sitting there, other things began to obtrude upon his consciousness. He realised just how wet he was. And whereas, in those first few moments on the ground, it had been a cooling, a reassuring consolation, now it was just plain uncomfortable. Everything was wet. It had soaked his flying coat and run through his uniform into the silk underwear he habitually wore. He felt cold and clammy. And that damned hand was pressing on his shoulder, bringing with it, he was beginning to realise, a nagging voice close to his ear. He supposed there was nothing for it but to open his eyes.

'Are you hit, sir? Does it hurt?'

It was a damn stupid question, really. Better directed at Foden. Any fool could see that Foden had been hit.

He opened his eyes and found himself staring into Sergeant Greene's face. With effort, he pushed himself slowly up in the seat and found that his head ached. He wondered vaguely if he had overdone it in the mess the previous evening. He looked down into the front of the nacelle but it was empty.

'Foden?' he asked.

'Still alive,' Greene said, 'but he's lost a lot of blood. MO's with him now.'

For some reason Miller felt it was incumbent upon him to look. Senior officer and all that. He half-stood and, leaning across the controls, peered into the front nacelle. An awful lot of blood, he thought. It was all pooled there, dripping through the wicker of the seat onto the floor. Swimming in it. He looked at Greene again and vomited over the man's uniform.

'Sorry, sergeant,' he mumbled as hands began hauling him out of the cockpit.

'Think nothing of it, sir,' Greene said, sounding unperturbed. 'Worse things happen at sea.'

Do they? He had often heard as much. But he wondered as he stumbled down from the aircraft, if it was true. If it was, then he would have to devise a new game. There would not be just the trenches to compare to his service in the RFC but the navy, as well. Being in the black bottomless water as your ship capsized above you — did being shot down in flames still trump that?

His legs wouldn't hold him and for a minute or two he had to sit on the wet

125

grass. One of the men was fussing around the back of his head and he passed a hand irritably over his hair to stop him. His helmet had gone and he felt the pain in his head again.

'Looks like you've had a close shave, sir,' the man said.

Miller staggered to his feet again. *Was that supposed to be a joke?* It was Jones, his servant, fussing. He had never been comfortable about having a servant — someone hanging on your every whim…

'There's blood on the back of your head,' Jones said. 'Bullet or shrapnel, looks like. Only a graze, though.'

Nothing to worry about then. The Man from Reading doesn't waste his time grazing people.

He looked across the field to where the other machines had landed. The light looked odd, as if they were under water. It was still raining; perhaps that was it. *They got the forecast wrong, then.* He saw Strouden talking to Chatterton. And there was Gregory strolling across the field. The word *insouciance* sprang into his head. That's what Gregory had, he decided, insouciance. He would have to remember that. Now, who else? Denham. Where was Denham? Then he saw Chacksfield. He had been in Denham's machine so they had got back. Who else? He looked over the field but there wasn't anyone else. No, there was the boy, Parry. If Parry was there Reynolds must have got back. He was glad of that.

'Best see the MO, sir,' Jones said.

'De-briefing first,' Miller decided. 'Then I'll go.' He took a few steps. The movement seemed to clear his head. He turned to Jones again. There he was, waiting on his every whim. 'Be a good chap, will you Jones? A bath. That's what I'd really like. A bath. Any chance of that? Not one of those canvas tubs. A proper bath, I mean.'

'Leave it to me, sir.'

He walked around his FE. The fabric on the wings had been shredded and he wondered how it had stayed in the air. Oil was dripping from the engine but the prop was still intact. Several of the wires had been cut and they were going to have to work on the struts again. Mackinnon was with Strouden and Chatterton. Miller nodded to the men that they could move the machine; a wave of pain ran over his head from the base of his skull and he decided it might be better if he kept his head still. He started walking towards the château falling in beside Watson. Grease smeared the observer's face from where he had handled the guns.

'We made a mess of their airfield,' Watson said.

Miller supposed they had. For some reason he had almost forgotten the airfield.

Waiting in the ops room, Budge sat with his paper and pencil while Strouden gave an account of the raid. He was filthy from oil that had sprayed him from somewhere and Miller couldn't understand why. It troubled him. That was one advantage of flying pushers, after all, having the engine behind; you weren't in line for the oil. For some reason, though, Strouden was covered with the stuff. A white line ringed his face where his helmet and goggles had kept him clean. It had even got into his mouth and onto his teeth. Miller watched as the CO kept running his blackened tongue over them.

He was numbering the hangars and sheds he thought they had damaged and the Hun machines he had seen destroyed. He looked around for confirmation.

Miller was finding it hard to concentrate.

Chacksfield confirmed the one Gregory had destroyed on the ground and Miller found he must have said something because suddenly they were all looking at him. He gave it a great deal of thought then said he'd seen Parry hit the one that had got into the air and driven it down. He was sorry, though, because he couldn't remember what it was, either a DFW or a Halberstadt.

Strouden looked at him oddly and told him not to worry about it. 'Did anyone see what happened to Springfield and Breconridge?' he asked.

Gregory and Watson shook their heads.

'They were right in front of me,' Miller now remembered, wishing his damned head didn't ache so much. 'It must have been a bomb in the rack,' he said. 'Jammed? Or a lucky shot from the ground hit a detonator, what do you think?'

Strouden was looking concerned. 'I didn't see it,' he said. 'No chance that...?'

Miller shook his head, remembering too late, and wished that he hadn't. 'That's when Foden got hit. Shrapnel, probably.' He looked at Strouden as if through a fog, rehearsing what he wanted to say. 'I'd like it,' he began, enunciating slowly, 'I'd like it entered into the log that, although severely wounded, Foden still managed to drop all our bombs.'

'Duly noted,' Budge said.

'Did anyone see what happened to Wynstanley and Bryce?' Chacksfield asked.

'I saw them go down,' Gregory said. 'That's all. There was smoke but...' he gave a small shrug.

Miller was trying to remember who the hell Wynstanley and Bryce were.

'We'll post them as missing until we hear to the contrary.' Strouden turned to Miller. 'Miller, get yourself to the MO. You're not looking too good.'

Miller mumbled something back as someone took hold of his arm and helped him to the door. In Doyle's hut the MO's orderly was scrubbing blood off one of the tables.

'If that's any indication of how you look after your observers, Miller,' he said when he saw him walk in, 'the sooner you get back in your One-and-a-half-Strutter, the better.'

'Foden?' Miller said. 'Is he going to live?'

'I'm not generally in the habit of betting on a man's survival but I'd take an each-way punt on it. He'd lost a lot of blood but I didn't find any metal in the wound. With luck he'll pull through. Providing they can keep the gangrene away, that is.'

With Doyle's help Miller stripped off his tunic and sat on the edge of a table. He had already found a tear in the back of his flying coat and now saw a matching rent in his tunic.

'Is he out of it?'

'You won't see him back here, if that's what you mean,' Doyle said. 'He's severed the tendons so he's not going to get much use out of that arm even if he does pull through.' He grasped Miller's shoulder and pulled him around, none too gently. 'Now what have we got here?'

He lifted Miller's tunic and pushed a finger through the tear. You've the devil's own luck, Miller. Barely a scratch. Another inch and you'd have smashed your scapula. That's shoulder-blade to the likes of you.' Then he leaned around Miller and peered at him. 'Or maybe you know a bit about anatomy. Would you have some experience in this sort of thing now?'

Miller just grunted.

'Mind you,' Doyle said. 'It was close enough to singe the hair on the back of your head and break the skin.' He bent Miller's head down. 'You must have been looking forward when it happened although what you've got to look forward to is beyond the likes of me.'

'Do you always treat your patients to this patter?' Miller muttered.

'I find it keeps their minds off the dying,' Doyle said. 'Hold still while I clean it up for you.' He took a swab from the waiting orderly. 'Now this is going to sting, as they say in Harley Street.'

Miller tolerated Doyle's ministrations for another ten minutes as the MO cleaned up the back of his head then lifted his eyelids and shone a light into his eyes. He asked him several inane questions and finally came to the conclusion that Miller had suffered a slight concussion and told him to take it easy for a couple of days.

'I'll let the major know you'll not be goin' up for forty-eight hours,' he said. He gave Miller something for the headache, then he tossed his tunic at him and pushed him out of his hut.

Back in his own billet Miller found to his amazement that Jones had scrounged a tin bath. The water was hot and waiting and, as Miller undressed, Jones brought it in. He luxuriated in the tub until the hot water began to turn cool then dried himself off and climbed into his bunk.

He never heard Jones empty the water or remove the tub, or even the four aircraft of the noon patrol taking off.

It was late afternoon before he woke. The headache had faded to no more than a dull depression at the back of his skull and he was thinking reasonably clearly again.

He was sitting up on the bunk and looking through Heyward's personal belongings. To begin with, the handwriting in Heyward's exercise books had swum in front of his eyes but he seemed to have got that under control. Now it had stopped swimming though what independent life and movement the words had possessed had departed with the cessation, leaving them lying like dead things upon the page.

Most of the exercise books appeared to have been filled with Heyward's early drafts of poetry. When he had been satisfied that a poem was finished, he had written it up in another book. Miller was therefore able to follow Heyward's process of creation — how, beginning with a fresh idea, he had chiselled and polished the notion until he had worked the life out of it, finally being left with little more than a memorial to what had begun as a living concept: an embalmed corpse.

He had been willing to give Heyward the benefit of the doubt, prepared to allow it was his own taste that was at fault, but he couldn't help thinking that there was something archaic about Heyward's style, almost gothic, as though he were working through a mode of construction that had been fashionable a century before. It might be, he thought, that he wasn't — in Foden's words — 'a literary chap'; then again, it might be that Heyward had not noticed that they had entered a new century.

Some of his prose was better; passages in the exercise books mixed among the poetry drafts. But even here his attempt at lyricism was too studied, too intent on leaving an impression rather than a reality; he did not float above a landscape, rather he ploughed through it with artisan thoroughness. Just like his flying, it seemed. Out of curiosity Miller looked through all the exercise books trying to find something relating to flight, yet there seemed to be nothing. It was as if the experience had not registered upon Heyward's consciousness at all. What he *did* find was some singeing on the back covers of two of the books, as if someone had tried to burn them. Or, perhaps more exactly, as if someone had decided to burn them and had then changed their mind.

The rest of Heyward's possessions were as Miller might have expected: there was a very nice gentleman's toiletry case — mahogany, with brass corner plates and escutcheons and engraved CWH; some books — Keats and Shelley, unsurprisingly; campaigning accoutrements — the kind of thing any Victorian soldier took with him abroad, very much of that vintage and of little practical use in an RFC squadron; and a few letters. They had all been opened. Two letters were from his mother, bore the squadron's address and a fairly recent postmark; the rest had all been forwarded from his home address in Yorkshire. There were no others, which suggested that either he did not keep his correspondence – odd, in one convinced of a literary posterity – or that Heyward was *so* convinced of it that he had been in the habit of sending it back to Yorkshire for safekeeping. Most of the correspondence that had been forwarded from his home address was from friends.

Miller read them all but found they held little of interest. Mrs Heyward always began, *My Dearest Boy*, and carried on mostly in that vein. She impressed upon him the need to keep warm and safe and to eat well, on average at least once in every paragraph, and filled the rest mostly with gossip from home. They were designed, Miller couldn't help thinking, rather as a protective umbrella of normality that might — along with a mother's love — go some way to counteract the insane abnormality in which her son had found himself. Although, Miller couldn't help thinking, it was an odd abnormality — if that was not an oxymoron — that had claimed him in the end.

Towards the end of the most recent letter Mrs Heyward had added some lines almost as a postscript, as if the news had only arrived just in time to catch the post:

Your Mr Gibson from London telephoned to say that although the extracts you submitted from your book were 'not quite their kind of material', he has taken the liberty of forwarding them to a Mr Fisher who was very interested indeed! He said a letter would be following. Does this mean you will not have to publish privately after all?

It came as no surprise to Miller that Heyward might have been contemplating self-publication. From what he had read of Heyward's work he thought it would probably be the only avenue open to him: a limited edition from a small press thoughtfully bound and printed was usually how material like that could be found. But it seemed, assuming Mrs Heyward was not gilding the lily for the sake of her son's morale, a publisher was interested in a book. There had been no book, though, not even any papers among Heyward's possessions that might have been described as a book. Nor had there been one in the hut. Suddenly curious about the burned edges of what he did have, he got off the bunk and went outside. At the back of the hut he found a small circular patch of burnt grass. The few ashes looked old and had been scattered and smeared by the rain and fresh shoots of green grass had already started to sprout in the patch. Miller wished he had one of Cody's Indians there to tell him how long ago the fire had been set.

The afternoon was warm after the rain. High towers of cumulus drifted on a southerly breeze that brought the smell of grass and turned earth. Doubting it was the plough that was raising the scents of summer, he carried the folding canvas chair from the hut again and set it by the door, facing the sun. The sound of running engines came from the maintenance sheds mingled with the voices of the men.

He had brought out his own notebook and a Dollards exercise book in which he obstinately attempted to bring form to the impressions that occurred to him in the air. He had the ability, he knew, to turn out the occasional decent enough phrase, but that was all it ever was. Somehow he never seemed capable of achieving an overview. The big picture always managed to elude him. Once again he tried stringing his decent phrases together in an attempt to make a whole but, re-reading the result, he found it resembled a rope made of knotted bed sheets — the most obvious thing about it was the joins. He wondered if he wasn't like Heyward, cherishing a view of himself that was only imaginary, a reflection preferable to the real thing.

He dropped the pencil onto the exercise book, closed his eyes and lifted his head to the sun. Perhaps that was why he had been singled out by Maxwell — his inability to see the bigger picture *because* of his eye for detail. That was the trouble with regular army men he often thought, too caught up with detail. By now it had to be more than just a careless entry on his RFC application form that had made him a marked man, that youthful misdemeanour that blotted an otherwise spotless record. He had, before this Heyward business, been assigned other details, being assured at the time that he had an eye for the detail of a thing. He now began to suspect that the larger perspective of *the thing* might well be lost on him. The minutiae of an incident was what he would inevitably find — that *this* or *that* happened — and that was the easy part; usually the *when* and even the *why* was within his compass. But when it came to the big picture — the moral imperatives, if you like — he generally found himself in deep water.

He was, he thought, on the whole able to deal with the meaner aspects of human motivation (he had, after all, the wonderful laboratory of the mining camps where almost every aspect of human nature was not only on display but pared down to the bone for everyone to examine) and he had witnessed most in the run of criminal acts.

He yawned and stretched his neck, deciding that concussion was really quite a pleasant state of fuzzy numbness.

Even in the case of Heyward, for example, one had to make the assumption that it was still a criminal act even if it was a suicide; for under present conditions suicide could be construed not only as dereliction of duty but also cowardice in the face of the enemy, and both were criminal offences under military law. Not that any due process was going to get much satisfaction out of Heyward's lifeless corpse. All that was left from which any retribution might be sought was Heyward's mother — retribution in the form, one supposed, of malicious gossip and social contempt — and that would only be spite and do nothing to advance the Allied war machine. But he was there, as far as he could understand it from Maxwell, to elicit the details to give their blessed minister ammunition against a bereaved mother. Best not look for the bigger picture there. From where in *that* morass of motive did one begin to pick the moral imperative?

Miller shifted his position and closed his mouth, aware that he had begun to doze off under the warmth of the sun. He had gone through it all in his head so many times before that now his powers of reasoning kept sliding into a tailspin. He didn't really want to open his eyes and break what had become a pleasant spell, but he knew he really ought to put some order into his thinking. Heyward's personal things had not elicited much so he reversed a little way and tried to come at it from a different tack.

The usual motivations in any crime, like money and sex and jealousy and love (he always kept love in a category of its own and not commingled with sex and jealousy because he was, despite everything, still a romantic at heart), were easy, he found, to tease out of most criminal incidents. It was when these motivations did not fit the bill that he started to struggle.

In Heyward's case he had to admit another conditional clause – rather like a wind vector that needed factoring in — it might be that sex *had* played a part in an accidental death. Had the idiot been simulating asphyxiation to heighten a sexual climax? He had come across this oddest of practices once before and decided that it should not be discounted although, as far as Heyward was concerned, the fact that he was fully clothed and hadn't even bothered to lock the hut door, made it a most unlikely eventuality. So (again) in Heyward's case, from the aforementioned, from what he had learned from the other members of the squadron, and from what questioning he was able to undertake in the whorehouse in Poperinghe, sex did not appear to be one of his preoccupations.

Did he have a girl back home? (He would have liked to have asked Foden, but poor Foden was now cruising at some unknown altitude between heaven and earth and did not deserve to be troubled by intrusive questioning). Anyway, as Heyward had not fraternised with the other squadron members to any degree and had not taken up with a girl *or boy* (for he would have to consider that possibility too given the public school background that many of the officers had enjoyed — or perhaps *endured* – despite the protestations of Budge and Foden concerning any inclinations Heyward might have had in *that* direction) it seemed that jealousy was something of a non-runner. And as for love, although he had found nothing to indicate that this might have been a motivation at all, under the conditions in which they found themselves men were just as liable to fall in love with girls to whom they would not have given a second glance under ordinary circumstances — case in point: Tozer. It was the old economic rule of supply and demand. But then, it had to be admitted that Heyward had given no indication of this either; if his letters home had spoken of a girl, there was nothing in the replies that he had read that had made comment upon the fact. As far as he had been able to elicit, none of the other men recalled Heyward mooning over any particular individual or even talking of any girl. *Or boy* — he must not forget the boys and Heyward *had* been friendly with Dunne before he had unfortunately killed him.

So, if it had been suicide over unrequited love, Heyward had been singular in not bemoaning the fact to someone beforehand, or at least in leaving a note in the vain hope that the object of his affections might have the scales drop from their eyes and, in remorse he supposed, have come to realise what they had lost.

Therefore, having eliminated the above, what was left? Money? Well, he supposed that that was a potent enough motive although, as far as he was aware, Heyward had not lacked money. There was no suggestion that Heyward had either advertently or inadvertently passed a dud cheque to his bank, to the mess, or to any of his colleagues. Budge had mentioned that his mess bill was negligible (he was not a mixer, after all) and, as far as he was aware, Heyward had neither borrowed money nor been asked for a loan that he had refused; apparently he hadn't been the kind of man one would have approached for a loan. Nor he assumed, the kind one would have needed to dun.

Dunne?

Perhaps remorse. After all, a fortnight before his death Heyward had smashed up his plane and killed Dunne, a man with whom he had been on friendly terms. But by all accounts it seems that Heyward had suffered nothing more than bruising and a shake-up and certainly not a case of remorse. His attitude had been that the crash had been caused by a mechanical failure even though Budge had seen Heyward come down that morning and judged the accident to have been an error on Heyward's part. Heyward had put the blame for the death of Dunne onto the fitter, Smith. *That* was not the action of a remorseful man; it was more the action of a man who lacked a conscience.

The accusation, though, left open the possibility of revenge on Smith's part,

132

somehow doing after the fact what Heyward had accused him of doing before it. This, of course, was to admit to Heyward's death being murder, and an elaborately staged one at that, and that was something he had already dismissed. Besides, both Foden and Doyle had remarked that Heyward had been a rotten pilot (Tozer had mentioned the fact, too, for what that was worth). And besides, Mackinnon was no fool and he would have had Heyward's engine stripped down to its last screw and there had been no suggestion of a fault.

Then, if not Smith, was there anyone else within the squadron who might have held an earlier grudge or been close enough to Dunne to take exception to the manner of his death? There was his friend, Parry. He would have to talk to Parry, but it seemed unlikely. After all, they lost men continually and their passing was greeted with perhaps no more than a wistful remark on how bad the man's luck had been and a raised glass in the mess that night. If anyone in the squadron was in the habit of holding grudges against the less personable members of the squadron then he would expect the demise of someone like Tozer to be imminent. It was true that Heyward's incompetence might have got any of them killed at any time, but if you started to take those kind of concerns seriously it would lead one into a line of reasoning likely to turn up all sorts of unpleasant forms of behaviour.

Miller's head had cleared. He had taken a walk across the fields, kicking his way through the rank grass until he could no longer see the airfield or any other evidence of the war. There was still a rumble of guns to the north but if he closed his eyes and really put his mind to it he could just about believe that it was thunder. Opening his eyes, though, spoilt the effect; the morning drizzle had cleared and the sky was empty except for a hazy suggestion of stratocumulus high beyond any altitude he had yet to achieve. Then far away he saw a formation of machines pointing south like distant geese and the war was back.

He found Smith, the fitter that Heyward had blamed for the accident that had killed Dunne, working on the C Flight FEs.

'It's Smith, isn't it?' he asked.

The man looked over his shoulder and made a gesture towards his temple with an oily hand holding a piston.

'Sir.'

'How are they looking?'

'We found a nick in your prop shaft, sir, and the oil filter was pretty much shot up. The riggers have patched up your wings and replaced that broken strut. We'll have her ready for the morning. I've seen worse.'

'I'm sure you have, Smith.'

'Must have been pretty hot all the same.'

'I've seen worse,' Miller said. He stood there a second longer then said, 'When Mr Dunne was killed, I'm told Mr Heyward blamed the accident on engine failure.'

'Yes sir.'

'In fact he suggested that you hadn't done the maintenance properly, didn't he?'

'That's right, sir,' Smith said flatly.

'Didn't that annoy you?'

'The engine wasn't damaged in the accident. I stripped it down in front of Sergeant Mackinnon. He said it was in good working order. The accident wasn't due to mechanical failure.'

'Had Mr Heyward criticised your work before the accident?'

Smith opened his mouth then closed it again.

'Well?'

'I'd rather not speak ill of the dead,' Smith said, 'if you don't mind, sir. Not about an officer.'

Miller stepped towards the FE and stood beside Smith peering into the engine. 'That's all right, Smith,' he said quietly. 'It's just between us.'

Smith put down the piston he was holding. 'Well, if you're asking, sir, Mr Heyward *did* generally find some sort of fault with his machine when there was a problem, sir.'

'What sort of problem?'

'When the machine didn't do what he expected, sir.'

'And was there ever a fault?'

'Yes, sir, but not generally with the machine, begging your pardon, sir.'

'Are you saying he was just a bad pilot?'

'Not in so many words, sir.'

'Mr Foden did.'

'He's likely to know better than me, sir. Do you know how he is?'

'Mr Foden? I'm told he's got a good chance,' Miller said. 'I thought I might try and see him in the hospital before they ship him home.'

'Perhaps you'd give him our best wishes if you do sir. From all the lads here.'

'I will, Smith. He'll appreciate that, I'm sure.'

Before dressing for dinner, Miller decided he had better send Maxwell some kind of report on his progress. The fact that he hadn't really made any was something of a hurdle to clear first, but he contrived to manufacture a couple of hundred words detailing the facts as he had found them (detail, he had found, was a servant disposed to work for anyone once you knew how to employ him). He wound it up by commenting on the stresses that weigh upon the men in an understrength squadron and hoped that Maxwell would draw his own conclusions.

He heard the evening patrol return as he read it through, then dressed and dropped it into Budge's office.

'Could you see that Colonel Maxwell at Wing gets this, Budgie,' he said.

Budge looked at it, seemed to divine what was inside as if he possessed vision like those new-fangled X-ray machines and said, a little too casually, 'Found out anything in particular, old man?'

'Nothing we didn't already know,' Miller said. 'I more or less suggested that it might have been the strain that did it.'

'Oh well,' Budge said, 'that seems reasonable enough.' Then thought a little more about it and added, 'As long as he doesn't get the impression that Major Strouden had *driven* him to it.'

'There's no reason he should think that,' Miller said, 'is there?'

'No,' Budge said, 'of course not.' Then, 'Gregory's missing, did you hear?'

'What happened?'

'No one saw.'

'Perhaps he was forced down,' Miller said. 'He might still turn up.'

'Yes,' Budge said. 'Of course.'

It occurred to Miller that he wouldn't get a turn on the DH2 now.

In the mess hall he was hoping he might have found himself a seat near Parry, but all the chairs around the young observer were taken. He happened to look up as Miller approached the table and averted his gaze as their eyes met. Miller had to content himself with a less congenial position opposite Tozer.

The B Flight pilot didn't look to Miller as if he was particularly happy about the situation either but Miller bid him a civil 'good evening' as he sat down and shook out his serviette. Miller couldn't help thinking that there was something markedly *lumpen* about the young athlete, although, given Tozer's background that could hardly be the case. Trying to put his prejudice aside, Miller decided it was a coarseness of feature more than anything: the nose was a little too fleshy, the lips a little too full, and, while on Parker full lips merely gave a hint of voluptuousness, on Tozer they suggested only appetite.

The conversation around him had inevitably focused on operational flying and Griffiths asked Miller what it was like in a scout squadron.

'If you mean single seaters,' Miller said, 'to be honest I've not been flying the Strutter that long. What makes the difference is having the interrupter gear. With that, all you have to do is aim the machine. What I've found is that those few seconds saved by not having to be first getting the machine into the right position and then having to aim the gun gives you a big advantage.' He moved slightly to one side as an orderly served him a bowl of soup. 'Of course, the biggest advantage is that the Hun's not expecting you to fire through your prop. *That* won't last long, though, now they know we can.'

'It must have given them a nasty turn the first time out,' Chatterton said.

Miller thought it had probably been no nastier a turn than his first Eindecker had given him. He said:

'Of course, having a gunner up front is just as good. The pilot only has to worry about positioning the machine.'

'As long as the man up front is any good,' Tozer said.

'There is that,' Miller agreed.

'I'm sure I could get some kills if I had the right machine,' Tozer said.

'It's mostly technique and practice,' Miller said.

'The thing to remember,' Chatterton said, 'is to do the job we're sent up to do.'

'What were you on before the Strutter?' Griffiths asked.

'FB5s,' Miller said. 'I have to admit that I never liked them.'

'I've heard some men have a dozen to their name,' Tozer said.

'A dozen?' Miller asked him.

'Kills.'

'Germans, perhaps,' Griffiths said.

Miller shrugged. 'I've not heard of anyone on our side claiming that many.'

'*They* know how to go about it,' Tozer announced.

'Don't let the Old Man hear you saying that sort of thing,' Chatterton warned.

'Oh rot!' Tozer said. 'Look at those fellows, Immelmann and... what's his name, Bulk?'

'Boelke?' Miller suggested.

'They say when they attack they've got the moves already worked out. Like rules so you can do it properly.'

'It's not a game, Tozer,' Chatterton said.

'No,' Miller said, 'Tozer's right. It's the future. If machines keep improving the way they have been we can only get more efficient at killing each other.'

'It's a bit thick deliberately trying to kill us,' Griffiths said. 'It's one thing to stop us spotting or flying recces, that's the job after all.'

'Why not?' Miller said. 'They're doing it on the ground all the time.'

'They're the top aces,' Tozer put in again. '*They've* got at least ten kills.'

Chatterton sighed affectedly. 'That's us you're talking about,' he said.

'Us?'

'Us, Tozer. The people Immelmann and Boelke are killing. That's us.'

14

The songs had turned sentimental. Chacksfield was stumbling through an Ivor Novello favourite on the piano, fat fingers tripping over notes like obstacles left carelessly on the keyboard. Moss and Trueman, standing either side of him, were bellowing out the words, whether to the melody Chacksfield was playing or to a completely different song, Miller was not sure.

The fact that Doyle had grounded him for forty-eight hours had given him the latitude, he had decided after dinner, to have a couple of drinks in the mess. But he'd had more than a couple and while he was still pretty sure of his latitude his longitudinal bearings seemed to have gone astray. Younger men with more stamina had gone into town, the few left who had not yet staggered off to their bunks were sitting around glassy-eyed. Second Lieutenant Parsons — together with Reynolds and Parry the last survivor from A Flight — had fallen asleep over a table. He had been Foden's observer and Miller wondered if he would now inherit him and if the boy was feeling vulnerable. It was a position Miller remembered all too clearly himself, being the last of a complement of men, and there was an inescapable feeling that it could only be a matter of time before the finger of fate inevitably pointed your way. Then new men would arrive and someone else would catch it instead of you and the feeling of being a marked man began to wear off. Or perhaps your skin just got thicker, he wasn't sure which.

He was sitting with Strouden and Budge. They had gravitated together but whether it was because of age, or experience, or simply because they didn't seem to know the words to the latest songs, he couldn't have said. Whichever, for some time they had formed a corner of tranquillity amid the earlier raucousness. Strouden had been drinking steadily all evening. It was the first time Miller had seen this and he wondered how much of a blow the loss of Gregory had been. The effects of the drink were not particularly noticeable on the CO — his enunciation was still as clear as ever and his eyes betrayed no loss of focus. The one thing Miller *was* aware of was the fact that the excess of alcohol masked any reaction to the blow of losing eight men and four machines over the past three days. Perhaps that was the point.

Garfield and Pollock looked pleased with themselves having survived their first operational flight on the noon patrol. They had returned unscathed — if one discounted the hangover they would have in the morning: a slim volume of survival between bookends of predation. Parker had led them in his now-recovered FE in Denham's absence — the C Flight commander's own FE having been badly shot up over Rumbeke — and he assumed that the laconic lieutenant would be given command of A Flight following Springfield's demise, a reward perhaps for getting no one killed. Strouden would not offer the command to *him*, he was sure; last man in would be the excuse but in reality it was because he had been foisted on the squadron. Whatever Strouden decided, he would have to recast the three flights following the losses and Miller assumed he'd be on FEs with Parsons. The CO had put in for more replacements, machines and men, but he was beginning to look like a profligate commander.

The empty chairs at dinner had been a reminder all evening. Places for them had been set — as was the custom — but they were not a subject for discussion. A glass was raised in their honour then dinner and the usual entertainment ensued. Out of habit Miller watched for signs that the losses had affected the men but he saw nothing in particular. The sentimentality of the songs might have been an indication of some hidden feelings, but then it might just be that sentimentality was popular on the stage at home at that moment. He did not know. What he did know was that sudden death had become a part of life. It was not for them an overwhelming tragedy now, that would come later; it was a steady *drip drip* of small accumulating tragedies which in time would overwhelm them when their defences had been eroded and their resistance was low. In the meantime alcohol manned the barricades.

Budge, he couldn't help noticing, was treading a fine line between drunkenness and insensibility. It had been some while since he had last contributed anything beyond a grunt of assent to the conversation and Miller was not sure whether he was still following it or not. Then again, neither was it exactly clear as to whether Strouden and Miller were still discussing the same subject or not.

They were talking shop; by now that was all they knew. It had been suggested that (by whom Miller could not now remember) the casualty rate being what it was and the probable expansion of the RFC being what it was probably expected to be, experienced officers would be at a premium. Strouden had implied that Miller might soon expect to be offered his own squadron.

He was not sure that this was sound reasoning on Strouden's part but he had drunk somewhat more himself than was his habit and was having trouble following the argument. The RFC was still army, after all, and they never seemed to lack officers ready to step into command posts. The quality had tailed off to be sure, but he was confident that that would shake down the longer the show went on. The rubbish would be weeded out and no doubt by the time it finished they'd have the best bunch of officers available from those who survived. That was always the way of it. Just as you've got the men you need the show's over. Then, by the time the next one was ready to start, they're generally too old, too stubborn and too set in their ways to adapt to the new show and the old merry-go-round would start all over again.

He might have been able to counter some of Strouden's arguments had he not, like Budge, ceased to contribute much to the conversation, having recently become aware of the fact that his own enunciation — unlike Strouden's — was not all it could have been. At that moment he was intent on using the major's precise speech as a benchmark for his own and falling some distance short of the mark. What he needed, he was thinking, was a spotter to help him get his range.

'Don't you see,' Strouden was saying, having in the absence of a reply, wandered off his topic and was now expounding upon the duties incumbent upon a squadron leader. 'One's primary duty,' here he frowned a little as if the concept had slipped out of focus, 'is to prosecute the war.' He took a little more whisky — to augment, Miller assumed, the prosecution. 'We have a job... *I* have a job. Orders to follow. Tasks to accomplish.' He lapsed into silence for a moment, looking into his glass at the shallow film of liquid that remained.

Miller was less concerned over prosecuting the war than he was about a personal problem he had noticed – he was beginning to slur certain words. Sibilants, he had been unpleasantly surprised to find, were falling off a clear 'ssss' sound and beginning to slush, as if they were dribbling out the side of his mouth and tobogganing down some wet snowy hillside.

'But I also have a duty towards these men – these boys — for that's all most of them are you know, really. Barely out of school...'

Miller touched his fingers to the offending side of his mouth almost expecting to feel the sliminess of escaped saliva. But it was quite dry. He dabbed with his fingers again and wondered if he didn't feel a slight flabbiness of the lower lip as if, despite the dryness, there was still a physical manifestation of the phenomenon, a slack point that allowed that damned toboggan to slide away.

'Now look here,' Strouden suddenly said.

Budge, across the table, started a little at the force of Strouden's imperative and, revived, blinked several times as if he hadn't quite expected to be just where he found himself. It was a moment or two before he seemed able to resume the attitude of benign tolerance he generally assumed as he watched his CO.

'I know what we all say about Brigade from time to time,' Strouden continued on another tack, 'and we sometimes wonder where on earth they get their intelligence from. '

Miller cleared his throat and concentrated. He had this impression that Strouden was trying to throw Miller off his tail, executing sudden unexpected verbal manoeuvres — a roll off the subject, then a loop that brought him back to the place he had been a minute or two before.

'And it must *be* intelligence,' Strouden said, 'after all, otherwise why on earth would they want to send us up on some beastly mission that commonsense says is just the kind of show an imbecile might dream up? But that's *their* job, don't you see? Just as it is mine to do as I'm told. But when that conflicts with my duty to do the best I can for the chaps it leaves one in such a devilishly awful spot. Do you see?'

'But shurely,' Miller said, risking speech although dissatisfied with the result despite keeping a finger against his lower lip, 'we're the fellowsh who provide Brigade with their intelligensh.'

'Well, of course,' Strouden agreed.

'Then it musht be a matter of interpretashion.'

'But they *know* more than we do,' Strouden insisted.

'*How* do we know they know?'

'The bigger picture.'

'The Bigger Picture,' Budge echoed, capitalising the phrase.

Miller rubbed at his jaw fiercely and pushed his glass aside. He had had enough. 'The offensive...' he began, then stopped in surprise. He said again. 'The offensive,' aware that, this time, he had not slurred the sibilant. He transferred his hand from his jaw to the top of his head and scratched it pensively, attributing his recovery to the decision. A mental pat on the back, a vote of perceptual confidence. He opened his mouth to pick up his thread but Strouden was talking again.

'The French were having a hell of a time at Verdun.'

'Take the pressure off...' Budge agreed. 'Punch a hole to let the pressure out – like a champagne bottle.' He reached for his glass and clinked his hook against it, knocking it over and spilling whisky across the table. 'Damn!' he said, then 'Damn,' again and apologised, sounding quite himself for the moment. 'Always forgetting... like champagne... let the bubbles out...'

'Not to worry, old man,' Strouden said as a hovering orderly reached over his shoulder and dabbed at the table with a cloth. 'Perfectly understandable.'

'The offensive,' Miller began for the third time, but by now he had forgotten what it was he had been going to say.

Strouden waited expecting more, irritatingly attentive now it was too late although too polite to make an issue of it when nothing more came.

Budge, having waited while the orderly cleared the spilt whisky and his glass, quite slowly and deliberately lowered his head to the table until his cheek rested upon it. He closed his eyes.

'Perfectly understandable,' Strouden said again.

Miller looked at Budge and then at Strouden.

'With the major's permission?' he asked.

'Carry on, Captain Miller,' Strouden said.

With the assistance of the mess orderly, Miller heaved Budge to his feet and, suspended between them, carried the adjutant to the door. A ragged cheer went up from those around the piano who were still sensible and somehow Chacksfield managed to play the first few bars of the Wedding March before tripping over his own fingers and collapsing in a discordant heap.

Budge had a room at the rear of his office and between them Miller and the orderly carried him down the corridor into the room and, with his limbs falling in every direction like loosely held rifles, managed to get the half-conscious figure onto his bunk.

'Thank you,' Miller said to the orderly. 'I can manage Mr Budge from here. Turn on the light as you leave, there's a good fellow.'

Miller watched the orderly out of the door, then heaved Budge's legs onto the bunk. He hefted the man so that he was lying comfortably on his back, noting how very light the recording officer was, then loosened his shirt collar and tie. He unlaced Budge's boots, pulled them off and put them neatly on the tin trunk at the foot of the bunk.

Breathing heavily despite Budge's lack of bulk, Miller dropped into the chair by the dressing table. The table was constructed, he noticed, of two planks of wood across empty bully beef boxes. Every officer's billet, he suspected, was better furnished than Budge's.

When his breathing had returned to normal, he took his cigarettes and lit one, looking around the small room as he exhaled the smoke. It was neat and tidy. A space along one wall had been curtained off, presumably to hang Budge's clothes; there was a washstand and toiletries, neatly arranged, and a shelf that held a row of books, some bound in leather.

He was curious as to Budge's taste in literature but found, when he made to get up, that his legs would not move. 'Disobeying an officer,' he told them. His tone was mild; he had never been a stickler for discipline. 'I could have you taken out and shot,' he added almost conversationally. But his legs didn't twitch. They knew, of course, that he wouldn't. Probably throw a counter-charge of shooting himself in the legs to get his ticket home. That's the trouble with war; you learn all the tricks. Officers weren't supposed to know them — that sort of thing was for Other Ranks — but they did. Of course they did. Courts martial every day. They were bound to learn all the tricks. How many officers tried them, though? That was the thing. He had not heard of an instance, but of course that sort of affair would be hushed up. Officers resorting to the tricks of Other Ranks? Unthinkable! Better to do what Heyward did. If Heyward did do what Heyward did.

Budge began to snore.

On the timber plank at his elbow, Miller noticed a journal. It lay open, the left-hand page dated for the previous day. Beneath the date, in a crabbed and untidy hand an entry had been made. Miller's eyes wandered down the page, only half taking in what he saw. Budge, of course, would have to write left-handed. His clerks did all the official writing; Budge merely signed his name to what he was obliged to. Here were words in his own hand. Despite only half-reading it, Miller was aware that the entry concerned the day's business of the squadron written for his own diary — from a private, rather than a recording officer's, perspective. The name, Gribble stood out — the man had been killed on the gunnery range when a jammed Lewis gun had unexpectedly cleared itself. Budge seemed to have had trouble forming the double 'b' with loops and had smudged the ink. He had recorded the young man's death, writing: *Gribble killed this morning clearing jammed Lewis. Good chap but clumsy. Wrote to his people in Southend. Forwarded back pay & £2.*

Out of his own pocket, no doubt.

Miller reached out a hand and laid it on the journal. Just a few pages back would be the day that Heyward had died. What, he wondered, had Budge written that day? He only had to turn back the pages. He was supposed to be a detective, after all. That *is* why he was there. But it was a man's private diary. Reading what he had already read was unavoidable, but to turn pages? To read it without permission would be an underhand thing to do. Was it justified? And what did this little matter of manners — honour, he supposed — what could this little matter of honour mean when weighed against the daily slaughter? There was no comparison. Was it less honourable to send men out on missions to get killed than to read another man's diary? Was that less honourable than to order a man like Borthwick to fill a bomb rack and blow himself to pieces? But, did that mean that if you were to do one dishonourable thing, you were then at liberty to do as many more as you wished? Did doing one dishonourable thing mean that forever afterwards you were without honour?

Miller lifted his hand and let it fall on his rebellious legs.

A head appeared around the door.

'How's old Budgie?' Strouden asked.

'Sleeping,' Miller said.

'Better leave him to it.'

'Yes.'

'Just heard over the blower,' Strouden said. 'Gregory. Forced down with engine trouble. All tickety-boo, though. Back in the morning.'

'Good show,' Miller said.

'Yes,' Strouden said. 'Good show.'

Miller stood up. Perfectly honourable legs now, smart and soldierly. He closed the door and followed Strouden down the hall.

We could all learn a thing from the smart and the soldierly, he supposed.

A hand shaking his shoulder disrupted his train of thought and Miller opened his eyes and was surprised to find himself in bed. He squinted up and in the lamplight saw Jones standing over him.

'Begging your pardon, sir,' Jones said, 'but Major Strouden's compliments and could you be getting ready for patrol?'

His head ached and he remembered the concussion. But he'd been through this before and wondered vaguely if it was a dream. Then the bad taste in his mouth suggested his headache wasn't concussion and, besides, Jones didn't look like he was in a dream.

'Something up?' Miller asked.

'Brigade's been on the blower again.'

So much for Doyle's having him grounded.

He moved his head experimentally. The ache seemed to have taken root somewhere above the eyes.

'Ops room?'

'That's right, sir.'

'Perhaps you'd bring me my flying gear.'

'All laid out and waiting, sir,' Jones said.

Of course it was. Why else would a man have a servant?

Strouden was waiting. A map of the salient and the surrounding country had been pinned to the easel and he was standing beside it fiddling nervously with his swagger stick. The hollowness Miller had seen in his eyes the previous morning seemed to have deepened but that might just have been the alcohol. Budge stood next to him, his face pale. In front of the easel B Flight was waiting.

'Are you up to this, Miller?' Strouden suddenly asked, as if turning out had been Miller's idea in the first place.

'Head's cleared now, thank you, sir,' Miller said, trying to keep it still.

'Mr Gregory's DH2 won't be available and I think we need you in your Strutter for this job.'

Miller took a chair behind Chatterton who turned and gave him a grim smile, looking like the lead actor in a production that was about to close. He had already been up on Strouden's bombing run the previous morning with his observer, MacMaster, as had Watson and they had all taken a second patrol later in the day. They looked a bit hollow-eyed themselves but were obviously prepared to see it through and Miller was damned if he was going to be the odd man out. Griffiths and Tozer sat directly in front of the easel; Boyes, Royston and the NCO observer, Sergeant White, with his pudding-basin haircut and prominent ears, sat next to them.

'Brigade want new pictures of the Hun rear lines from Hill 60 down to Armientières,' Strouden began without preamble. 'Mr MacMaster and Mr Watson are our experts and will be taking the snaps. So that Mr Chatterton can concentrate on doing what Mr MacMaster wants, I've asked Mr Denham to lead the flight.' He paused and looked around as if it was the best he could come up with at short notice and inviting anyone with a better plan to voice it.

Miller looked over his shoulder and saw Denham who had come in behind him, rehabilitated, Miller assumed, after the fiasco of the general's visit. Chacksfield was standing beside him, beaming at Miller and showing no signs of his evening in the mess. Miller supposed he had the constitution of an ox.

'Mr Tozer and Mr Royston will fly abreast of the cameras,' Strouden suggested when no one spoke. 'Captain Miller will be covering the rear in his Strutter.' He pointed his swagger stick at the map. 'You'll cross the lines over Hooge,' he said, laying the tip of his stick on the map at the town, 'and turn due south over Sanctuary Wood. At Hill 60 you take a bearing west-south-west towards Wytschaete.' He paused again and looked at Denham.

The C Flight commander ran a diffident hand through his hair and walked out in front of them.

'I'll lead in,' he told them, 'at nine thousand feet — '

'To give Archie something to shoot at,' Chacksfield called out from the back. Denham glared at him.

'Thank you, Mr Chacksfield,' Strouden said.

'We'll be flying,' Denham resumed hesitantly, 'a little east of the Hun reserve lines.' He looked at the map. 'When we're in position we'll drop to six and a half. Griffiths and Watson will be taking their photographs two hundred feet to my rear and Chatterton and MacMaster will follow them. We'll keep plenty of space between us so as not to give Archie a concentrated — '

'And Brigade want a decent width of photograph,' Strouden interrupted, 'so you'll stagger your approach.'

' — target,' Denham finished with a sideways glance at Strouden. 'Tozer and Boyes will fly cover on the Hun side. Royston and White on our right.'

'Our objective,' Strouden said, drawing the tip of his swagger stick along a line that passed through Wytschaete and Messines, south and to the west of Warneton then down to a point well to the east of Armentières, 'are some good

143

pictures of the Hun's rear trenches to see if there has been any marked reduction in troop concentration or missing artillery that might indicate they've pulled men out.' He waited expectantly as if there might be an objection to this.

'Most of us are pretty familiar with this stretch of the line,' he went on, 'so, photographs apart, I want you to keep your eyes open for any Hun activity on the roads or railways east around Comines and Menin.' He glanced at his watch. 'Unless you have any questions I suggest you get yourselves dressed and run your final checks. Brigade are partial to their shadow so let's get into the air while the sun is still low enough to give us some nice definition.' He stared at them intently for a second or two. 'What we want are good photographs. So, keep formation unless forced to defend yourselves and remember that it's Mr Watson and Mr MacMaster you're covering. Good luck, gentlemen.'

They stood up amid a scraping of chairs. Miller had long ago got used to the youth of the men he flew with, but he had never quite got over the feeling sometimes that he had wandered into a meeting of the upper sixth in the house master's study of a public school.

'I suppose you've done plenty of photography before,' Boyes said intruding upon the notion as he fell in beside Miller.

He was small and baby-faced and always looked to Miller to be lost in his clothes.

'We were doing a lot of it down on the Somme before I came up here,' Miller said. 'But mostly I was flying cover. I've only actually used the 'A' Type camera myself. I was usually so rotten at it that they always made me fly the machine instead.'

Miller could well remember his first attempt at photography, hanging over the side of a Vickers FB5 nacelle trying to keep the heavy mahogany camera level while the pilot threw the machine about the sky avoiding the Archie. Now the new cameras were all strapped to the side of the machine. It made the whole job far easier.

'All ours are 'C' Types,' Boyes said. 'Watson says there's nothing to it as long as you don't fumble the plates. Actually I'd like to try myself but I don't think Tozer could ever keep the Fee still enough for me to get any decent shots.'

'It does take nerve to keep it straight when Archie's bursting all around you.'

'Tozer's got the nerve,' Boyes said, 'it's just that I could never trust him not to go chasing after the Huns.'

Getting his height Miller circled with what seemed infinite slowness. The ground beneath him expanded as he rose — rather like one's awareness of life, he imagined, with one of those flashes of illumination that he suspected were a result of altitude rather than any sudden insight. Still, he followed the analogy even if it was no more than the effects of thinning oxygen on his brain. Like life, he thought again; horizons expanding as one grows older while at the same time growing less distinct until, with adulthood gained — like height — the view is one of limitless possibilities without any of them being sharp within one's focus.

He reached into the map pocket of his flying coat and pulled out his notebook, holding the stick with his knees as he wrote the thought down. He read it over and, as usual, he couldn't help thinking that it wasn't quite the same on paper as it had been in his head. There was something about thought that seemed to use concepts which bridged gaps that words couldn't span. Whilst in the head these constructs were not apparent; it was only when they needed to be converted to the currency of language he found what flimsy ideas they really were. Or was it that he lacked the facility to express them, that their nuances were beyond his talent? He put the notebook back in the pocket and took the stick back into his hand. Like Heyward, he thought again. Like Heyward.

At ten thousand feet he levelled off. A weather front moving through overnight had dragged a ragged formation of towering cumulus in its wake. Roiling cloud, anything from two or three thousand feet at its base, smeared red with the rising sun, to a soaring fifteen thousand feet or more at its top as it sailed along like a fleet of stately but distorted galleons on the north-westerly wind. High above this cumulus, serried lines of cirrus faintly etched the high pale sky.

Ahead of him, Denham had reached his height and Miller could see Chacksfield in the front nacelle scanning the sky to the east while he waited for the FEs to draw up into formation below. The sun had cleared the horizon, casting long shadows that on photographs would betray features otherwise washed out under full sun: bulky outlines of gun emplacements thrown with the jagged edges of a jigsaw piece, or a column of marching men seen as a dark wavelet lapping at a field's edge. Looking down over the side he saw the FEs straighten as they closed formation, Chatterton in the lead with Griffiths behind and Tozer and Boyes to the left, just a little higher and trailing at some distance. Royston and White had fallen in on the right flank as Denham started to drop to take the lead.

Over the lines Archie in Sanctuary wood began their barrage and Denham's FE started jerking unpredictably in the air, reminding Miller suddenly of severed frogs' legs goaded by electric probes. They passed over the wire-strung wasteland of Hill 60 and Denham took them down, dipping and turning to throw off Archie's range. Behind Denham, Griffiths and Chatterton positioned their FEs over the rear trenches, lining up on Wytschaete to begin taking the photographs, Chatterton and MacMaster's machine a little offset to increase the width of the shot. A few moments later the yellowing puffs of explosive got their range again and their wings disappeared behind a barrage of smoke.

Miller watched them with the detachment of a man observing a demonstration of nerve. With the cameras strapped to the sides of the FEs, the pilots would now have to hold height and direction all the time allowing for airspeed and wind-drift as Watson and MacMaster leaned over the nacelles and took the photographs, timing each of their exposures by counting before changing the plate to take another. Holding height and line was crucial as they flew along the German rear trench-works so as to get a series of photographs that could be overlapped in succession to build up a picture of the Hun line. What Griffiths and Chatterton had to do above all else was hold their position although the longer they held it, the more time the Hun gunners had to get their range. Resisting the temptation to throw the FEs around the sky to escape the exploding shells was where the nerve came in.

Miller looked around the sky again then down to what was left of the rail line that had once run through Ypres to Comines. Under the shade of a cloud, he saw a flash of fire that betrayed an artillery emplacement behind a rubbled building and he noted its position on the map spread across his knees then looked ahead beyond Warneton and the edge of Ploegsteert Wood to the spires of Armentières. The River Lys ran like a silver thread under the rising sun and, to the south and the rear of the hatched diggings that had become the Hun front line, the road that had once linked Armentières to the junction at Menin dipped in and out of visibility under clouds of dust raised by the boots of a column of marching men. Ahead of them a convoy of lorries was rumbling its way out of the tumbled ruins of Comines and he counted their number as they passed beyond sight beneath him and to his left.

To the right he saw that Chatterton had passed over Wytschaete and was approaching Messines in the centre of that westward lurch towards Mount Kemmel where the Hun forward trenches bulged like a counterbalance to the Ypres salient to its north. Griffith with Watson and Chatterton and MacMaster flew doggedly on although Miller could now barely see their machines for the heavy Archie they were attracting. Alongside them, but slightly higher and towards Comines, Tozer with Boyes in the front nacelle was darting this way and that, following in the wake of Archie's shells and suddenly looking to Miller like a flying bathtub pinned against the sky.

South of Wytschaete the front line took a dogleg around the stumped remnants of Ploegsteert Wood. New guns picked them up as Messines fell behind and Denham headed them in a drunken goose chase of his own, weaving between the exploding clouds of Archie. From the corner of his eye, Miller caught a movement of wings below him crossing the cratered ground beyond Warneton on the east bank of the Lys. It was a lone Rumpler at no more than four thousand feet, the Maltese crosses on its top wing etched dark against the fabric. He squinted automatically east towards the sun and raised a gloved hand against its brightness. Looking hard he could just make out small black flecks, like spectrographic lines in the glare.

Ploegsteert Wood dropped to their rear. Tozer had begun to lag a little and Miller eased back to keep him in view. East of Armentières, Chatterton, almost hidden beneath a pall of Archie and with the smudge that was Lille ahead, had reached the extent of the photographic reconnaissance and was following Denham, climbing to bank and turn around on Griffith's right. Miller glanced below to where the lone Rumpler had crossed the Lys River, still chugging along as if oblivious to the formation above him; in the east, Miller noted, the spectrographic lines had grown against the sun.

He looked ahead at the FEs again, expecting them to tighten their formation now they had finished their run, and saw a gap on the left where Tozer should have been. He scanned the ground beneath him, wondering abruptly if Archie had got them while he had been concentrating on the Hun machines that had hung east of the Flight in the sun. He looked for smoke or wreckage or a trail across the sky, then immediately saw Tozer emerge a couple of hundred feet beneath his own machine, diving on the tail of the Rumpler.

Miller muttered under his breath. He saw Denham's FE turn the rest of the Flight west towards the lines and Royston on the right drop to the rear of Griffith's machine, holding position where Tozer should have been. Then closer, moving between them and himself, he saw the looming outlines of two Eindeckers over his shoulder rising over the sun to dive on Tozer. Away beneath, the bait taken, Miller saw the lone Rumpler diving for home.

Boyes in Tozer's FE was having to stand on the combing of the nacelle, firing the Lewis back over the top of the machine at the approaching Eindeckers. Tozer had pulled out of his dive but he was already too low and Miller knew the Fokkers would give him no chance to gain altitude. He kicked his rudder and dropped to turn behind the Eindeckers as a line of tracer bullets arced past the cockpit of his Sopwith, stitching a crooked line through the fabric of his left wing. He snatched a glance above as a Halberstadt flew over the Strutter. He kicked the rudder bar again and put the machine into a right-hand roll, diving then pulling out as he came up behind and beneath the rearmost Eindecker on Tozer's tail. He was too far, he knew, but aiming the Sopwith's nose at the underbelly of the Fokker, he squeezed the trigger of his Vickers. The Fokker pilot turned as the fire sailed harmlessly past him and saw Miller on his tail. He slid sideways, spinning away to his left. Miller let him go, straightened up on the remaining Eindecker as it fell on Tozer.

Miller gave the Hun a burst as he closed on Tozer's machine then dropped below the FE and zoomed, turning to bring the Sopwith under the Fokker. Passing the FE he saw Boyes still standing, hanging on to the top Lewis gun for dear life as Tozer threw the machine into a half-roll. The Eindecker climbed and as Miller straightened to bring him within the sights of his Vickers, another burst raked across the front of the Strutter. He felt the judder of metal slamming into his engine block, banked left and climbed as the engine coughed and missed and a spray of oil flew back into his face. It coated his goggles and blinded him and he pulled them off, leaning sideways away from the spraying oil.

The Clerget kept running but its note changed, rising in pitch like a sentient thing capable of panic. Spitting the oil from his mouth, Miller wiped gloved fingers over his face. Blinking, he looked for the Eindecker but it had gone. He looked back over his shoulder and saw the Halberstadt slightly below and to his left, trying to climb onto his tail. He opened the throttle and climbed, putting distance between the Strutter and the Halberstadt before the Hun had completed his turn. Miller was too low and too far behind the German lines. Above him towards their own lines he caught a glimpse of the rest of the flight as it disappeared into the folds of a towering cloud. Archie had opened up again from somewhere to his north, the explosive puffs of smoke breaking high above him.

The Clerget engine coughed again as another spray of oil splashed onto his coat. He played with the throttle, coaxing the faltering engine and, with a sudden and overwhelming sense of exposure and isolation, realised he was holding his breath. If he stopped breathing, he reasoned, the engine would not catch fire. It was the only logical thing to do. He glanced back, waiting to feel the pressure from the hands of the Man from Reading on his shoulders. Behind and above the sky was clear. The Eindeckers and the Halberstadt had suddenly disappeared. The Clerget engine coughed on the edge of a stall. *Hold your breath. Hold it.*

He looked out for somewhere to put down, but there was nothing but churned earth and craters, the open wounds of trenches and strung wire like scars. Above the spluttering Clerget he heard the whining bullets of ground-fire. He played the throttle, caught her again and crossed the lines south of Ploegsteert Wood before she died. Looking up the sky seemed empty. Tozer and Boyes had gone. To the south, high at perhaps fifteen thousand feet and no more than pencilled ticks against the canopy of cirrus, another formation chugged slowly across the sky. Turning the nose of the Strutter towards the rise of Mt Kemmel, he hoped he had enough height to glide home. But he was cross-wind and too low.

Approaching the field he tried the engine again. She fired, coughed oil and spun and he eased back the stick. His chest was bursting. Small red explosions danced in front of his eyes and he tore off his helmet and felt the rush of air against his face. With a final gout of oil the Clerget rattled consumptively and died. He pulled upon the stick and sucked in a lungful of air. Smoke flared, blackened around the Clerget and burst into flame. He dropped the nose, skimming hedgerows, choking in the blinding smoke.

15

The fire-truck came bouncing across the grass with Mackinnon hanging off the side. Miller was out of the Sopwith before it had stopped.

'You all right, sir?' Mackinnon yelled as Miller jumped down.

'Hot!'

Mackinnon stripped the flying coat off Miller's back and pounded at his clothes. The fire truck began pumping water over the Strutter's engine and cockpit. Miller stumbled away from the machine as the dope burned, melting back the fabric of the wings. He saw Chatterton running towards him and, behind, the FEs and Watson and MacMaster handing the photographic plates down out of the nacelles to waiting aircraftsmen.

Miller's legs began to shake and he dropped onto the grass. Back where he had been twenty-four hours earlier, he thought.

'How are you feeling, old man?' Chatterton asked.

Miller almost told him but didn't.

'They jumped us as we were finishing up,' he said instead. 'I think Tozer and Boyes must have bought it. Two Eindeckers got on their tail.'

'No sir,' Mackinnon said, looking down. 'Mr Tozer came in a few minutes ago. His machine's pretty badly shot up and Mr Boyes took a bullet in the arm.'

Miller decided to trust his legs again. Mackinnon helped him up.

'I wouldn't have put a sou on his making it back,' Miller said. 'He dropped too low chasing a Rumpler.'

'I saw it,' Chatterton told him. 'You didn't see the Halberstadt, did you?'

'No,' Miller admitted.

'We couldn't come back, old man,' Chatterton said. 'You understand, don't you? We had the plates.'

'Of course,' Miller said. 'I'd have done the same.'

If he'd have done the same, he thought, he would have left Tozer to it.

Chatterton gave his shoulder a squeeze and walked back to the rest of the flight. Miller looked at Mackinnon.

'Have you any rag?' he asked Mackinnon. 'So I can get this damned oil off?'

'To tell the truth,' Mackinnon said, handing him a piece from his back pocket and lowering his voice confidentially, 'there was something of an altercation when Mr Tozer and Mr Boyes got in. They almost had to pull Mr Boyes off him despite his arm. He wasn't very happy with Mr Tozer at all. Not at all, you might say.'

'He broke formation to chase the Rumpler,' Miller said, wiping his face. 'Took the bait.'

'Mr Boyes knows better than to do that, sir.'

'I'm sure he does,' Miller said. 'It wasn't his hand on the stick, though.'

Tregoran retrieved the singed map on which he had marked the troop and vehicle movements from the Strutter's cockpit, then Miller walked to the mess hall for a mug of tea before the debriefing. He passed Tozer's FE and saw the fabric hanging off the wings and the dangling wires. Oil dripped from the engine and a smear of blood marked the side of the nacelle. Two men were disconnecting the machine guns while one of the riggers was shaking his head over the severed wires.

In the operations room Budge waited, perched on the edge of a table. Watson and MacMaster were comparing notes. Chatterton and White did not look happy. By comparison, Royston was sharing a joke with Griffiths. Tozer was sitting in a chair looking flushed.

Strouden looked grimmer than he had when they had left. A bullet in the arm and a couple of shot-up machines didn't seem much of a price considering the escalating cost of patrols, Miller thought, but then he wasn't the CO.

'I saw you come in,' he said to Miller.

'I was lucky,' Miller told him. 'Nothing serious. The Strutter will take a bit of patching up, though.'

'Well, Greene tells me they're still working on your Fee so I'm standing you down for the rest of the day. Get Doyle to look you over after breakfast and then put your feet up. Gregory's DH2 will be back this afternoon.'

Denham walked in with Chacksfield. 'Two Eindeckers and a Halberstadt,' he said to Budge by way of explanation. 'I saw them dropping on Tozer with Mr Miller here close on their tails. I decided the main thing was to get the plates back across the lines.'

'Quite right, Mr Denham,' Strouden said.

Denham looked at Miller and seemed about to say something then thought better of it.

Strouden glanced at the others. Tozer was staring at a point in front of him, apparently unconcerned.

'I saw them earlier sitting in the sun,' Miller said, 'I never saw them get their height.'

When no one else added anything, Sergeant White said:

'They put out a single Rumpler as bait.'

Tozer glared at him but White ignored him.

'How's Boyes?' Miller asked Tozer.

'Oh, he's all right,' Tozer said sulkily. 'The bullet only grazed his arm. It'll probably get him a month back in Blighty. I wouldn't mind one of those myself.'

'Say the word, old man,' Chatterton said with repressed anger, 'be happy to oblige.'

'Gentlemen...' Strouden said.

'Lieutenant Tozer broke formation chasing that Rumpler,' Denham said now that White had raised the point. 'He should have stayed in formation.'

'Mr Tozer?'

'We were finished,' Tozer complained. 'How was I to know that there was another crowd of them above us?'

Miller waited for someone to point out that that was precisely what he should have known, but no one seemed to think that would have been worth the effort.

'We were finished but we weren't home,' Chatterton explained slowly. 'Just think about it next time, will you?'

'Mr Budge?' Strouden prompted, and they began giving the recording officer details of the show.

'I think we got some pretty good shots, sir,' MacMaster said, glancing first at Watson then back to Budge. 'No cloud to worry about but Archie was a bit thick.'

'Too high to fog the snaps most of it,' Watson said.

The plates were already upstairs in an improvised dark room being developed by a corporal from the transport unit who had had his own photography studio in Brighton before the war. It was logical, Strouden had argued, to develop on site rather than transport the fragile plates back to Brigade. It also gave him the chance of vetting them and ordering another show if the photographs turned out to be duds.

Miller gave Budge his map with the guns and the column of men marked on it. The recording officer looked at the browned edges and gave Miller an enquiring look.

'I'd say they're moving men south,' Miller said.

With Jones's help he cleaned himself up in his hut then went into breakfast. In the mess hall he took a table with Chacksfield, Chatterton and Moss. Tozer sitting further along had been held back by Strouden after the de-brief and Miller assumed, had been torn off a strip for endangering the patrol. He sat now, still nursing the grievance which, Miller supposed, was probably as emotionally painful as Boyes's bullet in the arm was physically.

When he had finished eating, Miller looked down the table at Tozer and tried to give him some advice about calculating the percentages of any given situation, but judging by his response the younger man failed to grasp the content of Miller's counsel and appeared to resent the intent. Miller decided that if the CO couldn't get through to him he didn't have much chance.

'The trouble with pilots,' Chacksfield said apparently to no one in particular, helping himself to some more toast and marmalade, 'is that they're apt to forget that there's another man in the machine.'

'Don't be stupid,' Tozer said, taking the bait for the second time that day. 'He's staring at the back of the man's head.'

'I was speaking figuratively, Tozer,' Chacksfield said.

'What?'

'Figuratively, squit.'

'It's no good,' Moss advised. 'Tozer was probably playing rugger when philology was on the curriculum.'

'What's *that* supposed to mean?' Tozer demanded.

'Do you think so, Moss?' Chacksfield said. 'You know, I swear sometimes he can almost understand me.' He leaned across the table and peered into Tozer's face. 'Now and again one does catch the merest glimpse of intelligence, Moss,

151

wouldn't you agree?'

'Chuck it, Chacksfield,' Chatterton who was sitting between Tozer and Miller said wearily. 'I think the Old Man has made the point. Let's drop it, shall we?'

'I'm merely saying that a fellow ought to remember that he isn't the only man in the machine and should learn to hold position, not go chasing after every Hun he sees.'

'But that's why we're here!' Tozer said. He looked from one to the other and then along the table at Miller. 'Isn't it?'

Chatterton sighed, suggesting he was exerting extreme patience. 'Not when we're on a specific show,' he said. 'The whole idea, old man, is to protect whoever is doing the work, whether it's photography, spotting or whatever. Not to zoom all over the air chasing the Hun and being of no use to the chaps you're supposed to be escorting.'

'Then why doesn't the major ever ask me to fly cover?' Tozer asked. 'If *I* had a DH2, I wouldn't have to rely on windy observers.'

'I've never seen *you* standing on the edge of your nacelle,' Moss said.

'Anyway, you squit, you haven't got a DH2,' Chacksfield said. He buttered some toast. 'You're not even much good at keeping a Fee level long enough to do any spotting, not to mention taking photographs.'

'One supposes he must be good for *something*,' Moss said.

'Yes,' Chacksfield replied thoughtfully, 'I suppose if you *really* wanted to be of use to the squadron, Tozer, you could always ask the Old Man if we could get a cricket eleven together.'

On his way to the MO's hut Miller ran into Gregory. He was already dressed in his flying gear, the smooth skullcap of his flying helmet giving his face, with its slightly hooked nose, the appearance of a predatory bird.

'I hear you had a close shave this morning,' he said as Miller walked up.

'As close as I want,' Miller admitted. 'My Strutter will take some patching up. That'll mean more work for you, I'm afraid.'

'Heigh-ho,' Gregory said.

'How's the machine?'

'I'm just going to pick her up now. The men went over first thing this morning to give her a run through.'

'What was the problem?'

'Just some dirt in the carb, I think. Nothing serious.' He brightened. 'Fortunately I found a flat patch of ground to put her down so no damage.' A horn hooted and he gave Miller a wave and trotted off towards a waiting tender.

Doyle scratched at his red hair as Miller walked into the hut and motioned him to sit on one of the tables.

'I hear you lit up the sky like a roman candle this morning.'

'More of a bonfire from where I was sitting,' Miller said.

'And after I told you to keep your feet on the ground for a while.'

'It's the CO you want to tell, not me.'

'Now you know he won't listen to the likes of me. Any burns?'

'No, I managed to get out before it went up.'

'There'd be no point in testing your reflexes, then. Let me see that head of yours.'

Miller suffered some cursory prodding before Doyle grunted and let him off the table.

'Have you had any occasion to treat him?' Miller asked.

'Who?'

'The CO.'

'Now why would you be askin' me that?'

'He's under a lot of strain,' Miller said.

'Like the rest of us,' Doyle said, 'he'd benefit from a spot of leave but I don't suppose he'd take it even if it were offered. Now, if you've done examining me I've certainly done examining you.'

'How's Boyes, by the way?' Miller asked as he reached the door.

'Nothing but a grazed arm. I sent him off to the hospital anyway, otherwise I'd be getting the reputation for bein' an unfeeling brute. And it'll do him no harm to get away from the tender ministrations of Mr Tozer for a while.'

'There's something to be said for that,' Miller agreed.

Walking back along the edge of the field, he stopped to watch the FEs being pushed out and readied for the noon patrol. He knew he needed to talk to Dunne's friend Parry and also to find Woodward, the enlisted man whose brother had been friendly with Heyward, but the night in the mess, the lack of sleep and the flight that morning had taken it out of him. He thought instead he might read through Heyward's papers again in case there was something he had missed but, by the time he had got back to his hut, stripped off his tunic and lay on the bunk, he found it difficult to concentrate on anything except keeping his eyes open. He decided not to try.

It was late in the afternoon when he awoke. He could not remember having dreamed and felt more refreshed than he had for some while. Sitting up, he even found that the earlier muzziness that had been the result of the concussion — or more prosaically a hangover — had also left him. There was water in his jug and he washed, found a clean shirt and underwear freshly laundered by Jones, dressed and walked over to the Bessonneau.

Men were crawling over his Strutter like ants on a dead grasshopper. He circled around it. With its stripped engine, dangling wires and missing struts it looked lifeless. In the air they had beauty; here they were just agglomerations of materials.

New fabric had been stretched over the wings where the old had been burned and two riggers were coating it with dope. Smith was poking around the gutted Clerget engine and Miller watched as he worked, remembering the hours he had spent before the war in draughty sheds fine tuning under-powered, overweight versions of automobile engines that barely kept themselves, and the flimsy constructions into which they were fitted, in the air.

'How's it looking?' he asked Smith.

'We've had to strip her right down, sir,' Smith said. 'So Sergeant Greene decided we might as well rebuild her from scratch, just to be on the safe side.'

'That'll take a while, I suppose?'

'We've sent a man for the new parts we need, but yes. I don't think you'll be taking her up tomorrow. We'll have a better idea when the parts get here.'

'My FE's ready though?' Miller said.

'Yes, sir. We've patched all the holes. Whenever you need her, sir.'

He walked around the shed looking at the machines in varying states of repair. At one end he found Gregory's DH2, safely back with Mackinnon in the cockpit twisting backwards over the engine.

'I'm looking for a fitter of yours named Woodward,' he called up over the clanging of metal. 'You wouldn't know where I could find him, would you, Sergeant?'

Mackinnon looked down and straightened with a grimace as if his back were aching.

'He's taken a lorry to St Omer to pick up the spares for your Strutter, sir. Was it something in particular or can I get one of the lads to help?'

'Not to worry, sergeant. When he gets back will be fine.'

He left the Bessonneau and looked in on the mess. Gracey, the armaments officer was sitting in a battered armchair in the corner reading a newspaper. Puffs of smoke like towering cumulus were rising at intervals from his pipe and drifting across the room to where Grimshaw was restocking the bar.

Budge came up behind him. 'How you feeling, old man?'

'Fine. I've caught up on some sleep this afternoon.'

'Good for you!' Budge said cheerily. 'Tommy says to take it easy tomorrow. He means it, you know. We've nothing except patrols scheduled.'

'Thanks,' Miller said. 'Actually I was looking for Parry. Which hut is his?'

'I rather think you've just missed him, old man.' He cocked his head as a couple of Beardmore engines cleared their throats and purred into life. 'A Flight's rostered for the evening patrol. He'll be out on the field. Anything I can do?'

'No. I just wanted to talk to him about Dunne, that was all. Who's up with Parry and Reynolds?'

'Tommy's switched Parker to take A Flight and put that new pair with him, Garfield and Pollock.'

'Who is Parsons flying with?'

'Tozer. At least until Boyes gets back. He didn't get anything worse than a flesh wound this morning, luckily.'

Not so lucky for Parsons, Miller thought.

He had a beer with Budge then walked down the corridor and knocked on Strouden's door.

'Come in, Miller,' he said looking up from behind his desk. 'Mackinnon tells me your Strutter took a bit of a beating this morning.'

'Yes, sir. It should be operational again by the day after tomorrow apparently.'

'Good. I've never known Brigade go more than twenty-four hours without a flap of one kind or another. Sit down. What can I do for you?'

'I believe you used Heyward in an observing capacity rather than let him fly, is that correct?'

Strouden dropped his pen and let out a sigh. 'It wasn't *solely* to avoid having him fly, Miller, but I can't pretend it wasn't a consideration. As it happened I found myself two observers short. I could have used anyone but in those situations you keep your best pilots in the cockpit.'

'I'm told he was unhappy about it.'

'Men aren't here to be made happy,' Strouden said.

'No, of course not. Did you try to get him a transfer?'

'It did cross my mind. I rather hoped, though, that he'd take to the observer's job. Captain Budge told me he was rather good at it. Good shot, too.'

'But he preferred flying.'

Strouden looked doubtful. 'I can't say whether he preferred it or not. I think it was more a case of Heyward thinking we were doing him down by not allowing him behind the controls.'

'Injured pride, then?'

'Yes, I'd say that. He *was* a proud young man, as I recall.'

He had thought he would talk to Parry after the evening patrol returned but, once back in his hut, he found he felt too restless and decided upon a change of scene. Finding a lift into town he did some shopping then bought a postcard for his sister in San Francisco. He deliberated upon the card, not caring for the humorous ones nor the overly sentimental and had finally settled for an old card that showed the centre of Ypres from before the war with the Cloth Hall still proud and intact. He wrote the card over a glass of beer then strolled around until, back across the square, he found a small estaminet where the menu lacked both barkers and bully beef and he ordered mutton, eating slowly over a bottle of wine followed by coffee and cognac. Heywood sat across the table from him in the empty chair, stiff and unbending. A proud young man but still an enigma.

It was dark when he finally left, following the lights of the vehicles out of the square and looking for a lift back to the field.

16

The morning was clear. The only cloud was a haze that hung far to the north over the Channel misting the coast. Miller could see a formation of something big over Belgium and decided that, if they were theirs, they were returning from a bombing run on one of the Channel ports, or perhaps even Bruxelles; if they weren't theirs then someone was in for a pasting.

He could have done as Budge had suggested and taken it easy, but the patrol had been reduced to three machines; the loss of Hardy and Bartlett during Bovington's visit and Parker and Cliff being moved to A Flight left only Denham and Chacksfield, Moss and Trueman, and himself in C Flight. He might have let Denham and Moss fly the patrol by themselves yet he was still feeling restless and knew the best cure was to get into the air. In the absence of an observer to sit in the front nacelle, the fitter, Smith, had volunteered 'to go up for a spin'. Despite the ribald comments of his pals Miller could tell they were quite impressed. They were happy to work on the machines but it was only a small minority that ever wanted to get into one.

Major Strouden had said he was expecting replacements any day and that two squadron members who had been back home doing a stint of training were due back as well. Until then, C Flight would have to make do.

Brigade for once had not been on the blower and Strouden told them to run up and down the lines and not venture into Hun territory. As the Huns of late had kept pretty much to their own side since the Eindeckers had lost their dominance, Strouden had decided not to look for trouble until he had men enough to cope with it. It suited Miller. He was getting a little browned off with having machines shot to pieces under him and, with a novice like Smith in the front nacelle, a pleasure flight would fit the bill nicely.

Before lifting off he had told Smith to let off a few rounds with both the Lewis guns once they'd got their height to ensure that they were working properly and that he was familiar with the mechanism. He had done his share of training on the range, of course, but it was a different matter in the air and Miller watched as he first put several rounds towards the Hun lines with the front Lewis then turned around to reach the rear gun. Unlike Boyes, Smith was tall enough to man the top gun without having to stand out on the edges of the nacelle, but he still had to stand on his seat and Miller knew that that took nerve. For Tozer to suggest the day before that Boyes was windy was a calumny; it took even more nerve to do what Boyes did knowing that Tozer had little regard for him. Smith grinned at Miller as he clambered round in the nacelle and loosed off a clatter of shots over his head. There didn't seem much wrong with Smith's nerve, he decided.

Denham took them as far north as Dixmude at around eight thousand feet, the Archie light enough to be of no concern. An artillery barrage against the line gave them something to watch for ten minutes and the weather was so clear that there was no problem in pinpointing the Hun guns. At any other time, he supposed, they might have taken the chance of nipping over the lines and strafing the emplacements. Chacksfield, he knew, was always in the habit of taking up a few grenades on the off-chance of spotting a Hun *pickelhaube* to drop them on. It never seemed an effective use of resources to him but one could never tell when the disruption caused might just be enough to save some poor Tommy in his trench from getting a shell on his head. As it was, Denham was not about to blot his copybook again, having only just climbed out of the pit the general had dug for him, and they patrolled their own side of the line until their fuel dictated they turn for home.

Smith looked a little sheepish in the debriefing and only spoke when asked a direct question. Miller noted that he had seen everything there had been to see and, more to the point, had identified it correctly. As they filed out of the room Miller had offered, if Smith was keen enough, to have a word with the CO to put his name down if the opportunity arose again.

'I don't know I'd enjoy it as much if I had a Hun on my tail.'

'The idea is to get on theirs,' Miller said.

'Do you get to choose your pilot, sir?'

Miller laughed. 'I'm afraid not, Smith.'

The mess hall was quiet over breakfast, most of the other men having eaten. He looked for Parry so he might have a word with him about Dunne but he wasn't around.

He saw FitzHarris, the transport officer, morosely stabbing at a platoon of barkers at a table by himself and, after he had slid a pair of eggs and some bacon onto a plate, walked over and took a chair next to him.

'Do you mind?'

FitzHarris looked up in a mildly distracted fashion.

'Hmm? What? Miller, old man,' he said brightening. 'No, not at all.'

'Feeling all right?'

'Me? Fine, fine.' He paused, looking sideways at Miller, then said, 'I saw you come in yesterday.'

He wondered if there was anyone in the squadron who hadn't. 'I don't make a habit of that,' he assured FitzHarris.

'No, I should think not. Any damage?'

'Me or my Strutter?'

'You, old man,' FitzHarris said. 'Bugger the machine.'

'No. It shakes you up, though. CO's given me the rest of the day off.'

'Quite right, too,' FitzHarris agreed. 'I'd have thought it merited a weekend in Paris.'

'I think you have to get your tail shot off for that,' Miller said. 'I was thinking I might run into Pops today, though. Foden's being shipped home and I thought I'd see him off.'

'Good idea. Need transport?'

'If there is something.'

'Just nip round to the sheds. They'll fix you up.'

'By the way,' Miller said. 'You've got a fellow named Woodward in your unit, haven't you?'

'Yes, that's right,' FitzHarris said. 'Queer duck.'

'Oh, in what way?'

'Enlisted man. Could have applied for a commission. Gentleman... good family, you know...'

'Why didn't he?'

FitzHarris gave a shrug and reached for a mug of tea.

'Not interested, apparently. Not a conchie, obviously. Just preferred to enlist.'

'How do the men treat him?'

'Hard to say, really,' FitzHarris said, screwing his round face up as if the question were a ticklish one. 'Tend to go to him when they have a problem. You know, the sort of thing they'd normally take to an officer but don't like to. Makes my life easier, I know that. But then, of course, they don't fully accept him as one of them. I'll tell you one thing, though.'

'What's that?'

'He knows his wine.'

'Oh?'

'Spent quite a lot of time over here before the war, it seems. France. Germany, too... Italy... I try to take him with me when I'm buying for the mess. Sound judgement.'

'It's a bit hard on him if he doesn't get to drink any of it.'

'Oh, I let him have the odd bottle,' FitzHarris said. 'No worries there.'

'It's just I wanted to have a word with him,' Miller said.

'Oh? Right,' FitzHarris said, showing absolutely no curiosity as to why. 'You'll always find him in the machine sheds tinkerin' around. He's an absolute wizard with the vehicles. There's never a problem old Woodward can't get over.'

Miller found him in the machine shop, bent over a lathe. As Miller called above the noise of the machine, Woodward turned towards him and Miller saw an indentation and scar by the hairline on the man's left temple. He looked at the old wound with a sense of recognition.

'You're *Harry* Woodward,' he said.

Woodward turned off the lathe and straightened up. 'Sir?'

Miller gestured at the scar. 'I was at Brooklands when you got that.'

Woodward's fingers went to his temple touching the indentation with what seemed an involuntary reaction. Miller noticed a slight flickering of the left eye, a barely discernible tremble in the muscle beneath.

'I thought you were dead when they pulled you out of the wreck.'

Woodward smiled and the tremble in the muscle stilled.

'So did I, sir.'

He was tall with thinning chestnut hair over a refined and striking, if somewhat hawkish, face that almost kept the eye from being drawn to the depression above the temple. Had he not already known it, Miller might have guessed from his relaxed attitude in front of an officer that he was a man who had enlisted below his social class. It wasn't that he appeared insubordinate, more that he, unlike many enlisted men, did not display a degree of self-consciousness in the presence of an officer.

'When was it?' Miller asked. '1912… 13?'

'August 1913,' Woodward said. 'It put me out for almost a year. I'd only just started racing again when war was declared. In the crowd, were you sir?'

'Not exactly,' Miller said. 'I was working for Tom Sopwith in his sheds there.'

Woodward smiled. 'Good days, sir.'

'They were,' Miller agreed.

Woodward began tidying the bench. He tipped some paraffin from a can onto his hands and wiped them clean with a rag.

'I was just going off duty, sir. I'd planned to go into town for lunch. Was there anything in particular you required?'

Miller found himself smiling. Woodward had *planned* to go into town, not that he'd been given leave. There had been nothing remotely disrespectful in what Woodward had said, but he had still managed to convey the notion that he was now on his own time without resorting to the unspoken insolence that most enlisted men might have been unable to avoid.

'Going in with some of the other men?' he asked.

'No, but I've arranged to meet some chums of mine.'

'I was going in myself,' Miller said. 'I thought I'd see Mr Foden before they ship him home. Perhaps I can give you a lift?'

For the first time Woodward looked uncomfortable. 'If it's all the same to you, sir,' he said, 'I'll take my motorcycle. If you don't mind.'

'I understand,' Miller said. 'Riding with an officer?'

The muscle under Woodward's eye began to twitch as if Miller had issued a challenge.

'I'll give *you* a lift if you don't mind riding pillion,' he said.

'All right.'

'Give me ten minutes to put on a fresh shirt and I'll meet you here, sir.' He started for the door.

'Woodward,' Miller said, 'you're off duty; let's drop the rank, shall we?'

Woodward inclined his head like a dog hearing something he could not quite place. 'Righto,' he said.

The motorcycle was a 1913 Indian Twin. Or almost.

'I've made a few modifications,' Woodward explained. 'I've managed to get another twenty miles per hour out of her. I turned the luggage rack into a pillion, as well. I brought her back with me from my last leave.' He swung a leg over the machine and kicked the engine into life. 'She gives me the chance to get out on my own when I can find an hour or two.'

Throttle wide open, Miller supposed as he climbed on behind Woodward and took hold of the bars either side of the pillion.

They bounced across the field to the road and, as Woodward accelerated along the château's drive to the main road, Miller leaned forward into his back. The early June sun was hot on his face and, after the freezing wind to which he had grown accustomed at altitude, Miller felt the warmth of the breeze an odd sensation; a feeling of liberation as if he was turning his back on all the madness behind him. He thought he understood why Woodward rode the machine whenever he could and felt a sudden urge to shout at him to keep going until he was as far from it all as they could get — the machines and the sound of guns and of tramping men and the smell and the sights — especially the sights — of war.

Then they reached the junction with the road to Poperinghe and the sense of liberation drained out of him.

The road up to the front was choked with columns of marching men. Beyond the clanking of kit and the scuffing of feet an odd silence hung over them as they moved down the line, trudging in ragged formations, heads down, feet barely lifting out of the dust that rose in clouds and eddies around their puttees. Exhaustion was painted on their faces: hollow eyes, gaunt cheeks and unshaven chins. With only rare opportunities to wash or get out of their uniforms, the dirt lay caked on their hands and around their necks and faces giving them the appearance of troglodytes newly emerged into the light. Marching the opposite way were those moving up the line. They were in no hurry. It was easy to tell the new recruits from those who had spent time in the front trenches already. The new men eyed the returning columns with a slack-jawed alarm; the old hands kept their heads down. They concentrated on their boots as if they were only able to place one in front of the next through an act of will.

Between and through them moved motor ambulances carrying the wounded and horse-drawn carts carrying the dead. Motorcycles and staff cars jostled for space, breaking the unnatural quiet hanging over the men. Horns honked like curses at the slow columns that clogged the road, butting up against limbered guns and ammunition boxes making for the front.

Woodward threaded his Indian Twin into the slowly flowing morass and weaved his way to the next junction before turning off onto a side track. A few scattered men wandered aimlessly along the dirt road. Off it, in the ditches, Miller saw the occasional carcass of a horse, part-eaten by the packs of stray dogs and other scavengers, what was left decomposing under a swarm of maggots.

Flies droned lazily in black clouds and the warm June air hung redolent with the heavy scent of putrefaction.

Woodward opened the throttle and accelerated.

The town was no less crowded by day than it was by night. Streams of men meandered their way through the streets and around the stalls selling souvenirs and postcards and the few odds and ends that might possibly make life just that little bit more endurable in the trenches.

The casualty clearing station where Foden was held was housed in a bleak brick building that had the look of a market hall. Woodward pulled up outside and Miller climbed off the machine.

'As a matter of fact,' he said, 'if you've got time for a drink before you meet your friends, I would like a word with you.'

160

'There's a bar across the road,' Woodward suggested.

Woodward cut the Indian Twin's engine and lifted it back onto its stand. Somewhere in the distance Miller heard the clanging of shunting railway wagons.

Woodward gestured behind him. 'That's where the men who are going home are,' he said. 'Lieutenant Foden caught one when he was flying with you, didn't he?'

'Shrapnel,' Miller said. 'When Springfield's machine blew up.'

They crossed the road, edging through the traffic, and Woodward indicated a small bar with a table and a few chairs on the street. A medical orderly sat with two VADs drinking coffee. Inside were two or three other cramped tables and a bar against the far wall. The room smelt of cigarette smoke, coffee and beer. Men and women sat at the tables or stood, hollow-eyed looking at nothing.

'They come in here for a break,' Woodward explained. 'A pal of mine was here for a few days before they shipped him home.'

Miller bought two beers and took a table as two medical orderlies stood up.

'It was Foden who told me you knew Heyward,' he said.

Woodward drank half his beer before putting the glass down. 'I thought that was probably it,' he said.

'Word has got around, then.'

'That you were asking about Charlie Heyward?' He chuckled but there wasn't a lot of mirth in his laughter. 'Officers would be surprised how quickly the Other Ranks find out things.'

Miller said, 'I know. I was an NCO myself.'

'I thought you probably were.'

'Why's that?'

'When you suggested I drop rank. Officers do it socially between themselves, but not with enlisted men.'

'Not even a gentleman ranker?'

This time Woodward's laughter was genuine. 'Kipling? *God have mercy on such as we*? It's really not that bad. But no, no rank dropped, especially not with an enlisted man if he's what they regard as a "gentleman".'

'Why is that, do you think?' Miller asked. 'A betrayal of class?'

'It's what *they* think that matters,' Woodward said. 'Not me. But you're probably right.'

'Was that Heyward's reaction?'

'Possibly. As a matter of fact, I never had occasion to speak with him.'

'Didn't you find that odd, if you knew each other before the war, I mean?'

'I didn't know him, not really. He was a friend of my younger brother, Edward. We'd only met a couple of times — before the war, that is. I doubt we had much in common. He wasn't interested in motor racing and I wasn't interested in much else.' He drank some more beer, offered Miller a cigarette and lit one himself. 'Of course my enlisting in the ranks didn't help matters. It didn't go down too well with *my* family so I can't imagine what *his* mother made of it.'

'Did you know her?'

161

'No. Edward told me that she particularly asked him about my decision, though.'

'She had heard, then?'

'Provincial society can be a small world,' Woodward said. 'Particularly Yorkshire provincial society.'

'Why did you, as a matter of interest?' Miller asked.

'Enlist?' Woodward lifted his shoulders in an almost French gesture as if he wasn't sure of the answer himself.

'I've never cared for telling other people what they should or shouldn't do,' he said. 'Of course, my father puts it down to my unwillingness to accept any responsibility. Motor racing for him is an inherently irresponsible activity.' Woodward grinned at him. 'Great fun though.'

'But not flying?'

Woodward scratched at the side of his face. 'The truth is, I've no head for heights. I know,' he said, as if to forestall comment. 'It's a matter of great embarrassment. Silly, isn't it? When they first started building the things back at Brooklands I thought to myself, "this looks like fun", so I got a chap to take me up. I was as sick as a dog – dizziness, the works. I did try several times, but it was just no go.'

'But you joined the RFC?'

'I was in the Royal Artillery when they came looking for mechanics. I thought I'd get more opportunity to play around with engines in the RFC so I volunteered.'

'If you'd like,' Miller offered, 'I'll take you up in an FE. Sitting in a nacelle there's less sensation of being perched on a few struts of wood like you were in an old Boxkite or a Farman. The machines have come a long way.'

Woodward laughed, unconvinced. 'Don't forget I've seen how the observers have to stand on the damn things to get to the rear Lewis,' he said. 'But, I'm game to try anything if you're game to have a quivering wreck up there with you.'

'As a matter of fact I took Smith up with me this morning — the C Flight fitter?'

'Jim Smith? He probably had a bet with one of the lads he'd go up.' He finished his beer. When he put the glass down the smile had left his face.

'Have you any idea why Charlie Heyward did it?'

Miller exhaled smoke. 'To be honest, no. I wondered if it might have been remorse because he killed Dunne. But from what I gather I don't think he regarded himself as a rotten pilot. His first reaction was to blame it on Smith.'

'He's a good mechanic. He doesn't make mistakes.'

'Everyone makes mistakes,' Miller said.

'Not when you have Warrant Officer Mackinnon looking over your shoulder you don't.'

'Did your brother ever speak of Heyward particularly?'

'In what way?'

'Oh, I don't know. Girls, say. Did he have a girl at home? Perhaps he'd just been thrown over.'

Woodward crushed out his cigarette. 'I couldn't say, I'm afraid. I wasn't part of Teddy's circle. There was always some girl or other *he* was soft on but I didn't see much of him unless he came up to town, to tell the truth. Charlie Heyward didn't often come with him as far as I recall. Too fond of his weekend shooting parties and hunting, I think. I was never keen on that sort of thing — not enough grease involved for my liking.'

'Shooting?' Miller said. 'I was told he had literary aspirations.'

'Well, I don't know that the two are mutually exclusive,' Woodward said. 'It was one of Teddy's interests too and he wasn't averse to a weekend shoot. That's probably why they got on. I rather got the idea that Heyward thought of himself as one of these bucolic poets. Ruskin, was it? That sort of thing. And that American fellow. Thor something — ?'

'Thoreau?'

'That's the chap. *Walden*, wasn't it?'

Miller assumed Woodward had got this from Teddy. From what he had read of Heyward's work himself, the man had lacked the talent to do any more than ruffle the surface of Thoreau's pond never mind plumb the depths of *Walden*.

'But there probably *were* girls?' he persisted.

Woodward frowned then started to laugh again. 'You're wondering if his inclinations led in a different direction.'

'It has occurred to me,' Miller admitted.

'Anything's possible,' Woodward allowed. 'But I doubt if my brother would have been very friendly with him if that's how things were. Teddy didn't care for that sort of thing at all. Was pretty well down on everything Wilde wrote because of it.'

'Is your brother over here?'

'Yes, in a manner of speaking,' he said. He looked past Miller's shoulder towards the street and Miller was about to ask what he had meant when Woodward went on, 'Isn't it likely it was just the stress of flying that made him do it? Perhaps his nerve was gone.'

'That's the obvious answer,' Miller agreed, 'but the thing is he didn't have to. Major Strouden wanted to transfer him out anyway. He thought he wasn't up to it. I don't know that Wing would have been too keen to lose a pilot but I would have thought his mother could have arranged it.'

'But that would have meant going back to the trenches, wouldn't it? Not much of a choice when you consider it.'

'No, I suppose not,' Miller admitted. 'But there's always Staff. You heard his father was killed, I suppose?'

'Yes.' Then Woodward said, 'Did you know this is where they hold the courts marshal for cowardice and desertion? Here in Poperinghe. They've already executed several men.'

'No, I didn't know that,' Miller said.

Woodward looked at him intently for a moment before he said, 'It's not quite what we all expected, is it? In fact it's not much fun at all.'

163

Miller didn't reply. There wasn't anything he could think to say.

'When I told you I didn't want the responsibility of command,' Woodward went on, 'that was true. At least when I joined up. Now, if I had any men under my command I could never be sure that I wouldn't tell them to throw down their rifles and go home.'

'I'd keep that sort of thing to myself, if I were you,' Miller suggested.

'I do,' Woodward said. 'But I wanted you to know.' He played with his empty beer glass a moment. 'You see, when I said my brother Teddy was over here, I meant he was buried here. He was a subaltern with the Sherwood Foresters. He was killed leading his squad over the top at Neuve Chapelle in April last year. The family is very proud of him.' He looked down the street again and shrugged helplessly. 'So am I.'

Miller drank another beer after Woodward left then crossed the road to the hospital. An orderly directed him to the floor on which he would find Foden and a nurse took him to the bed.

He was lying with his eyes closed. His face was pale and the hair on the side of his head above his wounded shoulder had been shaved. Some cuts had been stitched and dried blood still clung to the sutures. Miller hadn't remembered a head wound. Then he recalled that he hadn't remembered much at all.

He was looking at the empty sleeve of the pyjama jacket where the arm had been when Foden opened his eyes.

'Hullo,' he said softly. 'Good of you to come.'

'They told me you were going home tomorrow,' Miller said.

'Boulogne for a few days apparently. Then a ship home. Not long enough to slip down to Paris and go dancing,' he said.

'No,' Miller said. 'It'll have to be London instead.'

'Yes, London.'

'The chaps back at the squadron send their regards.'

'Thanks. Old Budgie dropped by with some of my things. And Chacksfield and Moss. Capital fellows. I'm going to miss them.' He inclined his head ever so slightly to where his arm had been. 'Budgie says I should insist on a hook like his. I'd need a broomstick, too. Not very practical.'

'No,' Miller agreed. 'Probably not.'

'Still,' Foden said, summoning a smile. 'Better off than Springfield and Breconridge. Bad luck, that.' His face suddenly creased. 'I've tried to remember what happened but it's all a blank. Did you see?'

'I think their bombs went off in the rack,' Miller said. 'We were too close.'

'Bad luck,' Foden said again.

'Yes.' Miller took a breath and held it. He hated having to mention it. 'I've just been talking to Harry Woodward. Did you know his brother Teddy at all?'

'Bought it last year. Like Charlie's father.'

'Yes.'

'Met him once at a shoot. Nice chap. Good shot, I remember. Better than me, anyway. I don't suppose I'll do much shooting now. Rotten war, isn't it?'

Miller let it drop. He put a hand on Foden's good shoulder then left him, walking back between the beds without looking at any of them. He was a long way from the hospital before the smell of formaldehyde left his nostrils and he stopped hearing the groans of wounded men.

He started walking out beyond the edge of the town and through one of the transit camps, the tents pegged out in long olive-green lines with the grass between them scuffed and trodden down to hard-baked clay under the sun. Around them men lounged in vests or shirtsleeves or played soccer in rowdy clusters, kicking and chasing a ball. Beyond the camp he followed a farm track through unkempt fields that, after the 1914 crop had lain unharvested, had been abandoned by the plough altogether. Weeds and wild wheat and barley grew waist-high and he set up flocks of rooks and crows and larks with a raucous crying as he walked along the track, dust kicking up from his boots. He came to a small stream and sat on the bank for a while, watching a family of ducks squabble over a clump of weed that was waving hypnotically in the sluggish current. Woodward was right; it wasn't much fun any more. He supposed none of it ever really had been.

Sitting outside a café back in the square he watched the activity around him over a glass of beer until he caught sight of Tozer, Chacksfield and Moss jumping out the back of a squadron tender and making for a bar. They seemed chummy enough once more and he assumed that yesterday's disagreement had been nothing more than a schoolboy spat. Leaving them to it, he caught up with the tender and arranged a lift back to the field.

Dinner in the mess struck him as a muted affair. Glancing to the head of the table he saw there was something rancorous in Strouden's demeanour and if he spoke at all it seemed to be to do no more than to give a curt answer to a manifestly unwanted question. After a while his unresponsiveness had the effect of spreading over the tables to other conversations like some suppressant gas and talk became subdued and sporadic. Miller, arriving late and suffering a cold stare from Strouden had taken the first chair available. It was a moment before he looked up and saw he was sitting opposite Parry.

'Hullo,' he said. 'I was hoping I might get the chance of a word with you.'

'Yes,' Parry said. 'Jack said you might.'

'Jack?'

'Sorry. Pilot-Sergeant Reynolds. I know we're not supposed to call each other by first names but he's a good man and I think it's all a bit stuffy, don't you?'

'Yes,' Miller said, 'but all the same I don't think you'd better let the CO hear you do it. Is it my imagination or is there a bit of an atmosphere this evening?'

Parry glanced warily along the table.

'The Old Man's not best pleased, to be honest, losing Garfield and Pollock like that.'

Miller felt his stomach turn over. It was an odd reaction. He had thought himself inured to losses and he hardly knew the pair. At that moment, though, it seemed to somehow underline the waste.

'I hadn't heard,' he said.

'On the noon patrol,' Parry told him. 'There was only Ja– I mean, Reynolds and me left in A Flight. And Parsons, of course, so the major made Parker flight commander and gave us Garfield and Pollock, too.'

'Who did Parsons go up with?'

'Tozer. He's been moved to A Flight as well.'

'Did you run into trouble?'

'Not at first. We were only supposed to be patrolling over our own forward trenches. I think the Old Man's a bit worried over the losses we've taken the past few days so we were supposed to just keep our eyes open and not engage unless we had to.'

'What happened?'

'We were patrolling more or less the length of the salient — from St-Eloi up to Bixschoote. We saw the Hun machines pretty much from the off but they didn't seem very interested in us.'

'What were they?'

'Three Halberstadts and an Eindecker. They just kept circling over Polygon Wood.'

'Spotting probably.'

'Well, that's what I thought though there wasn't any artillery fire that I could see. In fact, it was all pretty quiet except for the usual Archie.'

Parry went back to his dinner for a moment and Miller caught Strouden's eye. They held contact for a second or two but Miller couldn't tell if the major was looking at him or through him; his expression never changed.

'We were on our way back south again,' Parry resumed, 'when two of the Halberstads detached and began moving north towards Passchendaele. Parker signalled us to get some more height — we were at around eight thousand and I suppose he thought they might be trying to work their way around behind us and cut our retreat. Jack started climbing, following Parker, and I was still looking out for Hun guns.'

'And?' Miller asked when Parry paused again.

He gave a small sigh, a mixture of frustration and reluctance. 'You know what Tozer's like,' he finally said pushing his plate away as if he had suddenly lost his appetite. 'When I looked back he had turned and was making for the two Huns left over Polygon.'

'I suppose the two moving north turned back.'

'Yes,' Parry said. 'We didn't have any choice then. We couldn't just leave him, four against one, could we?'

'Of course not.'

'I mean,' Parry went on, 'it's the sort of thing we've been doing all the time. It's just...'

'That the CO asked you not to engage unless you had to.'

'Yes.'

'What happened to Garfield and Pollock?'

Parry sipped at some wine. 'I didn't really see, not how it ended. We were pretty busy trying to get on to a Halberstadt. I saw Tozer get one — at least he knocked it out of the fight — and Cliff says he saw the Eindecker on Garfield's tail. Pollock was on the rear Lewis. I suppose Garfield must have done something to try and shake the Eindecker off. Pollock fell out.'

Miller reached for his wine.

'I didn't see much else until it was over. We'd drifted east rather and Parker signalled us to break contact and make for the lines. When I looked around Garfield's machine wasn't there.'

'Did anyone see him?'

'No.'

'Was it windy?'

'I'd say!' Parry said emphatically. 'Wasn't much when we went up but it was blowing pretty hard at eight thousand. Perhaps he was forced down.'

'Yes.'

'I dare say the Hun will let us know if he was,' Parry said.

Miller returned to his dinner. He found it to be one of the more curious aspects of the war that they probably *would* soon know. A code had developed which, despite having done their best to kill each other in the air, required whatever was left on the ground afterwards be treated with respect. The remains of airmen lost over the lines were given a decent burial and news of this, as well as any personal effects would be dropped back over the lines under a truce by one of the opposing aircraft. It was also known for airmen captured by the German Flying Corps to be given a decent send-off in the opposing camp's mess before being driven off to captivity. He found it curious because he supposed the practice stemmed from the social class that produced most of the flyers. Not the least curious thing about it was that, since it was a class to which he did not belong, it meant that in this particular respect the Germans had more in common with Miller's comrades than he did himself.

If Garfield had been forced down it meant that he had at least survived. But captivity was still captivity and while the treatment he might expect was a magnanimity to be welcomed, it was also one that Miller very much doubted was extended to captured infantry. Another card to be played in his game, he supposed.

'The Old Man tore us off a strip at the debriefing,' Parry said. 'Hard lines on poor old Parker, I say. First real time up as a proper flight commander, too.'

'Tozer shouldn't have broken formation,' Miller said.

'Well yes, I agree, but you know what it's like. No one likes to sneak on a fellow.'

Miller was suddenly exasperated with their schoolboy conventions. 'Didn't *anyone* say anything?'

'Well, Jack did actually,' Parry said.

'Reynolds?'

'Yes. He told the CO what happened. He doesn't have to share a mess with Tozer, of course.'

'Good for him,' Miller said.

'But if looks could kill…' Parry said.

It struck Miller that Tozer was quite capable of killing without the aid of looks; his thoughtlessness was just as lethal.

Strouden got up and excused himself before pudding. The room fell silent as they watched him leave then slowly the conversation picked up to the usual levels.

'I wanted to ask you about Dunne,' Miller said to Parry. 'He was a friend of yours, wasn't he?'

'We trained together,' Parry said.

'I didn't know that.'

'Not that it gives you much idea what to expect,' Parry added.

'Foden told me he was also quite friendly with Heyward. Not many of the others were, were they?'

'I suppose not,' Parry said. 'Heyward could be a bit stand-offish.'

'But Dunne got on with him?'

'The thing was Bobby knew Heyward had edited his college magazine and was publishing a book of poetry.'

'And was Dunne interested in poetry?'

Parry took a breath and said, 'He'd been writing a book.' He stopped again and looked sharply at Miller. 'Look, can we get out of here? I suppose there's something I should have told you.'

17
Cirrostratus

Milky translucence - sun seen with halo - ceiling rising -
visibility fair.

The sun had set leaving a rosy glow on the faint trails of high stratus. The last
patrols were down and the sky was empty. Out beyond Ypres towards the front
the guns were killing the last hour of daylight — and no doubt a few unlucky
men — by throwing a handful of shells at some target or other. Closer to, on a
patch of grass beside the Bessonneau hangar some of the men were finishing a
game of football, idly kicking the ball to one another or sitting on the grass
smoking. Without the distant sound of the guns Miller thought it could almost
have been a perfect summer evening.

They had walked across the field away from the château as far as a sagging
farm gate and turned, leaned against its rotting wood and looked back over the
airfield. They lit cigarettes and listened for a moment to the faint voices of the
men and the muted guns carrying on the evening air.

'We knew you were coming,' Parry suddenly said. 'Well, not *you* but someone
– a staff officer, we thought.'

'Did Strouden tell you?'

'Jack told me, actually. You know what the men are like, they hear everything
first. One of Budgie's clerks, I suppose. But then, they all seemed to know in the
mess, too, without me having to tell them.'

'It wasn't supposed to be a secret,' Miller said. 'After all, it was suicide. It was
just a matter of finding out why he did it.'

'I can't help you there, I'm afraid,' Parry said.

'What was it you should have told me, then?'

Parry dropped his cigarette onto the grass and ground it under his boot. 'I'd
been through his hut. Heyward's, I mean.'

'It was you who searched the place.'

'Yes.'

'What were you looking for?'

'Look, I know I shouldn't have done it, or at least should have told you when
you arrived...' he looked down and began to fidget with his belt. 'The thing is,'
he said, 'I'm rather fond of Bobby Dunne's sister, Phyllida.'

He continued to fuss with his tunic and Miller waited until Parry could find
nothing else to distract him. Finally he took a deep breath as if he had made up
his mind about something.

'Bobby had always had a bit of a bent for English at school apparently,' he
said, 'essays... that sort of thing? Phyllida told me. You see, she had quite high
hopes for him.'

'In what way?'

'Oh, I don't know. Journalism? Literary criticism? I'm not sure. After the war, of course, when things got back to normal. To be honest, it's a bit over my head. I don't really know why Phyllida wastes her time with me.'

'Go on,' Miller prompted when Parry showed signs of dwelling on memories of Phyllida.

'Bobby was awfully keen on the idea. I don't know that I should be telling you this but he was always keeping notes and writing something or other — you know, for pieces he might do for the magazines, that sort of thing?'

'Yes?'

'Look, I know it's against regulations, but Bobby thought that was all a bit stuffy.' He began to hesitate again.

'This is just between you and me,' Miller assured him.

'Well,' Parry went on, 'I told you we trained together and Bobby was keeping a record of our training and of the men we met... everything about it really.'

'A diary, you mean?'

'Oh no. It was more than a diary. He was dramatising some of the things that happened, if you get my meaning, turning it into a book, I suppose. A sort of record through the eyes of a young and... well, inexperienced pilot. The hero was a pilot, you see, because he thought being an observer wasn't quite adventurous enough so he was always pestering the pilots on how you do *this* and what happens if you do *that*. I think he would have trained as a pilot later if he'd got the chance.'

'And this is what he used to talk to Heyward about?'

'About being a pilot?' Parry laughed. 'Lord, no. No, it was the *writing* he used to pester Heyward about. Style, I think. Bobby called it "impressionistic" whatever that meant.'

'Why Heyward?'

'As I said at dinner, Heyward had edited his college magazine and was having his poetry published and, well, frankly Bobby would pester anyone he thought he might learn something from.'

'What did Heyward think of it?'

'I don't really know. He always seemed keen enough to talk to Bobby. Apart from Foden he didn't really have any friends here and at least they had this common interest. A couple of weeks before he died Bobby told me Heyward had offered to show some of his stuff to a publisher in London Heyward knew. Bobby was pretty keen to start with although, towards the end, I think he was having doubts about whether Heyward knew quite as much as he liked to make out. Well no, perhaps not *that* exactly... Anyway, Heyward showed Bobby some of his poetry and Bobby told me — in confidence, naturally — that he thought it was pretty poor. Derivative, Bobby called it.'

Well, Miller thought, at least Dunne had had an eye for what was good. Or rather, what wasn't good.

'Anyway, poor old Bobby got himself killed and I wrote to Phyllida saying how awfully sorry I was and that Budgie would be sending on his personal effects. Then a few days later it dawned on me about his book and I wondered if

Budgie had it along with all Bobby's other things. So I asked him in a roundabout sort of way, what with the regulations being what they are, but he told me there had only been some loose papers, that was all.'

'So you thought Heyward might still have it.'

'Yes.'

'Did you ask him?'

'That's the odd thing,' Parry said. 'He denied Bobby had shown him the book at all. Well,' he amended, 'that's not quite true. After a moment or two he said he *did* remember Bobby giving him some "outline sketches" to look at, as he called them, but nothing he'd recognise as a book. He said he certainly hadn't sent anything to London on Bobby's behalf. He maintained that all he'd done was give Bobby some advice but that it really wasn't particularly good work at all.'

'He said that?'

'A bit callous, I thought, to say a thing like that. Bobby being killed in *his* machine, after all, and it being his fault. Not that I said *that* in so many words. I mean, it's not everyone who has the skill, is it? I'm not sure I'd make much of a pilot myself to tell the truth and poor Bobby could just as easily have been killed with someone else, like Tozer — '

Or me, Miller thought, thinking of Etherington.

' — who knows how to fly but just seems to...to — '

'Lack judgement,' Miller supplied for him.

'Yes, that's it. Judgement.'

'When did you have this conversation with Heyward? How long after Dunne was killed?'

'A few days, I suppose,' Parry said. 'No, it must have been longer. A week? It's difficult to keep track sometimes. Not long before he actually did it, anyway. Killed himself, I mean.'

'And after Heyward hanged himself you searched his hut?'

'It makes *me* sound a bit callous, doesn't it?' Parry said. 'I did ask Budgie if he had found anything of Bobby's among Heyward's things but he said there wasn't anything in particular he'd seen, so I knew he couldn't have it. Then, when I heard you were coming — or someone from Staff, rather — I thought I'd better take a look for myself. I thought it might have just been overlooked. Foden was on a few days leave and the hut was empty... After all, Phyllida should have it really — they were very close, you see — and I was worried that if I couldn't lay my hands on the thing someone else might just throw it out not knowing what it was. Or even that the censor might have got hold of the thing and there'd be a stink about it. Do you see? I know I *should* have told you but...' he trailed off.

'Did you know Heyward had been burning papers before he hanged himself? Miller asked.

Parry looked at him, startled. 'No, I didn't.' He frowned. 'I wonder why.'

'Perhaps he burnt it.'

'No, it wasn't Bobby's book. I found that.'

'*You* found it?' Miller looked at him, surprised.

'Yes. Yes, I did.'

171

'Where was it, as a matter of interest?'

'It was under the bottom drawer of the bureau. There was just enough room there for it between the drawer and the floor.'

'It was hidden, then?'

'Oh yes.'

'Were there *any* signs of burning on the papers?'

'No, not that I noticed.'

'You sent it to Dunne's sister, I suppose?'

'No, not yet,' Parry said. 'It's still in my hut.'

'Would you mind if I took a look at it before you send it to Phyllida?'

'No, of course not,' Parry said. He started to say something else then thought better of it.

'Go on,' Miller said. 'What were you going to say?'

'Nothing, really.'

'Please, go on.'

'It's just that.' he stopped again. 'Well, look, would you mind telling Budgie that you have something of mine? I mean, after Heyward, if — that is...'

'You mean, if I'm killed, you want to make sure you get it back,' Miller said.

'Sorry,' Parry said.

'That's all right,' Miller told him. 'Just so long as the thing's not jinxed.'

'Oh my lord!' Parry said. 'I hadn't thought of that.'

'You're a dull dog, Miller, and I've come to shake you up.'

He had been sitting on his bunk with his back propped by a pillow, reading *Tono Bungay* by the light of the hurricane lamp when the banging on the hut door had pulled him out of a reverie.

Doyle was standing on the threshold, his brogue thickening and his flushed face lit by the lamp as it hung from the cross-beam that had supported Heyward. It swung a little in the wind coming through the open door lending Doyle the impression that he was swaying backwards and forwards. He might have been for all Miller knew; the doctor was drunk and he was waving a bottle of cognac in front of him as if he knew it was the key that opened most locks.

'You're conspicuous by your absence in the mess and I've been charged as the medical officer of this squadron to determine if you're sound in body and mind.'

'Well,' Miller replied nonplussed as he stood aside to let Doyle pass. 'I'd say I was as physically fit as any man in the squadron.'

'And your mental health, man? What's your considered opinion on that?' He put the bottle of cognac on the washstand and pulled two glasses out of his pocket. He filled them to the brim; his hand wasn't shaking.

It was to be one of those conversations, Miller decided.

He asked, 'What level of sanity is required to be here?' Doyle passed him a glass and raised his own.

'Now that's a very pertinent question.' He swallowed half his cognac. 'Clearly your out-and-out lunatic is of no use in an operational squadron and it's my job, Miller my boy, to weed these poor unfortunates out and make sure they're reassigned.'

'Oh?'

'Quite so,' Doyle said. He sat heavily on the chair beside the washstand, his face suddenly looking quite manic in the lamplight as if it was personal experience that informed his perspective. 'Those displaying signs of insanity of an obviously temporary nature — that is,' he particularised by pointing his half-glass of cognac at Miller, 'those who given the right treatment, would in time regain full use of their mental faculties — these men are to be immediately transferred.' He emptied his glass. 'I believe it is an order now enshrined in King's Regulations,' he added as an aside. 'These men are to be immediately transferred to a regiment in the front line and accorded all the duties and responsibilities of a junior infantry officer.' Doyle refilled his glass. 'Given the casualty rates the treatment's regarded as just as good as permanent cure.'

It *was* one of those conversations. Miller brought his cognac to his mouth, rather pleased with himself that he didn't spill any.

'And what of those who are obviously completely insane?' he asked, following the unspoken prompt.

Doyle drank some more and shook his head as if that proved no problem at all.

'Immediate promotion to the high command,' he said, 'and a black mark against the postings officer who so miserably missed the man's potential.'

Miller returned to his bunk and sat with his back propped against the pillow.

'And where in your medical opinion does that leave me?'

Doyle beamed at him. 'You, my dear Miller, I'm afraid are to stay on active duty but to remain under suspicion of not participating fully in the social activities expected of a Royal Flying Corps officer.'

'Ah,' Miller said, understanding.

'When, for instance,' Doyle asked, 'was the last time you threw a lamb cutlet across the dining table at the man opposite you? And I might also point out,' he added, 'that it has not gone unnoticed that on the last occasion a scrum was formed you, Captain Miller, did not immediately take up the position of tight-head prop for which your build has so obviously fitted you. Rather you were seen to hover around the position of fly-half, intent no doubt to hog the glory intended for younger — and I might add — more slender boys than yourself.'

'There,' Miller observed, 'I'm afraid you have grasped the nub of the matter.'

Doyle eyed him suspiciously. 'If you are intimating that your age entitles you to a position of greater responsibility during these sporting encounters and are angling for a recommendation from myself, I might remind you that the requirements of that job stipulate a perpetually fixed and paternal grin and a temperament for tolerance towards pranks and the shenanigans of schoolboys...' he waved an extravagant hand in the air, '...the glazed eyes are an optional extra.' He drank a little more cognac and added, 'I would suggest you study Captain Budge if you are serious in taking instruction in these matters.'

'And there I was,' Miller said, 'believing I'd served my apprenticeship.'

'Oh, indeed you have,' Doyle replied as if he had no intention of giving Miller an argument. He leaned back in the chair and stretched out his legs, crossing them. He stroked his moustache with the thumb and forefinger of his right hand and regarded Miller with what appeared to be some interest. 'In fact, Captain Miller, on that very point I believe I have a confession to make.'

'In that case perhaps you would have done better to take your brandy to the chaplain's hut,' Miller suggested.

'Padre,' Doyle corrected, 'and papist though he is, it might not be politically expedient to bare one's soul to a man who carries the King's Commission whatever his religious persuasion.'

'And are you sure it is politically expedient that I should hear your confession?'

Doyle shrugged and Miller was aware that the doctor seemed markedly more sober at that moment — despite two further drinks — than he had when he entered the hut.

'It's a small confession and I only give it now since it appears that I have been labouring under a misapprehension.'

'Go ahead, then.'

'I have an acquaintance in St Omer,' Doyle said, 'who — when he finds it opportune — has access to the RFC personnel records. He is by nature one of God's clerks and his facility with filing systems is something to wonder at.'

'And you asked your acquaintance to look at my record.'

Doyle sipped at his cognac and raised a finger. 'You go to the heart of the matter.'

'I would have thought,' Miller hazarded, 'that the King's Regulations would have something to say on that matter, too.'

'Oh, I don't doubt it,' Doyle agreed. 'They're a wondrous set of regulations and no doubt have a paragraph to cover every eventuality.'

Miller picked up the packet of cigarettes from the table beside the bunk and offered them to Doyle. The medical officer shook his head.

'I firmly believe they're bad for the health,' he said as Miller lit one.

'It's a small consideration, I would have thought,' Miller observed, exhaling smoke, 'when most days you're apt to meet a man with a machine gun intent on killing you.'

'You're not wrong there, captain,' Doyle replied narrowing his eyes, 'but being a man inclined to a little wager I'd be willing to stake a pound that in ten years' time — assuming you're still alive, of course — that you'll not be looking down the barrel of a machine gun but that you will still be smoking.'

'Assure me that I *will* still be alive in ten years,' Miller offered, 'and five pounds says this will be my last smoke.'

Doyle smiled. 'Ah, but those odds are a little long for my liking. Half a sovereign each way would be my limit.'

'I'm inclined to take your money,' Miller told him. 'But you haven't yet explained why you asked your acquaintance to look at my file.'

'Indeed I have not,' Doyle admitted, 'but you're no doubt aware how we Irish like to talk.'

'And I guess there *you've* gone to the heart of the matter.'

Doyle affected a look of surprise.

'It's a detective you are,' he said with admiration.

'A Pinkerton,' Miller admitted, 'and only briefly at that.'

'Ah well, it's in the file. But then, isn't that what we're jabberin' about?'

'I was trying to add a little glamour to my RFC application,' Miller confessed. 'I'm living to regret it.'

'At least you're living,' Doyle said, 'but now, you should have known it's no glamour to have been a Pink.'

'We weren't all strike-breakers and scabs,' Miller said.

'Try telling that to the Irish immigrants.'

'Well, if that's what's worrying you,' Miller said, 'I wasn't even alive when McParland infiltrated the Molly Maguires.'

'Sure I know nothing about it beyond that travesty, *The Valley Of Fear*. And before you ask, I'll not admit to a family connection to Conan-Doyle.'

'Poetic licence,' Miller said.

'There was precious little poetry about *that* meretricious pot-boiler.'

'So what *was* your interest?' Miller asked pointedly. 'Or was it literary criticism you came to talk about?'

Doyle nodded towards *Tono Bungay* on the bunk. 'I could give you the benefit of my opinion of Mr H.G. Wells if you wanted,' he offered, then sighed deeply. 'But these are parlous times for an Irishman and it's another matter entirely.' He raised his eyebrows in what Miller supposed he was meant to recognise as a gesture of frankness. 'I'm thinkin' you're aware — unless you are a complete ignoramus — of the rising in Dublin last Easter.'

'I read the accounts when I could get hold of the newspapers,' Miller said.

'Not what one might describe as an objective opinion.'

'How objective can they be?' Miller asked, 'when men using German arms rise against a government in the middle of a war?'

Doyle looked pained. 'I'm not trying to defend their actions, Miller. It was a nonsensical thing to do and those that weren't killed at the time will no doubt pay sooner or later with their lives. Public opinion, by all accounts, thought it a damn-fool thing to try. But I know the Irish and if they do hang them, by the time a year's out the poets will have wrapped the business up in some fine flowery phrases and we'll all be looking back on it through misty eyes and then, with the benefit of a drink or two, it's all kinds of trouble we'll be looking at.'

'I dare say you're right,' Miller said. 'But what's it to do with me?'

Doyle stood up, reached for the bottle on the washstand and poured himself another glass of cognac. He offered the bottle to Miller.

'I'm on the dawn patrol,' he said, shaking his head.

Doyle remained on his feet. He turned around and leaned back against the scrubbed pine top of the stand.

'I've never tried to hide my sympathies as far as Irish independence goes. Not that I've ever been one to think that everything in the shape of an Englishman is

175

necessarily a hound from hell, but we've been damned badly served over the years and the Lord knows we couldn't make a bigger mess of things if we'd been left to muddle through by ourselves. I'm a patriot but I'm no damn rebel. I'm not saying that if I wasn't at home things might have been different — we're a romantic lot of tomfools — but while I'm wearing this uniform I stand by my oath to the King and I'll do my best to patch up every damn Englishman, Irishman, Indian or Australian they put in front of me. I'll even help an American and I can't say fairer than that.'

'Has anyone suggested differently?'

'To me personally? No,' Doyle admitted. 'But there have been questions asked about the loyalty of some Irish-born men. And not just those of the Roman Catholic persuasion. That damn fool Casement has thrown suspicion on men whatever their faith.'

'As bad as that?' Miller said. 'Next you'll be telling me they're regarded as being almost as suspect as a man who didn't go to a public school.'

'There,' Doyle replied sarcastically, 'and didn't I just know you'd be a man who would empathise.'

'Well,' Miller asked, wondering if his first assessment of the doctor's drunkenness had been accurate at all. 'What's it got to do with me?'

Doyle didn't answer for a moment. Then he said, 'When I heard you were coming here I wondered if you hadn't been sent to....' He avoided Miller's eyes. 'I was only takin' precautions, damn it. And when this acquaintance of mine told me what was in your file — you having been a Pink and all — well, I naturally thought...' He didn't finish.

'You thought I'd come to spy on you,' Miller said.

'Well, the damned man had hanged himself,' Doyle said. 'Where's the mystery in that?'

'You didn't know that Heyward's mother supposedly has Kitchener's ear?'

Doyle stared at him in surprise. 'Well if it's Kitchener,' he laughed, 'from what I hear his ear's about all she'll ever get.' He looked down at Miller who hadn't moved from the bed. 'Well,' he said, 'I just wanted to clear that up.'

'There's nothing more to be said on the subject as far as I'm concerned,' Miller told him.

'Then you'll be wanting to get some sleep if you're up before dawn.' He tossed off the remaining cognac in his glass and slipped it into his pocket. 'I'll leave you the bottle. If you're flying that Strutter of yours, I know what those damned oil fumes can do to a man's stomach.'

Miller watched him leave and in the ensuing silence listened to the wind as it crossed the field and soughed through the huts and hangars. He emptied his glass then reached for his water bottle and took a long pull to counteract the brandy.

It was all so much simpler in the air. It was as if, in that moment of breaking contact with the ground, all the politics — the arguments and opinions, the prejudices and the grudges — were left behind. Up there the gravity-bound beasts that, when you were down, hounded you constantly, nipping at your heels and chewing at your life with their jealousies and their demands, could no longer reach you. Up there, unrestrained, they couldn't get at you at all. Earthbound, all they could do was wait for you to return.

Miller turned the concepts over in his head for a while and scribbled some notes.

The sound of engines, he had come to believe, was the sound of reassurance. He found it deeply comforting, a sound he could go to sleep to and one to which he was happy to wake. He could hear it now and he felt it bathed him in warmth, almost a sense of *liquid* security. It was as if they had always been there, muted, but always in the background, a part of his semi-conscious life.

He was not exactly aware of how long he had been listening to the engines. In fact, now he had begun to think of it, he had only really begun to notice them as a distinct and discrete entity when the volume of sound grew to such a pitch that it began to vibrate his bunk.

He opened his eyes.

There was no light. He could see nothing.

He was aware that he was lying in his bunk and that the hut was filled with sound. His heart began hammering in his chest and he realised with a start that he was not breathing. Then, as he opened his mouth to gulp air, a high-pitched whine that had been growing out of the noise of the engines began to overlay it and some rational part of his brain announced that he was not listening to the Beardmore engines of FEs but to the sound of completely alien engines.

The whine built to a scream and ended abruptly in a blast that shook the hut, threw him out of his bunk and got him breathing again all at the same instant.

He scrambled to his feet, hitting his head on the small table next to the bunk. Something tumbled off it and fell heavily on his foot. He took a few paces forward and crashed into the washstand. That gave him his bearings. A moment later he was standing outside the door.

Noise filled the world. Miller staggered back under its impact. Explosions were bursting all around him and he did not know which way to run. A fire was burning out beyond the Bessonneau, throwing the hangar into giant relief. An engine screamed overhead and he ducked without thinking. A span of wings flashed by, a hundred feet, perhaps lower. For some nonsensical reason he tried to identify the make of machine as if that might alter the fact that it was trying to kill him. Something got his legs moving, pumping, and his head, like a poor second in a foot race, told him to make for one of the gun emplacements at the edge of the field. He became aware of shadows around him, ghostly emanations that appeared and disappeared in an instant. His bare feet slipped on the dewy grass and, scrabbling up again, he realised he was dressed only in his nightshirt.

Behind him the explosions came quicker. He snatched a look over his shoulder and saw a second fire illuminating the château. The moon had risen, gibbous but bright enough to throw a bloodless luminescence over the airfield. Above it dark Hun machines were circling like bats in a gothic dream.

He looked back just in time to collide with another running figure. They tumbled into a heap on the grass and the other man came up cursing him.

'Watch where you're fucking going, man!'

He started running again and Miller saw it was Gracey, the armaments officer. He followed as the shadow of the sandbagged gun emplacement loomed up and scrambled into the dugout behind Gracey.

'Miller,' Gracey said as he fell at the man's feet. 'Sorry, didn't recognise you. Get on the Vickers. They're too low for anything bigger.'

Gracey had jumped behind the machine-gun and had already elevated the snout. Miller squatted beside him with his hands on the ammunition belt. A second later the Vickers began to shake, deafening him. It started to suck in the belt and he fed it through his fingers, keeping it straight to prevent a jam.

Between bursts Miller heard another gun start up across the field before a series of explosions around the machine sheds drowned everything else out. Light blinded him for a second then he lost his balance as Gracey swung the Vickers around to track a Hun machine as it crossed in front of the emplacement. It climbed as he raked its length, engine screaming, then suddenly canted over so that Miller saw the top wing. A second later a ball of flame erupted in the sky, belching fire and smoke for a moment before it tumbled to the ground, flattening on impact into a twist of burning wreckage.

'Jesus!' Miller said in astonishment. 'You got it.'

'I rather think they collided,' Gracey said.

The explosions stopped and the sound of the Hun machines began to fade. In their place came the rumble of the fire truck and the shouts of men. Miller, squatting on his heels sat down, lost his balance again and landed on his back. He lay there, not bothering to get up.

'At night?' he heard Gracey say. 'At night?'

18

At dawn the extent of the damage was clear. By good luck — or bad aim — they had missed the big Bessonneau; they had hit one of the smaller hangars, though, and destroyed two FEs. Worse, one of their first bombs had penetrated the roof of a billet and killed four aircraftsmen, Smith, among them. Half a dozen others had been injured, two seriously although the rest with nothing worse than cuts and bruises. Miller, walking around once it was light enough to see, decided it was not as bad as it looked.

He had gone back to his hut and dressed as soon as he was sure the Hun had gone and saw, once he lit a hurricane lamp, that it had been Wells's *Tono Bungay* that had dropped on his foot, bruising a toe. That was the extent of *his* injuries. The hut was a mess but that was mostly his own doing, blundering around in the dark. Once dressed and outside again, carrying the lamp for light, he did what he could to help with the injured men. Later, as soon as the dead and injured were loaded onto a lorry and on their way to a hospital, he checked on his Strutter and the FE. Neither had sustained any damage: the FE was ready to fly; the Strutter needed a little more work following the engine fire to get it fit for operations.

Out on the field he found a few bomb craters but by first light teams were already filling and levelling them and promising it would be back to normal by mid-morning. By then, he thought, the Hun would have had their breakfast and would be catching up on their sleep.

They had hit them at 3.30am when the moon was high and bright enough to give sufficient light to take off. A fair south-westerly had been blowing by then — he had seen the beginnings of it when Doyle had swayed in the doorway of his hut — and it would have helped speed them on their way home after giving the airfield a pasting. If it had been any stronger they might not have come at all. As it was, they had probably got back just as dawn was giving enough light to see to land. *They* had not managed to get anything up, of course. Nothing had been ready or in place and if they had tried the machine would probably have been destroyed trying to get off the ground; much safer simply to run for cover. They *had* managed to return some fire — from two of the gun emplacements and some odd ground-fire from a variety of weapons: Woodward had stripped a Lewis gun off an FE and had emptied two drums into the sky. He had not claimed to have hit anything, nor had anyone else, but Miller had wanted Gracey credited with the two Huns that had come down.

'Just luck,' Gracey had said. 'Doubt if I hit anything vital. The chap must have taken his eye off the ball.'

Budge had been keen, though. He said it would look good in the squadron records and be a bit of a boost for morale. Gracey conceded the point provided Miller shared the kill, so they had agreed on one each.

The wreckage of the Hun machines had fallen in front of the château by the road and the fire had more or less burned itself out by the time they were able to pay it much attention. There wasn't a lot left of the machines but what there was identified them as DFWs.

Three charred corpses still sat in the wreckage; a fourth lay unburned fifty yards away, telling the story of a man who had survived the collision but had preferred to jump rather than burn. Judging from the height Miller had seen them collide, he guessed that if the impact had not killed the other three they had probably died when they hit the ground and doubted that they had suffered much from the flames.

Strouden arranged a burial detail and that afternoon they stripped anything personal from the bodies that might have identified them then interred their corpses. The chaplain performed a short service and they had just finished singing the last hymn as the sound of an engine drifted out of the sky and over the field. It was another Aviatik flying a white pennant of truce tied to its struts and they all watched as it circled the field slowly — taking stock of the damage, Miller supposed — then dived low over them, waggling its wings as it went. The be-goggled observer had leaned out of the machine, given them a wave then dropped a bundle a few yards from them. The Aviatik circled again, climbed and headed for their lines.

Budge walked over to the bundle and opened it. It was an RFC flying coat and held the papers and a few odds and ends belonging to Garfield and Pollock. There was a note — in English — to say where they had been buried. Pollock's papers, Miller saw, were smeared with blood; given the height from which he had fallen he supposed that he had been a bit of a mess. He watched as Budge carefully re-wrapped the coat and carried it back towards the château. Miller turned to the others still standing by the graveside looking for Tozer. He wasn't there.

Strouden had cancelled the dawn patrol, bumping all the flights so that Miller went up at noon instead of dawn. B Flight was to take the evening patrol and A Flight dawn the next day. Two new replacements had turned up on the mid-morning tender while they were still clearing up and neither Strouden nor Budge had had much time to attend to them. They had hung around for a couple of hours looking bemused and generally getting in the way until it was time for the noon patrol. Denham and Chacksfield's machine had been one of the two destroyed and, with Parker and Cliff now leading A Flight, it left C Flight further under-strength. Strouden told Miller to lead the flight, find the two new replacements a machine and stay out of trouble. Miller relayed the message about finding an FE to Warrant Officer Mackinnon and went looking for the new men.

Taylor, the pilot, was stocky, a smaller version of Strouden, as if wartime shortages had necessitated economies. Proctor, his observer, was oddly porcine with thin, lank blond hair that kept falling in his eyes. There wasn't time to get it cut so Miller told them to get dressed and meet him on the field.

As he walked out onto the field, he took a deep breath and turned his face to the wind, the way the machines were pointing. It was no stronger but that was deceptive. It tended to vary at different altitudes.

Parsons, who at the moment seemed to have to play the rôle of spare observer, was standing by Miller's FE. Moss was waiting by his own machine, clutching his maps, with Trueman already in the nacelle making sure his forward Lewis was swinging freely. Mackinnon stood by the spare machine. Its wings, Miller noticed, were beginning to resemble a patchwork quilt where the fabric had been repaired so many times.

'Whose is that?' Miller asked.

'Mr Tozer's, sir,' Mackinnon said. 'He's moved to A Flight and not due up till tomorrow morning so I thought it would be all right.'

'Didn't he mind?'

'Couldn't find him to ask,' Mackinnon said.

Miller certainly didn't mind; Tozer's sensibilities didn't rate particularly high on his scale of concerns.

'Is it in good order?' he asked.

'Better than it looks, sir.'

They stood waiting a few minutes for Taylor and Proctor while the fitters and riggers walked around the machines giving them a final check. When the replacements arrived they looked somehow lost under the flying coats and helmets.

'You haven't flown an FE before, I suppose,' he asked Taylor.

'First one I've seen, sir.'

'Right. Get up in the cockpit then and I'll show you the ropes. Proctor, go over there where Mr Trueman is and he'll show you the two Lewis guns.'

'I've already fired a Lewis,' Proctor said.

'The Huns better watch out then,' Moss observed.

'It's just a normal patrol,' Miller said to them. 'We'll fly up and down the lines, recce their rear areas and come home. Got that? We're not looking for a fight today.'

'What if we see Huns?' Taylor asked.

'We'll wave at them and give them a wide berth,' Miller said. 'We lost two machines this morning and we're short-handed so all we'll be doing is showing our faces, got that?'

'Yes sir,' Proctor and Taylor chorused.

Miller spent the next few minutes telling Taylor what to expect from an FE then said, 'Just try to get her off the ground in one piece. We'll worry about getting down again when the time comes. Just remember the golden rule: if you stall on take-off try and put her down in front of you. Never, *never* attempt to turn back to the field. You won't have the height or the speed for a turn. You'll end up going in nose down. Got that?'

'Yes sir.'

'Good,' Miller said. 'Let's get up then shall we, gentlemen?'

Climbing through the low, dough-like piles of cumulus Miller thought about

Tozer and how the man would be better off in one of the new fighter squadrons they were forming now — or if not there, at least in a rôle like Gregory's with his DH2. He was thinking about Tozer because he was watching the man's machine, hoping that Taylor would get it into the air in one piece and at the same time glad that Tozer was not flying it that morning. All he wanted to do was attack Hun machines whenever he saw them. That made him either brave or stupid.

They all wanted to do their bit, do their duty, do whatever they were there for — call it what you like — but some men he had met wanted to take it further than that. According to Strouden the newspapers had begun writing about pilots at home — Knights of the Air and rubbish like that — and perhaps men like Tozer craved the fame. It wasn't something Miller could understand. Perhaps it was merely a desire to kill Germans. After all, he knew war gave opportunities to men who, in civilian life, might otherwise end their days dangling from a hangman's noose. For most men their more ignoble desires would never surface, but war gratified the baser cravings of humanity and unfortunately also gave it a respectable sheen of heroism.

He had met a few men like that during his time with the Pinkertons, and had found that there were as many of them working for the agency as there were being pursued by it. Maybe that was what Tozer required — an outlet for a tendency towards homicide. God knows, the war gave men like that plenty of scope.

Up past the scattered piles of cloud, somewhere near the FE's ceiling, a thicker layer of stratocumulus obscured the sun and, away to the north, hazed the horizon into a mist. Miller didn't need to climb that high and at eight thousand feet turned north towards Bixschoote, keeping Pilckem to his east. Here the Hun line regained its roughly northwest orientation after the bulge of the Ypres salient and continued its move through western Belgium towards the channel coast. Below, around Dixmude, the flooded Yser reflected the dull sky in mud-brown tones like the heavy varnish on a Flemish canvas. Beyond, towards the coast, he could make out the specks of half a dozen machines hanging in the sky without movement. Closer, and at a comparable height to their own, a pair of Rumplers patrolled the sky between Passchendaele and Langemarck.

He glanced back at Taylor's FE and saw Proctor in the front nacelle gesturing vigorously at the Rumplers. Miller nodded with an exaggerated movement of his head and waved his gloved hand backwards and forwards along the length of the Hun trenches. Moss, on his left, had turned towards him and although he could not see much beyond the goggles, Miller knew he was grinning. He flew on towards Oostvleteren. After a few minutes the Rumplers moved east and dropped back far behind their own lines.

He kept the flight up for a couple of hours patrolling the line. A few puffs of dirty Archie discoloured the sky each time they passed the batteries around Bixschoote but he was pleased to see that it did not overly disconcert the new boys. Parsons, in the nacelle in front of him, marked his map with anything he saw of note while Moss, trailing behind like a bored schoolboy on a nature ramble, darted through the air this way and that as if chasing gnats. As the cloud began to thicken and the ceiling dropped to ten thousand feet, Miller took one last turn and brought them back over Poperinghe towards the airfield.

Coming down first, he had time to jump out of the cockpit and watch Taylor cut his engine for the glide in. He was too high as he approached the field but Miller thought he would be all right as long as he realised that he had plenty of field to work with. But he had only arrived that morning and didn't know and tried to come in too steeply. The wheels hit hard and it passed through Miller's head that Proctor must have been holding on to something with his little piggy hands or he would have been bounced out of the nacelle. Something gave, though, for although the wheels ran for a few more yards a supporting strut suddenly snapped and the FE slewed around and dipped nose-down. The tail came up but she balanced without somersaulting although Proctor tumbled out in a tangle, springing to his feet an instant later like an ungainly gymnast.

Sergeant Greene and the other men ran over and by the time Miller had arrived both Taylor and Proctor were on their feet, bloodless as ghosts but otherwise unhurt.

'A little too high,' Miller said, 'but not bad for the first time.'

'Thank you, sir,' Taylor croaked but he didn't look as if he believed it.

'Get yourselves a cup of tea. We'll see to this.'

They walked off unsteadily as Greene looked over the machine.

'Could be worse, sir,' he said to Miller. 'We'll have her fixed for Mr Tozer in the morning, no problem. He won't even know she's been up.'

There wasn't a lot to report. Parsons and Trueman had both made some observations but they didn't amount to much. Taylor looked desolated by the result of his landing and tried to evade eye contact with anyone. Miller doubted that Strouden noticed; the CO wasn't making much eye contact with anyone either. He looked more haggard than usual. His skin had lost its colour and appeared to hang flaccidly as if it had given up its grip on his skull. His eyes, retreating back into their sockets, looked like those of an animal peeping warily out of a cave.

Miller didn't think Strouden had gone to bed the previous night, never mind slept. He had first noticed him slightly after four that morning, not long after the Huns had dropped their last bomb and flown off home for their breakfast. Whereas everyone else had been running around in various stages of undress having pulled on whatever was to hand, Strouden had been fully dressed: uniform, belts, buckles and boots. He hadn't had his cap with him or his swagger stick, granted, and his tie had been loosened, as if that was the one concession to unpreparedness he had allowed himself to make while being bombed by the enemy in the middle of the night — but that aside he was much as one would have expected to find him behind the desk in his office.

'Miller,' he said suddenly.

Miller realised he had been staring at Strouden while everyone else had been getting to their feet and leaving the room.

'Sorry, sir,' he began, 'I was — '

'The new men...?'

'Taylor and Proctor.'

'Any good?'

'Taylor made a hash of his landing and broke the undercarriage but apart from that...' he finished with a shrug, adding, 'Sergeant Greene says he can get the machine back in the air for the morning.'

'Are you fit?'

'Sir?'

'To go up again?'

'If you want me to, of course. My Strutter still needs some work but the FE's ready to go. Has something come up?'

Strouden began patting his pockets.

'Care to have one of mine?'

Miller took his cigarettes out, gave one to Strouden and lit it. He lit another for himself.

Strouden sat down and nodded Miller into a chair.

'Brigade's been complaining about a Hun sausage,' he said, drawing on the cigarette. 'They've been spotting our artillery south of Ypres and have been pretty damned accurate. Brigade want it taken down.'

'I've never liked sausages,' Miller said.

'One of the other squadrons saw it over the eastern edge of Sanctuary Wood. They took a crack at it and lost two machines.'

'They're never easy.'

'Quite.'

'So now it's our turn.'

'I went over those photographs we took the other day with Chatterton and Watson and I think we spotted it. Maxwell got on to Brigade and they agree. The swine think it's hidden but we think we've got a pretty good fix.'

Miller was momentarily taken aback, not sure whether Strouden was applying his epithet to Brigade or to the Hun, but he didn't elaborate so Miller let it pass.

'We're giving it priority.'

Miller sucked on his cigarette. Observation balloons were never an easy target. He had had his share of them in the past and would not have been sorry if he never saw another. The artillery spotters were suspended in baskets beneath the balloons while it was let up to a sufficient height to give them a view behind the lines. They were big enough and cumbersome enough that the neophytes always thought they were an easy target. But at the first sign of aircraft, the Hun would haul the things down or, if they were not quick enough, the spotters would jump out of the basket with parachutes. Ideally, of course, you wanted to kill the men, too; balloons could be replaced whereas experienced spotters were a scarce commodity. Good ones could call in artillery with pin-point accuracy in no time at all as it was easier from a stationary platform; spotting from a moving aircraft always involved relative positions. But the fact that they were stationary did not make them easy to hit. The Huns could get the things up and down in a matter of minutes and, on top of that, they were generally protected by plenty of anti-aircraft guns. It was also usual to have a formation of Hun machines on hand when the balloon was up. All in all, it was never one of Miller's targets of choice.

'The gunners want first crack,' Strouden was saying. 'You know what they're like. They think they can flatten anything given the range.'

'Not if they're well dug in,' Miller said.

'You don't have to tell me that. But you can't argue with them and some of those jokers at Brigade still regard aircraft as little more than toys.'

'I'd have thought we'd proved our worth by now.'

'Of course we have,' Strouden insisted, beginning to puff and colour. 'But we're not the ones the Whitehall Warriors listen to, are we?'

Knowing the signs — and before Strouden had the chance to expound on all those high-ranking men in uniform in London who never got close enough to the front to even mistake the sound of guns for thunder — Miller said quickly, 'So, they want us to spot for them, I suppose.'

'Yes,' Strouden said succinctly, as if disgruntled by having been pre-empted. 'And being a small target we'll need to get close. Chatterton will lead. Gregory will be up with you in his DH2 to provide cover.' He looked inquiringly at Miller. 'You haven't met York and Hunt, I suppose?'

'No, sir.'

'They came in while you were up. Brought a new machine with them from the Aircraft Park. I'm told we're to expect two more tomorrow.'

'We could do with them.'

'They've been home doing a stint of training. Both good men so they'll be up with you.'

'It sounds as if it could be a tough show,' Miller said. 'Don't you think they might be a bit rusty?'

Strouden looked affronted. 'They're both experienced. I can't feather-bed men, you know.'

'No, sir.'

He looked at Miller grimly. 'And it's worth keeping in mind that if the gunners don't get the job done we'll have to go back and take the thing down ourselves. Boyes is back, by the way,' he added, 'so you can take him with you in the front seat.'

'Doesn't he fly with Mr Tozer? Or are you pairing him with Parsons now he's in A Flight?' Hardly good news for Parsons, he thought.

Strouden's face twitched as if he had suffered a stab of pain. 'What? No, I decided to stand him down after yesterday.'

Miller reflected that that left little distinction between punishment and feather-bedding.

He said, 'You spoke to him about yesterday, then? Garfield and Pollock...'

When Strouden didn't respond, Miller went on, 'If I'm speaking out of turn...'

'What's that?' Strouden said.

'Well, it's just that it... well, it seems to me that he'd be better suited in a scout. He's headstrong,' Miller said. 'Single-minded, if you like. It's not that he's a bad pilot.'

'No,' Strouden echoed. 'Not a bad pilot.'

'I've heard they're forming new fighter squadrons. All scouts... BE2s and Sopwiths. It might suit Tozer's talents better.'

Strouden stared at the end of his cigarette and then at Miller. 'I tried to get him a DH2, you know. Wing wouldn't hear of it. Hadn't served the time, you see. Would have to have been put in ahead of other chaps... wouldn't hear of it.' He exhaled noisily and took another deep breath. 'Well, there it is and we'll just have to make the best of it.'

'The sausage,' Miller said. 'If the artillery can't get the job done and we have to go back...' he hesitated, knowing he was going to regret the suggestion, '... why not let him take a crack in my Strutter? I can always fly the FE.'

He wouldn't have put it past Tozer to go and wreck the thing but, after all, it wasn't as if they'd refuse to give Miller another machine if he did.

Strouden peered at him. 'That's very decent of you, Miller,' he said. 'I'll give it some thought. You know, I did wonder when Maxwell sent you here... Well,' he finished, 'that's decent of you.'

Below, the green fields and hills of the west gave way sharply to a landscape of pitted greyness, like a pox that had crept out of the east, and spread its infection over the land. He could trace the lines of trenches amid the craters that, from his height, looked little more than scratches paralleling some, converging on others as if, under an overseeing eye, a hand had scribbled a nonsensical doodle across the country. Darker blotches, sometimes marked by the few remaining trees, indicated artillery emplacements and, back from them like traces that kept everything in harness, lines leading to somewhere in the rear where that mystical controlling hand and eye dictated all the madness beneath.

Below him, as if they were birds riding thermals, the other machines described circles as they inched up towards him. Chatterton with MacMaster, Griffith and Watson... A minute or two later they had been joined by the two men who had arrived while Miller had been on the noon patrol. Lieutenants York and Hunt had been in England instructing for the past few months. He had met them briefly over lunch and found they looked oddly similar, both above average height with long-limbs that somehow appeared disjointed, giving the two the air of badly operated marionettes. His height had made Hunt, the taller of the two, develop a slight hunch as if reluctant to tower over his fellows and it gave his gait something of an ambling, simian aspect not ameliorated by the fact that, since his arrival, he had not found the time to shave. The pilot, York, on the other hand was quite startling. Blue-eyed with a tanned, flawless complexion he possessed the sort of looks that Miller thought would not have been out of place on a recruitment poster, the kind with his flying helmet unbuckled and his blue eyes fixed on some distant future — the epitome of indomitable youth.

He glanced above him to where Gregory's DH2 had already got its height and Royston and White, the sergeant-observer, had almost climbed to join him. Relative to them, Miller found himself drifting towards the German lines. The wind was stronger than it had been on the ground and he banked slowly and turned his circling climb into an ellipse to maintain his position. The three machines below had grown into distinct shapes of wing and strut and tail-plane, and he could see Chatterton and MacMaster in the nearest clearly, the top of their heads smoothed and rounded by their flying helmets. Back on the ground to the east of Poperinghe, he made out two centipede columns of men slogging up clouds of dust as they marched towards the front.

He was unsure what to make of his conversation with Strouden. It made him remember what Maxwell had said about 'taking a look at him'. He hadn't understood it at the time and he didn't understand it now but the remark had lodged in his head and wouldn't go away.

York, he saw, had caught up with Chatterton and MacMaster. He wondered how different he found it now after a few months back in England instructing. You weren't supposed to notice changes if you lived through them — like watching people age — but Miller often felt as if he were sufficiently detached to note even the smallest of changes so that he found constant reminders of how things had been once and now were no longer. What he had said to Strouden about scout squadrons, for instance, had been inevitable, but that was not how it had seemed at the start; the sense of inevitability had only come *with* the change. Now there were machines designed for no other purpose than to shoot down other machines in an offensive capacity and he couldn't help thinking that that was murder. The thought made him laugh out loud and, although the wind blowing into his face and the roar of the Beardmore behind him drowned the sound, Boyes still turned in the nacelle in front of him to look at Miller questioningly. Miller shook his head and the observer turned back.

Miller's line of thought was undistracted. It was ridiculous. After all, what was any of it if not murder? He looked down over the side. *That* had always been one of the problems — the detachment that altitude gave to what they were doing. On the ground it was obviously murder. He supposed that was why he was plagued by that damned voice in his head nagging about taking the easy option up here, despite the evidence of the casualties they took. It was no easy option, he felt like shouting, though, and through the noise of the engine he knew he'd still hear the reply:

Tell that to the poor bastards stuck down there in the mud.

Regardless of that, he could not escape the sense of detachment. It was a cliché to believe that, above it all, he had a god's eye view, but clichés, he supposed, began with truth. Despite himself he could not help but regard the activity on the ground as something apart from life, as nothing more than the scurryings around a disturbed ant's nest. And the higher one went, the less apparent could any pattern to it all be discerned. Perhaps politics and power were thin-lunged creatures that couldn't survive in the rarefied atmosphere above ten thousand feet.

Chatterton was suddenly beside him, his machine rising and falling on the air as he made a signal gesturing east beyond Ypres and the Hun front line. Miller looked out across the lines before nodding.

A high formation at around sixteen thousand feet lay off to the north, BE2s from their shape, moving east along the coast towards Dunkerque. A few thousand feet below them, slightly in advance but moving in the same direction, was another formation, heavier Avros most likely carrying bombs for the docks. Below them was the coast, indistinct in the late afternoon haze. Further still, a hinted-at reflection in silver and grey, was the Channel.

Chatterton slid back out of his line of vision and MacMaster, in the front of the nacelle, turned his goggled eyes in Miller's direction and waved. Boyes in front of him waved back then looked over his shoulder to where York and Hunt had dropped into formation behind. A little below them now were Royston and White. Miller climbed to allow Chatterton to edge ahead then took position above and to the left of Chatterton's wing as they crossed the German lines and moved south.

19

Ypres slid behind them, a grey ruined stain surrounded by haphazardly churned countryside. Black smudges began to appear like little charcoal clouds that made small plosive sounds even above the noise of the engine. A closer explosion juddered Miller's machine and he followed Chatterton's lead, diving, turning and climbing again to avoid the anti-aircraft fire. Archie followed like a faithful dog, running ahead and around them but never quite closing. To his right, he saw York making his jerky adjustments, wings waggling and tail-plane nodding like a child's toy as the charcoal smudged the blue of the sky all around him.

Welcome back, Miller thought.

The observation balloon had been seen on the eastern edge of Sanctuary Wood, south of what had been Gheluvelt on the old Menin road. The front line where the Germans had originally entrenched in November of 1914 had advanced to the western end of the wood during the gas-led advances made in April and May the following year. Since then little had changed. Sanctuary Wood was now a wood in name only; riven trees were nothing more than bleached and blackened stumps pointing in crazy angles from the fragmented land, like a life model for one of the Cubist paintings Miller had seen in Paris before the war.

They flew over the western edge of the wood, peering down through the thickening Archie as Chatterton dropped them in slow spirals to eight, then seven thousand feet. MacMaster fired a red flare that arced above them as Chatterton tightened his circle and Griffiths closed in. Miller could see Watson in front of Griffiths, half out of the nacelle as he tried to pick up what MacMaster had seen then, waving his arm above his head to signal Chatterton, Griffiths took the machine up and Watson began to call in the artillery strike. A few moments later the ground along the Menin road erupted. Earth and smoke belched into the sky. Miller looked at his watch: 7pm.

He took the FE in a long circular sweep above the other three FEs following Gregory in the DH2, scanning the sky as he went. Watson was directing the bombardment and Miller saw the shell blasts creep forward towards the edge of the wood where MacMaster had seen the tethered balloon. Archie grew thicker and Royston's machine disappeared behind the jaundiced-grey detonations as they ignored the higher machines and concentrated on the artillery spotter. As he watched, York's machine jerked violently sideways under the shockwave of an impact.

Boyes started waving his arm and to the west, in the glare of the setting sun, Miller caught a movement and, adjusting his position, saw the aircraft above them, coming out of the sun like a flock of mechanical phoenixes. He counted eight machines only there was no phoenix, just Eindeckers and Halberstadts. He banked, then slid off his turn and climbed to meet them, putting his FE between the Hun and the other machines.

He saw Gregory climbing fast on his left flank five hundred yards away as Miller singled out a pair of Eindeckers from the pack. One was flying slightly behind and below the other and, as he closed, he saw Boyes swinging the forward Lewis into position on the leading machine. The pack held their formation and at a thousand yards he wondered if they had seen him, then — at six hundred — four Halberstadts peeled off towards the FEs below. Miller ignored them keeping his two targets in Boyes's sights. At two hundred and fifty Boyes squeezed the trigger of the Lewis in a short, testing burst. At one-fifty he opened the machine-gun for a longer raking burst and Miller pushed forward his stick as the sky between them disappeared in a rushing gale. Raking from propeller and cockpit along the fuselage of the first Hun, Boyes stitched a path down the length of the machine. A spattering of fire from the second Eindecker passed in front of Miller above Boyes's head as the tail of the first Hun shattered in a sunburst of splintered timber. A second later Boyes was on his feet, standing in the nacelle as the second Eindecker slid into the sights of his top rear-facing Lewis gun. He emptied a drum at him as the Hun spun away.

In front of him Miller could see Gregory jousting with a Halberstadt but the rest of the Hun formation was behind him now and he pulled the machine around in a steep bank and levelled out as Boyes fumbled in front of him, replacing the Lewis drums. Over the side of the FE he caught sight of their first Eindecker with its shattered tail spinning to the ground. The second had pulled out of his dive to join the attack on the other FEs. Miller eased the stick forward to follow and saw Chatterton with MacMaster standing at the rear Lewis gun waiting for the attack.

Behind and to the southern edge of Sanctuary Wood, York was manoeuvring his FE for Hunt to cover Watson and Griffiths who were still calling in the artillery. A few hundred yards away three Halberstadts had dropped on Royston and White. Below them, the Hun Archie had died away as their own machines closed in and, as the sky cleared, Miller glimpsed the edge of the wood where the British artillery was pounding the earth.

Chatterton pulled his FE into a turn across Miller's path and exposed a Halberstadt that had hooked itself onto the flight commander's tail. Too far to do any damage, Boyes put a scaring burst past the Hun machine's wing and it slid off and dived away. An Eindecker and another Halberstadt were closing on York who was dropping in a slow spiralling circle and, as he watched, he saw Hunt in the front nacelle jerk suddenly upright. Then, as York straightened the FE and pulled her nose up, Hunt slid down from sight.

Beneath Miller a Halberstadt raked a burst through his right wing, tearing the FE's cloth into tattered fragments. Miller kicked the rudder and swung around, angling the nose of the machine and the Lewis gun's snout down onto the passing Hun. Boyes gave him a short burst but the Hun had already passed beneath. Turning, he saw Griffiths, now several hundred feet above him with an Eindecker on his tail. Miller pulled back sharply on his stick and he felt the FE's nose rear up in front of him as he zoomed. He climbed then turned, slid off the parabola and came around, behind the Eindecker. He saw the Hun turn in his cockpit, swing right and dive but Miller's speed in the dive closed the distance between them and Boyes, sighting the Lewis in front of the Eindecker's propeller, squeezed the trigger. The pilot jerked upright as the machine flew into the rest of the burst, then he slumped. Miller slid off left, and came around, seeing the Eindecker nose down in a spin beneath them.

He had no time to watch the Eindecker down and he climbed again, looking around. Above him he saw Gregory's DH2 raking the underside of a Halberstadt, angling his Lewis up to its maximum elevation and swinging it round, leading the Hun like a pheasant on a shoot. Behind him Griffiths was attempting to evade a Halberstadt on his tail, banking the machine to give Watson a target with his rear Lewis gun. Moving to help, Miller caught sight of two enemy machines closing in on him. He saw Chatterton waving in the direction of their lines, then was past him and looking at the approaching props of two Halberstadts. York and Hunt were gone. The artillery strike was over. There was suddenly no advantage in staying over the lines. Boyes squeezed his trigger as the two Halberstadts closed and the Lewis rattled for a second then jammed. Miller cursed, watching Boyes's back as he detached the drum, yanking at the mechanism. Miller pushed violently on the stick as the closing Halberstadts opened up on them and, falling sideways in a sickening slide, he straightened the stick and kicked at the rudder bar, climbed and turned with the sun at his back.

Below he glimpsed the remaining Hun machines swarming over Royston and White like wasps around over-ripe fruit. A thin trail of smoke was curling from their engine in a dull funereal streamer and he saw Gregory above turning to help. But it was already too late. A burst from an Eindecker had smashed one of the FE's struts and the right top wing suddenly crumpled and hung uselessly like a broken limb. The machine lurched to the right then swung in a sweeping radius around the broken wing. The Eindecker on its tail pulled up sharply to avoid the careering machine and, too late, saw the Halberstadt above it. The Eindecker's propeller churned through the Halberstadt's fuselage like a circular saw then found the fuel tank. A burst of flame erupted and engulfed both machines, the debris spinning away. Burning, the interlocked Huns fell, guttering like a candle, past the slowly twisting FE of Royston and White.

Transfixed by the collision and with the sun behind him, the remaining Halberstadt didn't see Gregory until it was too late. He emptied a drum into the machine and Miller saw the fabric of the wings tear as the startled pilot slid off and dived for his lines. Gregory circled round, peering below as Royston's FE dwindled and shrank like a closing flower.

The last three Hun machines broke off the pursuit as the remaining FEs turned towards their lines, Gregory's DH2 bringing up the rear. Closing up on Chatterton's machine, Miller looked around as the Archie opened up again. Griffiths and Watson were above him, Gregory behind. He had seen Royston and White go down. York and Hunt had disappeared.

191

Clambering from the FE Miller watched as the smoke began billowing from Griffiths's engine. The pilot and Watson jumped out as the fire truck bounced up and the men unrolled the hose and dowsed the front of the machine. He waited for Boyes to get out of his nacelle, said, 'Well done,' then looked across the field as Chatterton landed. The nose of the FE tipped up, pushing the tail down until Miller thought he must stall, then he levelled out, dipped again towards the field and bounced his wheels down. He hopped another ten yards before touching down again and this time the tail skid hit as well and the machine trundled along in a series of hiccups that shook the wings with a spasmodic fever.

Miller waited until Chatterton and MacMaster had both climbed out of the FE then turned towards the château where Mackinnon, arms akimbo, was watching. As they walked towards him, the sergeant strode to meet them.

'Mr Royston and Sergeant White?' he asked quietly.

Chatterton shook his head and walked on past.

There would be an empty chair in the sergeants' mess that evening.

'Lieutenants York and Hunt as well,' Miller said to Mackinnon as he passed.

'They came in a few minutes ago,' Mackinnon said. 'Mr Hunt's taken a nasty one but Captain Doyle is with him now. We've got their machine in the hangar already.'

Strouden and Budge were waiting. York was already there. He didn't look up as the others came in. Miller dropped his gloves, goggles and helmet on the table in front of the easel and began unbuttoning his flying coat. Grimshaw brought in tea from the mess. Miller took a mug and fell into a chair.

Chatterton took one next to York.

'How's Hunt?' he asked.

York turned to him, rubbing his eyes between thumb and forefinger. 'Caught one in the back,' he said. He shook his head as if in disbelief. 'It cut the strap of my helmet going past me. Never drew blood, then hit Hunt in the back. Can you believe that?'

'Bad luck,' Chatterton said automatically.

'Sorry about...' York started hesitantly. 'You know ... getting back. I — ' He stopped abruptly.

'Don't worry about it, old man,' Chatterton said.

'That was bloody,' Griffiths said, taking a chair. His face was white and he was shaking.

He sat heavily and stared at a spot on the floor just in front of his boots. 'Bloody,' he said again.

Miller looked up at Strouden. His face was grim with black rings circling his eyes like his own identification roundels. Miller doubted if he'd caught up on his sleep yet.

'Poor old Royston,' Watson said to nobody in particular, scratching his head where his flying helmet had flattened his hair.

Budge scribbled a few notes with his left hand on his pad then began nervously tapping the pencil on the desk. Strouden glowered at the offending hand as he glanced at his adjutant.

'We just heard that the balloon is back up,' he said.

'Oh, fuck it!' Griffiths said. '*Fuck* it!'

'Mr Griffiths...' Strouden cautioned.

Griffiths looked up from the floor. 'Sorry, sir,' he said, then went back to the spot on the floor and cursed under his breath.

'They're giving our reserve trenches behind Hill 60 a pasting while there's still some light,' Strouden said.

'I don't see how we missed,' Watson said. 'I called them in right on top of that spot on the photograph.'

'It wasn't up?'

'No,' Chatterton said.

'Could it have been a dummy?' Budge asked. 'On the photograph, I mean?'

No one replied.

After a moment Miller told them what he had seen.

'I counted eight of them. Eindeckers and Halberstadts. They'd worked around west of us and came out of the sun. Boyes and I were higher than the others. Like Gregory. They weren't interested in us. They went for York first.'

'I'm sorry,' York began again. 'Once Hunt was hit there wasn't anything else I could do, you see.'

'No one thinks there was, old chap,' Chatterton said.

'I thought they'd got you,' Miller said.

'I managed to get into some cloud,' York explained. 'When I came out they'd lost interest in me. I could see that Hunt was bad so I thought I'd better come home. It's not that I didn't — I'm sorry,' he finished again.

'Only thing you could have done,' Budge said.

'Boyes got one Eindecker and forced another down,' Gregory said.

Budge made a note.

'Only because Captain Miller put me in front of it,' Boyes said.

'Royston?' Strouden asked.

'They were all round him, sir,' Chatterton replied.

'I tried to help but they took a hit before I got there,' Gregory said.

'You got one, though,' MacMaster said. 'I saw it. You definitely got him.'

'I can confirm that,' Miller said. 'They took out one of Royston's struts. Then the two Huns closest to him collided avoiding his machine. Gregory got the third.'

'I wish I'd seen that,' Chatterton said. 'I just saw the explosion.'

'They'll go down to Royston and White,' Budge said. 'I'll see they're credited.'

'Good,' Strouden nodded, as if already composing the letter to Royston and White's families. *Something to tell them.*

'I'm pretty sure I got a Halberstadt,' MacMaster went on, looking hopefully at Miller.

'Sorry,' Miller said, 'I must have had my hands full.'

'Anyone?' Budge asked.

'I really don't see how we missed the sausage, sir,' Watson said again. 'I was sure we got it. We peppered the whole area. I don't see *how* we missed.'

'It could have been a dummy, old man,' Budge repeated.

'Colonel Maxwell is getting some photographs in the morning,' Strouden said.

'We'll have to go back?' Griffiths asked.

Strouden looked at him and stood up. 'Finish up here, will you Frank?' he said, and walked out.

They sat in silence a moment longer before Budge took them through it all again. When they were leaving he grabbed Miller's arm.

'I'll walk you back to your hut,' he said.

They were outside and well away from the château before Budge said what was on his mind.

'Lieutenant Tozer seems to have disappeared,' he said.

'Missing, you mean?'

'Well, disappeared. As far as I can tell no one's seen him since yesterday evening.'

'He's not in town or up, or anything?'

'No. His FE's in the Bessonneau being patched. Those new boys had it up with you this morning and nothing else is out. He's supposed to be up with A Flight on the dawn patrol tomorrow.'

'Hasn't he been stood down, then?'

Budge frowned. 'Stood down?'

'I thought Major Strouden said — '

'That's just it,' Budge said. 'I haven't told him yet. He's got enough on his plate as it is.'

'What do you expect me to do about it?' Miller asked, a little more curtly than he had intended.

Budge hesitated, as if he hated to ask. 'If you could talk to the chaps?' he suggested. 'See who saw him last?'

'Are you sure he hasn't just gone for a walk or something? Who does he bunk with?'

'Boyes,' Budge said. 'But he only got back earlier today. He didn't miss him.'

Who would, Miller wondered, but he said, 'I saw him in town yesterday evening. Maybe he got drunk last night and curled up somewhere.'

'All day?'

'The bombing last night...?' Miller suggested. 'He might have caught one.'

'We'd have found *something*,' Budge said.

'I'll have a word with Chacksfield and Moss,' Miller said. 'When I saw him he was with them.'

'Good of you, old man,' Budge said. 'I'd just as soon not worry Tommy with it until I have to.' He opened the door of Miller's hut for him. 'You'd better get cleaned up and have your dinner first.'

'Yes,' Miller said. 'Thanks.'

At dinner he found a chair near Chacksfield and Moss. Denham was eating fastidiously and glanced only momentarily at Miller. A skinny and sallow Cockney who couldn't have been more than seventeen was serving at table and

194

Miller couldn't help wondering if this sojourn in Belgium was the first time he had actually come up out of whatever east London cellar it was he lived.

'I've been looking for Tozer,' he began, having the feeling he'd been through that conversation before.

Chacksfield across the table from him was wolfing down a plateful of boiled beef. Death, sitting in the empty chairs, didn't seem to have dimmed his appetite much. Miller watched him as he played unenthusiastically with his own food, still hearing guns but unsure whether they were in his head or at the front. Denham, he noticed, didn't seem too hungry either; he had probably heard that C Flight would be the ones to take down the balloon.

'You were in town with him last night, weren't you?' he asked Chacksfield.

'Was I?' Chacksfield said. 'Couldn't say, old man. Seems a long time ago, now.'

'I thought I saw you,' Miller said.

Unconcerned, Chacksfield shook his head over his beef. 'If you say so. Actually, I rather think I drank something that disagreed with me. Between that and the bombing, everything's a bit of a blank to be honest.'

'No one appears to have seen him, that's all.'

'What do you want the squit for this time?' Chacksfield asked.

'To find him. He's not been seen.'

'Perhaps he's done a bunk,' Moss suggested, suppressing a giggle.

'Tozer hasn't got the imagination to do a bunk,' Denham said. 'Hasn't he got the patrol in the morning?'

'I went into town to see Foden yesterday before he went home,' Miller said to Chacksfield. 'I was in the square and saw you and Moss with him.'

Chacksfield glanced at Moss. 'Is that right? Were we there?'

'You were squiffy,' Moss said.

'Me?' Chacksfield said. 'Wait though. It's coming back now. We ate then went on to...' he stopped and gave Miller a meaningful look.

'To the brothel?' Miller said.

'Keep your voice down, old man,' Chacksfield objected. 'No point in letting the whole squadron know.'

'I rather think you're too late, there,' Denham observed.

'I was just thinking of the parsons' sons, that's all,' Chacksfield said. 'As old Breconridge used to say.'

Miller had to pause for a second to remember which one Breconridge had been.

'Tozer didn't come on with us,' Moss volunteered.

'He was even squiffier than Moss,' Chacksfield remarked, his case of amnesia apparently cured. 'He went to the restaurant where that girl works, to moon over her I suppose.'

'Arlette?'

'Arlette,' Moss repeated for no apparent reason other than to articulate her name.

'Refused to come with us.'

'You came back in a tender?'

'That's right. We didn't see Tozer there, did we Moss?'

'I doubt you could see much of anything, old chap,' Moss said.

'Actually,' Chacksfield said. 'I was feeling a little under the weather to tell the truth. Then when I finally got off to sleep all that beastly bombing started.'

'How was Tozer planning on getting back?'

'I've no idea, old man,' Chacksfield said. 'He didn't want to come with us, that's all I know. Quite adamant about it. You know what Tozer's like. Perhaps he was in luck,' he suggested, offering up his plate for a refill, 'with Arlette, I mean.'

In the mess after dinner Miller asked a few of the others if they'd seen him but no one could remember having done so. He had a couple of drinks and then returned to his hut. The beastly bombing had disturbed his sleep as well and it had been a long day. He sat on his bunk and pulled towards him the package that Parry had given him. It was Dunne's manuscript wrapped in brown paper now torn from handling. The pages inside were dog-eared and creased. The first, a title page, read: *Heavier Than Air* by Robert Dunne. This had been crossed out and above it written in a different hand: *Memoirs of a Flying Officer.*

Miller poured himself a glass of cognac from the bottle that Doyle had left and sipped at it as he turned the pages.

Dunne had had a neat looping hand and, although written in pencil, the script was perfectly legible. The pages were all loose-leaf, as if they had been taken from a writing tablet. Given what Parry had told him about Dunne keeping a record of his training and writing at every opportunity, he assumed that the manuscript was a fair copy written up from earlier drafts. He had understood Parry's reticence about the book, it being against RFC regulations to keep any sort of account of training or operational duties beyond one's log — even the day to day observations one might make for oneself about life at the front. But many men broke the regulation, as did Miller himself. They kept dairies or journals, but if they wanted to *keep* them they kept them to themselves. All mail went through a censor and — depending on the man with the black crayon — at times little could be left of postcards and letters beyond the mundane.

Miller suspected that Dunne's manuscript, with the best will in the world, would have begun with *Chapter 1* and ended with a full stop with nothing but pages of blackness between. When sending the personal possessions of the dead home, a commanding officer might be more sympathetic, but even on one of his best days Miller could not see Strouden letting Dunne's book through his office unscathed. Parry would have to smuggle it home on his next leave if he wanted to give it to Dunne's sister, Phyllida.

That might account for why Heyward had hidden the thing in the first place. What it didn't account for was why he lied to Parry about having it.

Not that Miller found anything particularly controversial in it as he turned the pages. The book began with a character called Richards reporting for his first day's training as a pilot, then took him through the early days and weeks up to his posting to a squadron in France. But what Miller did not find controversial was not necessarily the same as what the military mentality might regard as innocuous. The fact that fellows training alongside Richards died in accidents would have raised their blood pressure at the outset, he supposed. That it was *true*, was irrelevant; it was not the sort of thing one ought to blab about. Neither would they care for the fact that Dunne had suggested that some men were scared of the prospect of being sent to the front.

But it wasn't the content of the book that interested Miller most. It was the style and, more particularly, some of the amendments that had been made to the text. While many of these were in the same hand as the manuscript itself — Dunne's, presumably — others, usually grammatical corrections to the text but including the alternative title, had been made in a different hand, and a hand that Miller recognised from Heyward's exercise books.

20
Cirrus

Dense patches may obscure sun - ceiling otherwise high - visibility good.

It was still dark when Miller opened his eyes. The hurricane lamp shed a faint glow, illuminating Jones who was standing over him, shaking his shoulder.

'What is it?' Miller asked. 'What's the time?'

'Four-thirty, sir,' Jones said. 'Mug of tea on the table.' He turned up the lamp. Miller pulled himself up onto an elbow.

'I'm not on the patrol this morning,' he complained. His head felt thick from the cognac he had drunk.

'No, sir.'

'Do they want me to go up again?'

'Captain Budge said to tell you that Mr Tozer hasn't reported for patrol this morning.'

Idiot!

He groaned and pulled himself out of the bunk. Doyle's cognac bottle on the bedside table caught his eye. There was only an inch or so left. To have an early night rather than stay drinking in the mess had not been such a good idea. He began pulling on his clothes as Jones tipped hot water into his basin, saw Dunne's book on the floor and re-wrapped it. He washed his face and hands and tried to clean the taste of stale cognac out of his mouth. Then, with the faint suggestion of dawn creeping over the still dark field and lights shining from the château, he trudged through the grass towards the latrines.

He found Budge in the operations room bent over an enlarged photograph of the eastern end of Sanctuary Wood. Parker and Cliff were already there. Pilot-Sergeant Reynolds and Parry followed him in.

'We've got to get more photos of that beastly balloon,' Cliff said as Miller walked up. Beside him, Parker stood looking down at the enlarged photograph. With his smooth skin and unclouded eyes, there was something almost objectionably healthy about him that suggested a regimen of physical exercise. It would never have surprised Miller if Parker, at any moment, had burst into a round of athletic jerks. He possessed a kind of animal litheness upon which even his time with the squadron had failed to leave a mark.

Miller stood at his elbow and looked at the photograph. The first time he had ever seen one it had been a mystery of disjointed lines, oddly symmetrical circles and uneven shading, bearing little relation to the country he was used to flying over. It had been some while before his eye had adjusted sufficiently to read the information hidden within the hieroglyphs.

'That has to be the dummy,' Budge said, pointing to the small grey and vaguely lozenge-shaped object they had taken for the observation balloon. On the enlargement the feature was quite clear, if still indeterminate as to its nature; how anyone had spotted it from five thousand feet seemed a mystery. He suspected it had been more a case of wishful thinking than observation.

'Then where is the beastly thing?' Cliff said.

'Perhaps there's some sort of cover they can keep it under,' Parry suggested. 'So they can tow it out when it's needed.'

'In that case,' Reynolds said, 'we'd need to look for a length of road, or even rail tracks. Suppose it's on a railway bogie?'

Parker bent closer, running a magnifying glass over the photograph. Second Lieutenant Parsons walked in.

'Am I up with you, sir?' he asked Miller.

'I'm not sure,' Miller said. 'I was with Boyes yesterday.'

'A bit rough, wasn't it?'

'A bit.'

Budge took Miller's arm and drew him aside.

'No sign of Tozer,' he said.

'Am I taking Parsons up?'

'No.' He looked unhappy. 'The CO insists on taking a look himself,' he said. 'You know what Wing thinks about *that*.'

'He's taking on too much,' Miller said.

'Do you want to be the one to tell him?'

'What about Tozer?' Miller asked, changing the subject. 'Does he know the idiot isn't here?'

'No. I thought I'd hold off telling him until he gets back. No point in upsetting him further.'

'Isn't he going to miss him? After all, he's the one who put Tozer in A Flight.'

'Do you want to go into Pops and look for him?' Budge said, ignoring the question. 'There's a girl he's keen on. She might know something.'

'Don't you think I'd be better employed with the flight?'

'He's for the high jump unless we get him back.'

'It's up to you,' Miller said. 'Chasing balloons before breakfast isn't my idea of a good start to the day.'

'Perhaps you might try the casualty clearing stations as well.'

He didn't much care for the thought of that. 'They'd notify us, wouldn't they? He'll have identification.'

'Yes, of course.'

'Besides,' he said, 'that might take some time and the CO will want me back if we need to go after the sausage.'

Budge sighed.

'One other thing,' Miller said. 'Did any mail arrive for Heyward after he died, by any chance?'

'Heyward?' Budge repeated, as if he'd forgotten all about him. 'There might have been.'

'There wasn't any with the effects you gave me. All that mail had been opened.'

'What generally happens when a man dies or gets shipped home is that his mail is held then returned. Anything for Heyward wouldn't have been put with his effects.'

'Would you mind checking?'

Budge slipped out to his office as York arrived in his flying gear looking even more like a poster boy for the service.

'Who's Parsons?' he asked.

'Are you going back there again?' Miller asked him.

York stepped up to the photograph. 'Let me take a look,' he said. 'I thought I might have spotted something yesterday.'

Miller stood over the photograph again until Budge returned with three letters.

'This was all there was,' he said.

Miller buttoned them into his tunic pocket.

'Who's the CO taking up with him?' he asked.

'Chacksfield,' Budge said. 'He volunteered.'

'He would,' said Miller.

He managed to avoid Strouden, went back to his hut, had a decent wash and found a clean shirt. He was tempted to read Heyward's letters but decided that could wait. As he was dressing he heard the flight taking off to recce the balloon. It was still early and only Boyes was in the mess for breakfast. Miller helped himself to some rashers of bacon and two eggs and sat beside him.

'Tozer didn't come back, then?' he ventured.

'The chump,' Boyes said.

'I don't suppose you saw him at all after you were injured, did you?'

'No, sorry.'

Miller reached for some toast. 'It looks as if we'll have to go after the sausage again.'

'Will I be with you?'

'I think the major will want me in the Strutter,' Miller said.

'Pity,' said Boyes. 'It makes all the difference when you trust the man on the stick.'

'You don't trust Tozer, I take it.'

'Oh, he can fly all right. I never have any worries about getting up and down. It's the bit in between that I worry about. He can never resist a Hun, regardless of the circumstances.'

'You wouldn't have said he was getting windy, would you?'

'Enough to bolt, you mean?'

'Yes.'

'No, I wouldn't,' Boyes said. 'Not a chance. He hasn't got enough imagination to get windy.'

'No, that's what I thought,' Miller said.

FitzHarris walked in, bade them 'good morning' and heaped a plate with everything on offer. He took a chair opposite them, saw Miller glance at the size of his breakfast and looked back guiltily.

'You need a good start to the day,' he explained.

'I'd never get off the ground if I started the day *that* well,' Miller told him.

FitzHarris chortled into his eggs.

'I've got to go into Pops,' Miller said.

'The tenders are bringing in replacements,' FitzHarris said, 'but I can find you a lift if you need one.'

'What about a motorcycle?' Then he thought about what he would do if he found Tozer. 'Got anything with a pillion?'

'Sidecar,' FitzHarris said.

Miller thought about having to weave a motorcycle combination through the traffic around Poperinghe, then said:

'Do you think Harry Woodward would let me borrow his Indian Twin for a few hours?'

'You can always ask, old man,' FitzHarris said. 'Harry's a good egg. I don't see why he should mind.' He grinned. 'Pull rank.'

Woodward was already at work in the machine shop. He saw Miller and wiped his hands on a rag.

'I was giving Sergeant Greene a hand with your Strutter yesterday, sir' he said without preamble. 'We're short-handed after the bombing what with poor old Jim Smith catching it. The piston rings had gone again of course. It's one of the drawbacks of the Clerget, the rings being brass. A few hours is all you'll ever get out of them and I was thinking you'd get a longer life out of a Le Rhône.'

'Change the whole engine?'

'I believe they're fitting Le Rhônes in the new ones.'

'Could you get one?'

'It's worth a try,' Woodward said. 'I'll have a word with Sergeant Mackinnon. Captain Gracey is a wonder at procurement.'

'If he can,' Miller said. He paused and scratched at his head, not quite knowing how to put what he wanted to ask. In the end, he just jumped straight in. 'I know you didn't personally know Heyward,' he began, 'but you said your brother was a friend of his.'

'That's right,' Woodward said, waiting.

'From what your brother told you — or rather, from what you might have understood from what he told you, do you think Heyward was an honourable man?'

'*Honourable*?'

'I don't suppose I've put it very well,' Miller said. 'What I'm really asking is, do you think he was the kind of man who would consider doing anything dishonourable?'

'In what way?' Woodward asked.

'Well, for instance, he tried to blame Jim Smith for the accident that killed Dunne. Was that a dishonourable thing for him to have done?'

Woodward ran an oily hand through his hair. He smiled pensively. 'That's not a straightforward question.'

'I know.'

'And I can only tell you what I might have inferred through his friendship with Teddy.'

'Understood.'

'Then, from Heyward's standpoint, no, I don't believe it was,' Woodward said.

'Why?'

'Persistent, aren't you?' Woodward said.

'That's why Maxwell sent me here,' Miller replied.

'I don't suppose Heyward thought of himself as a rotten pilot, or a rotten anything else come to that. If he had trouble getting the machine up and down he would probably have regarded it a mechanical defect rather than a lack of competence on his part. I don't know, but I should think a man with a sense of his own self such as Heyward had would assume he was capable of mastering anything.'

'Would that have been his mother's influence?'

'Probably.' The muscle around his scar began to twitch and Woodward's face creased as if grasping for a concept that was barely within his reach. 'It might sound odd, but somehow, if he hadn't totally believed in the superiority of his own class, there would have been something hypocritical about him, a falseness that Teddy wouldn't have tolerated.' He gave an almost apologetic shrug. 'My brother shared his attitude about such things, you see. It's what they teach them at school — a regard for their value. Breeding, I suppose you'd call it. It's why Teddy never understood why I enlisted.'

'Why you wanted to grub around with engines.'

'Yes,' Woodward said. 'Unless a man was an enthusiast he'd employ a chauffeur. After all, one doesn't get one's hands dirty out of choice. The war has changed things in that men of Heyward's class are required to fly aeroplanes and if duty requires it that's what they do. It's just a matter of mastering the technique, rather like riding a horse. Of course, he added, 'the difference there is that that skill is more or less socially obligatory.'

'And if it ever dawned on him that he *was* a rotten pilot?' Miller asked.

'Well,' Woodward said, 'it's only my opinion, of course, but I think if it ever actually dawned upon him that he was never going to be any good he might have refused to go up again.'

'And taken the consequences?'

'Ah,' Woodward smiled, 'that's a different matter. Disgrace? Court martial? No, he wouldn't have put his family through that. I dare say, if he flew single-seater scouts, he would have gone up regardless. But in two-seaters? No, I don't think he would have wanted to continue risking other men's lives. He probably would have switched to observing and convinced himself that the observer was the senior man in the machine, anyway. Otherwise he would have transferred out.'

'But he transferred to the RFC to get out of the trenches,' Miller said.

'No, he transferred out to please his mother,' Woodward said. 'His father had been killed and she thought the RFC was a safer billet.'

'*He* didn't?'

'No, I'm not sure he did. After all, his mother *could* have wangled a staff job for him, or some other cushy job at home. In fact I know that that was what she wanted. Teddy told me.'

'So it was Heyward's idea to join the RFC?'

'Yes, I've always assumed so. He wanted to please his mother but not at any price. He knew Arthur Foden was in the RFC, so perhaps he thought if his old school chum could do it, it couldn't be that difficult. He must have had some idea of how dangerous it might be. He was no brainless fool. He would have looked into it if only to find out the kind of men he would be messing with. The point is, he was the sort of man who knew he had a duty to perform and was prepared to do it regardless of the dangers. But then,' Woodward finished, 'he wasn't alone in that, was he? France is full of men who see things that way.'

'Yes,' said Miller, 'I suppose it is. Why then do you think he hanged himself? Surely he would have been aware of the disgrace that would have brought upon his family.'

Woodward blew out his cheeks. 'There you have me. A guess? Perhaps after Mr Dunne's death he finally realised that he could kill people through his own incompetence.'

'And couldn't live with the knowledge?' Miller asked sceptically. 'No, I can't buy that. After all, he could have transferred out to avoid harming anyone else. In fact he didn't even need to do that — the CO wanted to ground him or restrict him to observation. It might have injured his pride but I can't see a man hanging himself over a blow to his esteem. No, I think there must have been something else, something that cut deeper... something got closer to the man Heyward thought he was.'

'Such as?'

'I'm not sure yet,' Miller said. 'It might have been something someone else might regard as trivial but, given the strain everyone is under, the trivial can sometimes be magnified out of all proportion. Under those conditions doing something out of character isn't unexpected. Which,' he said, looking at Woodward, 'is why I've got to go into Poperinghe. Someone has done something out of character and I've got to go into Pops and straighten it out. Except all the tenders are out picking up replacements.'

'Mr Tozer?'

'Word's got around, has it?'

'Only that no one's seen him and he was due up this morning.'

'Captain Budge has asked me to see if I can find him.'

'You want to borrow my bike?'

'Would you mind?'

'She's out the back of the shed,' Woodward said. 'Watch her, though. She's faster than you think.'

'I'll be careful.'

Woodward nodded. 'She's not too good on the loop, either.'

203

The roads around Poperinghe were still choked but the town itself was quieter in the early morning. An old man sat and scratched at his grey-stubbled chin outside a bar in the square that Miller knew was popular with some of the squadron. Miller parked the Indian Twin, pushed his goggles onto his forehead and walked inside. A barman stood cleaning glasses and talking to a customer. They turned and looked at Miller as he walked up, the barman straightening in anticipation of an order.

'*Je cherche un officier de volant...*' Miller began. 'A flying officer?'

The barman looked at him vacantly. '*Un officier de volant?*' he repeated.

'*Un pilote,*' Miller said. '*aviateur.*' He pointed to the RFC wings on his own tunic, suddenly aware that he was almost shouting. 'Lieutenant Tozer. *Aviateur,*' he repeated,

The barman shrugged dismissively. His customer looked pointedly down at his glass.

Miller bought a packet of cigarettes and walked out onto the bright pavement. He lit one, swung his leg over the Indian Twin and kicked it into life. The old man watched indifferently as he pulled away across the road.

The restaurant in Priesterstraat was closed. The shattered window had been boarded and he banged on the door until he saw through what remained of the cracked glass the fat waiter crossing towards him. Miller could see him muttering to himself. He pointed to the *fermé* sign hanging on the door. Miller shook his head and indicated he wanted to come in. Reluctantly, the man unlocked the door.

'*Je cherche un aviateur ,*' Miller started again.

The waiter stared back at Miller with a face devoid of interest.

Miller pointed to his RFC wings. 'A pilot.'

The man muttered to himself again, '*Un pilote?*' He pointed at the ceiling and said, '*aviateur... aviateur.*'

'That's what I said,' Miller replied. '*Aviateur. Est-il à l'étage?*'

The man turned, looked around the room then offered his variation on the other barman's shrug.

'There is no one here, monsieur,' he said in English. 'You can see.'

'Upstairs,' Miller said again, pointing at the ceiling. Then, 'Arlette? *Arlette est ici?*'

The man's shoulders slumped a little and he gave Miller a look of exasperation. He turned around and stomped off behind the bar and through a doorway. A moment later Miller could hear him calling for Arlette.

If Tozer was upstairs, he thought, he was going to give him a thrashing. Resisting arrest could do as an excuse.

He looked around the restaurant, shabby in the morning light. From the inside he could see that some of the glass still hung in the frame of the boarded window. The chequered tablecloths had been removed showing the cheap wooden surfaces to be scratched and scarred with cigarette burns. Paint was peeling from the walls and a large crack had appeared on the wall where the *charcuterie* next door had collapsed. It ran from floor to ceiling and then across that, loosening lumps of plaster. The advertisements and posters that hung around the room had an almost quaint air about them, something of the last century, and were dog-eared and faded.

The girl, Arlette, came through the door and around the bar. He hadn't got her out of bed, he noticed, as she was dressed in a blue frock decorated with white flowers. It had a wide neckline and the short sleeves bunched just below her shoulders leaving her slender arms bare. Her eyes widened a little in recognition as she saw him. She was shorter than he remembered, and to achieve eye contact she had to raise her head in an attitude that pushed her chin out pugnaciously. Her dark hair curled around her face in an unkempt cascade.

'*Monsieur*?' she asked.

'*Un aviateur*,' Miller said again.

'A pilot?' Arlette asked, accenting the last syllable.

'Lieutenant Tozer,' Miller said.

'Tozair?'

'Close enough,' he said. '*Est-il en haut*?' he asked, pointing at the ceiling again. 'Upstairs?'

'*A l'étage*?'

'He said a pilot was upstairs,' Miller repeated slowly, pointing at the waiter behind the bar.

'Phillipe said a pilot is with me?' she asked in broken English.

'Yes,' Miller told her. 'He pointed at the ceiling.'

She glared at him then turned sharply to Phillipe and there was a rapid exchange in French that Miller caught little of.

'He points to the sky,' Arlette said accusingly, turning back to Miller. '*Un aviateur*.'

'Oh,' Miller said, embarrassed. 'Sorry. I didn't understand. You haven't seen him, then?'

'Who?'

He began to describe Tozer only to find that, in *his* description, Tozer was much like every other young officer.

'We were all here the other evening,' he said. '*L'autre soirée.*'

Arlette frowned again.

'Here,' Miller said and walked to the table at which they had sat. He pulled out a chair and sat where he had himself been sitting. '*J'etais ici*,' he said. Then pointed across the table to Chacksfield's chair and mimed a big man with fat fingers. He repeated the exercise, pointing to where Moss had sat and trying to imitate Moss's quick nervous movements and his falling off the chair.

Arlette stared at him as if he were mad, the corners of her mouth turning down.

Then there was Springfield, but in the middle of it he suddenly recalled that Springfield was dead. So he tried to convey Denham's superciliousness and failed miserably, only succeeding in making Arlette laugh. When it came to Tozer's chair he merely sat down and shrugged and said, 'Tozer.'

She looked at him blankly.

'Tozer,' he repeated. 'He is in love with you. *Il vous aime.*'

'*Moi?*'

'*Oui.*'

She made a small plosive sound with her lips — 'poh' — and shrugged her shoulders under the thin dress. '*Ils m'aiment tous,*' she said accusingly. '*Est-il ma faute?*'

'*Faute?*' Miller repeated.

'It is not my fault,' she managed in English. 'Soldiers...' she added dismissively. '*Et vous?*' she asked.

'Me?'

'*Es-tu amoureuse avec moi?*'

Miller laughed. 'No,' he said, 'I don't even know you.'

She lifted her eyebrows in mock surprise.

Miller sat there a moment longer as he and Arlette looked at each other, then he slapped his hands on his thighs and stood up as if to demonstrate he had arrived at some decision.

'Well,' he said.

'You go to look?' she asked.

'*Mais où?*' he asked.

She regarded him meditatively for a moment as if deciding whether or not to tell him, then made up her mind.

'*Attendez,*' she said and Miller waited while she disappeared again through the door behind the bar. He heard a brief conversation, too muffled for him to understand any of it, and then the unmistakable clink of bottles. A few seconds later Arlette returned carrying a woven raffia bag. 'Come,' she said and steered him towards the door.

On the street she stood for a moment looking right and then left.

'*Où est-il votre voiture?*'

Miller pointed at the Indian Twin. 'I came on that,' he said.

She looked at him wide-eyed and then back to the motorcycle. She stood still a moment as if reconsidering then pushed the bag at Miller.

'*Attendez,*' she said again and went back into the restaurant.

Miller held the bag. He looked inside, saw a bottle of wine, a stick of bread and some parcels wrapped in paper.

Arlette came back carrying a rug. She put it on top of the bag.

'*Allez,*' she said, pushing him towards the bike.

Miller swung himself onto it and looked over his shoulder as Arlette sat astride the pillion, the bag between her and his back and her dress pulled back above her knees onto her thighs. He glanced down at her legs and she hit him sharply on the shoulder with the heel of her hand.

'*Allez,*' she said and pointed down the road.

Miller pulled his goggles down over his eyes, kicked the starter and wobbled off into the road, adjusting for the added weight on the rear of the motorcycle.

He followed her directions south and west out of the town. He assumed she was taking him to Tozer even though in the restaurant she had seemed not to know who he was talking about. He wondered if she made a habit of hiding pilots — any serviceman — who had decided to desert; or perhaps she just knew where they went. Whichever, he was not going to give Tozer the opportunity to consume any of the contents of the bag that was sticking in his back. He would be lucky to get away with as little as a charge of Absent Without Leave.

After a couple of miles, Arlette pushed him in the ribs several times and indicated a track that led off the road up a slight incline towards a wood. He slowed the Indian Twin, turned along the track and weaved around the cart ruts up towards the trees. He slowed and put it into neutral in response to her tapping him on the back of the head.

The wood was a sparse growth of larch and birch. The rise on which they had stopped looked down upon the town and beyond to patchily uncultivated fields. Towards the front the green of the grass and the uncut weeds started to give way to the churned brown and grey earth that marked the boundary of the enemy shelling. Over to the northeast a smudge on the horizon marked the ruins of Ypres.

He waited until Arlette had dismounted and then got off the machine and pulled it back onto its stand.

Arlette put the bag onto the ground and took out the rug. She walked a few yards to a spot beneath the trees and spread it over a level piece of grass. She came back for the bag and said, '*Voilà*.'

Miller looked around. He had been half expecting a path into the trees, a hut or some other kind of shelter.

'Where is he?' he asked.

'*Quoi?*'

'Tozer,' he said. 'Where is Tozer?'

'Tozair, Tozair...' she repeated, scowling at him as she sat on the rug. 'Who cares for Tozair?'

It was then — belatedly — as Arlette began placing the contents of the bag on the rug in front of her that he realised they were there to have a picnic. He began to laugh at his own denseness.

Arlette looked up at him questioningly. 'Why do you laugh?'

Miller sat down beside her. 'I thought,' he began. '*Je croyais que vous m'emmenez à —* '

'You think I know where Tozair is?'

'Yes,' he said, looking at her a little obliquely.

'Why should I know?'

'Your English has improved,' he said. 'What is it, the altitude?'

'Altitude?' she queried, breaking the bread stick into pieces.

'The height,' he said. 'Up on the hill.'

She rested her black eyes on him for a second and laughed mockingly.

'*L'aviateur*,' she said. 'Altitude. Always the things mechanical.'

'You're evading the question,' he said.

'*Je ne comprends pas*,' she replied.

Miller picked up the bottle of wine and the corkscrew and drew the cork.

'You speak better English than you admit.'

Arlette shrugged. 'If I speak no English I do not have to talk so much.'

'And maybe they say things about you they would not say if they thought you understood,' Miller suggested.

'Yes,' she said. 'The evening the bombs fall... When you tell that one he should speak of me like a lady,' and she looked snootily down her nose at Miller, catching Denham's own sense of superiority perfectly.

'Denham,' he said, laughing. 'You understood, then?' and he suddenly felt embarrassed, not knowing if it was for her or for being caught defending her.

Arlette's lips formed a small pout and she shrugged.

'They are not so bad, your *aviateurs*. Flight officers. Some of the others...' she allowed the criticism to pass unsaid.

'Oh, we're a better class of person altogether,' Miller told her, but the irony he had intended concerning his own position was lost on her.

Arlette unwrapped paté and cheese and spread it on the bread. Miller poured two glasses of wine then took the bread Arlette offered him.

He bit into its crusty freshness and swallowed some wine. It was cheap and sharp but somehow still managed to complement the cheese and the paté.

'Tozair,' she said, eating, flakes of bread clinging to the side of her mouth. 'He has run away?'

'Maybe,' Miller said.

'Then he has more sense than the others,' she said, tapping a finger to her forehead. 'I have seen them. They come to eat and drink for a few weeks, then *pouff*, they come no more. *Ils sont morts.*'

As if to underline the precariousness of mortality, Miller caught the distant thunder as an artillery barrage opened and looked up and saw smoke begin rising into the June air over Ypres. He shaded his eyes and gazed up into the deep blue of the sky and after a moment his practised eyes caught the minute specs of black, like drifting midges on a breeze, that were the machines up over the lines artillery spotting for the British guns.

'Do you have a husband, Arlette? *Un mari?*'

'*Il est mort,*' she said quite complacently. 'Dead.'

'I'm sorry,' he said.

'Last year he was killed in the German... *printemps,*' she said.

'Spring advance,' Miller prompted.

'Spring advance.'

She shrugged as if it really didn't matter and drank some wine. She looked at him, taking his concern for criticism. 'Why?' she said. 'Thousands have died. What is one more?'

'But he was your man.'

'*Tout le monde appartient a quelqu'un,*' she said.

Miller looked at her blankly.

'Everyone is someone's,' she explained. 'And you?'

'No. I have a sister, that is all. There is no one else.'

'She is in England?'

'America.'

Arlette's eyes widened. 'America? She is in the moving pictures?'

Miller laughed. 'No. Not all Americans are in the moving pictures. She is married to a banker. *Un banquier.*' It was, he thought, the one financially positive result of the years their father had spent dragging them from one gold strike to the next. Catherine had met a man who had had the sense not to try and claw the gold from the ground but to finance those who would.

'You are an American?' Arlette asked. 'You do not have the accent of the others.'

'No,' he said, 'but I was there as a boy.'

'And you come back for this?' she asked incredulously, flinging her thin arm wide as if trying to encompass the whole of the Western Front. 'You are mad?'

'I came back several years ago,' Miller explained, 'to find a man who knew my father. Then the war started...' It was hardly worth explaining. It was what one did. 'And what about you? You have always lived here?'

'Poelcappelle,' she said.

Miller knew the town as nothing more than a heap of rubble. He had flown over it a hundred times. After the initial movement of the first few months of the war, when the stalemate had begun and the armies had spread north in the hope of outflanking each other but had, in the end, just settled down to the stalemate of trench warfare, Poelcappelle had found itself just behind the German front line and had been bombarded mercilessly. The German gains of the previous spring had left it in their rear as they had flattened out the salient in their attempt to take Ypres.

'Maman had a patisserie,' Arlette said. 'When the Germans came we went to Ypres. Last year when — how you say? — *évacuation...?*'

'Civilian evacuation,' Miller said.

'Maman and my sister, Liselle, went to Paris. I stayed because my husband was with the *Quarante-cinquième L'Algérien.* They were near Poelcappelle. The Boche used gas. He was only one day at the front.'

Miller could think of nothing to say. He remembered the attack. He had been serving in this sector and was up over the trenches. It was April 22nd and a fine spring day. In the afternoon the wind had shifted and down over the lines, where the French and the Canadians were holding the front at Poelcappelle, a mist had sprung out of nowhere and drifted towards the trenches. He hadn't been able to see much until it had cleared and then the men he could see were just lying in the trenches, oddly still. Then the Germans had come over the top and he'd been too busy to take much notice.

They'd lost ground that day and it wasn't until he'd got back to his squadron that he'd heard that poison gas had been used for the first time. They had all gone up strafing the next day, up and down the line of the German trenches and to the rear where they thought the gas might have been stored but he was not sure it had done any good. Not beyond giving them some sense of retaliation, anyway. Just revenge.

'Why don't you join your mother and sister in Paris?' he said to Arlette after a while.

'There is no money, trains, no automobile... how?' She pushed her chin at the Indian Twin parked under the trees. 'You take me on that?'

Miller smiled. 'If I could,' he said.

They finished the bread, the cheese and the wine and Miller took some francs out of his tunic pocket to offer them to Arlette.

'For the food,' he said.

She shook her head. 'Phillipe...' she began, then shrugged, not caring.

He lay back on the rug and looked up into the sky. He could barely hear the guns and he had grown so used to their regular and incessant *crump crump* that he hardly noticed it anymore. The birds in the trees behind them made more noise than the war did... Blackbirds, he could hear, and somewhere up high a skylark was singing. He looked out of the corner of his eye at Arlette. She was sitting up, hugging her knees and looking out across the field towards Ypres and perhaps as far as Poelcappelle. He wondered idly why *he* was there with her. Because it happened to have been him that turned up that morning and not one of the others? Or because he had told Denham to treat her like a lady? He supposed so.

He glanced at her again and found she was watching him. There was a look of amusement in her dark eyes but also something more, almost as if she were trying to read his thoughts. She had laid a hand on the ground between them, leaning slightly towards him, and without thinking about it Miller placed his hand over hers. She looked at him questioningly for a second and smiled, turning her hand and entwining their fingers. He leaned closer to her then stopped at the sound of an engine overhead. They both turned to look.

'Boche,' Arlette said without rancour.

Miller saw it was a DFW, probably on a reconnaissance. He looked around the sky but couldn't see any of their machines.

Reluctantly he took his hand from hers and pushed himself up. 'I have to be getting back to the squadron,' he said.

'Yes,' she said and smiled at him. 'Phillipe will be running around like *un poulet.*'

'A chicken...' he jerked his fingers across his throat, 'a headless chicken.'

Arlette laughed. 'An 'eadless chicken,' she repeated.

Miller brushed the breadcrumbs from his uniform. He helped Arlette pack the ruins of their picnic back into the bag then took it over to the Indian Twin while she shook out the rug. She held two of the corners towards him.

'Tozair?' she asked.

Miller shrugged, taking one end of the rug. 'He might be back at the squadron by now,' he said, doubting it.

They folded the rug and stepped towards each other, Arlette gathering the corners into her hands. She was looking up into his face and as their fingers touched again he closed his hand over hers once more. She smiled at him, then glanced reluctantly towards the motorcycle and folded the blanket. She picked up the basket.

Miller took it from her and threaded the handles over the bike's grip. He swung his leg across the Indian Twin and Arlette climbed behind, putting her arms tightly around his chest and holding on. Her head was resting against his back and he sat a moment without moving, rediscovering the sensations of having another body so close to his own. Then he heard the guns again and felt himself coming back to earth.

They rode into town and he stopped outside the restaurant. Through the open door he could see Phillipe fussing over two young army officers who were sitting by the window. They were gesticulating towards the rest of the room while Phillipe stood over them alternately pointing towards the menu and opening his hands, palm up and shrugging, as if to convey that things were beyond his control.

'Will you get into trouble with Phillipe?' Miller asked as Arlette stood beside him on the pavement.

She smiled and smoothed her hair which was tangled from the ride.

'He will be in more if I leave,' she said. She leaned over and kissed him quickly on the cheek. 'You will come back, *Capitaine*?'

'I'll come back,' he said.

She made to leave and he put a hand on her arm to stop her, pulling her gently back towards him. She looked questioningly into his face and he bent towards her and kissed her lightly on her parted lips.

'I'll come back,' he repeated.

He watched her walk inside and greet the army officers, touching one familiarly on the shoulder. They smiled at her and stopped gesticulating at Phillipe, one taking the opportunity to glare through what was left of the grimy glass towards Miller on the motorcycle. Arlette turned and aimed a stream of invective at Phillipe that he could hear even above the rattle of the Indian Twin. He laughed, revved the machine and swung it out into the road. At the crossroads he turned towards the airfield, weaving back into the heavy traffic.

He knew he should have felt some guilt for not trying harder to find Tozer but at that moment he couldn't. He wanted to think about Arlette not about Tozer. The closer he got to the airfield, though, the more Tozer intruded.

A man should be responsible for his own actions, he told himself, and if he was old enough and therefore responsible enough to fly in what was, in reality, no more than an arrangement of plywood, fabric and wire — *and* avoid others who were intent on killing him — he could presumably take the consequences of his own actions; even, he realised, if that meant a court martial and all that that might entail.

Near the airfield he caught sight of four FEs losing altitude as they approached the field. The wind had shifted from the south pushing high cumulus in its wake and the machines had altered their approach to land into the wind. He pulled the motorcycle to a stop and watched them dropping steadily, adjusting their speed to avoid bunching over the airstrip.

The leader, he could see even from that distance, had been badly shot up. Fabric flapped in a loose tear to the rear of the cockpit and part of one strut

211

appeared to have broken, hanging uselessly between the two planes of the wings. Then he heard the restart of an engine and a gunning roar and saw one of the following FEs raise its nose suddenly and climb above the others before banking and taking another circuit. Miller watched him circle the airfield again.

By the time the stray FE had cut its engine and checked its speed for the landing, the other three were down. Miller pushed the Indian Twin into gear again and bumped over the ridged grass towards the shed where Woodward parked it.

He was walking back across the field when he noticed Watson waving his arms wildly as he jumped down from the front nacelle of Griffiths's FE. He was shouting something at the aircraftsmen walking towards him then abruptly broke into a sprint towards the southerly edge of the field.

Miller watched as the two of them accompanied Watson while Griffiths followed at a more leisurely pace. A third aircraftsman ran off towards the château. Miller, curious, turned to follow Watson. After walking a few paces and beginning to feel an odd sense of disquiet, he began to run.

Watson and the others had climbed over a gate and were running along the other side of the hedge by the time Miller reached the field. He looked back from the gate towards the château and saw that the third aircraftsman was running towards him followed by Strouden and Budge. He climbed over the gate and walked along the hedge.

The group had stopped under an elm tree that formed part of the hedge. They were standing in silence in a semicircle, looking down at the ground. Miller joined them. He edged alongside Watson as one of the aircraftsmen turned aside and vomited on the grass.

Miller looked down and he saw that he hadn't needed to ride as far as the town to find Tozer.

21

Tozer was sitting on the ground with his back to the elm's trunk. His legs were straight and spread like the hands of a clock. Twenty minutes before five from where Miller stood, but that was not going to be of any help. His arms lay limp at his sides with his head lolling towards his right shoulder. His left hand was empty. His right held a service revolver. Miller couldn't see the chamber from where he stood but he knew there had only been one bullet fired; the one that had taken off the top of Tozer's head.

'Good God,' he heard Budge say as he and Strouden reached them.

Flies were busy around Tozer's skull and Miller waved them away as he knelt and put his fingers against the inside of the man's left wrist. There was no doubt that he was dead but, aware that the inside of the wrist was one of the areas of the body where the veins were closest to the surface, he wanted some indication of the warmth of the body.

'I'm afraid he's dead,' Budge said.

'Cold, too,' Miller told them, looking up. He lifted the arm. It moved stiffly against his pressure. 'This is full rigor. He's certainly been here all night and judging by the flies quite a bit longer.'

He patted down Tozer's uniform as behind him he heard Strouden tell one of the aircraftsmen to fetch a stretcher. Miller pushed his hand beneath the dead man's left buttock. There was only a vague sensation of dampness where he was making contact with the grass. It had been a warm night with no rain and little in the way of a temperature fluctuation so he wouldn't have expected a dew that morning. Tozer had been shot beneath the chin and the bullet had taken the top back of the skull away as it had exited the head. Some blood and brain material was smeared over the bark of the elm behind Tozer's shattered head and there was more, Miller noticed, clinging to the trunk a few feet above the body. He leaned across the dead man to get some idea of the angle of the bullet in relation to the tree but it was only an approximation.

Strouden came around the other side and knelt over Tozer. He felt in the man's pockets then shook his head at Miller.

'Doesn't seem to have left a note,' he said.

He prised the revolver out of Tozer's stiff fingers and checked the chamber.

'Just the one,' he said, then stopped as he became aware of Miller's expression. He handed him the gun. 'We've no facilities here to get the weapon finger-printed,' he told him as if in answer to Miller's unspoken complaint. 'Anyway, this comes under military jurisdiction and no one's got the time to bother with something that looks like an obvious suicide.' He looked up questioningly at Watson. Parker and Chacksfield had now joined them, standing at the observer's shoulder.

'I saw him as we were coming in,' Watson said. 'I just happened to look down and saw him sitting there. I signalled Griffiths to go round again for another look.'

'All right, Mr Watson,' Strouden said. He stood up and turned to Budge. 'Get them back, will you Frank? Miller and I will see to this as soon as the stretcher gets here.'

Miller glanced up at Strouden as the major watched the others walk slowly back along the line of the hedge, then he leaned over Tozer's body again and pushed the man's chin up so that he might see the entry wound. There was blood and what appeared to be fragments of teeth down the front of the tunic, dried to a sort of gritty dark brown residue.

'Over here,' Strouden called and Miller saw the men with the stretcher hurrying towards them.

Miller took Tozer under the arms while one of the other men picked up his feet, trying to force them together against rigor mortis in his legs. He was aware of Strouden watching him and probably thinking he ought to leave it to the men. Getting one's face over the top and within a few inches of the shattered pulp of a head, though, never mind the buzzing flies, was not a job he would have wanted to delegate; he regarded it as one of the responsibilities of rank never to ask a man to do something that he was unwilling to do himself.

'Take him to the MO's hut,' Strouden told the men, following with Miller to the gate. He closed it after them then, alongside Miller, outpaced the stretcher back towards the château.

'We got a good look this morning,' Strouden said when they were out of earshot of the stretcher bearers. 'We know where they're anchoring the sausage now. Artillery's no good for this job. As soon as it's up again we're going after it.'

'We shouldn't take any of the new men with us,' Miller said.

'No, I agree. Five squadron at Droglandt is on standby until 1800, then we take over. If they follow yesterday's pattern they'll put her up while there's still two or three hours of daylight left.'

'Do you want me to take up the Strutter?'

'Yes,' Strouden said. 'I've briefed Chatterton, Denham, York and Moss. Reynolds will be up, too. He's a solid man.'

'And Gregory?'

'No. He's already been up several times in the last few days so I'm standing him down.'

'We could really use that DH2,' Miller said.

'You're right,' Strouden agreed. 'That's why I'm taking it up myself. I'll lead.'

Miller said, 'There's no use in reminding you that as CO you're non-operational, I suppose?' he said.

'None at all,' Strouden replied.

They fell silent for several yards. Approaching the château, Miller said:

'You really shouldn't have touched the gun.'

'I'm aware of that, Miller,' Strouden answered irritably, 'but it'll do no good to have the men think it was anything other than suicide.'

'The men will think what the men will think,' Miller said. 'Particularly after

214

Heyward.'

Strouden looked at him sideways. 'Damn it all! The job's hard enough as it is without this kind of distraction.' He grunted and strode off towards his office. Miller waited until the stretcher had caught up then followed behind towards the medical officer's hut.

Tozer lay on one of the two scrubbed board tables. Miller leaned against the wall while Doyle examined the body and washed away the blood from around his throat.

'Entry wound's under the chin,' Doyle said. 'Bullet went up through his pallet.'

'Don't suicides generally put the barrel of the pistol in their mouths if they're going to shoot themselves in the head?' Miller asked.

'As a rule,' Doyle confirmed, 'if they don't put it at the temple. But I've seen both methods. See, just here.' He pulled the point of the chin back and indicated the puckered, scorched skin where the revolver had been pushed into the soft flesh under the jawbone.

Miller leaned forward for form's sake. He was perfectly willing to take Doyle's word for it.

'He's lucky the gun was held firmly,' he said. 'I've seen people with half their face shot away and live because of the recoil.'

'Well,' Doyle said, 'luck's not a word I'd use in this context but you're right. In my experience,' he went on while he dabbed the cloth around Tozer's face, 'those who give it any thought put the gun in the mouth so they don't miss. But even then they really need to clench the thing with their teeth to stop it jerking about. Nerves, I suppose. I assume they're squeamish about breaking their teeth, though it does seem a bit odd when you think that what they're trying to do is blow their brains out.' He looked up questioningly at Miller.

Miller wondered if he'd give *his* teeth any thought if he ever reached that extremity. He decided he probably would. He had always noticed teeth. It was something of a fetish for him ever since his boyhood. He remembered those old miners with their irregular stumps like old pit props, black and rotten and giving the impression they might snap at any moment. Good teeth for Miller was a relative term, given the low base from which he started his comparison, but they were something he always noticed nevertheless.

'If Tozer was thinking about it,' Miller remarked, 'it didn't do him much good. There were bits of tooth on the front of his tunic.'

'Molars, I should think,' Doyle said. 'From the back.' He swatted at the last of the blowflies that had come in with Tozer with a newspaper he had rolled for the purpose.

'How long do you think he's been dead?' Miller asked.

'Some while if I'm any judge. Rigor mortis has reached its full extent.'

'I noticed that.'

'I'd say he did it some time the night before last. It's a wonder that nobody spotted him earlier.'

215

'The wind's shifted,' Miller said. 'The patrol had to approach from a different direction. He must have been hidden by the hedge until then.'

'Do you think he did that on purpose?' Doyle asked.

'If it was the night before last,' Miller said, 'I'd guess it happened not long after he got back from town.' He was sure that Tozer hadn't done anything on purpose. 'Some of these blowfly eggs have started hatching,' he added.

'So, Miller, you do have some medical knowledge, then.'

'No. I've just seen a few dead bodies, that's all.'

'Haven't we all, man,' Doyle responded. 'Haven't we all.'

Miller finished his cigarette as Doyle cleaned up the rest of Tozer's face. They had tried to shut the eyes in the field but a tautness in the skin around the cheeks and the open mouth still suggested an expression of alarm that the half-closed eyelids did little to soften. Miller remembered how the face had looked in the restaurant and the lovesick expression Tozer had worn as he had gazed at Arlette. Even if she didn't remember him, Miller decided that he would not want her to know what had happened. He supposed that someone like Chacksfield would blurt it out without a thought, though, the next time he was in town and drunk.

'But if you don't mind my saying so, Miller,' Doyle was saying, 'it's a curious way of putting it.'

'Putting what?'

'About the gun being held firmly,' Doyle said. 'It's almost as if you're suggesting he might not have been holding it himself.'

Miller said, 'Well, since you broached the subject perhaps after you've stripped him you'd let me know if he's got any bruises anywhere that might suggest he'd been held.'

'Now I'm not the Pink, man. You do your own detecting.'

'Don't you think that two suicides in ten days might be a bit more than statistically significant?'

'I'm thinking that a man will go to any extreme to get out of this bloody mess.'

'Perhaps,' Miller said. 'But this is a little more final than shooting yourself in the foot.'

Doyle nodded in the general direction of the ground — or it might have been hell. 'That's them down in the trenches, Miller. They're all good upper-class English gentlemen here. You might say they're bound by etiquette. They don't shoot themselves in the foot. They're expected to do the decent thing.'

When Miller didn't reply Doyle looked over at him and added, 'I'm speaking as an Irishman you understand, an outsider.'

'You're speaking as a volunteer.'

'You're not wrong there, Miller,' Doyle said. 'I'm an Irish patriot, but then this is the real world. Dreams are one thing and mud's mud. Anyway, what is it that makes you think this benighted soul didn't just up and decide to shoot himself?'

'He was in love,' Miller said.

Doyle snorted. 'Aren't we all, man. Aren't we all.'

By mid-afternoon the tenders had arrived from Boulogne with the new replacements. Miller watched them pile out with their gear, shouting and laughing.

There were six of them and they were young. But he had expected that. For two years he had watched replacements arrive while a certain trick of relativity had them grow younger whilst their ages remained the same. There was some new theory in physics he had read about that was making a stir and challenging the accepted notions of the passing of time; or was it our perception of it that had been challenged? He couldn't remember and couldn't understand much of what he had read anyway. It was a flaw in his education of which he had always been aware: he possessed a wide knowledge of many subjects yet it was rarely more than skin deep. He had never had the correct education that would have fitted him for a deeper understanding or, rather, the means of acquiring a deeper understanding. In his eyes, that always put him at a disadvantage to those around him and he wondered if it was this that governed their attitude towards him.

Oddly enough, though, the longer he survived, the more marked the change in the way that the new arrivals — like these new replacements, still public school educated for the most part — viewed him. Now they were beginning to look on him as someone to whom they could come if there was something that they did not understand. Perhaps it was just that they sensed he had knowledge that might keep them alive, or it might just have been a matter of age. The workings of relativity again.

Budge was shepherding them all into the operations room whilst the enlisted men unloaded their baggage. Miller followed on behind, giving the odd smile and nod of encouragement to any face that turned towards him: the keen, the wide-eyed, the apprehensive.

No replacement aircraft had arrived. They would have been ferried over the Channel to the aircraft park and would then be flown on to the squadron by anyone available. If no one was, he supposed some of them would have to go and fetch them. In the meantime the replacements would have to make do with what they had.

A respectful silence fell over the room as Strouden introduced himself and welcomed them to the squadron. He outlined the kind of work the squadron undertook and what he expected of them. As welcoming speeches went, it went quickly, and within sixty seconds Budge was on his feet calling for names and checking them against his roster. Formally — after the first had done it — they stood in turn as they called their names. One — Canning — nervously called, 'Canning Two, sir,' suggesting an older brother somewhere who had preceded him through school. The others laughed and Budge smiled and said, 'You'll just be Mr Canning here.'

Miller wondered where Canning One was, but it was the sort of question that one had learned not to ask.

'Any flown together?' Budge asked. 'Happy to stay a pair?'

217

A couple of hands went up and Budge made a note of their names. The rest he allotted to fill the gaps.

'Best get settled in and cleaned up for dinner,' Budge said. 'We'll see to the paperwork later. The mess hall is the big barn behind the château.'

He asked the few officers present to escort the new boys to their billets and Miller took the two who had become a pair to Breconridge's old hut.

'Ward, isn't it?' Miller asked on the way to the château.

'Yes, sir.'

'I'm Miller,' he told them.

They offered their hands.

'Williams, sir,' said the other one.

'Which of you is the pilot?'

'Me, sir,' Ward said. He was an unprepossessing youth who gave the impression of still needing time to grow into his uniform, having empty space around the limbs and body that made the material wrinkle untidily. His face wore an eager-to-please expression that Miller found difficult to concentrate on as a lank lock of hair bounced with every step he took, falling continually across his face. He swept it back in an action that looked mechanical.

'Much time up?' Miller asked.

'Twenty hours, sir. Maurice Farmans mostly although I got a couple in on an FE.'

'Smashing machine, sir,' Williams piped in with a high pitched voice that was going to give the mimics something to imitate.

'This is your hut.'

He opened the door. The bunks were made and tidy, the shelves and cupboards empty and waiting. It was as if Breconridge had never been there. He tried to remember who the observer had shared the hut with but couldn't.

'Thank you, sir,' they said almost in unison.

Miller looked at his watch.

'You've got a few hours before Mess. I suggest you settle in then take a look around and get the layout of the place before Captain Budge catches up with the paperwork.'

'Yes, sir. Excuse me, sir,' Ward said, 'but are you an American? You don't mind my asking, do you, sir?'

'That's all right, Ward. I don't mind you asking. But I'm English. I used to live there, that's all.'

'I've got an uncle who lives in New York. It's just that I'm hoping to visit him, you see, sir. After the war, of course.'

'New York's a grand town,' Miller said. 'I'm sure you'll like it.'

He was halfway to the Bessonneau when, breathing heavily, one of Budge's clerks caught up with him.

'Colonel Maxwell on the blower for you from Wing, sir,' he gasped. 'Wouldn't leave a message. Had to talk to you direct. Mr Budge's office, sir.'

Miller trotted back to the château and the office, picked up the ear-piece and spoke into the telephone.

'Miller here.'

'Miller?' a gruff voice crackled down the line. 'Maxwell. I've just seen the report you sent.'

Miller waited for him to go on.

'The report on Heyward, man. The chap who hanged himself!'

'Yes, sir,' Miller said. 'I know who Heyward was.'

'You didn't say why he did it.'

'No, sir. I don't know why he did it.'

'That's why I sent you there.'

'I'm aware of that. I'm afraid there's no obvious answer.'

'Obvious? If it had been obvious, man, I wouldn't need you to find out why, would I?'

'No, sir.'

'I had expected more,' Maxwell said.

Miller wondered if it might be worth trying to sound contrite.

'Anyway,' Maxwell went on, 'why I'm phoning is that the situation has changed.'

'In what way?'

'Kitchener is dead.'

'What?'

'The news has just come in. He was in the *Hampshire* on his way to Russia. It struck a mine near the Orkneys. Went straight down. Only half-a-dozen survivors.'

'Poor bastards,' Miller muttered. Then, to Maxwell, 'I suppose that changes things.'

'Yes. Heyward's family... Well, back to proper channels again.'

Miller hesitated, almost deciding not mention it, but he knew Maxwell was going to find out soon anyway. 'There's been something else.'

'What?'

'An officer named Tozer appears to have shot himself.'

'Oh, good lord!'

'We found him a couple of hours ago across the fields.'

'What did you say his name was? Grocer?'

'Tozer.'

'Where have I heard that name before?'

'I was wondering if Major Strouden hadn't tried to get him transferred recently,' Miller said.

'I think you're right, Miller. He wanted me to put this chap Toaster in one of those new scout squadrons they're forming. I told him it was too early yet to allocate personnel. Besides, with the casualties you've been taking recently I can't afford to transfer experienced men out.'

'No, sir.'

'And now you say he's dead?'

'Yes, sir.'

'Good God!'

There didn't seem much need for Miller to comment.

'What in God's name is going on there, Miller? Is he riding them too hard? Do I have to pull him out? He's taking more casualties than any other squadron. I need to know why, Miller. You need to tell me why.'

'I'm not sure yet,' Miller said.

'Well find out, man. That's why you're there.'

'I'll try.'

'The sooner you do that the sooner you can get back on the Somme.'

'Thank you, sir,' Miller said, but Maxwell had already broken the connection. Budge walked into the office as he replaced the telephone.

'Hullo, Miller,' he said. 'Can I do something for you?'

'No. I've just had a telephone call from Colonel Maxwell at Wing. He said Kitchener's dead. Drowned when his ship went down.'

'I'll be damned,' said Budge. 'Does that mean you'll be leaving us?'

Miller lit a cigarette. 'Not immediately. With our casualties he's not keen on taking men out of the squadron just yet.'

'I'm glad to hear it,' Budge said. 'I don't think the CO would want to lose you.'

'You may be right,' Miller said. He made a vague gesture towards the telephone. 'Maxwell told me Major Strouden had been on to Wing trying to get Tozer a transfer to one of the new scout squadrons.'

'That's right,' Budge said, 'after that unpleasantness over Garfield and Pollock.' He made a gesture of helplessness. 'No go, unfortunately. Wing wouldn't hear of it, not after we put in a request for six new men.'

'Did the CO tell Tozer?'

'Couldn't say. If he did, perhaps that's what tipped the balance. What do you think?'

Miller didn't think so for a moment. It was hardly serious to suppose that a man like Tozer would react in that way because a transfer had been turned down.

'Maxwell's wondering if Major Strouden isn't riding the men too hard.'

Budge looked affronted. 'I think that's hardly fair.'

'Two suicides on top of casualties.'

'We do the work they give us. I trust you stood up for him. You know how things stand. You must have served under a few COs, Miller.'

He did and he had – and COs of varying quality. He hadn't quite made up his mind where on the spectrum he would place Strouden. He was a career soldier, but not one of the kind who saw commanding a squadron as merely a step on the ladder and used it to squeeze out every last drop of kudos they could to impress their superiors. Nor did he fall into the category of the friend whom you sat next to at breakfast only to find he had become your CO by lunch; that kind, often promoted through necessity, could easily find themselves caught between leadership and friendship and generally fell into the chasm separating the two. Strouden wasn't either of these. There was something paternalistic about his command, but he kept it within the bounds of the work he had to undertake. If there was a chasm between his regard for those under him and the responsibilities of his job, it was one he kept within himself.

Miller merely said to Budge, 'He needs a rest.'

Budge had begun sorting papers on his desk, but without any method. 'I know,' he said. 'A couple of months back home and he'd be on top of his form again. But he thinks he can't leave. Not the way things are.'

'They're not going to get any better.'

Budge looked up. 'Why don't *you* have a word with him, Miller,' he said, as if it was an idea that had just occurred to him. 'As a — ' he searched for the right word but didn't look far ' — an outsider.'

'Isn't it already too late for that?' Miller said. 'After Tozer, I mean.'

Budge went back to his papers, abrogating responsibility. 'You'd better do what you think best, old man.'

The door to Strouden's office was closed. Miller walked by and got as far as the front entrance to the château before he stopped, turned around and walked back. He knocked on the door, waited a moment then opened it. Strouden was sitting behind his desk, as still and solid as a stone Buddha. After a moment he raised his eyes slowly. Perhaps it was just a reflection of the conversation he had had with Budge but he thought the somewhat disdainful look with which Strouden regarded him was another reminder that Miller — if any reminder were needed — was not a member of the club. Not 'one of them' and, although some temporary dispensation might have been granted, Strouden's paternalism didn't stretch as far as him.

Foisted not fostered.

'I've just spoken to Colonel Maxwell on the telephone,' Miller said when it became apparent that Strouden was not going to speak. 'Field Marshal Kitchener was drowned when the ship he was on went down. They think it hit a mine.'

Strouden barely reacted. After a long moment he dropped his eyes to his desk. In contrast to how he had been earlier when they found Tozer it now seemed to require a great effort for Strouden to do anything more than move fractionally in his chair. It was as if, once he had stopped moving, he had become locked in immobility and Miller sensed how much it was costing Strouden to drag himself back from wherever he had been. He looked like a man who had physically to pull his life back on like an old suit of clothes. When the task was finally accomplished, something of the animation returned to his face, though worn and haggard and slowed by its re-assumption. He looked up to where Miller stood, breathing deeply like a man who had just come up for air.

'Shut the door, Miller,' he said. 'And sit down.'

Miller closed the door and took the chair facing him across the desk.

'You said something. What was it?'

Miller repeated that Kitchener was dead.

This time Strouden reacted, but only to raise an eyebrow to signal a passing interest.

'I doubt if it will mean much,' he said after a moment. 'He'd been pushed too far up the ladder, past what he was best at. He was no more than a figurehead, really.'

'The Huns will think it's a feather in their cap,' Miller said.

'My father was with him in the Boer War,' Strouden suddenly said conversationally. 'Did you know that?'

'No, I had no idea.'

'A soldiering family, you see. I'll be the last, Miller. No brothers and I'm not married. No children.'

'There's still time,' Miller said. He didn't know that he believed it, but he knew that it was what one generally said in that sort of situation. 'You're still young.'

'Am I? I don't feel it.'

'The work,' Miller said. 'Away from here things will look different.'

'He was utterly without pity, my father said. Kitchener. He showed that in South Africa.'

'I suppose that is what war does to us,' Miller said.

'Oh, no,' Strouden said. 'I wouldn't agree with you. We are what we are. War merely exaggerates what it finds in a man and a man should always retain a certain amount of pity. I often think that without pity there is little to distinguish us from common murderers.'

The statement was stark and Miller wondered if they were still talking about Kitchener.

'War is no more than a job we have to do,' Strouden continued, 'particularly for the regular soldier. That is his choice. Having undertaken to do it, he must do it to the best of his ability. I'm not saying it is pleasant. It costs the lives of our best young men, but that is the price we have elected to pay. But even if we are willing to pay that price it does not mean we should forget our humanity while we are paying it. You agree, surely.'

'Yes,' Miller said, 'but it is still a dehumanising experience.'

'Only if you allow it to become so.'

'Not an easy thing to avoid, I would have thought,' Miller said, 'giving what it is we are asked to do.'

'Perhaps that is what differentiates us from the enemy.'

'My worry is, given what it is we *are* asked to do, does it justify *anything*?'

'Anything?'

'Doing whatever we might regard as necessary,' Miller said.

'Necessary?' Strouden repeated, more to himself as if he were stepping carefully over Miller's words. 'That, I suppose, must remain the judgement of the officer class. It's their decision as to what is necessary and therefore justifiable.'

What Miller wanted to ask was – *and supposing an officer's judgement is impaired?* But he hesitated and the moment passed. Strouden seemed to shake himself out of his discursive mood and returned to the business at hand. They began discussing the best way of attacking a balloon and the chances of success. Miller couldn't help thinking that, even if successful, they were going to take casualties and, sooner or later, another balloon would take the downed one's place.

He was beginning to wonder what the point was. Balloons equalled dead men; consecutive balloons would mean consecutive dead men. Perhaps the point was the few who might live by slipping between the two, survivors of the hiatus. Did it all come down to some geometric corollary, then? Or was it an algebraic formula? He didn't understand it. Like the rest of the dunces he just did what he was told.

22

'Looking in the wrong bloody place altogether,' Parker said shaking his head in bewilderment. He was in the operations room examining the map where the balloon was now believed to be. He ran a finger around the area then stabbed it in the centre. 'Bloody great hangar, so Watson said.'

Miller looked at the spot. 'Then why don't they call in another artillery strike?'

Parker dropped into a chair, draping himself over it languidly. 'Your guess is as good as mine,' he said. 'Too much egg on their face already, I should think. Don't want to bodge the job again.'

'So it falls to us,' Miller said.

'Damn decent of them, don't you think?'

'Well, I hope it's not going to be another dud show.'

'Watson says the bloody thing's big enough to house two of the buggers,' Parker said.

'Shouldn't be able to miss them then, should we?'

In his hut Miller stripped off at the washbasin. Hanging his tunic on a hook, his hand touched the top pocket where, that morning, he had put the letters that had arrived for Heyward after his death. Riding into town had put them out of his mind and he took them out, dropped them onto the bunk then washed. He dried himself, sat down and began examining them.

There were three, all still sealed. One was from a friend in the Yorkshire Yeomanry who had sent an earlier letter that had been among Heyward's personal effects. The latest missive was dated two days after Heyward had killed himself and merely detailed a couple of days' shooting the friend had spent while on leave, along with some local tittle-tattle. The second letter was from Heyward's mother and dated the day Heyward had hanged himself. It contained the usual mix of gossip and concern for his welfare and the fact that two of Heyward's acquaintances had become casualties: one dead, the other badly injured. The last paragraph, however, sounded a different note:

Charles, I do wish you would reconsider your decision as regards to your book. I realise that artists go through periods of disenchantment with their work and this is only natural but I am sure it will pass. Once you have had time to reflect you will see that I am right. After all, if Mr Fisher from Carver & Fisher thinks your work worthy of publication your disillusion can only be a temporary feeling. So my dear boy, I must insist upon exercising a mother's prerogative and disobey your instructions to destroy the chapters you have directed Mr Fisher to return. I am certain that in a few days you will see that I am right and would be regretting any hasty decisions...

Miller laid the letter on the bunk and opened the third. It was postmarked London, dated three days after Heyward's death and had been typed beneath the letterhead of Carver & Fisher & Co., Publishers.

Dear Mr Heyward,

I am sorry to read that you have decided not to submit the remaining chapters of your manuscript, Memoirs of a Flying Officer, and that you wish us to return the material already with us to your Yorkshire address. We will, of course, comply with your instructions but would ask you to reconsider as it is our opinion that, on the strength of what you have submitted to this office, the work has real merit and is deserving of a wider audience.

It may be that you have been approached by another publishing house and if this is the case then, naturally, we will respect your decision. However, before committing yourself might I be so bold as to suggest you consider the terms Carver & Fisher might be in a position to offer. Any decision, of course, would be dependent upon an appraisal of the complete manuscript.

I remain etc.

Gerald Fisher

Heyward, naturally, had never had the opportunity to read the letter. It was always possible that, had he known what Gerald Fisher was going to write, he might never have made his fatal decision. But Miller was beginning to think that that was not the point. He pulled out the box of Heyward's effects from beneath the bunk and went through the letters in it once more. There was nothing from Carver & Fisher and the only other mention of Heyward's book was in the few lines his mother had written informing him that the opening chapters had been forwarded to another publisher. But she had known an offer had been made and the three-week gap between the date on this letter from his mother and the one from Carver & Fisher that he had just read gave plenty of time for a communication from the publisher, even if it was not there. He supposed that Mrs Heyward had received the returned material by now and that, as she had said, she had disregarded her son's wishes and had not destroyed them. She would, no doubt, be expecting to receive the rest of her son's book along with his effects. *That* was going to beg some awkward questions.

Parry was out on the field looking over his FE with Pilot-Sergeant Reynolds. The rest of the makeshift flight's machines were being readied on the assumption that the squadron at Droglandt had not been advised that the Hun observation balloon was up and that they would be stood down at six o'clock. Strouden had already briefed those chosen for the operation and now they were filling in time as best they could. Chatterton was there, talking to Warrant Officer Mackinnon, and, in the front nacelle of Moss's machine, Trueman was helping one of Gracey's men fit the Lewis guns on their mountings.

Reynolds looked up as Miller approached.

'Any news, sir?'

'I've not heard,' Miller said. He glanced at his watch. It had just gone 5pm. 'I think we'd better assume we'll be up.'

'I've never had a go at a sausage,' Reynolds said.

'Have you got a minute?' he asked Parry.

They walked a few steps away from the machines.

'It's the waiting that's the worst, don't you find?' Parry said.

'Yes. I'd much rather just climb in and get going.'

'Was it something about Heyward? I've been thinking it over since we spoke, wondering if there was anything I might have done. You know...'

'I don't think so,' Miller assured him.

Something he'd *not* done, perhaps, but he didn't say that. 'I was just wondering how long it was after you'd asked Heyward about Dunne's book that he actually killed himself.'

'I've tried to remember,' Parry admitted. 'Certainly not more than a day or two. I do remember I tackled him about Bobby's work the same day that Captain Pearson caught it.'

'Pearson?'

'Captain Pearson was C Flight commander before Denham. They were on patrol and got jumped by Rumplers. Denham thought Appleyard — he was Captain Pearson's observer — must have got hit and wasn't able to defend them. The captain had been with Major Strouden since the beginning and it was a bit of a blow for the squadron.'

'And you asked Heyward that day if he had Dunne's book.'

'Yes. I thought he was up with the patrol but someone told me he had turned back with engine trouble or something. That's why C Flight was under-strength. Denham said that the Rumplers might not have fancied taking them on if there'd been an extra machine up.'

'So you went to see Heyward?'

'Sorry,' Parry said. 'Yes. I went to his hut when I found out he wasn't up with the patrol. It annoyed me when Heyward said he didn't know anything about Bobby's work when I knew very well that he did. But one can't call a fellow a liar to his face, can one? Well, not unless there's evidence. I'd made up my mind to tackle him again later then the flight got back and I heard that Captain Pearson and Appleyard had been shot down. Heyward and Dunne's book went straight out of my head.'

'And you can't remember if this was the same day that Heyward killed himself or a day earlier.' Miller said.

'I know it wasn't the same day,' Parry said, 'because there was a bit of an atmosphere in the mess that night. Denham more or less came out and said that if Heyward hadn't turned back we wouldn't have lost Captain Pearson. There was nothing wrong with his machine, you see. He probably wasn't keeping the revs up, or something. Captain Budge would know, of course.'

'Know what?'

'Which day it was that Captain Pearson was killed.'

'Yes,' Miller said, 'of course.'

He left Parry and returned to the château. Budge was going over papers at his desk.

'Nothing from Droglandt yet, I'm afraid,' he said as Miller walked through the door.

'No, it was something else,' he said. 'Can you tell me what day it was that Captain Pearson was killed?'

'Henry Pearson?' Budge asked, stopping what he was doing. 'Why on earth would you want to know that? Didn't know him, did you?'

When Miller didn't reply, Budge frowned and reached for the squadron log book.

'May twenty-fourth,' Corporal Donaldson said from his desk before Budge could open the log. 'A Wednesday it was if you recall, sir.'

'Yes, you're right Donaldson,' Budge said as Strouden walked in behind Miller. He was already dressed in his flying gear as if eager to get up.

'Get on to Droglandt, will you Frank? Let them know we've got the ball now. Then let Brigade know we're ready to go as soon as the balloon is up.'

'Rightyo,' Budge said, reaching for the telephone. Then he said, 'Miller here is asking about Henry Pearson.'

'Oh?' Strouden responded belligerently. 'What's your interest in Captain Pearson, Miller?'

'I'm told Heyward turned back on the patrol the day Pearson was killed.'

'Did he?' Strouden said. He glanced down at Donaldson who had pointedly turned back to his typewriter but was making no attempt to type, then he looked at Budge again. 'Right away if you would, Frank.' He held Miller's gaze for a moment. 'My office?' he said, in the manner of a headmaster summoning an errant schoolboy.

'It's going to be a good clear evening for spotting,' Miller said in an attempt to pre-empt Strouden.

The CO grunted as he sat down behind his desk, looking bulkier than ever in his flying gear.

'They're bound to supply air cover and won't want to spoil their dinner,' Miller went on, 'so I doubt it'll be much later than six-thirty.'

Strouden eyed him sardonically. 'And do you think Brigade would take our dinner into account if it was one of our sausages that was going up?'

'Probably not,' Miller admitted, 'but they're the golden boys, aren't they? The Hun have always thought more of their air corps than we have of ours, wouldn't you say?'

'I'll pass on to Brigade your suggestion on not having our dinner interrupted,' Strouden said.

'May I smoke, sir?' Miller asked.

Strouden looked up at him. 'Yes, of course. There's hardly a need for formality.' Adding testily, 'And sit down, will you. I didn't think you were a man for form, Miller.'

'I'm not, as a rule,' Miller said. 'It's just that you're a difficult man to read, if you don't mind my saying so.'

Strouden didn't comment.

'You were asking about Henry Pearson,' he said.

'He'd been with you for some time, I'm told.'

'Since the beginning,' Strouden said. 'We met in training. We were good friends.'

'Apparently Denham more or less told Heyward that if he hadn't turned back Pearson and Appleyard wouldn't have been killed.'

'Appleyard?'

'Pearson's observer.'

'Was that his name?' For a second Strouden frowned. 'Yes, Appleyard. A good man.'

'Heyward had reported engine trouble but it seems there was nothing wrong with his machine.'

'Yes, I recall now,' Strouden said. 'Mackinnon had them go over it. Not for the first time, either. But some machines can be temperamental for no apparent reason.' He paused. 'You've had no problem with it, I suppose?'

'Heyward's Fee? No.'

Strouden grunted again as if he hadn't expected that Miller had.

'Did *you* blame Heyward for Pearson's death?' Miller asked.

Strouden didn't reply. He looked at a spot on the wall above Miller's head then breathed deeply. He reached for his cigarettes.

'No,' he said eventually. 'The Hun killed Henry. What might have happened if Heyward had been there is pure supposition.'

'Is that how you felt at the time?'

'Does this have any bearing on Heyward's suicide?'

'It might,' Miller said.

Strouden exhaled smoke. 'Very well. I did speak to him afterwards. I'd seen him turn back. He was sounding off to his fitter, Smith, about his Fee. The only man who didn't seem to mind was the observer who had gone up with him — White, I think it was.' He drew on his cigarette again and looked at Miller. 'We lost White as well, didn't we? Another good man.' He breathed out the smoke with what was almost a sigh.

'I'd had Heyward fly as an observer after he'd damaged a machine a week or two earlier,' Strouden went on, 'when Dunne was killed. But he complained that having been trained as a pilot, flying as observer reflected badly on him. Maintained it looked as though he couldn't be trusted. We were short-handed so I was persuaded to give him another chance.' He ground out the cigarette. 'After Mackinnon had checked over the Fee and found it perfectly serviceable I decided enough was enough. Trained as a pilot or not, having a man one couldn't trust to stay up when he was supposed to was worse than having no man at all.'

'You told him that?'

Strouden scratched at his head. 'I told him that I found him unfit to fly and that there was no way I could allow him up again behind the controls. I told him he could continue in the squadron as an observer or that I could have him transferred to another squadron where they could find him a ground job.' He looked pointedly at Miller. 'I wasn't about to foist a bad pilot onto someone else, don't think that. I made that clear. I told him to think it over.'

'How did he take that?'

'He hanged himself,' Strouden said. 'I had no idea he would take it as badly as he did.'

'I don't believe that was why he killed himself,' Miller said. 'At least, if it did have any bearing it was only in a peripheral way. The last straw, perhaps.'

Strouden's shoulders sagged a little, as if some of the air had gone out of him.

'Well, that's something. I don't mind telling you, Miller, it's been weighing on my mind. Heyward was a decent chap. Not the kind one could grow fond of, I admit, but decent enough.'

'Wasn't Tozer a "decent chap"?'

Strouden looked up, his eyes suddenly growing cold. 'What has Tozer got to do with this?'

'When I first spoke to Maxwell he told me you had applied to transfer Heyward but that he'd turned you down. He couldn't have his squadron commanders cherry picking, he said.'

'Well, what of it?'

'You were ordered to keep two men you didn't want and now they are both dead.'

'This squadron has seen a lot of dead men,' Strouden said. 'Casualties are to be expected.'

'Like the men killed in training?' Miller countered.

'That's just sheer waste.'

'Isn't it just another way of weeding out the duds?'

'Perhaps it is,' Strouden said, 'but it's beyond some men to be anything else. Just because they're duds doesn't mean that they have to die.'

'Not even in times of war? When they cost the lives of others?'

'That's a different circumstance,' Strouden said.

'Is it?'

'Are you playing devil's advocate?'

'Perhaps I am,' Miller admitted. 'The point is Tozer wasn't a dud but he was still costing lives, lives of better men. Wing wouldn't transfer him and I'm wondering if you came to believe that the time had come to take responsibility for him yourself.'

Strouden said nothing.

'Who do you believe is ever authorised to make *that* kind of decision?' Miller persisted.

'All kinds of decisions have to be made,' Strouden said. Then, when Miller made no comment, 'By those of a rank delegated to do so.'

'Heyward's suicide must have looked like a convenient solution to an inconvenient problem.'

Strouden regarded him contemptuously. 'You're making assumptions, Miller. Command isn't easy and you're not fitted to pass judgement until you've borne that weight upon your shoulders.'

He locked his gaze onto Miller's. The dark rings of exhaustion were still there but his facial muscles had tautened, firm again. He looked suddenly resilient.

Miller returned the stare. There was a line he was about to cross and he had

229

no idea what lay beyond it. He knew that he could back away, then and there, and that nothing further would be said. That would be the end of the matter. But Miller couldn't help asking himself if it would be the *right* end.

He took the step.

'When Tozer got back from town — '

There was a rap at the door and Budge put his head into the room.

'Sorry to interrupt Tommy, but the balloon's been spotted. Brigade want us up right away. Mackinnon's getting the machines started.'

Strouden stood and picked up his flying helmet. He looked down at Miller and there was a challenge in his expression.

'We can continue this later, Miller, if you want.'

Miller followed him out of the office, no longer sure if he wanted to or not.

The early evening sky was clear. Trails of high nimbus streaked the upper reaches, tinted almost gold by a sun setting somewhere over Normandy. Closer to Heaven, Miller thought as the Strutter climbed through the thinning air. Fifty yards east of him Strouden sat in the bathtub of the DH2's cockpit; below them the rest of the flight were strung out like great winged insects droning above the salient. To the east a heat haze hung over no man's land mingling with the darker mist of artillery smoke. A bombardment was rattling up and down the Hun trenches, its thunder drowned by the roar of the Strutter's Clerget engine into soundless gouts of mud and earth that blossomed into the air like scenes from a picture house two-reeler. Due south a Hun formation patrolled to the rear of their lines; to the east, hanging seemingly motionless against the ribbed strands of nimbus was a high blur that at any other time and place might have been a flock of migrating birds.

The conversation with Strouden kept running through his head like a constantly replayed phonograph record. He needed to clear it, to empty his head of everything except the business at hand. Distractions killed. Yet each time he focused on the machines around him, the ground, the sky, his mind slid off in a different direction, banked and turned to skim over a course already run and sit on his own tail.

He knew what had happened to Tozer but had no evidence and wasn't sure that he really wanted any. Tozer was just stupid enough to hand over his service revolver and lift his chin if ordered to do so. He probably never realised what was happening until it was too late.

Heyward was a different matter. Miller couldn't get into the man's head. The gulf between their respective experiences was just too great. He could infer from what he knew and even make assumptions but that's all they could ever be; he could never know for certain.

He found it difficult to think of Heyward as a young man although that was what he had been; his attitudes and prejudices had, to Miller, the taint of middle-age about them. He didn't share them so he was unable to understand how Heyward had reacted under their sway. The pressure from the squadron was understandable — he was a bad pilot unwilling to admit the fact even to

230

himself. Dunne's death was due to his incompetence and on some level he must have known it but, what Miller suspected must have been infinitely worse, was for Heyward to have come to realise that Dunne was a better man than he was — better, that is, in the *kind* of man that Heyward aspired to be. His own writing was turgid, unimaginative and third-rate; if he hadn't already known it, he must have realised as much when Dunne gave him his own work to read. And then Dunne was dead and he found himself in possession of his manuscript.

Under any other circumstances Miller was sure that appropriating Dunne's work would never have crossed his mind. But under the circumstances in which Heyward found himself his judgement must have been impaired. He had probably already sent a few pages to the publisher he knew while Dunne was alive as Parry had suggested; he didn't suppose that, at that time, Heyward had had any intention of passing the work off as his own. But then Dunne was killed and the publisher made the erroneous assumption that Heyward was the author and had passed the work on to another firm. Perhaps. He was dead and Miller thought he deserved a little charity. But however it had happened, Miller was sure that, once he had had a favourable reply, Heyward had copied out the opening of Dunne's manuscript in his own hand and sent the first chapters to the publisher as his own work.

And then? Pearson is killed on a patrol from which he had turned back on a spurious excuse; Strouden tears a strip off him, tells him he will be transferred and given some other job because he wasn't up to the one he had been trained for... Wouldn't Heyward have felt that second transfer to be another retreat, like his move out of the trenches?

Finally, Parry turns up looking for Dunne's manuscript. Perhaps this was the first he knew that someone else was aware of Dunne's writing. Perhaps Parry even told him about Phyllida Dunne and of her hopes for her brother. It would be like Parry, eager to talk about the girl he was in love with and using the boy's family as the excuse for demanding Dunne's manuscript back. Once Heyward had denied ever having seen it, given a petty lie to a fellow officer, what could he expect except to be caught attempting to pass off the work of the man he had killed as his own?

Under those circumstances it might be that even the disgrace to his family of hanging himself did not seem too extreme. In one way, considering Dunne's death, he might even have thought it to be a fitting punishment.

That's when Heyward had burned any more of the manuscript he had copied out, he supposed. And momentarily thrown his own work onto the fire as well, judging by the burnt edges of the exercise books he had seen. But perhaps destroying his own work was something Heyward couldn't bring himself to do; he'd wanted to leave something behind even if it was second-rate. And neither had he destroyed Dunne's manuscript. Just why he hadn't ensured that it had got to Parry, Miller didn't know. By then, he supposed, Heyward had other things to think about. After all, Miller imagined that throwing a rope over a cross beam and tying a noose in it would be the kind of thing that's apt to concentrate the mind...

He was suddenly aware of the DH2 and Strouden, a bald owl in helmet and goggles, flying alongside him, gesticulating wildly. Miller shook the train of thought loose from his head and tried to concentrate. He raised a hand to pacify Strouden and looked around. Reynolds and Parry were to his right, Denham and Chacksfield ahead. Over his shoulder he saw Trueman in the front nacelle of Moss's FE. Somewhere, York was flying with Boyes and Chatterton and MacMaster were close but Strouden began waving again before Miller had the chance to pin them down. He was pointing east and a moment later had banked the DH2 and was slipping towards the Hun lines.

23

The Hun must have tired of being shelled because now an artillery bombardment of their own was targeting Poperinghe again. Below them Miller could see smoke rising but couldn't make out whether it was the railway junction or the transit camps they were after this time. It was quite immaterial really, the shells would be falling all over the town like randomly thrown dice. He wondered if perhaps it would have not been better just to let the *Luftschiffertruppen*, the Hun balloon battalions, get on with it, get the spotting right, so that it wasn't such a damnable lottery for the poor devils under the barrage. He could imagine how a suggestion like *that* would go down with Brigade.

A particularly concentrated pattern of fire threw up a swirling black cloud of smoke to the west of the town, closer to the camps, and he thought he might have to reassess his estimation of the balloon spotters. He scanned the sky around him, supposing that some other squadron had machines up to spot the Hun guns but he couldn't see them. There were some vague flecks against the sky to the north that might have been machines but it was difficult to see in the haze and, anyway, they were too far away to be interested in this barrage. These guns would be well behind the Hun front line, probably big beasts reserved for long-range work, and he wondered how high the arc of the shell needed to be to reach its target. He had heard men claim to have seen shells in flight passing their machines during a bombardment, but he never had. Considering how close the damn thing would have to be to be spotted, he was quite sure he never wanted to.

Strouden was taking them over the lines with the setting sun at their backs. This made them lower than he usually liked to be over Hun territory but it would also make them far harder to spot as they approached. Maintaining their usual altitude would be pointless; the balloon would see them coming from miles away and be winched down before they could get anywhere near it. Their only chance of taking the thing down was to get on top of it before the Hun realised they were there.

Moss and Trueman, slightly below and to his right, had drifted out of formation — Moss translating his erratic movements into a vector — and the phrase *quantity with direction and magnitude* sprang into Miller's head from the mathematics he had been taught as a boy. Old Larson, he remembered, a Swede who had given mathematics lessons in one of the mining camps to raise enough money for a grubstake. Men like Larsen were not uncommon in the goldfields and, in a moment of clarity, he saw the camps as a microcosm of what was below: a sinkhole into the descent of which useful men wasted their lives.

Beneath him Moss jerked his FE back in formation and the thought skittered away in Miller's slipstream.

They still didn't know what kind of sausage it was the Huns were using. Strictly speaking, he thought to himself pedantically, cocooned as he was within the cacophony of his engine, it was only the old *Drachen* that were truly sausages — completely cylindrical as they were with rounded ends and one fat stabilising fin like a growth on its rear-end. Now the Hun had started copying the French *Caquot*, a balloon with more of a teardrop shape which had three fins. Not that it made any difference: they were all still known as sausages. The *Caquot*, though, was a better balloon. It was more stable in high winds and could fly higher, well over 4,000 feet. The *Drachen* couldn't get that high and, if Miller had been a *Luftschiffertruppen*, he was sure he wouldn't want to; the baskets in which they were suspended beneath were flimsy wicker affairs that a few well-aimed rounds could rip to pieces. The spotters were equipped with parachutes, it was true, but they would only jump as a last resort. It was a fifty-fifty chance whether or not the thing would open and Miller had seen one poor devil take the gamble and be rewarded with nothing more than a tangle of cord and flapping silk.

He hoped the one they were going after was a *Caquot*. It may have been a better balloon but a *Caquot* would be higher. That would give them more time to get on it before it was winched down. The damned *Drachen* were never much more than one or two thousand feet up and at that height the Archie and the heavy machine gun fire on approach was murderous. *That's* what made them so difficult: if you managed to get through the screen of aircraft the Hun generally put up to protect them, all you had to look forward to was a hailstorm of hot metal.

Strouden was waggling the DH2's wings, dancing like a tipsy maybug, then he slid off his course and took them down another five hundred feet. They were over the Hun lines now and had attracted some ground-fire — ineffectual pot-shots you could swat away with the back of your hand if you could ever reach it. Then Archie spotted them and began lobbing up shells that seemed to explode out of nowhere in puffs of grey and yellow smoke that muddied the sky.

Miller stuck on Strouden's tail, edging in front of the rest of the formation. The two of them were to engage the Hun machines when they found them so as to allow the five FEs a clear run at the balloon. The pilots were going to have enough to worry about just getting their observers in gunnery range through the Archie without having to keep looking over their shoulders for Rumplers or whatever it was the Hun would have up in defence. They needed to get close, too close, if their rounds were to be of any use. Ordinary bullets would pass right through the skin of the sausage and do no more damage than let a little air out. To ignite the hydrogen, they had to use tracers and for them to be hot enough to detonate the gas they had to be close, otherwise they cooled down too quickly and just fizzed prettily over the sky harmlessly trailing smoke.

Below, Polygon Wood slid away as they picked up the pitted road towards Passchendaele. Archie thickened. Gouts of smoke blackened the sky as it found their range and ahead of him, Miller saw Strouden's DH2 lurch violently as a blast rocked him. He crabbed sideways for a moment then straightened as Miller once more closed on his tail. The heavy Archie might mask their machines but

Miller couldn't help thinking that it was like waving a red flag at the Hun, signalling that *something* was approaching and, even as he looked up, he saw a formation of machines a thousand feet, perhaps two thousand feet, above them. Halberstadts and Rumplers, he thought. He pulled the nose of the Strutter up a little and moved over and above Strouden. Not quite done in hunt circles, he supposed, nosing in front of the head huntsman, but at least it would get Strouden's attention. The major looked up at him and Miller waved his arm towards the Hun formation then let the Strutter slip back into position.

If they were up, the balloon couldn't be far away. He looked along the road beneath them to the line of trenches and fortifications that had marked the front line in 1914 when the opposing sides had first dug themselves in. Through the smoke and to the southwest of Passchendaele, he could just make out the looming bulk of a balloon breaching the horizon. He looked across at the DH2 and knew immediately that Strouden had seen it. He had climbed slightly, now positioning himself between the Hun machines and the FEs below and behind him. Miller followed him, glancing down at Chatterton and MacMaster in the lead FE and saw that they were maintaining their course and were heading for the sausage. From above, the Archie looked like a dense grey smog and he saw one of the FEs suddenly buck like an unbroken stallion and its right wing tear loose. It canted around and for a moment lay on its side and Miller recalled the wounded horse in Poperinghe that had lost its leg. Then the FE started to spiral, twisting around and down in uneven jerky turns and somehow he knew that it was Moss.

Above, two Rumplers had detached themselves from the group and were diving on Strouden. The other three, two Halberstadts and another Rumpler, were slower and had to bank and come around once they had seen the flight.

Miller began to climb, getting above and between Strouden and the remaining three Hun machines. As he closed with them, he looked again towards the balloon, across through the clearer air that the Archie had not yet polluted. Closer now, the great grey bulk had grown fatter and somehow elongated and he realised that there were two balloons, both *Caquots*, hitched in tandem by a stabilising wire cage strung between them, invisible except for the occasional sharp glint, like an exploding flash bulb, where the setting sun caught the metal frame.

Then the Huns were in front of him and he saw the trail of a tracer arc away to his left. Too far, he thought, kicking the rudder bar, banking and easing back the stick so that he was climbing on their flank before they could adjust their course. By the time he was above and behind them he realised they had lost interest in him and were heading for the rest of the flight. He dropped his nose and dived. He looked around for Strouden and the other two Rumplers but they seemed lost in the haze thrown up by the Archie. At three hundred yards he singled out the rearmost Halberstadt, dropping onto his tail as the other two Hun machines paired off towards the leading FE. He reached up for the Vickers and closed a finger on the trigger. Two hundred and fifty... two hundred... He squeezed. The Vickers rattled for a second, his tracers cutting a trail over the

Halberstadt's top wing. Then it jammed. He cursed and hit the gun with the flat of his hand. The Hun machine dived away to his right and Miller eased back on the stick, levelling out as he worked to clear the jam.

He snatched a glance at the FEs below and saw an observer he thought was Parry standing in the nacelle at the rear Lewis, firing a burst over his own top wing at a Rumpler trying to get into his blind spot. Miller cleared the jammed Vickers and dived onto the Rumpler. They were nearing the balloons now and he thought they had lost height, the motorised winches below trying to get them down before the machines closed on them. He saw three or four great roiling balls of fire rise towards the FEs, those curious defensive weapons they had nicknamed 'flaming onions'. He had never seen them anywhere other than near balloons and was still not sure what their exact purpose was, whether to set the machines alight or merely to distract the pilots. They were easy to avoid, though, and he caught a glimpse of Strouden's DH2 dodging one as he dropped towards the balloons, the Rumplers that had gone after him seemingly having disappeared.

The Archie had ceased close to the *Caquots* for fear of igniting them and Miller saw the leading FE put a burst into the nearest balloon. But they were too far and their tracers fizzed harmlessly into the thick skin of the sausage. A Halberstadt picked them up before they could get any closer and Miller saw the observer, MacMaster was it?, swinging his forward Lewis around to stitch a diagonal line of fire across the Hun's fuselage. Then a Rumpler crossed unexpectedly above him and Miller pulled back on his stick to line up the Strutter on him. He emptied a drum into the machine and watched with grim satisfaction as it turned, quite gracefully, upside down before losing all momentum and begin to fall, inverted, past the balloons.

Two FEs had reached them now, so close he thought they would have to pull up or collide. The first, slightly ahead and twenty feet higher, rattled a continuous burst into the hide of the sausage. A gout of flame erupted and in an instant the sausage skin started peeling back as it was consumed by fire. A black plume of smoke rose into the sky above it and Miller saw the basket beneath tip and a man fall out, end over end, arms and legs working like a panicking swimmer as he tried to get purchase on the thin air. The second man still clung to the wicker basket as it hung beneath the limp skin of the sausage, held up by the wire cage that linked it to the second balloon.

Miller almost found himself willing the man to let go and open his parachute, then, as he watched, the man and the basket exploded in a starburst of flame and he saw Strouden's DH2 angle past him, guns still firing.

The smoke began to clear and he saw Chatterton's FE climbing up above the wrecked balloon. He looked for the second machine and saw it, sickeningly, hanging in the crumpled metal cage that had connected the two *Caquots*, trapped like a fly in a spider's web. The wings had folded into an upright 'V' like a crude gesture of defiance with the nacelle suspended between. Miller closed in and saw the pilot slumped over the side of the cockpit and the observer clambering out of the forward nacelle onto the twisted metal. He had lost his goggles and, as Miller flashed by, the observer's head turned and he saw Parry's startled face stare back at him. A second later he was past, climbing around the rear of the second balloon and suddenly looking into the spitting nose of a Rumpler.

Bullets zinged by between his wings on his left and he grabbed his Vickers and fed them back across the closing distance between the two machines. Fabric ripped and he felt something tear through the wood of the cockpit dashboard. He kicked the rudder and slammed the stick sideways and the Strutter and the Rumpler passed within feet of each other in a gale of rushing air.

Miller's stomach turned and his chest heaved. He felt the vomit rise in his throat and with a shudder of repulsion swallowed it down again. Moving away from the balloon and banking for another pass he saw Denham's FE with Chacksfield hunched in the front nacelle gripping his Lewis gun. Beyond him were York and Boyes angling down on the top of the balloon. Tracers spat out of the two machines and arced in a burst onto the sausage. It seemed to shudder for an instant like a fevered elephant before splitting open as if ruptured at a seam. A ball of fire roiled in its gut and spewed out like flaming entrails and the whole balloon seemed to turn inside out and quiver as it fell. The burning skin wrapped itself onto the twisted metal of the cage, over the tangled FE and Reynolds and Parry and fluttered like a monstrous leaf to the ground. Beneath it the winches were enveloped in a wave of flame and smoke.

He was low. They had followed the balloons down and now, as the smoke cleared, he could see that he was no higher than five hundred feet. Ground fire peppered the air with shot, heavy machine guns stitching patterns like a lattice around him. They had got the balloons and there was no point in staying around to get shot at. With the sausages down the Archie would start again and the remaining Hun machines would be on their tails like vengeful wasps. They couldn't afford the luxury of wasting time getting their height; it was going to have to be a run for home and every man for himself.

Ahead, on a bearing that would take them back over their own lines he could see two FEs flying abreast. The third — Denham, he thought — was lagging behind and he pushed the Strutter's Clerget in an effort to catch him. Two Halberstadts were diving on the FE from different directions and Chacksfield was going to have to concentrate on one or the other. Miller adjusted his course to intercept the nearest and hoped that Chacksfield would see him. Then, a foot from his cockpit, machine-gun fire ripped through the fabric of his lower wing and instinctively he kicked the rudder to avoid it, knowing even as he did that by the time he had seen the fire it had already missed. *You never see the one that has your name on it*, the saying went. Miller wiped the spraying oil from his goggles and prayed the one with his name on it hadn't come out of the munitions factory yet.

The first Halberstadt had opened up on Denham and Chacksfield, but he was too eager and hadn't closed sufficiently. Miller could imagine Chacksfield's fat fingers curled around the Lewis, holding his nerve, then he saw the trail of the tracers as the observer opened up on the Hun. The scorching fire seemed to envelope the Halberstadt but somehow he flew through it, screaming over

237

Chacksfield's head. Miller couldn't see how Chacksfield had missed. Then the second Halberstadt filled his vision. He was almost as close to the Hun as the Hun was to Denham, but he couldn't wait. Another few seconds and the Halberstadt would have the FE in its range. Miller opened up the Vickers and saw the Hun pilot turn a startled head in his direction. The Halberstadt zoomed, lifting itself over Denham's FE and climbing out of the fight. Miller banked and turned, swinging the Strutter behind and above the FE to protect its blind spot.

The ground-fire had lessened as they moved out of the balloon's protective perimeter and Miller had just begun to breathe again when a line of tracers whined over his head and past the nose of the Strutter. He twisted round in the cockpit. Strouden in the DH2 was sitting on his tail.

In one heart-stopping moment he realised that Strouden had no intention of continuing their conversation back at the field. Miller knew what had happened to Tozer — so was *he*, like Tozer, now an inconvenient obstacle to the orderly prosecution of the war? Had he become another piece on the board to be removed after all due consideration?

Miller sat paralysed at the controls. Unable to do anything except sit and wait for the unwinding of his fate, he felt the winds of chance turning into a whirlwind about to suck him out of existence. Then the Strutter lurched violently and the tip of his top right wing crumpled and hung by the fabric, swinging in the slipstream for a second before tearing loose. A Rumpler screamed past and the Strutter began to pitch and yaw, careening across a sky filled suddenly by Strouden's DH2 as it swung over Miller's damaged top wing as he chased the Hun.

Miller hadn't seen the Rumpler, but Strouden had. He was protecting Miller's tail not sitting on it. Life flowed back into his hands. He eased the stick over, compensating with the rudder until he found a kind of equilibrium that kept the machine level. Below, the DH2 was sticking to the Rumpler's tail, tracers smoking like rockets ahead of the two machines.

But Strouden was too close. He couldn't depress the snout of his Lewis far enough to sight the Rumpler. The Hun, pinned beneath him like the unwilling partner in a violent sexual union, dipped and wriggled unable to slip free. They were low now, fifty feet, less, and the Rumpler was dropping still. Then, as the ground ahead of them rose towards the blasted remnants of a hillock, the Hun ran out of room to manoeuvre. He rose to avoid the cratered surface and locked the DH2's undercarriage beneath his top wing. For a second they flew in tandem, in a final consummation, until with one last climactic spasm Strouden's DH2 rolled nose down, pulling the Rumpler up and over as they somersaulted in a tangle of wire and wood and fabric into the hillside.

Cirrocumulus
Some vertical turbulence - ceiling unlimited - outlook
settled, temporarily.

There was a cold January wind blowing across the Boulevard Saint-Michel from the Luxembourg Gardens. He had recently been reading *The Old Regime And The Revolution* in the original French by De Toqueville, in part to improve his grasp on the language but also because he had developed an interest in the subject. The French Revolution had formed a bridge between two worlds and, in a way, he was aware that he had lived through a similar cultural upheaval — at least, an event that promised equal change.

He was sitting not more than a stone's throw from the old Cordeliers Club, where men like Danton and Desmoulins had fanned the fire that had forged that bridge. Pulling the collar of his greatcoat higher around his neck he felt little of the heat that 1789 had generated, or, come to that, the subsequent fire of the following years. The Revolution, he was aware, had ended badly but now they had another chance to remake the world. They owed it to the men they had fed to their own modern form of the guillotine to get it right this time.

He had still not quite managed to outdistance his surprise that he had survived when so many others had not. He had never been able to divine why *he* should have eluded the grip of the Man from Reading; words like *fate* and *chance* would occasionally flit through his mind, but there were no metaphysical pegs upon which to hang them and certainly there were no spiritual ones. Perhaps it was because he had found someone to survive *for*. Yet to dwell on reasons — or worse, nihilistically dwell upon the lack of them — seemed somehow a betrayal of those who, by any other twist of fate might have been sitting where he was sitting. The thing to do, he had finally decided, was to live a life as best one could. It seemed to him, even on that cold January day, that Paris was as good a place as any to do that. He had his notes and his thoughts and — perhaps most poignant of all — he had his memories. The least he could do was to make the effort. That, surely, was a debt owed to those who could not.

He closed his notebook and slipped it into the pocket of the greatcoat, sitting back in his chair. There remained some cognac rimming the bottom of his glass and he sipped at it, letting the alcohol run over his tongue. The wind seemed to have dropped a little and the sun was straining through the high cirrostratus, forming a weak yet persistent halo, as though the effort might still be worth the endeavour.

He looked at his watch. He had an appointment with the printer in an hour. There were still a few decisions to be made but by the spring the first run would be off the presses and he would at last be able to get *Heavier Than Air* into the bookshops. He had been promised several reviews, even if each assurance had been accompanied by the proviso that it could be too soon for the public to be reading about the war. He didn't disagree but he was afraid that, in a year or two, people would want to forget the horror altogether. Dunne and all the others surely deserved more than that.

It was one of his regrets that he had never got to meet Dunne, yet he supposed he had got as close as was humanly possible. For a moment, an unbidden eidetic image of poor Parry clambering out of the broken FE onto the metal cage beside the balloon overwhelmed him. He didn't know why those few days in Strouden's squadron stayed with him so vividly while much else had misted in his memory; Dunne's book, perhaps, or that sight of Strouden's last moments as his DH2 and the Rumpler fused in death below him.

Chacksfield had also seen how Strouden had taken the Rumpler off Miller's tail and between them they had told Budge what had happened, the recording officer stoically filling the log as if Strouden's had been just another death. Budge had held himself together for the rest of the evening then, that night, had got heroically drunk. They had lost Moss and Trueman and Pilot Sergeant Reynolds as well. With Strouden gone there had been some talk of Miller filling the post of squadron leader. After all, as an outsider, he would have had the requisite distance from the men. But he was too distant, it seemed, and the job had gone to Chatterton. Miller had got his squadron in the end, but that was as high as he ever got. He never heard what had happened to Chatterton and Chacksfield, Gregory and the others. Except for Denham. He had run into him again. Denham had made wing commander by the summer of 1918, still as supercilious as ever but by then somehow having grown to fill the job.

In the aftermath of the raid on the balloons, the others had said they had not seen Parry on the cage when they took the second balloon down, although at the time Miller had not been convinced. There was nothing anyone could have done for him, of course, and the last balloon had to be destroyed. His death had left Miller with the responsibility of Dunne's book and somehow the thought of that had added purpose to a growing certainty that he wanted to survive, a feeling which had been slipping away. Anyway, he had got through and the book was with the printer. He had never told Phyllida quite how Parry had died, or even, come to that, how useless the death of her brother had been.

He had taken the trouble to call on Mrs Heyward, though. She had never been told the true cause of her son's death and had always believed that he had died honourably. Miller had fabricated a plausible story to explain how he had come to read Heyward's letters and how, although he had never met Charles, he had heard so much about him that he had come to feel as if he *had* known him. She had surprised Miller then by admitting that she had indeed honoured her son's wishes and had burned his papers. She had not, she had confided, even had the heart to read them first.

Across the Luxembourg he saw the girl approaching him, coat pulled tight against the wind, her features pinched by the cold. Around her face, from beneath her woollen hat, errant black curls projected like wisps of dark cloud. Then she saw him and smiled, waving her arm. At the sight of her he felt his

240

spirit rise, that same feeling that climbing into the sky in a machine had once given him.

Miller waved back.